THE RENEGADE
BODIE NINE

THE CHRONICLES OF BODIE NINE

THE RENEGADE BODIE NINE

ERIC N. LARD

4 Horsemen
Publications, Inc.

DEDICATION

We shared very few things in common—we didn't even choose each other—but we both loved my mom. Besides that one great unifying factor, my stepfather and I shared stories—sci-fi and action movies, like *Star Wars* and *Aliens*, but also a few books; The Dark Tower series by Stephen King and a handful from Louis L'amour, of which *Hondo* stands out in my memory. In a story where sci-fi tech and alien monsters battle it out across the lonesome hills and expansive skies of the high desert, it seemed only fitting that I dedicate this one to him. Thank you, Tony, for finding something we could share together and, in so doing, unleashing an imagination and inspiring still more stories in the process.

CONTENTS

Chapter 1...1
Chapter 2 21
Chapter 3.. 44
Chapter 4 49
Chapter 5.. 67
Chapter 6 84
Chapter 7 111
Chapter 8 127
Chapter 9 152
Chapter 10 166
Chapter 11..183
Chapter 12.. 200
Chapter 13..211
Chapter 14.. 222
Chapter 15.. 229
Chapter 16.. 250
Chapter 17.. 264
Chapter 18.. 280
Chapter 19..291

Chapter 20 308
Chapter 21. 319
Chapter 22 331
Chapter 23 342
Chapter 24 357
Chapter 25 368
Chapter 26 377
Book Club Questions. 381
Author Bio. 383

CHAPTER 1

PHANTOM LIMB

A wad of stringy, brown spittle splashed across Bodie Nine's metallic hand. That hand still formed a protective shield around what was left of a tiny sapling that'd been smashed upon the floorboards of the Sever cabin.

"Haven't you had enough, boy?" a man in dusty cowboy boots asked, exasperation heavy in his gravelly drawl. He spat again.

"No. I have not," Bodie responded, curling his hand more tightly around the biology experiment. The sapling had belonged to the youngest of the Sever family, Justine. Bodie had promised to protect it.

The man turned and strode away. Bodie watched from floor level, idly noticing that one of the points was missing from his spurs. Outside, he could hear the clatter of men on horses and the crackle of fire. This was getting out of hand.

Moments later, the man returned just as an axe handle swung down in a looping golf stroke of an arc.

1

It struck Bodie on the side of the head with a crack that echoed loudly off the stacked log walls.

Static buzzed in Bodie's circuits before his sleep mode forcibly engaged. A lower level of his operating system attempted a feeble override, but his master processor was incapable of parsing the avalanche of garbled sensory data and glitched on a circular piece of code. Hardware fail-safes took over. A sideways view from the floor of the abandoned cabin was the last thing stored in his conscious memory files.

< 0 0 1 0 2 0 x x 1 2 1 3 ? a 0 0 … 0 0 1 0 2 0 x x - 1 2 1 3 ? a 0 0 x 1 1 0 1 0 0 … 0 0 1 0 2 0 x x 1 2 1 _ a00x110100xxbxx01111>

The startup sequence scrolled across Bodie Nine's ocular circuits before the background resolved from darkness to a dim, monochrome, night vision-filtered image of his surroundings.

<Cabin floor>

<Occupants: Absent>

<Significant physical trauma. More on that in … 4.178s>

<Subject of interest … unsalvageable>

Bodie's ocular circuits focused on the crushed sapling as facts aggregated into his OS consciousness level. This was where more complicated arguments were processed. Where conflicting arguments sought resolution.

Here was one: his Primary Directive was missing. *Still.*

In spite of that fact, Bodie's startup protocol was allowed to initiate. And he had no programming that told him how to replace a missing directive. He was quite certain it had never been done. He should not, under any circumstances, have been allowed to start up without one.

Yet here he was. This was hour 73,489 of autonomous operation without one. What was worse, Bodie hadn't the vaguest idea how to find a primary directive.

What was his purpose? Did he just accept any command offered by a human? There were numerous recent commands to choose from:

"Go to hell, iron-ass."

"Get bent, toaster."

Or just yesterday, "Stay down and don't get up."

That last had been offered while scoundrels smelling of liquor, stale sweat, and testosterone were harming other members of their species. Bodie didn't have specific programming about how to interact with humans, so he processed information while he sought a directive within the flurry of activity. A woman in a white bonnet and light blue dress carrying a hand-made satchel was struck across the face when she'd protested the agitators' actions. She lost two teeth for her troubles. Bodie had tried to retrieve them for her and received exactly three lead slugs to the torso and another to the face.

The blow to the head by the .44 caliber ball had caused a forced power cycle and reboot. Thirty-seven seconds later, when that process was completed, he'd relieved the four male humans of their firearms, as well as several teeth of their own and the ability to walk without a severe limp. Broken femurs, according to Bodie's declarative and semantic memory files, were particularly painful. This appeared to be the case, as the men were wholly distracted from their previous endeavors after receiving such injuries. Kung fu was a thing, and it was quite effective. However, he had made modifications to the patterns of movement since being dug up in that Chinese labor camp some miles south.

Bodie rolled onto his back and was dismayed that his right leg did not roll with him. He reached through radio waves and found that his leg was attached to a rope that was attached to his horse and that his horse was running north, along with the pack of outlaws who'd fallen upon him here at the abandoned cabin— the former Sever residence.

<The cabin is on fire>

This observation percolated into his awareness as well as another.

<Right leg missing>

That seemed a long 4.178 seconds.

Other information aggregated. Most of it pertained to his physical well-being. Most of it wasn't good. Bodie sat up and was greeted by a significant number of alarms, one of which pertained to low-pressure levels within some of his internal hydraulics. He found himself relieved that hydraulic fluid was, for the most part, non-flammable. Flames didn't bother him much but still, having one's inner liquids set afire was unsettling, no matter who you were. And it'd be hard to replace his favored Batterson Boss cowboy hat.

The robot Bodie Nine stood up and instantly fell over, breaking the cabin's lone table on the way down. Apparently, that leg was more important than he'd realized in the moment.

"Well, Sheeyit," Bodie drawled his favorite expletive authentically.

He got back up and retrieved his trampled Batterson and the ax handle that'd been put to such effective use upon him earlier. He then further demolished the table and picked through its scraps. Grabbing a clothes iron from its resting place atop the potbelly stove, he pummeled an already worse-for-wear teakettle into a couple of socket-shaped objects and then whipped all the articles into a rather effective crutch with a hand-spooled bundle of used baling wire. He'd found that last bit resting upon the low wall of mortared river rock backing the stove. The rocks were for re-radiating heat and for protecting the wood framing, he surmised. Smart. Functional. The crutch, too, was functional, and he wasn't falling over anymore. That was a little better, at least.

Searching under his poncho, he found the pistols he'd commandeered the day prior still magnetically attached to his torso. Two nine-inch-barreled Walker Colts, a Bergman Simplex semi-auto, and another semi-auto whose manufacture he was unfamiliar with. Probably something I-talian. It looked like a cross between something you'd find in a physician's kit and something on a cobbler's bench. Utterly horrific. The filigree was nice, but otherwise, its design would be a justifiably truncated appendix to the flow of tech-nology, he was sure.

Personally, he was a fan of the Walker platform. Five pounds of deadly accuracy at fighting distance and quite a ways beyond. Bodie fancied himself some-what of a marksman but found suffering punishment until the offending human had worn themselves out was just as effective most times and built up less bad blood besides. And Bodie worried about karma.

He didn't worry about much else. Sure, his direc-tive problem was a nuisance, but the concept of karma weighed on him something fierce. A system of credit based on actions that lacked a clear-cut definition for every possible interaction, but which had the potential to impact one's very existence in this and possibly even the next life...? The implications were daunting.

For instance, the altercation the day before. Did he incur good karma, bad karma, or both? Did they cancel each other out? Did the amount of good he did outweigh the harm he'd caused, and did it matter if the men he'd harmed were bad? He recognized that a bad human was a subjective qualification anyway... Humans were not wholly good or wholly bad, but they were, largely, of no help in sorting all this out and seemed to understand it even less than he did.

Bodie extinguished a flaming corner of his poncho between metallic thumb and forefinger as he hobbled through the threshold and away from the now fully engulfed cabin. Orange and yellow tongues of fire flicked up into the sparse canopy of pines. No worry about them catching fire, as there was still a smattering of late-spring snow clinging to their needles. Smoke roiled heavenward. Timbers crackled and popped. Bodie considered coming back to rebuild the Sever cabin, but the Universe seemed to be prodding him northward again. It was a pattern with no constituents, no framework, just outcomes. It was as relentless as a glacier. He would go. His leg, after all, had already started north without him.

Frozen snow crunched under his boot and improvised crutch. Bodie stopped and turned to gaze upon the cabin and the valley invisible through the trees beyond. It was midnight on a moonless, high prairie night. He tried his night vision filtering but found it impossible to tune in the distant valley with the flames in the foreground, bathing the entire area in a dancing miasma of orange-white light. Just as well. There was nothing much to see. He was just feeling a bit moody and sentimental, was all.

Was that a thing? He was certainly experiencing what he considered to be feelings. He wasn't sure if they truly qualified according to human standards, but he quietly offered his respects to the Sever family's home, regardless.

Justine, the daughter of Josiah and Merrideth had given him the sapling before the three of them had high-tailed it off their claim just that morning. It had been her biological sciences project, and she had entrusted him with it. Patting him on the head as he sat holding the small plant, she had called him "nice" and "enigmatic." Bodie considered the odd comment and then logged the day's activities into his karmic ledger. Again, this was all subjective, but at least when he finally met the "Great Fabricator," he'd be able to provide an accurate account.

The Severs had been warned of the men's approach by neighbors, the Montalvos, one valley over. They had sent their youngest boy on far too lively a mare at great risk to themselves. Sometimes humans could be decent, Bodie acknowledged.

The Sever girl, Justine, had a bit of the magick in her. Bodie had sensed it, though he wasn't sure by which of his sensory systems that information was gleaned. The girl didn't have as much magick as the men believed, but that wouldn't stop them. They would still take her from Josie and Merr. That's what he'd been instructed to call them, Josie and Merr, rather than Josiah and

Merrideth. They, for whatever reason, had taken a shine to Bodie and offered their home after the incident the day prior. Apparently, they knew the toothless lady in the bonnet.

Bodie's fear was that the men would take young Justine back to one of the mining camps he had seen. Or one like it. There was a mining boom going on; for coldbright. The appearance of this new mineral breathed life into the idea of manifest destiny—the obligation to conquer the land, subdue or subjugate its inhabitants, and liberate its lucre. The children, apparently, were the key to unlocking this reservoir of riches. The details on that were unclear to Bodie. He just knew that coldbright was near impossible to mine without magicks and magicks were in the kids.

What was clear was that only children that were born here in the Alta Estranyazie had it. He supposed adults could have it, too, but people had only just started to settle this region in the last decade or so. Other than that, there were no people here at all. Not like the lowlands, peppered with savage nations as they were.

Bodie sighed. He didn't know if the Severs had gotten away or not, but there was some good news. His disembodied leg was waiting for him to catch up. Bodie guessed that the rope had finally frayed and the pack of desperadoes hadn't noticed when it'd flung off into the bushes, tumbled down a slope, and finally came to rest at the bottom of a river gorge.

Joy of joys, he had a leg ... but no horse. Carole had been a particularly good horse. A pinto Appaloosa. Her coloring was ink-splatter on wet parchment; a curious arrangement of charcoal on bone. She didn't have magick, but she sure could fly. Bodie loved Carole. The feeling seemed mutual. He hoped to get her back. To Bodie's sense of justice, karmic or otherwise, stealing a man's horse—even if that man was a robot—was low. Definitely a femur-snapping offense.

<Kung fu> Bodie's tertiary level OS, where procedural memory resided, provided eagerly.

Yes, very helpful, he acknowledged patiently as if speaking to a child.

His fourth or quaternary level OS, where Episodic and Semantic memories were processed, not wishing to be outdone, provided a montage of instances where kung fu had been used to effective resolution. In spite of being quite lengthy and focusing, perhaps gratuitously, on the more gruesome details, it took only fractions of a second to observe. A helpful reminder.

Again ... thank you, he provided in a near constant stream of inner dialogue between the various levels of his main consciousness levels of OS and the two devoted to memory. Though his persona was supposedly just a composite of several such layers of programming, he found that, somehow, in an inexplicable way, his "self" seemed to float above the bits and bytes in an ephemeral fog of data and actions directed in response to it. That was the extent of his existential reasoning. He was an automaton, a robot, and yet in some strange way ... a person.

That thought process operated concurrently with hundreds of others. Meanwhile, Bodie had stopped to address the leaking fluid from his abdomen—a problem that was slowly being rectified by his self-regenerating systems anyway—when something rustled in the darkness off the trail. There was a weak flutter.

A dark spot bobbed in the snow beneath a mid-sized pine. It fluttered again.

Bodie veered off the trail and found a small bird in a spherical depression it'd beaten into the snow. *A downy woodpecker*, he thought, though it was young, which made it hard to tell from other varieties. This one was either injured or had fallen from its nest and not been able to fly back up. He scooped up the snow beneath it and let it crumble away so that just the creature remained.

It fluttered some more but seemed short on energy and before long settled into an internal pocket of Bodie's poncho. His vest was too tight fitting to accommodate the bird's fragile body. Bodie's own metal body produced some heat, but not much. The location on his torso was as likely as anywhere on his body to provide the bird the warmth it needed, but it would still be insufficient.

Bodie drew the Walker and fired straight overhead. It cracked viciously in the stillness of the night, a bright flash like a photographer's tray brought the forest scene around him into high contrast. The bird jumped but settled again, its tiny heart beating impossibly fast. Bodie returned the long, blued-steel wheel gun to the magnetized resting place on his torso where its warmth would keep the bird comfortable through to the morning, at least.

Bodie Nine returned to the path, his boot and crutch crunching on the gravel and frozen patches of snow. If he continued through the night, he'd find his leg by morning light. He was sure he could track the men after that. But weather was always an issue in the

Estranyazie. *If you didn't like it, wait five minutes*, people said. It was an exaggeration, but not far off, really.

A soft plunk issued from a snow patch a few paces ahead of him, and he kneeled down and retrieved the .44 caliber bullet head he'd just fired into the air, which had landed as intended, only yards away. He inspected it casually.

<Undamaged>

He'd have expected a typical lead ball to be so, but this was a dragoon bullet, shaped like a pointed dome. He found them to be more accurate. He'd be able to reload it. The rectangular cluster of light tubes on Bodie's face—his visual emotive indicator panel—configured into the approximation of a smirk and he continued on.

Dawn did not break as such. Dark clouds hung low over the hills and thick snowflakes glided softly down as if cast from some celestial pillow fight. Bodie looked up and a quarter-sized flake landed on his nose and then on his eye, and then another on his cheek. He vocalized a thought in his cowhand drawl. It was a Haiku:

Quiet its approach
Justice, constant as snowflakes
Bodie catches them

He nodded in solemn appreciation of his own work. Why not? No one else was around. Except the woodpecker, and they weren't known for their artistic appreciation.

Bodie didn't produce enough heat to melt the flakes on his face, so he had to wipe them away with one leather-gauntleted hand. The index finger was cut away like some of the Texas kids, the quickdraws, liked to do. He looked down. Crumbling red sandstone tumbled down to the river at the bottom of a two-hundred-foot embankment. That embankment was quickly becoming covered with a thick layer of white. This was going to take some doing.

He made his way down with his one good leg and his crutch and managed to do it without landing on his iron ass. It was actually not iron, but he never bothered to correct anyone who called it such. After shedding his clothes and hat and carefully tucking Downy away—that's what he'd named his new bird companion—Bodie walked out on the loose rock shoal deposited at the outer bank of a bend in the swift-flowing river.

Jaybird naked, he hobbled in and was overhead within yards and leaning hard against the current to stay upright. His radio connection assured him that his leg was only a few yards farther on when he was struck by something large. It was dark, heavy, and dragging him quickly downstream. Bodie twisted in the water and before long was grappling with the semi-submerged timber. In the process, one end of it jammed against the bottom of the river and the whole thing cantilevered up and over, launching him out of the water another dozen yards. He splashed down just in time for the timber to find him again and further drag him away from his prize.

He struggled mightily to right himself, but missing a leg was really beginning to cramp his style. After a minute or two of being battered by yet more of the displaced timbers, he was able to work his way to the water's edge and onto a worn, smooth red rock ledge.

Just in time, he realized. The river gorge narrowed significantly, the water moving treacherously fast and then pitching over a sizable drop. Lucky. Here in the narrows, there was nothing but smooth walls, where further up there'd been at least a little slip of sand. He guessed that he was maybe a quarter-mile from where he'd started and where his kit and the adolescent woodpecker lay unprotected.

More and more of the timbers flooded in from upstream and many were lodging here, creating a goodly pile. Given long enough, it would turn into quite the logjam and probably raise the waters significantly. His thoughts went to the bird. Downy should be safe for now.

One good thing though—his leg was also heading downstream. Slowly, at least.

Bodie reached out through the radio and commanded movement. Bending knee and ankle, he wriggled the leg remotely, freeing it of snags and letting the river bring it to him. It was an agonizingly slow process. In the meantime, the logjam was materializing, and Bodie found he had to clamber over timbers to stay on the right side of it. For Bodie, tripedal locomotion was growing tiresome.

Twenty minutes later, he dove into the water to capture his leg but was slammed into the logjam and pinned underwater. But he had his leg! The rushing river current acting on the timber cinched him in tight, and he found he wasn't able to maneuver much at all. He let his leg do the rest of the work as the severed bit found his hip socket and began to self-regenerate the connections. Again, not a swift process.

An hour passed and more deconstructed logs gathered, but finally, his leg connection was complete. Bodie dug deep, unlocking seldom-used reservoirs of strength, and pressed with all his might. Making a little gap here and there, he wiggled his way up from the darkness to the water's surface and then still further until he was able to extricate himself wholly from the convoluted mess.

He would have been sweating if his body was equipped to do that. Of course, he'd also have drowned if his anatomy was any more human in functionality. Appearance was something else. He was vaguely human. Similar but metallic. Gray, white, or bare metal predominated. Framework and skeletal system rhymed, but musculature, not so much. For instance, he had pectoral-shaped features but not chest muscles under elastic skin. Inside, he was all gizmo and clockwork. He was hairless, but his face shared angulature of a not unhandsome, thinner man, but with lights where his mouth would be—his VEIP, or visual emotive indicator panel. He didn't need a mouth, per se. He didn't need to eat or drink. The energy he used came from some internal source, but he didn't really know exactly what that was and he'd never run out of juice, so it was a bit of a non-issue. He'd just go until he couldn't anymore. Just like humans did.

With his newly returned appendage, trekking back to his gear was fast, even if it meant he had to venture back into the water on several occasions and risk being swept away again. But now that he had full use of his body, this presented less of an issue. He reminded himself not to allow himself to be disassembled again. It just wasn't worth it. *Boundaries*, he thought. *Boundaries are good.*

Bodie came upon his gear and found that sometime in his absence, his little companion had left. Apparently, the woodpecker just needed some warmth and a little rest. *Good luck, little buddy*, he thought, and then he saw one downy little feather resting lightly atop the snow, and then another a bit further away. And then another. And then he saw a whole pile of them near the water's edge. Bodie's mouth VEIP settled into a thin line of disappointment as he sighed heavily. He considered offering his favorite expletive but thought it in poor taste. He dressed in contemplative silence. Some critter, a raccoon or a river otter, had found an easy snack. Bodie couldn't blame them, but he could certainly blame himself.

Bodie pulled on his dark brown work pants and rawhide vest as his thoughts wandered to the girl, Justine. Best if he rejoined the trail sooner than later. He held little hope that Josie and Merr stood a chance against those men. And in Bodie's experience, cowards loved the company of other cowards. Bodie's eyes wandered back to the pile of feathers slowly scattering in the wind. He turned solemnly back to the hill and started climbing up to the top of the bluff.

North it is. Bodie started jogging, the fringed edges of his poncho flapping in the increasingly urgent wind. Snow crunched rhythmically beneath his boots. He patted his Batterson down further on his head and cinched the chin strap that he ordinarily left loose except when running Carole at a full gallop. He missed that horse. And now he missed a woodpecker. He wasn't very good at being a robot, he realized. Mucking about in Dara knots of complex emotions instead of just getting things done was a decidedly human endeavor.

"Get yer brain in the game, iron-ass," he scolded himself.

Bodie knew it wouldn't take the men long to catch up with the Severs if they were able to find them. Josie struck him as a shrewd fellow. If they'd managed to elude the men long enough for the snow to cover their tracks, there was a chance. As it was, Bodie was having to use some very sophisticated tracking methods to stay on their trail.

Hours passed. Hints of sun behind the high gray vagueness that'd started in the east transited the entirety of the sky and Bodie hadn't stopped. He traveled through sage-covered valleys with washout gullies and rambling hills, worn round by the actions of weather and dotted with sparse pines. And then he'd climbed a switchback hillside skirted with jagged boulders sloughed off of a cliff wall through millennia of weathering. This was an actual wagon trail put in, no doubt, to service the coldbright mines that dotted these hills. In fact, at one point, rusted rails jutted out into the air like two solitary whiskers from a great cat. He could see no other remnants of the rail that must have clung to the side of the canyon wall. Reused, most likely. What could be reached, anyway.

Little accompanied him but the solitary cry of an eagle far above or the evaluating eyes of a large coyote, contemplating whether Bodie could be a meal or might leave the remnants of one. No on both counts.

Bodie knew he'd never be able to overtake the party, mounted as they were.

<21-35mi ahead>

Thank you.

An image appeared in his mind showing the Alta Estranyazie. It started in high resolution at the bottom and faded into cartoony, sketchy detail near the top, north of where he was currently. The reason for the sketchiness was simply that he'd never been there and there wasn't much available lore.

Also, thank you, he told his lower-level OS, toying with the idea of referring to it as Helga. He didn't know why; it was just a thought he had. If he did that, he would probably refer to the sub-sub layer, as Dmitr. Again, no reason...

He had noticed that Helga and Dmitr had a tendency to get panicky when innocents were in danger.

However, Bodie thought this loudly for the benefit of the other two, *if the men have had any trouble tracking the girl and her family, it will slow them down.*

This appeared to be prophetic, as when a faint light in the western sky yielded entirely to darkness, Bodie sensed a divergence in the tracks. It was faint, but there were definitely three sets that veered off and traced their way back to a gully about a half-mile back. "Shrewd indeed, Mr. Sever."

The man had led them up a runout gully made up of large rocks and boulders to obscure their footprints. The gully ran up a hillside. He, his wife, and daughter had exited that gully partway up amongst a smattering of blackbrush and juniper that had either grown up through the rabble or simply survived the original slide.

Bodie dared not follow. He'd just leave a fresh set of tracks in the newly laid snow. The men would surely see it if they doubled back. Instead, he pressed on over a small rise and was greeted by a low ridge that cut across the path ahead. With the aid of his night vision, he could see that it was made up of thick, unevenly weathered layers of sandstone. He assumed red and white but could only make out tonal differences in the low light, not the colors themselves. Stunted trees dotted the hillside and the ridge. He didn't need his low-light filters to pick out what he saw next: fire. Or the glow from one.

Far to the left, in a pocket shielded by a free-standing boulder taller than a two-story building, someone had a campfire and wasn't too concerned about who could see it.

His audio circuits picked out a holler off in the distance. And then, closer in, the crunch of gravel.

"Yer hands, pardner."

To Bodie's ears, the word "partner," in this instance, did not carry a very neighborly tone.

Bodie's hands had been tucked into his poncho and the rawhide vest beneath it.

"Dammit. He's a toaster," another, gruffer voice called out. "Meanie Moe, you got a bead on him with that, Henry?"

"Mmhmm—" a voice about twenty yards out began to reply before a .44 caliber, dome-shaped dragoon bullet interrupted him—a bullet fired twice that very same day. This time it would not be salvageable, as it had passed through approximately a quarter-inch of human bone above the man's eye and then ricocheted off of several interior surfaces, making a frappe of brain matter in the process.

The shot had been fired across Bodie's chest as he'd extended his arm from just under his poncho—so as not to damage the wool. The movement had been blindingly fast, and indeed, the first two men had only begun to raise their eyebrows in surprise before Bodie had turned more fully to his left and the other Walker protruded, similarly cross-chest from the right side of this poncho.

Both men's heads tipped back as the high plains were illuminated by flashes of light and booms of pistol rounds fired at nearly the exact same moment. The shots echoed off the cliff wall while horses nearby neighed and stamped in fright. More hollering from far off evidenced that whoever was gathered at that campfire had heard the multiple reports.

Bodie quickly scavenged the bodies of the three men and came away with two bandoliers and the octa-gon-barreled carbine. He considered the Henry a fine tool, but he was most taken by a long bowie knife. An actual Wostenholm, complete with acid-etched I*XL stamp. Likely stolen, Bodie assumed, so he wasn't sure it warranted noting in his karmic log. He did it anyway. Along with the deaths of Dewey, Mars, Meanie Moe, and everything he'd prized from their bodies. He'd remembered their names from earlier.

A shout from a closer hip of that same ridgeline interrupted his activities.

"Dewey? Mars? You guys up to no good?"

"Damn 'winder in Dewey's bedroll. Dead now, though." Bodie approximated from the first man's voice.

"Izat you, Mars? Wuza matter with yer voice?"

Bodie didn't respond. He was too busy hustling through blackbrush and sage, circling around the man's position.

"Moe? Meanie Moe?"

A horse whinnied again, covering Bodie's movements as he drew within twenty meters of the newcomer.

"Dammit. That's it," the man cursed under his breath, making ready to return to the main camp and warn the others. Then there was a whirring of something heavy and unaerodynamic cutting through the air before he was struck in the head by a flying five-pound hunk of L-shaped iron that looked conspicuously like Bodie's Walker Colt. The newcomer's eyes fluttered, and he found he was looking up at a metal-faced man with lights for a mouth and a wickedly gleaming knife in his hand.

"Nice Wost," were his last words.

CHAPTER 2

BLACKIE LUNG

Bodie agreed. The bowie knife was a nice specimen of a Wostenholm.

But now it had tasted human blood … and it sang for more. Or that's what Bodie thought would have made a great entry if he'd been writing his memoir. However, it was just a stupid anthropomorphism. The blade did not, in fact, *sing* for more human blood. It was just a hunk of steel.

The Henry lever-action, on the other hand, was a thirsty sonofabitch.

Shots rang out. Bullets hurled through the night, whizzing as they split the air around and overhead, splintering branches and ricocheting off rocks before spending their inertia.

<Three or four subjects. Closing from two vectors.>

Thank you.

A close-in map of the hip and cliff wall, the brushy depression between them, and the large camp in the converging pocket overlaid Bodie's ocular circuits. This was not a nuisance at all. Two well-placed shots from the Henry echoed in under a second, and Bodie vacated the location from which they'd issued, having learned that to stay put was to invite bodily harm. The two corresponding targets dropped—one spun ostentatiously while a wad of moist black tobacco leaves and spittle sprayed away in a wide arc, the other simply folded in half, crumpling to the dirt without so much as a whimper. The other two men and others besides poured forth like paper wasps from a burning nest.

Bodie cycled and fired several more times. To his thinking, there was nearly nothing in the world as satisfying as the well-lubricated action of a lever rifle—each click announcing a new action in a chunky, crunchy expression of mechanical logic. *Shik-chik. Bang. Shik-chik. Bang.* It was gloriously straightforward. The amount of pure robotic glee he derived from it probably should have been noted in his karmic journal, but that would have to wait until he could apply more processing power to it. Abstracts required time to process. He was short on that luxury, and right now, there were other issues at hand.

Bodie rabbited forward into the scrub between the trails, converging on his position. He swung out the Henry, spinning and cocking it in a fluid, one-handed blur. It swung up and came to a stop, fully loaded, and aimed at the head of a man just rounding a cluster of rocks.

At the same moment, his other hand whipped the Walker out from under his poncho, pointing it upslope to yet another of the desperadoes sliding not-so-stealthily down the hill. Bodie timed the hair-trigger of the cocked Henry with the long double-action pull of the Walker without any trouble, and they fired simultaneously. It was an unnecessary flourish. He recognized that. Was it showing off? Maybe. Was it a tiny bit self-indulgent? Also maybe. Was it effec—

Bodie's feet flew up mid-thought as his body keened backward as if attached by rope to a startled express pony. Two seconds later, a crack could be heard echoing off the bluffs.

"Meanie Moe Sheen. Dewey Dahl. Mars... What was Mars's last name?"

"Favereux."

"Mars Fa-ver-eux. Earl Johns, whom we identified by the fact that the headless body that was found only had three fingers on the left hand, which was consistent with his living self, and a living Earl is still unaccounted for. Je-ho-sha-phat Mon-toy-ez ... and Chin, who only had the one name. Identified solely by his signature bamboo hat. 'Zat it?"

"Yeah, that's about the long and short."

"Sonofabitch! Who knew these toasters could be such a nuisance? Ordinarily, they're pretty mild in humors. What do ya think's gone an' made this one so froggy?"

"Got me."

"Hmm..." Childers Lung finished scrawling the names of the recently fallen into the robot's inverted torso with the bowie knife.

"This is a nice Wost, though," he said, admiring the acid-etched scene on the dully gleaming blade. "Hoist him up!"

The troublesome android's body, tied at the ankles, began sliding up the side of a very large, smoke-charred boulder.

"Wait, wait, wait!" Lung yelled at the person on the other side of the large rock. He walked up to the bot and pulled off the poncho that'd been hanging down and obscuring his face.

He turned around to make his point. "You gotta be able to see his face," he said, pointing at Bodie. "When the mouth lights up, that's when you know he's rebooted and about to wake up. That's when you gotta pop him again with that beastie .45-70 o' yours."

"Got it."

"Be sure you do. You gotta give us a day's ride. Then you tie him to a big rock and drop him in the gorge. It ought to be nice and deep now that we've dammed up the narrows and flooded out those rat Hooties mining down there."

"Got it."

Childers Lung turned back to his companion and then back toward the boulder.

"Okay! Pull him up," he hollered.

A blink of lights fluttered across Bodie's visual emotive display.

"Wait, wait, wait!" Lung yelled, peeling a highly polished silver Peacemaker from his hip and placing it on Bodie's temple. A loud crack from the pistol rocked Bodie's head violently to the side, and the display lights faded.

"Goddammit!" Childers holstered the pistol and his hand flashed to his face, where a crimson streak had just formed on his cheek. "Goddammit. My eye. Shit ... shit." He stood up straight, blinking as he dropped his hand. Blood streamed down the side of his face from multiple lacerations, and his eye was a gory red.

"Shit. I can see, I think, but … shit."

"Ricochet?"

"Yeah, no fucking shit, ricochet," Lung barked and pressed his kerchief against his face. "Fuckin' toasters."

"You okay?"

"Yeah, I'm fucking peachy. Fucking toasters and their fucking metal-headed... Fuck." He seemed to run out of curse words as he peeled his kerchief back and saw with his good eye that there was still fresh blood coming from his face. Lung pressed the kerchief back to his tortured flesh and resumed the conversation.

"Anyway. You pop him every time he wakes up. You give us a day's ride. After that, you dump him in the gorge, but make sure it's in a spot we can get to. Cuz after those worthless sacks of shit Hooties clear out, we're coming back. We blow that dam, take their claims, and fish out Mr. Iron-ass Toaster here. Then we weld him to a Coldbright cart so he can atone for his many sins by hauling ore for the rest of his ever-lovin' days. 'Zat make sense?"

"Sounds like a reasonable plan. As long as yer not a Hootie."

"Ya think?!? Well, thanks for that vote of confidence, Mr. Klamath, suh. And while we're deliberating, maybe you can remind me to ask for yer fucking opinion on my plan the next time I wanna hear it! Which is not ever. *Comprendee*?"

Klamath said nothing but stared back in mild amusement.

"Mr. Lung?" a gravelly voice called out as a bow-legged man of barely four feet in height skipped up to where the two men were still staring each other down. He saw Childers's gory eye and retched a little.

"Oh, for Pete's sake, Horntoad, I seen you turn a man into a canoe with a boot knife," Lung said, irritatedly kicking a piece of gravel and checking his kerchief again.

"Sure enough," he retched again a little before swallowing it, "but I was so full of corn liquor at the time I couldn't piss on a campfire for fear of roasting my beans and franks," the newcomer said in a voice that was as deep as he was not tall. He said this last while looking anywhere but at Childers's eye. "Is that your shootin' eye?" he asked.

"Yes, but I can see just fine."

"Whatever you say, boss."

"Never mind. What's the—"

Another shot rang out, clanging loudly off Bodie's metal skull.

"Ow! Fuck. Goddammit." Childers's hand flew up to his face. "My other fucking eye! Are you kidding me? Dammit. That fucking toaster's gonna pay for this, I swear it."

Childers pulled his hand from his face. Horntoad took one look, stepped into the bushes, and retched for real.

"Fucking Horntoad. What good's a fucking henchman with a weak stomach?"

Horntoad looked over at Childers and turned and retched again.

"Klamath? You wanna warn me next time?" Childers asked the man holstering his own Peacemaker.

"Shit boss. The odds..." he said with a disbelieving shrug.

"Fuck you very much about the odds," the bleeding man told him and then turned to the short, bow-legged Horntoad who looked at him and then turned away quickly before he had to throw up again.

"Are you quite through?"

"Uh-uh," the man said, shaking his head, still facing away, hands on chaps and leaning over in the ready position.

Hank "Klamath" Pettibone stepped forward. He was nearly half a head taller than Childers Lung and looked every inch the understated ranch hand; capable of subduing a mustang or even the hounds of hell with nothing but a stare and the patience of the very roots of the earth. Even Childers blanched a little when Klamath brought his full attention to bear. There was an unsettling hollowness in his gaunt features and gray eyes.

"Here." He offered Childers a black kerchief with two eyeholes cut out, perfectly folded, perfectly sized and spaced.

Childers looked at it imperiously with his blood-shot and bleeding eyes and then looked back at the man. He paused and then grabbed the kerchief from his hands. Childers removed his black, wide-brimmed hat, tied the kerchief over his eyes, and pulled his hat back on, looking much more like the outlaw than the boss man he was.

A peeked Horntoad turned around, squinted, and then shrugged. "Better..." he provided in his outsized, gravelly baritone.

Childers turned to get Klamath's impression. A tight-lipped nod was silent agreement. He turned back to the sawed-off Horntoad. "So?"

"We found the girl 'bout a mile back."

"I see."

Klamath grimaced and turned away to keep from laughing out loud at the ironic remark.

"How'd we miss her?" the man in the black kerchief persisted.

"Sneaky fuckers trotted up the runout rubble to cover their tracks. We seen 'em when they was making a break the other way. Back home I'm guessin'."

Childers Lung nodded. Thin streams of blood leaked out from under his bandana, navigating blond stubble on a sun-darkened face. "Is everyone mounted up?"

"Pretty much," Horntoad provided in his ultra-low baritone, looking skeptically at Childers's eye arrangement. "You sure you can see 'nuff to ride?"

Childers drew on him in a flash, losing his own hat in the process and revealing greasy blond hair pressed flat across his scalp as the barrel came to rest between Horntoad's saucer-round eyes.

"Toad? 'Nymore questions before I make that head o' yours a sight more hollow?" Childers asked in a strained, noticeably higher-pitched note that suggested the faintest twitch would cause that trigger to nestle back beyond the point of no return.

Horntoad shook his head slowly.

"Alright, then," Childers announced, snapping back into his typical upbeat delivery. "Let's get her back to Low Camp with the others before the wagon train from Puro Pura shows up and leaves empty-handed. That'd be all our hides."

He kneeled down, dusted off his black hat, and eased it back onto his head.

"Boss," Klamath warned, his bushy brush guard of a mustache swaying gently in the breeze. The rest of him remained motionless, causing him to appear more like a wizened old mossy oak than a man.

"I know. I know," Childers said as he started away toward the trail and the horse he already had prepared. His mid-length black duster flapped in the breeze as he walked. He stopped to let a steer-sized sage brush tumble past and then continued on around the corner.

"Just wait until I'm on the other side of the boulder before you shoot him again," he hollered over his shoulder. Horntoad looked at the robot hanging from the boulder and then to the towering Klamath.

"Best you get, before Blackie Lung there loses his shit."

Horntoad looked back at the robot.

"Did you mean that to rhyme?"

Klamath just looked at him. Lightning bloomed amidst dark clouds way off in the distance. The wind whipped up ash from the campfire and the short man had to turn away to shield his eyes. The wind smelled of dusty sage and ozone. He looked back at Klamath, nodded, and then skipped off through the bushes to catch up.

Hank "Klamath" Pettibone looked across the short distance to where Bodie was examining him. Their eyes were even though the robot was upside down and hanging from a boulder, slowly brushing a clean spot on the charred, towering rock that had acted as a wind-break and campsite for time immemorial.

"Well, tin-ass? Got anything to say for yourself?" Klamath asked.

No response.

"Looks like my ol' Trapdoor here caused you to spring a leak," he said, patting the long-barreled Winchester cradled in his arms and nodding in the direction of Bodie's abdomen, just above his right hip, where a healthy stream of gray-green metallic ooze was running down his torso and dripping onto the sand and rocks.

Bodie finally spoke. "That was you on the cliff with that elephant gun? Nice shot. Five hundred yards. In the dark..."

"What're you getting at?" Klamath asked, still looking at Bodie with those dead, gray eyes.

Again, no response.

"Suit yourself. We got the girl," he said, spitting a stream of gritty brown saliva into the sand below where Bodie was hanging.

"Ya know that, right?" Klamath asked.

Bodie nodded. His mouth was a thin row of lights.

Klamath chuckled a bit at that. "Yer an odd one, for a toaster. Ya know Childers isn't bluffing about welding you to a cart, right?" One eyebrow lifted questioningly. "Having to push an ore cart till yer circuits burn out... What was running through yer mind? Wading into a mess of vipers, expecting not to get bit? Thought toasters were smarter than that. Where do you all come from, anyway?"

Bodie said nothing.

"Whole mess o' you up in Low Camp. A mess more up in Puro Pura where the big man's got his place. But you toasters are just here in the Estranyazie. Nowhere else... And then the kids, with their strange magicky ways. All a bit odd, isn't it?"

Bodie again remained silent. Swayed gently at the behest of the increasingly urgent wind.

The brim of Klamath's hat flipped up on the windward side, revealing shaved, short, white-gray hair beneath a longer mop of scraggly gray that curled down into a thickly braided ponytail halfway down his back. He pressed his hat down firmly and cinched the drawstring, squinting against the scouring grit.

"I'm gonna wander off a ways yonder," he said, motioning with his head toward the sheltered pocket where the cliff and the nape of the low hill converged.

"If I see you move, I'm gonna punch more holes in that pretty metal skin o' yours."

Bodie's mouth formed the same flat line, and Hank Pettibone's dead eyes assumed an amused twinkle. He took Bodie's silence as acceptance of his terms. He then turned and walked away into the scrub, not bothering to look back until he was positioned far up in the notch, out of the direct wind and approaching weather but with an easy shot at the strung-up tin-ass.

Justine Marie Sever was scooped out, dried, and hollow. Tears, long gone, were just salty streaks where fair skin peeked out from grit and grime. The wagon wallboards bucked at her with each bump in the trail, of which there were many. Her butt and hands were numb from sitting, and the dry, cold wind tore at her hands and cheeks, like haunting laughter through an abandoned mill.

Frontier life was no easy thing, and it took a person of determination and resolve to stomach it.

Thirteen-year-old girls were no exception. Born of the Alta Estranyazie, she knew how to take care of herself and just how much the high plains would take in return if she let them. Her ma and pa had known it, too. All too well.

Despite her attempts at bravery, Justine's facade of stoicism crumpled at the thought of them—the fresh memory of their deaths at the hands of the men who now held her freedom. She had a good idea at where they were taking her, even if just in a general sense. Kids were for mining.

She wondered how little Pete Montalvo had got on—foolishly risking his life, and that of his family, to warn hers. She'd always suspected he was a little sweet on her, though it'd been a couple of years since they'd shared more than a handful of words together.

They didn't have to kill them. Her mind rabbited to that thought and just as quickly corrected itself. *Yes … yes, they did.* It didn't make it right, but they most certainly couldn't have the likes of Joseph Sever hunting them down to retrieve his daughter. And no less that of Mrs. Sever. The fate that would have befallen these men would be legendary if left in the hands of that God-fearing frontier woman.

Despite her generally hospitable demeanor, she had a streak of the severe that'd raise its head when injustice was allowed to germinate. Unlike some kids her age, Justine had never taken to stealing that which wasn't hers on account of never—absolutely ever—wanting to be the target of her mother's ire.

The image of their lifeless bodies jumped into her mind, and she pressed her palms into her eyes, squeezing fiercely to make it go away, but all she could see was blood. Blood on their clothes in big blotches. Blood on their faces. Pools of it, midnight black, under the storm-darkened sky, seeping into the sand like crude oil returning to the earth.

She swallowed down bile raking at the back of her throat. The hollowness inside her was cavernous. It felt like she could drop a stone into it and never hear it echo back—could only imagine its depths.

Somehow, now, her capacity for doing right or doing wrong seemed a concept just as unknowable. How would she divine the difference between them now that the evil she'd been exposed to was so vast?

Yesterday, she might have considered killing a bug, the morality of the act, weighing it thoughtfully before execution. Today, she could not in any way consider the killing of every single man in this company with the same regard.

In her present dark mood, she had exactly zero inhibitions about doing just that. Monsters make monsters. Is that what she was now? A monster? Justine took solace in the fact that at least monsters had teeth. At least the ones that haunted her imagination and kept her up as a small child did.

The wagon jostled her out of her thoughts and she looked out across the snow and red dirt that stretched on into infinity beneath a swirling carbon sky. The wide-open lonesome was... Well, it was home. The emptiness that pressed in around her that felt so final, so resolute? It was home, too. It was around her. And it *was* her. And nothing that was left in the world could change that.

She pulled her knees up close, tucking her dress tight around her ankles and between her knees to keep the biting wind, nipping at her exposed skin and shifting grit up into her eyes and mouth, out. And then she did something she told herself she'd never do. She reached down deep inside for that old connection. The silver strand of magick she'd pressed down so fearfully when she was young—when it first presented itself and threatened to sweep her away with its power.

She stretched for it now. Once a shimmering, ephemeral stream, it was now a molten river. Through her mind, she descended. Through the madness, the malevolent chaos, she traveled to land firmly on its shores. Now she bared herself to the pressure waves of its crushing heat. Now she tasted sweet sulfur on her tongue. Now she could think of nothing so comforting as the image of all these men, their bodies, scattered; entrails, blood, and viscera nurturing the thirsty soil.

Smiling a Mona Lisa smile, Justine pulled her braid over her shoulder and worried at it idly. Sandy-brown strands, dry and split, poked out of the ratty plait. Her perfect hair, meticulously looked after by her ma, was now ragged after her harrowing flight and subsequent capture. She stroked it now as she stared off over the plains and reached into that glowing, super-heated morass. Justine drew up a manageable bit and watched as a man's horse stumbled. It righted itself quickly, shaking its head, its eyes rolling wildly before it settled and resumed its plodding pace behind the wagon. She smiled a little. Not a pleasant one at all.

There were other kids in the wagon with her. She hadn't spared them a second glance until now. She recognized one or two from town: Joseph Moberg, but not his sister Janicee, and then Harriet Pickfordshire, the preacher's daughter. That was about it. They all looked as cold and miserable as she was. She assumed they'd suffered similarly. They certainly looked as wretched and lost in their thoughts as she had been. She would not be like that. Though outwardly she could appear that way, it would only be because her situation required a certain amount of discretion. She didn't want to stand out. Not until the time was right.

Justine thought it, and the gray, speckled mare stumbled again. This time, its cowboy sat up in his saddle, jerked out of some meandering of the mind. Snapping at the reins and clinching an ashed-out cigarette between his teeth, he trotted the horse up past the wagon, presumably to freshen up himself and his mount by stretching her legs.

<001020xx1213?a00…001020xx1213?a00x110100… 001020xx121_a00x110100xxbxx01111>

The alphanumerics scrolled across Bodie Nine's ocular circuits. The background resolved from a darkness to dim, monochrome night vision.

<Scrub brush>

<Sand>

<Wind>

A ricochet somewhere close and then the crack of a large caliber gun from a distance.

<Time between impact and audible report … 0.513s>

The image he was seeing was inverted. He was upside down.

Klamath, Bodie realized, recalling some of what had occurred before losing consciousness. He jerked up, grabbed the rope that bound his feet together, and heard another ricochet right where he'd been a moment before. Gripping the rope in both hands, he broke it before hearing the rifle's report and dropped, rolling to the ground before the soot-covered wall of the boulder he'd been hanging from. Dirt kicked up near his face and he dove for cover. Another report. His foot ripped away mid-flight, causing him to land awkwardly. Two more sharp claps echoed off the cliff walls, but Bodie was around the corner and running as fast as his demolished foot would take him.

He judged it'd take Klamath a few seconds at least to reposition so that he could get a shot off with the boulder impeding his line of sight. Bodie was unarmed, on foot, with a remarkably accurate assailant with a high-powered rifle tracking him. His lower-level OS, Helga, attempted to provide odds of survivability and he shut her down. Too, the endless stream of gruesome images provided by Dmitr.

Appreciated ... but no.

Bodie angled left, judging that Klamath would have gone right based on the lesser slope of the hip versus the sheer face of the cliff wall. Something ripped him from his feet and spun him in the air. He landed awkwardly on his head and shoulder, grinding to a halt on the sandstone. He realized he'd been wrong about Klamath taking the easy slope. He lay there, listening intently for movement, but the wind and sand gusting through the bushes masked anything more than a few feet away. The wind was warmer, he realized. A cold front was pushing in.

Was Klamath moving or waiting? Oddly, the smell of decomposing flesh entered Bodie's senses like a sickening wave. He wondered if his sensory circuits were addled with all the beatings he'd taken of late, but no, it was clearly rot … decay … old, old death.

Bodie tuned his senses in the direction of the wind and heard something moving through the night-shrouded brush.

Long, heavy steps. The sound of sniffing, something animal, something large was in the swale with him. Bodie remained still.

Most animals, like wolves or puma, would have nothing to do with him, but not all animals required flesh for fuel. Some of the Estranyazie's more unusual denizens found Bodie as interesting as any warm-blooded creature. He didn't know why this was. There was an inextricable link between the esoteric and humankind. The darkest of these creatures fed on souls, or so the lore seemed to indicate. Bodie could find no sense in why such creatures would be intrigued by his presence, him being a robot, but then he found much that didn't seem to fit with the natural order of things here in the high plains.

Again movement, but this time, it was from the far edge, near the cliff. A horse whinnied. "H'ya, h'ya!" He heard Klamath's voice, an edge of terror in it, and then horse hooves as the beast pounded a retreat, racing along the cliff and out toward the main trail he'd followed just the day before. Movement close by, closer than he'd realized, and the large creature brushed the bushes within an arm's length of him. Long, thudding strides pounded the hard-packed earth and rock, cracking branches echoed sharply in the night air as it pursued its prey.

"H'ya!" Klamath yelled madly, reins snapping as he pushed his mount as fast as it would go in the low light.

Bodie tracked the increasingly reckless noises of the creature as it cut more of an angle on the man's retreat. He hazarded a quick peek above the bushes and saw massive elk-like antlers but knew he'd been hearing a massive bipedal creature. Nothing of what he saw or heard was right by nature. This was an unholiness.

Man was the largest upright critter of natural origin. This creature was very tall. Taller than even a grizzly bear on its hind legs. And then there was the stench of decay. The natives of the lower plains had a word for it, he thought.

Wun-dee-go. A skeletal man-beast that fed on human flesh. An account by Wilford Smyyd, by most accounts credible, suggested the creature could reach upward of fifteen feet in height. Bodie had been skeptical, first of its existence and second of it being quite that tall if it did in fact roam the blasted wastes of the Estranyazie.

He felt no confidence that the creature might not find him of similar interest as it did the man Klamath. Bodie wondered only briefly about the horse. Perhaps he'd be lucky and the Wun-dee-go would eat Klamath and leave his horse? Bodie admitted that he was not feeling all that lucky. Best to beat a hasty retreat while the creature's interest was elsewhere.

His lower consciousness started calculating odds about the Wun-dee-go leaving the horse unharmed again and he suppressed it.

Bodie heard gunshots as he cut back up to the ridgeline opposite the cliff and kept pushing until he was well up onto the plateau—angling west for a ways before he dared attempt to parallel the northerly trail.

The sounds of pursuit, either of Klamath or the creature, had gone swiftly quiet. Probably not a good sign.

That still left him with no guns, just the clothes on his back, an oozing wound on his back where the right side of his ribcage would be, and half a foot, also on his right side. Needless to say, his boots were in need of repair. And his hat, his favorite wide-brimmed Batterson in Colorado cream, was missing.

He wasn't worried. A fine hat like that would turn up somewhere...

After a bit, Bodie reached an arroyo and was forced to turn north. Always north. He breathed in a deep sigh and followed fate, perpendicular to the path of travel of the now-setting moon.

The sun would be up in a few short hours. Best to cover whatever ground he could before he had to worry about being seen.

Something tickled his senses. He pulled up abruptly. An echo of a memory caused him to lie down in the sand, an ear to the earth.

An odd slithering sound could be heard. Something like grain in a grindstone but vaguely ... digital? It was haunting and beautiful and captivating. The sound grew closer, and Bodie sat up as a pool of silver light bubbled to the surface and gathered into a puddle the size of a small plate. It looked like mercury but was ever so slightly luminescent. It could have been the light of the moon, but Bodie was sure it was not. For once, Helga and Dmitr were silent.

He reached out, and the liquid metal slithered into his hand. It felt hot. Molten hot but ice cold at the same time. He shook his head in disbelief. This was cold-bright, he realized. He'd only, to this point, heard it spoken of. It was too valuable to be left about and its use too specific to be utilized by the common folk of the Estranyazie. They said it was… Well actually, they didn't say what it was used for. Bodie felt certain that it was for rocket ships. There was no such thing, of course, but that which existed in the wild imagination of the strangest of writers and illustrators. But he felt no less certain that this was the case.

The liquid jiggled and shivered in his hand and then split of its own accord in several directions, shooting up his arm, and then crawling all over his body. His eyes shot wide as it dove into the holes in his torso, while another tributary ran up his neck, and yet more oozed up from the ground and latched on to his foot. He repressed panic as the sensations of heat and ice prickled at the open edges of his many wounds.

<Percent deterioration of capability: Thirty-five… Thirty-two… Twenty-nine> Helga provided.

Bodie's terror dissolved slowly into cautious relief. He felt tingling from no less than thirteen distinct areas of physical trauma throughout his broken body. Discovery of the liquid metal seemed to be a good thing. He stretched his neck and pulled himself upright. Most fortuitous. Maybe luck was favoring him now?

<Percent deterioration of capability: Twenty-six>

Well, that was a start, he thought. His foot looked better, and he was no longer oozing. He would definitely be paying attention to sensing more of the coldbright. He was certain that was not the material that he was originally cast from, but it definitely worked in a pinch.

Something came to him, a ghost of a thought. In his mind's eye, he saw a blue-white saucer suspended in a sea of stars. No, a sphere. Like the moon but alive.

Water, clouds, and earth. Was this the world as viewed from the heavens?

And like that, the image was gone.

Bodie looked down and could see that where his foot and boot had been sheared away by Klamath's rifle, his new metallic skin had fused with the leather remnant. He didn't have a foot sticking out of half a boot; he had a boot, half made of leather and half made of metal. It moved like boot leather. It was creased in the same way. For all intents and purposes, it was Bodie's boot. That would do. For now.

Bodie pressed on along the ragged edge of the escarpment until it drew into a thin copse of leafless trees, with ghostly white puzzle bark. He moved forward, but something in his circuits warned him to be cautious. Nothing was out of the ordinary. He scanned for creatures and came up with nothing. Well, *that* was out of the ordinary. On a typical evening, the desert would be a menagerie of critters going about their stealthy business. Maybe it was the incoming storm?

Bodie pressed forward but more slowly. He'd had the sense that the dry gorge was pushing him northeast, which he imagined would rejoin the trail he'd departed when waylaid by the black-masked man's outlaw gang—the trail the tall man with the dead eyes had fled down, and the Wun-dee-go had pursued him on.

Bodie slowed his approach a little more. Wind whistled through the branches. Movement off to his right startled him but turned out to be a large tumbleweed bounding across the gently sloping hillside. It bounced into the tree line and stuck fast, quivering in the wind like a fly in a spider's web. Bodie's visual emotive indicator drew a thin line across where his mouth would be.

It'd been exactly forty-three minutes since he'd heard anything of the chase. He wasn't sure now what he'd hoped would happen. Bodie decided to skirt the wooded area and head for the road. He walked along the edge as the wooded area dropped further down an embankment and into a snarled lowland he imagined must collect a substantial amount of water in the torrential rains that happened from time to time.

A branch snapped in the woods below and he dropped to a crouch, waiting, listening. Seconds went by and no other noises carried to his audio circuits. He waited another dozen or so and opted to continue.

Was it possible for robots to get freaked out? Yes. Yes, it was.

Bodie's next step did not feel firm. In fact, it felt downright squishy, and then, in the blink of an eye, he was tumbling down the embankment in an avalanche of rock and dirt and bushes before colliding with ghostly white trees and carrying on down slope a full thirty yards farther into the snarl of brush, briar, and fetid grasses at the bottom of the depression.

Bodie sprang to his feet and paused, listening. But all he heard were the remnants of dirt and rock still trickling down the crumbled hillside above. He took one hesitant, sucking step. It sunk halfway up his boot. He took another and cringed as it slurped loudly in the still night air before slopping back down. He scanned for biologicals again and came back blank. Well, there was nothing for it but to press ahead. It wasn't like he was going to be able to get out of here without making a ridiculous amount of racket.

He trudged on, slopping and slurping loudly, and then spotted something shiny a few yards beyond. His enhanced vision made out the side plate of a lever-action rifle. The breach half disengaged. It rested against a blackened stump. Beyond it was another metal object, partially obscured by what looked to him like the decomposing ribcage of an adolescent moose. There were moose in the Estranyazie. Some anyway. The scene before him seemed an unlikely pairing.

The wind clawed at the tree branches above him and he used the sound to cover his own racket of movement, but then something rose over the roar of the wind. Something loud and haunting and absolutely lubricant-curdling. It was a howl but deeper. Something … not wolf and not bear and not puma. Lower, louder, like the wind itself, but filled with eons of yearning if that was possible. It was no more than a quarter of a mile away.

Bodie bolted forward, scanning the terrain for more weapons, but something not broken or packed with mud. He stomped and splashed, and the sound felt like it was all he could hear. The howl echoed again, louder. Closer. Bodie burst forward, scanning now in the muck and in the trees.

He saw them now … the bodies. Desiccated, shredded, and decomposed, they littered the trees like ornaments swaying in the wind. Trophies. Terror flooded his circuits. The howl boomed again. It could be no further away than the edge of the tree line. He splashed on, but there were no weapons he could find that weren't destroyed in some way. The branches tore at him as he passed, blinded him as he pushed through, and then something caught his foot, and he plunged headlong into a deep, putrid pool and lay there. Face down … waiting to die. Or worse…

CHAPTER 3

ELDRITCH SPIRITS

Bodie sensed that the sun was up. He was face down in muck about two feet below the surface of a stagnant puddle, deep in the haunted wood decorated with the bodies of the Wun-dee-go's victims. But—small victory—he was still alive and his robot soul hadn't been scooped out with a broken moose femur or some similarly horrible instrument. That was probably impossible, he conceded. Probably.

He turned his head just enough for his ocular circuits to make out a vaguely prismatic illumination playing across the surface of the gray water above him, an oddly spiderweb-like effect.

Correction, he thought to himself, *I'm resting face down in the muck about a foot below the* frozen *surface of a stagnant puddle.*

During the night, he'd calmed his feelings of desperation and terror by counting backward from the square root of pi. That may not sound like much since the square root of pi is less than two, but if you take the whole number of 1.77245385091 and throw in

Mississippis, it can take a while. At some point, after realizing he wasn't dead or dismembered yet, he relegated himself to just waiting things out, thinking that, maybe in the morning, the creature would be sleeping or doing whatever it was that Wun-dee-gos did when they weren't stalking the night, slurping entrails, or generally acting creepy.

Bodie lifted his head slowly. His sensors pinging the area for critters he knew still would not be there. However, he was proved wrong again. Twenty feet up in a tree just yards from where he languished, waterlogged in the black water, was a woodpecker. Ironic, considering his earlier encounter with the baby Downy—missing under conspicuous circumstances.

Bodie chided himself not to be too sore about it. It was the cycle of all things, after all. He'd just been luckier on this go-around than Downy had.

Bodie's mouth (visual emotive indicator panel is such a cumbersome title and VEIP just seems a silly thing to say) formed a flat line of dim lights as he pushed himself up, breaching the surface like a cautious frog, through the thin sheet of ice. He pinged the sensors again and still came up with nothing but that solitary bird that was not Downy. In fact, from where he was, he could tell that it was a yellow-bellied sapsucker. *Really?* he queried Helga, and she confirmed it. Dmitr provided an image. *Huh...*

It started pecking; the noise echoing off the barren trees and cliffside. Bodie Nine turned to sit on his metal alloy ass and marveled at the sunlight brushing the tops of the ghost trees with blushing neon amber, pink, and gold, playing magnificently off the withered bodies. Muck and mire dribbled down his metal face and shoulders. He was naked. Robot naked wasn't all that weird to the folk of the Alta Estranyazie, but it felt weird to him. Maybe he was different, like the sharpshooter had suggested. Bodie searched his circuits for the man's name, but he'd been in and out of consciousness throughout the night. The coldbright must be doing something wonky with his circuits, he speculated.

<Klamath> his sub-self provided.

That was it.

The silence of the fetid, dead-tree Wun-dee-go marsh was complete, so Bodie deemed it safe and got up and walked off. North ... of course.

Helga and Dmitr were chattering nervously back and forth; one with statistics, the other with archived images. Bodie was trying to ignore them. The whole experience with the Wun-dee-go had shaken them up something fierce, and he was concerned that they were losing focus on the mission—the directive, he realized.

He had given himself a directive? Wonder of wonders...

The thought caused him to pause in the middle of the trail, which he'd begun following only a mile or two back. He'd given himself a directive? He wanted to search the processes that had led to that conclusion but was a little concerned to do it. He'd probably find an error, and he really didn't want any reason to question his intention to go and find the girl. That was it. That's what he was going to do.

Off to his right, between where he stood on the trail and a prominent, flat-topped boulder overlooking a wide, sandy gorge, he caught an image that didn't quite fit the surroundings. He zoomed in and saw that it was an upward-pointed boot sole. Implying that its owner still occupied it and was, most likely, lying prostrate on his back.

<87% likelihood deceased> his lower-self provided.

"Yeah, I'd figured as much," he said out loud to no one in particular.

A montage of corpses ensued, and Bodie pushed the stream of images aside so he could focus on the issue at hand. The two OS layers *were* getting more and more preoccupied with things of a morbid nature. He wasn't sure what to do about that. But for the time being, he had more pressing concerns.

"Map areas of sensory anomaly within a two-mile radius," he suggested, thinking that this would bring up a very large number of items and keep his lower selves busy for a while.

He made his way off the path. There were pockets of snow down here on the low side of the trail in the shadiest spots. A minute later and he was staring at the boot just poking out from under a medium-sized sagebrush, its branches silver-gray and the buds a dusty, faded ochre.

The boot *was* attached to a body. The body was a lot newer than he was expecting. It was hours old.

A man—late thirties, shortish, with bushy brown hair and a bushy mustache and goatee to match. He was a rider from the look of him. Not an outlaw. Bodie had surmised that this man had likely been delivering post. He deduced this much by the mailbag lying an arm's length away. It was full, meaning that whoever had fatally harmed him had not done so to steal the mail, but, likely, to steal his pony.

A quick scan of the area suggested that a solitary man had struck the express rider on a narrow section of the trail that wrapped just below the location of the man's body, which had been drug to this point and left to natural processes. The other footprints were large. The whole thing smacked of a desperate man needing to get somewhere in a hurry. A man without a horse. *Klamath.*

Bodie guessed that he was beelining it to Low Camp to warn the others and deal with the girl. Bodie was precious low on time. He already started filing issues in his karmic log before he even started undressing the dead man and scavenging his clothing and provisions. He'd have to leave the bag lest he be instantly recognized as a mail thief—a federal crime punishable by hanging. Not that that'd do much to Bodie, but still, the last thing he needed was to have his character impugned and be branded an outlaw.

Bodie said a few words over the body of the deceased, not to relieve his karmic debt in any way but just because it was the right thing to do. Besides, the man had a fine mustache and well-worn spurs, just like a cowboy should. He said as much to the gallery of quivering sage.

Bodie stacked a bunch of rocks on the corpse to dissuade vultures or coyotes. There was no shortage of rocks in the high plains. And then he walked down to the switchback section of trail and continued down into the valley on his way to Low Camp and to what he knew was a whole mess of trouble waiting for him. He sighed and then picked up the pace to an easy jog.

CHAPTER 4

AND HELL'S
COMING WITH ME

Justine woke with a jolt as the wagon came to a halt. Images of her ma and pa were fresh in her mind. She'd replayed those last few moments before they'd run, abandoning the home of her childhood, possibly for good.

Her father had been talking about taking her up to the far end of their claim to hunt for raw gems in the scree-covered hillside. Her ma wanted none of it and hated the idea of her girl tromping over every inch of God's creation, possibly stirring up one of the terrible creatures of the Estranyazie in the process. It was a dangerous and unnecessary risk, in her opinion. Justine had defied her and taken her father's side. Despite the wood-burning stove nurturing a healthy stoke, it felt to her as if the temperature dropped ten degrees in that cabin. The look on her mother's face, warring between anger and woundedness, would never go away.

The wagon lurched and then stopped again as the driver set the brake and jumped down to go talk to a couple of the men from the camp. She looked around, and the terrain was foreign. She couldn't place quite where they were. North for sure. Maybe a bit west into the hills?

They'd stopped only briefly in a busy town that she heard someone call Low Camp. Then they were corralled into another wagon pulled by a forlorn-looking shaggy gray mule. After hours of travel up a winding canyon, they were deposited at the bottom of a stepped wall of bare rock. The revealed stone was white, brown, and red, with a smattering of blackish-blue streaks thrown in for good measure. This had been part of the canyon, but much of it had been stripped away.

The canyon floor was a wide washout with a bump of a hill wreathed by well-weathered clapboard shacks. In a hard rain, she imagined much of this would be underwater. No doubt they'd redirected the flow upstream for their own purposes.

After a while, she and the other seven captives were sat down in the dirt in a row facing an ominous hole in the mountain. Two at a time, the children were placed in mining carts which lurched forward into the darkness, pulled by some cable or rope that Justine could not see. And then lastly, she and the preacher's daughter, Harriet, were loaded into a cart and then plunged into the cold dark of the mine. Harriet had screamed when the cart jerked forward, but Justine did not. She neither spoke nor expressed any emotion on their journey from Low Camp. Nor would she now that they'd arrived at their final destination.

Inside her mind, the fires of hell still burned hotly. And in those fires were the faces of every man who'd participated in their incarceration in any small way.

"Justine," Harriet whispered urgently, her face unseen in the cloying darkness around them.

"Justine!" she hissed again. "Talk to me. Say something," she pleaded, but Justine ignored her. Her mind was busy devising the plan for her escape. That plan, however, was increasingly crowded out by an ethereal, ephemeral murmur—an aggregation of low voices like warm wind through barren trees.

It was the coldbright, she realized. Her hate burned inside her, and somehow that chorus surrounded her, surrounded the hate, and, in some mysterious way, amplified it. It was cold in the mine, but Justine couldn't be bothered to feel it. Inside, she burned, and within the roots of the earth, the coldbright called to her.

She reached out and let her fingertips drag along the rock wall as they continued their journey into the mountain, and with each bump, each crease in the rock, she felt the element more and more. When she pulled her fingers away, the tips were covered in a dimly illuminated substance. She turned to look back in the direction from which they'd come, and a thin stream of light, like a distant river's reflection on a dusky plain, trailed behind them. A trail of quicksilver on the ground between the steel rails that carried the carts. The coldbright. It was drawn to her somehow. And her to it.

Inside her, the fires grew as billows to a furnace. The fires and the hate were comingled now, the white-hot flow of magick bubbling and steadily rising. And with it, murderous voices, a demon choir roaring in her ears.

Justine sat back against the wall of the rattling cart and smiled alone in the darkness. Soon...

Soon, she would have her justice.

"I'm just a bad man tryin' to be a good man. It's the human condition. We're all of us afflicted." This was stated at volume by the boss man, Blackie Lung. His point was punctuated perhaps by his black clothes, black cowboy hat, and black bandana covering his eyes. Also, there were tears of blood flowing slowly over coagulating streaks of dark crimson upon his blond stubbled cheeks. Though horrific, it lent him an air of earnestness, at the very least.

Bodie heard this argument after having entered the town of Low Camp, seeing a poster for his arrest, following a young Indian boy through a series of back alleys, and finding himself here, just inside the entrance to a two-story warehouse of some sort. The building was old but refurbished somewhat recently. It had an upper level that ringed the large open space in the middle and, at the far end on a raised platform of some sort, was the man Bodie knew only as the man in black.

<Childers "Blackie" Lung> his lower self provided. *Thank you.*

Blackie Lung was the one who'd shot Bodie in the head and inflicted much injury upon his own face in the process. Judging by the bandana and tears of blood, the injuries were extensive.

"Profiting upon the suffering of others ain't got no good in it, Mr. Blackie," Bodie hollered across the space. "Subjugating children, forcing them to labor under the earth for personal gain? That just makes you a bad man doing bad things. No sense trying to gentrify it." That was the entirety of Bodie's called response, but then no one in the Alta Estranyazie put much account on the words of a robot, even one as dashing and handsome as Bodie Nine.

"Well, if you can't *be* good, you might as well *live* good. Am I right? Now..." And this is where Blackie looked around broadly to encompass all the hired guns hiding throughout the warehouse trap. "Kill this proselytizin' renegade toaster before his sermonette puts me off my supper."

Movement echoed throughout the upper and lower spaces. Via radio frequency that was beyond the ability of human anatomy to perceive, Bodie had already pinpointed each of his would-be assailants. He ascertained roughly what armaments they possessed and formulated his plan of attack. Actually, it had little to do with attack and a lot more to do with running and hiding if he were to be honest.

He proceeded with haste. Diving to the side and dodge-rolling, he came up with an explosive jump that landed him at an opening in the railing of the second-floor catwalk. Bullets careened wildly after him, a cacophony of gunfire. Within seconds, the smell of gunpowder pervaded the room, and billows of smoke and dust were struck through by shafts of light peering in at the activity through open windows and the occasional hole in the roof.

Bodie lunged left, coming upon a man struggling to follow his movements fast enough, and Bodie decided maybe an attack was in the cards after all.

He deposited the man on his back, unconscious, with a broken jaw and teeth several yards away. The man's rifle lay where he'd been kneeling behind a pile of draft horse tack.

Bullets continued to pepper the railing and column next to him as he snagged the rifle, dove to the side, and came up behind another column. Bodie's arms extended the rifle around the corner of the column, and he fired without sighting down the barrel, just using his scrolling map and robust targeting capability. Which, he thought, was an odd sort of thing to have for a robot whose purpose seemed to be to just fetch odd parts and pieces. There was a man behind this business. A man named Zilich, they said, lived just beyond Puro Pura, high in the mountains that ringed the northern edge of the Alta Estranyazie. Bodie imagined he'd have to pay that man a visit. After he saved the girl, Justine. And that, after he extricated himself from his present predicament.

Two outlaws on the opposite catwalk dropped quickly from well-placed shots. Another dove behind cover just as a bullet slammed into Bodie's back. He spun with the impact and fired the .44 carbine from his hip, dropping the man who'd shot him. Behind him was another who stared down at a growing dark stain on his dingy undershirt.

"Two for the price of one," he vocalized, amused, and then logged a negative tick in his karmic log for deriving too much pleasure in the killing of a man. Best to err on the side of the conservative when calculating one's own place on the continuum of good and evil.

Presently, a heavy rhythmic thudding issued from the far end of the warehouse. With each thump, explosions of wood from the catwalk deck and surrounding walls, columns, and stored materials burst into the air. Bodie spun and started sprinting up the catwalk, away from the chaos of dust and splintering wood. Daring a glance down, he caught the sight of Blackie Lung, turning the crank on a wheel-mounted gun with multiple barrels. Smoke and fire exploded from it while the masked man hooted with glee and followed Bodie's movements with lead and pandemonium.

<Survivability decreasing precipitously>

Bodie ignored the less-than-helpful statement of facts and dove headlong into a pile of straw behind a stack of large wooden barrels. A pile of straw which, oddly enough, concealed a neatly arranged row of smithing anvils. Bodie struck hard and struggled to maintain functionality while the lower half of his body, not quite concealed by the pile, twitched convulsively.

The maelstrom of wood and lead raced down the floorboards, and then the barrels exploded with some liquid or another, covering Bodie in straw and a sticky morass of amber.

< 0 0 1 0 2 0 x x 1 2 1 3 ? a 0 0 … 0 0 1 0 2 0 x x - 1 2 1 3 ? a 0 0 x 1 1 0 1 0 0 … 0 0 1 0 2 0 x x 1 2 1 _ a00x110100xxbxx01111>

Bodie's eyes sprang open. The air was filled with dust, settling straw and feathers, and an eerie silence.

"How 'bout it, bwah?" a man hollered. "You gonna come down with yer hands up? Or am I going to continue to poke holes in this perfectly fine building until I poke enough of them in you to be 'sured yer dead?"

Bodie's mind jerked back to the present. *Blackie.*

Also, Bodie now heard a few muffled groans coming from wounded men throughout the structure. He knew there must be at least a dozen left unharmed, not willing to come out of hiding until their boss was done raining unholy hell on the place.

Bodie sat up. Looking down, he realized that the rifle's barrel was ruined—bent at a point where the metal looked like a piece of unfired clay that had a finger jammed in it.

Bodie cast the firearm aside and stood up, a little unsteady still.

"If I give myself up, will you let the girl go? The one named Justine Sever?"

"Sure thing, toaster. What's one little girl to an operation like this? 'Sides, you gone and killed a good dozen of my men. I can't abide you carrying on like that. I might not be able to hire anyone at all 'nymore," Blackie Lung crooned in his most persuasive voice.

Bodie stepped forward to the edge of the catwalk, and presently, half his skull exploded back and to the left of him.

He dropped like a sack of flour as a deafening boom echoed through the silence of the building, shaking dust from the rafters.

Blackie's eyes snapped to the side door, where he now saw Klamath returning his .45-70 to the cradled position across his chest. He wore a self-satisfied smile under his bushy mustache, nodded acknowledgment, and spit a brown stream of saliva into the dirt and sawdust.

"Well. That's one way to do it," Blackie muttered under his breath. Then more loudly, "I rather liked my mechanical unit here, but, yeah. That'll do. Didja pack that load yerself? Course you did," he said, referring to the obviously overpowered rifle shot that'd just crippled the troublesome robot.

He looked around at the men straggling into the open space from their various hidey holes. "Tie him up," he hollered, making a circular motion with an upward pointing finger and then pausing to think. "With *chains* this time. From the rafters here. I wanna be sure he's dead and not just in one of those toaster-naps or whatever it is they do."

At the back of his thoughts, something wriggled. Not a thought as much as an ... ill-ease. And then a low moan arose to fill the air. Blackie's eyes snapped to Klamath, who was suddenly alert, eyes scanning the space.

The moan grew in intensity, and a wind whipped up a minor dust devil in the middle of the floor. It hung there improbably and refused to move for several seconds before dissipating and leaving the space in an eerie silence.

Justine stood in the center of a ceilingless room hewn from rock and lit dimly in the flickering orange light of scattered lanterns. Her eyes glowed brightly. Something whiter than the lanterns and fueled from a different source entirely. Eight or nine of the mining kids huddled in a cluster against the wall—terror etched on their faces and reflected in their eyes.

In the air around Justine, gently undulating streamers of silver hung in the air, emanating out toward the walls. The streamers seemed to pulse with power, and at the ends of five of those tentacle-like streams hung the lifeless bodies of the men who'd forced the children to work and who provided little food and meager accommodations for their efforts.

Rippling pools of metal bubbled to the surface before her and lifted into the air. They slithered under each foot like stairs as she stepped upward until, when she stood some five or six feet off the ground, they congealed into a disk beneath her.

And then the disk itself began to lift further off the ground. Justine looked up, peering into the darkness of the shaft as it continued several hundred feet to the entrance tunnel.

The bodies of her jailers bumped dumbly along the rock walls as she rose until she heard a cry from below. "Wait!"

She slowly came to a halt. Blinked her eyes and looked down.

The other children would be stranded and starve to death if left here. Justine felt nothing. But still, she dropped the men, and the silver strands shot down at the group huddled against the wall.

Screams of terror echoed off the walls but then slowly dissipated as one by one they realized that the liquid coldbright, rather than impaling them as they had the jailers, had simply wrapped them up and were lifting them up to safety.

Above them, Justine rose more and more swiftly, more and more certain of her power. She had barely tapped the reservoir within her. Only dipped a finger in that flow. It had been nothing to overpower those men, to break them like toys. A dark satisfaction swelled within her but then stopped abruptly. There was still more to do. More ... justice.

Minutes later, the children sat upon a tall-wheeled freight wagon with that same shaggy mule from before. They knew how to drive a wagon, even a heavy one like this. They were children of the Estranyazie, after all.

When the men of the camp came to quell this minor revolt, they had no idea of what awaited them. Justine had let the escapees round the corner of the canyon wall, out of sight, before she uncovered the mouths of the men who'd come to stop her. She let them yell, to curse her, to beg as she raised them further and further up on the ends of living metallic tentacles, and then, when as one they thrashed and struggled and screamed to be let loose, she obliged them. After all, who was she to keep them captive against their will?

Their broken bodies littered the sand and rock of the canyon floor. Not one survived. Wind whined through the rocks. Justine repressed a chuckle. She knew how it would sound, echoing off the canyon walls, infused with the power of the coldbright magick and her own mania. It would sound twisted and cruel and carry with it the wails of the recently deceased. She shook her head to clear her thoughts. She couldn't let a moment of weakness, of loathing and self-pity-fueled introspection, break the magick's thrall. An image of her parents' faces, their lifeless eyes, pierced through her thoughts. And her resolve returned. *Death for death. Murder for murder.*

Now, where was that little town again? Down the canyon, through the notch, and then down into the next. Justine looked south, and then moments later at treetops, and then down at the rocks and low scrub, and then the walls of the canyon as it passed beneath her. The silver disk beneath her feet, continuing to pick up speed as it rose, edged gently forward.

Streamers of luminescent liquid silver trailed behind her as she glided through the air. They looked like something between flowing faerie wings and the tendrils of a jellyfish. Images she'd only seen in picture books, of course. If only her parents could see her now. Or little Pete Montalvo on that muscular nag, so eager to swoop in and save the day...

She thought again of where she was going. It'd taken them half a day to get from Low Camp to the mine, the one they called Lucky. She snorted. Half a day by freight wagon, and she'd make the journey back in less than an hour.

Blackie Lung, Klamath, Horntoad, and eight or nine other outlaws—or company men as they called them in these parts—stood around looking at the swirl of dust in the middle of the floor. Soon a faint glow seemed to trace those spiraling wisps, and then it was obvious. Silver trails in the dirt and sawdust of the floor were circling a spot about the circumference of a barrel. It looked to Horntoad like the empty circles that sometimes developed within a school of fish.

He huffed out and then, in his low, gravelly voice, echoed the thoughts of every man present, "What ... the ... fuck?"

The men jumped as a screeching, snapping clatter came from above them. They watched slack-jawed as a hole peeled back in the roof, and then as gentle as a feather, a young girl descended the thirty-some-odd feet into their midst. She looked to them like an angel. She trailed silvery light, and her eyes glowed as with the very fire of heaven.

Bodie, a good portion of his robotic brains leaking out onto the floor where he'd been strung up, recognized her but was unable to vocalize as such. He may be woefully impaired, but that was no angel. That was Justine. Or what was left of her.

What Bodie could clearly see and the others could not was that she was a thing of the Estranyazie now. An esoteric creature, maybe Uktena, the flying serpent that was spawned from anger or envy and represented the underworld. Or possibly Ishkitini, an owl witch. *Or maybe*, he speculated, *something new...*

For the first time ever, Bodie Nine voluntarily initiated his shutdown sequence. No need to witness what would come next.

The men, awestruck, stared at Justine and then stepped back involuntarily as her body began to emanate an eerie silver light. Her tendrils drifted slowly down, spreading about the space, one subtly closing a side door, two others drawing the large cargo doors firmly together.

Blackie Lung noticed this, lifted his hat back to scratch at his greasy blond hair, and cocked his head suspiciously. "Just what kinda angel are you?" he asked.

Justine's eyes intensified, and she smiled.

```
< a 0 0 x 1 1 0 1 0 0 … 0 0 1 0 2 0 x x 1 2 1 _
a00x110100xxbxx01111>
```

Some minutes later, Bodie's waking protocol ran smoothly for a change. That was nice.

He studied the space before him. Though it was upside down, it was evident that bodies were everywhere. Blood ... was everywhere.

Someone definitely did not leave the space better than they had found it. Then he spotted a torso attached to the head of a man whose face was familiar to him. Klamath. Well ... maybe he needed to adjust his initial poor assessment. Some things were better.

For 0.0023 seconds, he wondered what happened, but then Helga and Dmitr provided a quick recap.

Justine had happened. The poor innocent girl with the biological project that he'd tried so desperately to save, and then to save her family, and then when they were gone, to save her. His record up to this point, he conceded, was dismal. What was that, a double-bogie?

Somewhere, a downy woodpecker sat in unsympathetic judgment.

It may be time for him to rethink his directive. His directive... Maybe that's why robots were forbidden to create their own. Maybe they needed a human to do it, to dumb it down, to make it more ... manageable?

Then a silver disc, feet, the hem of a dress, and, after a moment, the face of a girl slid into view from above him.

When her feet came to rest on the floor, they were eye to eye, him suspended upside-down and swaying slightly.

"You *are* an enigma, Mr. Bodie," she said in a voice that was sweet but contained a disturbing undertone of madness.

Of damnation and madness, Bodie thought.

"You, as well, Ms. Sever," he managed out raspily, cognitive circuits reforming rapidly but still a far cry from functional.

"The coldbright has given me some little knowledge. I go to kill the man at the center of all this, the one from the north, named Zilich. He's the only one that knows the truth about you. Please don't try to stop me."

"Don't think I could," Bodie replied honestly, gray-green liquid still dripping from the wound in his head.

She patted his cheek and looked at him wistfully, and there was a hint of sadness. Just then, silver strands flew from out of the shadows, gripped his limbs, and then ripped them from his body. Justine casually floated up through the hole in the roof, mercurial tendrils trailing behind until the last one slipped from sight and she was gone.

Bodie lay on the floor. And the platform. And the catwalk. Various bits of him lay in several places, actually. Carnage was everywhere. Flies were multiplying, buzzing enthusiastic circles through the air that smelled of gunpowder, death, and dust.

He'd seen Justine go but now could *feel* the absence of her. The coldbright had altered them both in ways he could only guess.

Bodie called through radio to his various bits. They responded by articulating and bending, and either dragging themselves or worming their way back to him. There was a small remnant of coldbright here still. It, too, slithered in response to his call. He wondered at it. It was just a metal, but under the influence of Justine's hatred, it was a malevolent, violent, and chaotic catalyst.

To him, it was soothing. It sang, in fact, longingly of beauty, of the cosmos, of far-off worlds. It told him stories, too. It told him a little of himself. Of a great battle in the sky. Of two men and two great ships. The coldbright, itself, the living metal that made up an outlaw craft. Bodie was a private audience to its ballad of that action.

It told of a pirate captain named Zilich who gathered the most dangerous creatures of the galaxy. Bodie was sworn to stop him and bring him to justice. But there was a great calamity and a double-cross.

Some of the coldbright drawn from the extents of the warehouse encountered the pool of inner goo that had gathered in the dirt below where Bodie was strung up. A glimmering silver thread grew up from it, and Bodie felt the coldbright slither into his exposed cranial cavity. A shock of light burst through every layer of his consciousness and his eyes shot wide open as the liquid metal tapped into his circuits and an orchestra of information spilled into his mind.

Visions burst into his mind as if he were living them. Bodie, his two lieutenants Helga and Dmitr, and a boarding party of his crew fought tooth and nail against Zilich's sentry bot minions. When they finally gained access, they found the man gone and the ship armed for self-detonation. Bodie's team evacuated, but Bodie himself turned back. He had to be certain that this wasn't a ruse and that Zilich wasn't waiting for them to beat a hasty retreat from what appeared to be a ticking time bomb, only to leave him with his ship and its cargo intact. Bodie hunted desperately until the clock ticked past the point of escape.

Out of desperation, Bodie downloaded his mind into one of the fallen Neinhelen sentry bots—the one thing he knew would survive the explosion. His team jumped out of local space per his emphatic command. He rode the disintegrating ship into the ground, along with its contents: a host of creatures so dangerous that it was illegal to hunt them or remove them from the worlds from which they came.

Now he understood how the Wun-dee-go and the other nightmare creatures of the Alta Estranyazie came to be. And why they existed here in such peculiar concentration.

But the story wasn't done. The coldbright longed to be reunited. To be whole again. The man in the north, beyond Puro Pura, was trying to do just that. To rebuild his ship.

Bodie looked across the dusty floor to the metal hand steadily working its way back toward him, looking not unlike a metallic tarantula dragging a hunk of driftwood.

"I have to talk to him. I need to know the rest of the story. Who I am, where I'm from... And did I leave anyone behind?" A void began to grow inside Bodie's chest. In his zealous quest, *did* he leave someone behind? His heart told him so. He sighed.

Justine was heading to Puro Pura to destroy Zilich. Bodie's thoughts careened wildly. *There must be another way.*

Perhaps with enough coldbright, he could piece all the information together, all the things he couldn't remember? No, he realized. Coldbright was the ship. But the man, his enemy, would know much, much more.

He could not let Justine get there before him.

A thump came from the vicinity of the main doors. Light spilled through, and then a silhouette appeared, accompanied by clopping hooves. Bodie's eyes zoomed in on the figure. As it drew closer, texture and color resolved until, finally, he could make out a familiar face. It was white, speckled with black, and it came up and nuzzled him, snorting dust into his face.

"Carole. I missed you somethin' fierce."

Bodie's arm found its socket just as something bumped him from behind. A leg. His leg. But it couldn't get to the shattered joint beneath him. Using his head for momentum, he rolled onto his back. Bodie couldn't use his arm yet to position it correctly, but the leg managed to work its way around without assistance. More streams of coldbright slithered across the floor, and he felt the metal enter his body, repairing and augmenting without need for instruction. He would be better than new soon. He looked around again. There were plenty of guns to choose from. Plenty of ammo. And then his ocular sensors picked up something he'd not seen before. A cowboy hat. It was dusty, but the Colorado cream beneath was undeniable—the signature color of a Batterson Boss.

A row of lights across Bodie's visual emotive indicator panel spread into a broad smile. "Well, sheeyit," Bodie drawled.

Maybe his luck was changing after all.

CHAPTER 5

MORE CRYPTID FAUNA OF THE ALTA ESTRANYAZIE

A little bit of darkness poofed up into the air like coal dust from a dropped boot. That dust coalesced into a shadowy form, and then there was Vohl the Devil, an imp-like creature that was actually something called a Nawri. Three feet tall on a good day, he had short pointy ears, a broad shark-like nose, his eyes were not black like a shark's but were larger, golden sunbursts with metallic flecks. They were beautiful if you ever had the misfortune to gaze upon them. For Nawri largely cared less about appearance and only about wealth. And magic. And they were cruel.

Vohl sniffed the air. His thin, potbellied body stepped lithely across the dirt floor of what appeared to be a working warehouse. His tail swished in irritated twitches. He didn't much appreciate the smell of human blood, of which there were gratuitous amounts.

Someone had been busy. He sniffed again, and then his hand slid down to the floor, where a trace stream of coldbright slithered up to meet it. He lifted the mercurial strand and watched as it gathered into a pool in his palm. And then he raised his hand and poured it into the other. He listened to its whispers as it fell.

Vohl's eyes grew round. He looked up at a shredded hole in the roof and then around for a second look at the bodies strewn about like discarded playthings.

A proper pilot's been born. One who can do more than just draw the coldbright from the earth. He surveyed the carnage once more, his eyes crinkling at the corners with the hint of a smile. "Zilich must hear of this," he said in a breathy whisper, though it was unlikely anyone would hear it. And then in another poof, he was gone.

Klamath heard it. He should have been dead, what with his head and torso separated from his limbs. That certainly would have been the end of him had he been any more human. The tin-ass had danced dangerously close to the truth when he'd questioned Klamath's ability to hit a far-off target in the dark. Of course, Klamath had dodged the question by suggesting that it was the light from the robot's VEIP or Visual Emotive Indicator Panel that had helped him acquire his target. But it was not.

Turns out, Klamath could see quite well in the dark. He was also pretty far from human these days. Unlike the robot, who was able to reattach his limbs, Klamath was going to have to grow them back. In fact, he'd already started. Flat, fleshy, ochre-colored tentacles extended from stump shoulders and stretched outward like shoots from a peapod seeking sunlight. Same for his legs, though they were a little further along. If anyone found him like this, it would make for an awkward conversation, especially since his face was pressed against the blood-soaked dirt and sawdust of the warehouse floor.

He'd heard the small raspy voice but had been unable to identify its source. All he knew was that it had to be yet another of the unusual denizens of the Alta Estranyazie—the xenozoological freakshow that it was. He was sure the voice wasn't human, anyway.

In his time with Blackie's gang, he'd heard of Zilich. In fact, before that, he'd been hunting the man for some time until he'd dropped off anyone's scope about a dozen years back. And then, he'd stumbled upon a story about an Arkhveran marshal who'd caught up with him and had apparently died while apprehending the notorious collector of the galaxy's deadliest creatures. A bounty having brought him near, in relative terms, to the scene, he'd decided that it would behoove him to verify the account.

It proved wildly inaccurate.

Klamath sucked in a dusty, gasping breath as his lungs finished repairing themselves. Eyes rolling wildly, they finally came to focus on his surroundings. At least what he could see from the floor. A writhing, transparent clutch of tentacles was his protean arm. It wriggled in the dirt, stretching and growing visibly but still interminably slow for his liking.

That girl had really done a number on him. All of them. Ordinarily it wouldn't be worth the effort, but the enormous bounty on Zilich was still active. Surprising for someone presumed to be dead for over a decade. Klamath had figured if he could prove the story, he might be able to claim at least some of it. But now that he knew the man was alive, well, that was another story entirely. Not that he'd have chosen to be dismembered in the pursuit of said reward. But such was a galactic bounty hunter's lot.

He pulled his arm tentacles up in front of his face. They were weak and sickly looking but growing. Though pathetic, he secretly praised the decision to ingest that alien goo he'd appropriated from a smuggler's hold rather than reporting it. He'd heard enough stories to know what it was and what it could do. That xenogeneic elixir, plus a multitude of cybernetic enhancements—too many to number—ensured he always came out on top. And he would do so again.

His arm was getting close enough to fully grown to help him assume a more dignified position. He pushed and pushed on translucent spaghetti arms but was still unable to roll over and flopped back down. Oh well. Patience was one of his many attributes. Soon enough, he'd be walking. He could steal some clothes, find a horse, and hightail it north to Puro Pura. As long as he was still able to identify Zilich's body, he'd be more than happy. That might be getting ahead of himself, though. Zilich had proven to be quite resourceful.

Of course, there was still the matter of the tin-ass. He had to die.

Bodie had great form. Elbows close to his ribs, upper body silent, he guided mostly with his knees, the reins just something to hold until it was time to stop. He was good, but Carole was a gift from the horse gods—damn near magickal. She intuited his commands, glided over challenging terrain with such ease, and was smart as a whip. It was good to have her back.

He let out a whoop. Sheets of water arced to either side as they plunged into the waist-deep waters of Big Rocky Ford. The name was misleading; not that it wasn't a broad section of river, but that it was actually gravel and sand through this section rather than cobbles that could break a horse's leg. As such, the pinto Appaloosa charged through it, hit dry sand on the other side, and launched up the embankment like a fox on fire.

Bodie marveled at her stamina. In another mile-and-a-half, they'd drop down to a comfortable trot to let her breathe, he thought. They'd made great time so far, but it was a solid two-day ride to Puro Pura, and then who knew where Zilich was from there. He wasn't sure how fast the girl, Justine, could travel, but he and Carole could only go so fast. He hoped it'd be enough. He reached out through his array of sensors for the girl but still came back blank.

<Sustained heart rate—233 bpm> Helga provided

Dmitr rifled through morbid images of dead horses and Bodie got the message.

Thanks, you two.

He dipped left under a bone-white branch and then right as they navigated what was a tight S-turn at their present speed. As they exited the corner, Bodie stood a little into his stirrups and reined Carole in. The mare pounded the earth four-footed twice before dropping into a canter and then a petulant trot. She shook her head, then whinnied and snorted as if insulted by the very idea of slowing down. Her flared nostrils and heavy breathing betrayed her need for it, though.

Still, Bodie found her behavior strange. She was charging north like her life depended on it. He wondered what she knew that he didn't.

The land on this side of the river was made up of sage-covered mounds that looked like rumpled folds of furry flesh leading to some taller hills and then a snow-capped ridgeline beyond. The brush was tightly packed and would be very difficult to navigate off the road.

He'd seen a ranch or two on the plains outside of Low Camp but nothing that looked like it was still in use. Bodie's mind flashed back to the huge skeletal creature with the elk-like antlers that adorned trees with the bodies of its victims: the Wun-dee-go. He worried about that and wondered what else might prowl these hills. As it was, they had a haunted look to them, whatever that meant. He couldn't quite articulate how something could look haunted. It was just an eerie feeling you got when you saw it. He got that feeling now. A tingling in the arms and the sensation that something was riding on his back, breathing in his ear.

Bodie turned his head to scan the terrain behind him, but nothing was out of the ordinary. He'd scanned it with his sensors already, so knew it was a pointless gesture. Carole twitched her ears and shook her head again as she trotted along the pale tan hardpack of the road.

Bodie turned again, unable to help himself, and thought he'd seen the ghost of an image. A bit of blackness where the shadows didn't sit right. He pulsed another scan that came back ought.

<Barometric pressure dropping precipitously>

Bodie pinged Helga to elaborate as he noticed for the first time that what had been a warmish wind had turned a sight colder. Snow again?

<Trend: average millibar drop over the last three hours is 1.03347>

Bodie turned in his saddle again but to look at the skies in the direction of the wind. He saw two things: a dense bank of clouds that turned to dark and extended all the way to the valley floor, and something that looked like a six-legged panther with a pair of long tentacles along its back and burning golden eyes. Both were alarming, but the creature quite a bit more so. And then it disappeared, as in it crouched and turned completely invisible.

Bodie snapped the reins, and Carole launched forward, and in barely a second, she was head down, ears back, and flat-out flying.

Dmitr was stumped and just kept rifling through images. Helga had nothing in terms of Indian lore that could account for such a beast but kept digging. Bodie just held on.

They flew over a rise into a hard right, and Carole was scrabbling to slow down before pitching them both into a thicket of cacti and thornbrush. She cut hard, the embankment rising to their right. Before them, a switchback came into view.

Bodie scanned with sensors, optics, and audio. He heard crashing in the bushes ahead just as the creature bounded from the bushes at the top of the cut, already head high. Bodie had both Walkers out and hip-fired with no need for aiming.

He expected to see it crumple but was surprised when, suddenly, the creature was coming at him from a completely different angle. It hit him hard, knocking him out of the saddle and onto the trail in a tumble of flailing limbs.

The nameless creature rolled to its feet and roared. One tentacle whipped out, catching Bodie's feet out from under him as he tried to rise. He rolled as he hit the ground and fired from his back. But again, the creature was not where he'd seen it last, and a black tentacle clubbed his head to the side as the creature lunged for the kill.

Bodie dropped into another layer of consciousness. He called it Zen-mode. Time slowed down as his processors spiked. He let all of his sensory inputs float in at the same priority, hearing all, seeing all, feeling some broad fabric of space that was greater than the sum of its constituents.

He replayed the attack, the tentacle batting his head, then he saw/felt something else. Footprints in the dirt slipped left while it appeared to still be standing in the same spot. Calculations upon calculations branched out, streaming through his mind, and then his hands whipped up to catch the jaws of a creature that wasn't there, except it was.

The fake image to his left faded while the real creature exploded into vivid color before him. Its fanged jaws held wide by his perfectly placed hands, its momentum driving Bodie skidding on his back across the buckboard road.

Bodie drove a leg into the beast's stomach as it gripped his head with its claws and tried to rip out what should have been Bodie's throat. The creature was big, fast, and powerful, and Bodie was losing the fight. One of its rear legs clawed at Bodie's stomach and caught on his hip joint, threatening to rip his leg completely off.

Bodie, in Zen-mode, noticed a large snowflake landing on the beast's head as tentacles whipped from either side to wrap around his outstretched arms. He noticed Carole, nervously stamping, eyes wide, furious, and scared just a dozen paces up the road. He noticed his leg beginning to separate from his hip, the rocks beneath him screeching against his metal skin. He noticed how both tentacles wrapped around just one of his arms and how the other arm pressed the Walker Colt into the beast's ribs and fired three quick .44 caliber rounds into its chest.

And then Zen-mode faded, and the beast was yowling deafeningly, its tentacles thrashing, casting rocks and dirt and branches into the air. Then it bounded into the brush to find some dark place to hide and lick its wounds, or, to Bodie's dearest hopes, just to die.

Carole knickered and stamped.

"Yeah. Good riddance," he agreed.

The snow was falling now. To say that it was falling, though, was inaccurate. The wind had picked up significantly, and the snow was now whipping sideways. Also, it was dark, getting much colder, and they'd need to find shelter for Carole's sake.

Bodie would need to worry about the nameless beast later.

Branches whipped at Justine's face, arms, and ribs, and then she bounced off the dirt of the hillside so hard she was sure she heard a crack. And then she was tumbling until she found herself in a tangled mess at the bottom of it. She couldn't breathe. She gasped but nothing came in or out, and then slowly, when she thought she was going to black out, a pitiful wheeze found her ears and she was sucking in shallow breaths until she finally managed a full one.

She didn't know what happened. The magick ... just stopped. Luckily, she'd just cleared a low ridge and was close to the treetops when it happened. Now she didn't know what to do. Cold crept in, fighting against the burn of raw and bleeding skin. And then she felt an aching hollow in her stomach. Hunger.

She pushed against the ground and yelped as pain sliced through her left arm. Was it broken? She wasn't sure, but she definitely couldn't use it. And she needed to find something to eat. Judging by the cold, she needed to find shelter as well. The air smelled like snow. Of course, it didn't actually smell like snow since snow was just water, but her senses told her it was storm weather, and in this cold, it was going to be a doozy. She could die of exposure.

Well, *if* she could die. She didn't know what she was anymore. The fire still burned within her, but she could feel none of its fury. Her mind flashed through dozens of faces with a cold distance. Faces of men she knew she'd killed, but somehow, it didn't feel like her who'd done it. She couldn't even bring herself to feel the satisfaction of avenging her parents. They were like a distant memory even though it'd only been days. Hadn't it?

Justine remembered seeing a rooftop in the trees before losing all sense of what was going on and ending up here, on the floor of the pine forest. She knew she was somewhere between Low Camp and Puro Pura but not where exactly. Didn't matter right now. Right now, she just needed to survive the night.

She stood, careful not to put too much weight on any one limb till she was upright. *Maybe it's okay? Maybe I can make it to the cabin?* Justine started limping in that direction.

It took her nearly half an hour to find it: a two-story log structure with a stable and a large woodshed. Empty. She thought it looked spooky up here all by itself but then chided herself for being so soft. She was a mass murderer, for crying out loud. A witch, or something like it. Somehow, that didn't help. Right now, she felt like a little girl that just wanted her ma and da. What a wreck she'd made of things. But how could she have done any differently?

You could have saved those kids and left it at that.

No, she couldn't. Saving the others was one thing. There had still been some small vestige of herself that wasn't crowded out by the glorious blaze of hate and magick that the coldbright amplified. But sparing those men? No, that was never going to happen. They would burn in hell. And now, for the first time in her life, the question of where she'd reside for eternity was also quite thoroughly laid to rest.

"I'll definitely be joining them," she mumbled as her body shivered violently enough to again upset the inflamed tissues within her arm. She still couldn't tell if it was broken. She kept it tight up against her body as she walked, holding it in place with her good hand.

Justine's brooding carried her to the threshold, and then the door was swinging open, rusty hinges grating against the silence of the darkened interior. Nothing stirred. She stepped inside and stamped her boots to free them of dirt and the little bit of snow that had begun to fall. The wind was loud in the trees but diminished greatly down here.

A stone fireplace stood off to one side. She saw that there was kindling and a small bucket filled with dry tinder. She judged that the wood at hand was enough to start a fire and sustain it long enough for her to fetch some logs. *Hopefully, there's dry wood in that shed.*

And hopefully, she could carry it with her one good arm. The thought brought her attention to the other one, and it throbbed dully. Her fingertips felt numb from the cold and from keeping it immobile.

She struggled through setting up the wood and was faced with her first challenge: how to start it. There was a large hunk of flint and up against the hearth was a hatchet. She could lay the hatchet down and strike the flint upon the side of it. That could work.

It took a few tries and finally, she got the angle and pressure right, managing to spray some embers into shredded wood. She leaned over quickly and blew it into life, but then nearly fell right into flame as she became lightheaded from hyperventilating, on top of being so drained.

Wearily, she stood up to go fetch wood but paused and reached back down for the hatchet. Something about this place didn't feel safe. Her eyes darted to the loft area upstairs, but it was too dark to see anything until the fire came up. Which she realized would come and go before she fed it if she didn't fetch that wood in a hurry.

Justine nearly stumbled going down the short set of steps from the front door but then made it to the shed easily enough. The snow was laying down quite thick; there was already an inch on the ground. She could get snowed in, she thought. Well, maybe if she managed to get a little rest, her magick would come back and she could fly her way out of here rather than tromping over miles of fresh snow to find the man named Zilich.

Of course, there was little worry that word would get to him about the happenings in Low Camp any time soon, what with the storm and the whole mess of Blackie's men being dismembered and rotting in a warehouse. A small smile crept onto her face, but then guilt and fear and shame eroded it. She thought on her ma and what she'd think of her actions. She shook her head clear of the thoughts, and the full force of the early evening cold embraced her.

The door to the shed stood before her. She stared at it, reading every grain, every knot, and square nail as if they were tea leaves. *Don't open it,* she told herself. She was certain she didn't need whatever was in there. Something was wrong with it. Wrong about this whole place but—

A soft thump from inside interrupted her thoughts. Justine's heart jumped. A chill drenched her neck and spine. She swallowed with a dry mouth, tried to lick her lips but just settled on chewing on the top one a little bit as she thought. She could find wood elsewhere. There were two pieces cast to the side right there.

That thump happened again, and Justine quietly slid a thin chunk of kindling into the hasp on the door she'd only just realized was there. Then she laid the hatchet down on top of the two logs and scooped everything up against her chest, cursing each tiny scrape betraying her movements. Slowly, she retraced her steps backward, away from the door. It faded quickly into shadow as she neared the house.

She'd left the door open she realized, but then when she looked down, she saw two snowy footprints on the threshold.

There'd been no one here, she was sure. She'd only been a dozen or so paces away. She would have heard it. Yet, there they were. And what was worse, it was completely dark inside. The fire she'd started was out. Justine tried to reach inside herself, and though she could feel the fire there still, she had no connection to it. She breathed in slowly, cast another look in the direction of the shed, and stepped inside, closing the door behind her. She listened for a long moment, but there was nothing, no movement, no breathing but her own. So, she sidled slowly over to the fireplace, quietly laid down the logs, and picked up the hatchet with her good arm.

There were still some embers in the barren fireplace, kept alive by a draft coming down the chimney. She needed that fire to see. Making a quick decision, she sat the hatchet down, grabbed more of the dry tinder from the bucket, and hastily scattered it on the embers, which quickly ignited. Without real kindling, she threw some of the bigger chunks onto the meager flames and then grabbed the smaller of the two chunks of wood, which was good because it had a split down the length that would make it easier to catch fire. She set it down so that it was propped up a little and could get good ventilation and then reached back down for the hatchet.

It wasn't there. Justine yelped and sat down with her back against the cold stone of the hearth. No one was there. Nothing moved. She knew exactly where she'd put it, and now it was gone. Justine's eyes drifted back up to the loft and that impenetrable darkness. There was nothing that she could see, but she couldn't take her eyes away. Beside her, the fire popped, and she jumped, but still nothing moved.

"Wh-who's there?" Justine's voice sounded small and weak.

"Wh-who's there?" her voice came back to her, only it wasn't her voice exactly.

"I mean it." She cleared her throat, putting force behind it she didn't feel. "Tell me who you are."

"I mean it..." There was a pause and then, more loudly, the voice mimicked, "Tell me who you are."

Light from the growing fire slowly began to fill the room, causing the shadows to flicker and shift. Upstairs, one shadow remained fixed. She could see two reflections from the fire, but then they blinked. Justine let out a shuddering breath, fear gripping her stomach like a vise. The shadow moved forward without seeming to move at all. It was tall and blacker than night, and its silhouette was almost shaggy, which had to be some trick of the light. But then it slid over the railing and landed on the floor on all fours. The eyes blinked again, and she realized she was looking at something like a wolf. A lanky, black wolf. A low, guttural growl rattled from it. She didn't know how, but it sounded like amusement and arrogance ... and menace.

The wolf, sniffing at something from outside through the open door, padded across the cabin floor, baring its teeth and looking like something from hell itself. It drew up so close Justine could smell wet fur and something else. Urine, she realized. It was her own, but she didn't dare look down to confirm it. Instead, she reached inside and found the connection, the weakest, barest thread, but it was there, and she pulled on it. Justine felt the power, some of it anyway, fill her bones with heat. The creature drew back slightly, looking a little perplexed and, again, a little amused.

A noise from outside caused it to turn and growl. The creature's ears flicked back briefly as it stared in the direction of the shed, and then it looked back at her. It sniffed the air again and then sniffed at her dress. It glanced back up, paused, and then trotted casually out the door.

Justine sprang up and slammed the door shut, barring it from inside. She heard another loud thump from the direction of the woodshed and thought about the way the wolf had reacted. It almost seemed afraid, or maybe it just didn't like whatever was in there. *What's in there?*

She would be happy never to find out. She walked back to the fire and dropped the other log onto it. A flurry of embers scattered to the sides, and she felt a rush of heat from the blaze. *Thank goodness.* The heat she felt from the magick within her was fading again.

Justine turned and leaned against the hearth, arms on her knees, head hanging, when she realized her arm was feeling a little better, too. Doing this earlier would have been an excruciating reminder of her injury. Then she heard a rustling sound, but it wasn't something that made her worry, for it had the jingling of chimes in it. She looked at the floor, and a thin little stream of a mercurial substance rolled across the floor, following along each straight or perpendicular seam in the boards but steadily heading in her direction.

Some of the coldbright had found her. Maybe if she got her strength back, she could find the rest. For now, she would just sit here and watch the door until the fire burned out and she was forced to venture outside or freeze.

The woodshed waited. She knew she had to go in there but was terrified by what she would find. The dark, beastly wolf creature even seemed wary of it. A chill raised goosebumps on her arms, and then as the coldbright reached her, she felt its scalding, cold fire on her skin.

It slithered into her palm and drew up into the shape of a flowering thistle that she held in her mind and then melted back down into a quivering puddle. She sat it back down on the floor and watched as it morphed into various geometric shapes, seeming not to know what to do with itself. Justine could relate. Just a little time. That's what she needed.

The fire behind her popped, and she watched a small chunk of blackened wood tumble across the hearth. One side flared orange and then quickly dimmed. She looked at the fire. Maybe an hour, maybe less.

Forget it. Whatever was in the woodshed held no power but what she gave it, she thought, but knew it was false bravado. This was the Estranyazie, whatever was in the woodshed was put there for a reason. She would just have to overcome it. Justine stood up, and she felt the wooziness from either the injury to her arm or lack of food. Or maybe lack of sleep. Probably all three. *Oh well*. It couldn't be helped. She raised her chin, drew a calming breath, and headed for the door.

CHAPTER 6
ANTIGONY VON RICHE

odie spied a strand of tall cottonwoods huddled along the base of a low ridge. It seemed there were as much of the stark gray-and-black trees strewn across the ground and generally in chaotic repose as there was any of it standing upright. Through the low light and obscuring snowfall, Bodie could make out a tumble of aspens upon the hillside beyond, intersecting the grove. There was probably a creek in there some-where, but Bodie only cared about getting relief from the gusting wind and the gathering snow for Carole's sake. They veered off the road, clomping across pads of snow buoyed by tall grass as they headed into a gap in the wall of trees.

The forceful wind cut to half once they entered the tree line, and quickly, the patches of white snow gave way to dark, moist ground cover. They'd still need to create a windbreak and a form of shelter, how-ever crude.

Fallen limbs with scraggly little branches abounded. Bodie tied a few of them behind Carole and added a few more for good measure, and then they headed in deeper along what seemed an obvious path. Another fifty yards in, when Bodie found a nice, live split cottonwood with even more cast-offs gathered around its base, he began to heap their haul on top and, after only a couple of minutes, called it good. Carole's ears perked at what sounded like voices deeper in the thicket.

Bodie slid up beside her, quietly patted her neck, and massaged her muzzle. All the while, he tuned his senses in the direction of the disturbance. It was several voices. And they sounded like they were having one heck of a good time. Given the miserable turn in the weather, he found this odd. Bordering on disquieting, in fact.

Slipping his hands beneath his purloined poncho, he drew out his Walker Colts. Besides being efficient weapons, they were equally effective negotiators. He dropped low and eased forward into the darkness. His vision, already tuned to a monochrome filter suitable to low light, revealed a shack another eighty yards farther on, just visible through the trees.

The lay of the land suggested that it sat at the edge of a slope that most likely concealed the suspected creek. Flipping through heat imagery, air density, humidity, and a slew of other sensory filters confirmed this hypothesis as well as suggested that this area was also a spring of the geothermal sort.

Ahh, that makes sense.

Whoever was over there was indeed not worried about the weather. Now that he was closer, he could hear the sounds of a small waterfall accompanied by splashing and cavorting that was previously lost in the hush of the thickly wooded grove.

Bodie approached, still cautious, but could not detect even a single sentry. As he rounded the corner, he found half a dozen people lounging in the shallow waters. They looked like merchants, or maybe entertainers. It was hard to tell. And they seemed very relaxed. Too relaxed. Drunk wasn't quite right, though it was close.

"Heyyy! Buddy," a topless brunette called from across the wide pool that Bodie could now see was part of a damned up creek. The waterfall emptied into it from one side and then the pool trickled over a half-moon-shaped dam built of river rocks opposite.

"Heyyy! Buddy," the woman said again, almost identically to before.

Definitely operating sub-optimally.

Bodie looked around, and it seemed clear that she was speaking to him. He stepped forward into the light of a lantern that'd previously been obscured by the shack.

"Ho-lee Cannoli! It's a for-real toaster!" the woman shouted, her severely cut bangs framing dark eyes, round with surprise or maybe amusement. The others turned from their hushed conversations and fooling around.

"Come and have a seat!" she said, patting the water next to her, and then pulled her long black mane over her shoulder, which rather than obscure her healthy bosom, simply framed it in much the same way her bangs framed her eyes. "Take a load off. Have a squirrel." She gestured to a smoldering smoke box made of flat rocks a few feet beyond the edge of the water upon which rested the charred remains of no less than half a dozen of the varmints.

"Much obliged. Maybe later, on the ... fare du jour," Bodie replied. Something bumped him from behind, and he realized it was Carole, nudging him forward. She was probably letting the cold from their journey obscure her better judgment.

All eyes were on them as the two stepped down the slope into the pool. The occupants shook their heads and murmured in surprise at the odd pair joining them. Carole just stood in the pool awkwardly for a moment and then sat on her rump, saddle and all.

Bodie waded across and sat next to the woman who had invited him. "I'm Bodie Nine. It's a pleasure to make your acquaintance," he said, tipping his soaked Batterson.

The woman brightened but was still a bit bleary. "Well, I'm Antigony Von Riche," she said, looking both ways. Then she whispered, "You may have heard of me."

<...> Helga provided.

Dmitr, too, came back with nothing.

Bodie played a flat line across his VEIP, which seemed to irk Miss Von Riche.

"Icehouse Von Riche? Tig the Kid?" she asked.

Bodie shook his head in the negative. Internally, Helga and Dmitr confirmed the lack of data.

"Felicity Noir?" she asked, batting her eyes and placing both hands demurely upon her submerged knee. "Huh. You must not get out much. I was kind of a big deal in Arapaho City before the old Western Star burned down." She shrugged. "Never would have found my true calling if it hadn't, I guess."

"Your true calling?" Bodie asked, suddenly more engaged in the conversation. He'd fallen into the mistaken belief that he was maybe the only one in the world who had no idea what their purpose was. For him, it'd all come in a flash less than twenty-four hours prior, but it was still fresh enough for the idea to hold considerable intrigue.

"Why, yes. Dancing for scoundrels and rough men with rough hands. Had its disadvantages. Why, I was in such dire straits that at one point I had to boil the leather of my very own shoe just to have something to eat. So, I thought to myself, if you can't beat 'em..."

"So, that's your calling? To be a rogue and a scoundrel?"

"Exactly," she said, tapping the tip of her nose with her finger. "That's how I got this security gig."

Bodie's eyes dropped to the woman's bare chest and shot back up. He would have blushed if he wasn't so shocked by the idea that she was somehow protecting the other travelers while sitting topless in a hot spring. And if he was biologically capable of doing such a feat.

"Like what ya see?" Antigony asked, an amused look on her face that morphed into something slightly more devious. She slid a little closer to Bodie and placed a hand on his knee.

Several things happened all at once and in just milliseconds. Dmitr started in with a highlight reel containing all manner of human copulation. Helga started and stopped a handful of observations, complaints, data streams, and conjectures, and finally gave up. She seemed to be as distraught and befuddled as Bodie himself was. The last thing that happened was Bodie felt the uncontrollable urge to swallow and clear his throat. Like blushing, both were functions that held zero anatomical relevance for him as a robot.

Though he didn't have an esophagus, he managed to approximate the sound that clearing his throat would make if for no other reason than to avoid continuing to sit there and stare at the woman as if he'd blown a cognitive circuit.

"Umm…" he said.

She nodded slowly up and down.

"Ummm…" she agreed and slid a little closer, her hand inching up his thigh.

He didn't know what she had planned once she made it all the way up to where it would be evident that he did not share every anatomical feature with a male of the species. He realized that a small part of him was embarrassed by this. Another was a little disappointed. It felt good to be the object of desire rather than consternation for once. Even if that objectification was misguided and most likely aided by some judgment-impairing chemical concoction.

"So," he said, "you're the … um, bodyguard, for this group of travelers?"

"Uh-huh," she replied as she closed the distance between them so that her hips were pressed up to his, and then she slid a leg over his lap.

It would be unfair to say before he knew it, because, he did know it, but he was just so surprised by the turn of events and then embarrassed by his own foolishness that he failed to react. In under a second, she had relieved him of one of his firearms—the Bergman semi-auto—and had it pressed up under his chin.

"As I was sayin'… Yes, I am the security around here, and I'd very much like to know what it is that one of Zilich's metal minions is doing sniffing around these parts."

Dmitr ceased his slideshow immediately.

<The gun is not loaded> Helga provided.

I know that, but she doesn't. She would realize it's a bit too light if she wasn't high as a kite.

And no, I did not mean that to rhyme.

To Antigony, he responded, "Actually, I'm a free agent, of sorts. A lone ranger. My sights are set on the man himself. Only ... I need to find him before someone else kills him first."

Antigony raised an eyebrow but kept the clip-fed automatic pressed firm into the hollow beneath his chin.

"You mean to kill him?"

"That seems inevitable. But I do need information first. And the other one after him is ... a force to be reckoned with," he replied, staring off into the darkness between cottonwoods dimly illuminated in amber light by the roasting squirrels.

Something pinged his sensory circuits but vanished as quick as it appeared. Helga was tense. Dmitr, too. He just had no idea what it had been that'd caused them both such unease.

"Ms. Von Riche, tell me about this place. Y'all seem to have become quite familiar with it. Are there none of the usual denizens of the Estranyazie in these woods?"

This got her attention. "You mean like owl witches, Wun-dee-go, skinwalkers, and the like?"

Bodie nodded.

"There are. But we've locked 'em out," she said, a self-satisfied smile spreading across her face. Freckles were almost obscured by tanned skin and there were fine wrinkles at the corners of her eyes. Bodie placed her in her late twenties to early thirties.

"You don't say? How'd you go about doing that?" he asked.

"Well…" she replied, settling in to make herself a little more comfortable. It appeared to Bodie that Antigony Von Riche's favorite topic was her own endeavors. "On account of my gypsy heritage, I know a thing or two about the esoteric. And monsters. We encountered such a creature. El Pantera del Diablo, Marcus called it," she said, nodding toward a bald man with an impressive mustache and beard braided into two long strands that rested on broad slabs of tattooed chest muscle.

"It came upon us sudden and fierce, all claws and teeth and tentacles. And those eyes … eight of 'em. We lost half our number within minutes. I gathered everyone I could, and we made for cover. The creature, contenting himself on the carcasses of our fellow travelers, made no overtures on the rest of us. However, I saw this for what it was: just a pause in the slaughter. We rallied here and then, using some of the supplies we carried, I created a warding circle out of salt. One continuous line within the woods. A circle unbroken, as my great-grandmother used to say."

"Ahh," Bodie replied, attempting to hide his growing concern as Dmitr replayed imagery from earlier when Bodie and Carole had gathered brush in order to make a windbreak. They had encountered such a line of salt. And had unsurreptitiously dragged the brush directly and thoroughly through it.

"So, if the circle remains unbroken, then you're safe from creatures of a … mythical and horrific nature?" he asked.

"Exactly," she replied with a wink and patted his leg where her hand once again rested, much to his discomfort.

One of the other travelers, a pale, heavy-set man with no hair on his face or head, began to recite a poem in the sloppy fashion of someone well-distanced from sobriety.

"Tyger, tyger burning bright,
In the forest, of the night..."

Antigony and Bodie turned to one another, eyes squinted, and then returned their attention to the man.

"What fearful, symmetry—"

He managed to get out before a roar from the forest echoed through the night air. It was not far away.

Bodie was still trying to extricate himself from Antigony's serpentine grasp while drawing the Colts when the Pantera del Diablo burst from the trees, lunging for the poem-reciting man and, within seconds, reducing him to so much as roadkill.

Shots boomed and flashed. The pistol that Antigony had commandeered clicked impotently without cartridges loaded in the clip.

"Dammit, you men are all the same! Even when you're robots. Give me one of them!" she demanded, one hand out, the other on her hip.

Bodie fired three more times but to little effect. The creature was in the blood now and couldn't be bothered. Two more travelers met a messy end. Bodie fired again and realized the futility of the situation. It shrugged off .44 balls like hail to a tin roof.

"How many squirrels have you had?" he hollered back at her.

"Three. Why?"

"You're all high as a herd of mountain goats. And I don't see any liquor. I'm guessing those squirrels have been infused with some drug or another?"

"Shit. That makes a lot of sense. I just thought this was some sort of magickal watering hole, but I think yer right. There's a truffle called Witch's Knickers that the injuns used for ceremonial stuff. I'd bet a nickel them squirrels been into it. Still, I'm sober enough for some shootin'. Trick is, if you're seeing three targets, ya aim three guns. Easy."

Bodie shot her a sideways glance as the Walkers boomed. He flipped a Peacemaker he'd taken to replace the stillborn I-talian auto he'd been carrying around. She caught it with ease, and he stopped to reload his and hers.

"Don't shoot yerself. Or me," he told her, leveling a gaze her way. She had pretty eyes. *Dammit. Am I a robot or not?!?* With every passing moment, it seemed that the bots were getting outweighed by the nots.

The Pantera wheeled on the two while they were mid-load and growled threateningly. Bodie flicked cylinders closed and sent two rounds down its throat. The creature yowled, lurched erratically, then bolted into the trees. They listened to it crashing through the underbrush until the sound died out.

"That won't be the last of him," they both muttered identically before turning and staring at each other in mild surprise.

"Right," replied Antigony. "Best beat a hasty retreat."

Bodie nodded in the direction of her bare chest. "You might wanna cover up."

She didn't bat an eye. "It's my Amazonian heritage. This is how I like to fight," she said defiantly, clearly lying to save face.

"Well, it's cold out there. You could freeze to death," he said. Then mumbled to himself, "Or put an eye out."

Antigony huffed but then looked around. A body tumbled over the falls. It was someone that didn't appear to have been with the rest of the group. She waded over and removed the man's shirt and put it on. When she turned around, Bodie was surprised to find that the black shirt had a clerical collar. He was going to object, but then another body flopped down the falls. A gaucho hat followed.

The woman grabbed the hat and pulled two bandoliers off the new victim.

"Where do you think these guys came from? They look ... fresh."

"Probably just another band of innocents," Bodie replied.

She looked down at the bandoliers. "Maybe not *that* innocent. No one in the high plains goes far without getting blood on their hands." She looked around. "Least they had the sense to carry .44. Whadaya say we get while the gettin's good?"

Bodie nodded. That was the first thing she'd said all night that made any sense. Now, to figure out how not to get eaten by the devil panther. And then, how to log this in his karmic ledger since it was clear he'd been the one who'd let the drawbridge down and didn't put it back up. That was six bodies by his count. Not counting these other two.

<Correct>

Please, Dmitr ... don't. He already had the images of all the dead men and women in his memory circuits. When the victims were members of Blackie Lung's gang? That was one thing. These traveler folk? That was another. He had definitely crossed into negative territory. In fact, he was so deep into that territory he damn near had his own postbox.

Two hours and twenty-seven minutes later, Bodie, Carole, and their new companion were huddled in a tight stand of aspen within the larger wooded area. They were barely a mile from the hot springs. Going had been very slow, trying to stay quiet in the tangle of fallen tree limbs and underbrush. Plus, Bodie had resorted to attempting a sort of short-range echoloca-tion technique using bursts of high and low-frequency radio waves in an attempt to track the elusive monster. He found he could formulate an image from the signals, but it was limited and pretty sketchy. He stuck with it out of a lack of anything better to try.

"Antigony?"

"Yeah, Bodie?"

"You ever worry about karma?"

"Karma? What's that?"

"Uh ... well, it's all the right and wrong you ever done."

"Oh, like, if you're going to heaven or hell? Shit, robot. I stopped carin' bout that a long time ago. Who can waste time thinking 'bout that when we're all so busy just trying to get by? 'Cept preachers o' course. But it's their job, isn't it? Me? I'm just doing life minute by minute. Day by day."

"I suppose that's fair."

"I mean, if you just, ya know, count yer blessings and shit. It'll all work out in the end, won't it?"

"I hope so."

"Take it from ol' Icehouse. You mind yer business. And it'll mind you."

"I'm sorry. What does that mean?"

"You just live yer life. Doing robot shit. Just do robot shit, Bodie Nine. Ya think there's some big automaton in the sky looking down on all of this? Judgin' yer work? Yer *worthiness?*"

Bodie had to confess, he kind of did. Maybe not a robot since Bodie himself wasn't exactly a robot. For sure a robot body, but he was fairly confident that, somewhere deep inside that convoluted maze of synthetic material, there was a soul. Whatever *that* was.

Sounds of rustling bushes and wet leaves issued from a stand of trees not twenty yards away just as a hazy, vaguely feline image appeared in his echolocation tapestry of radio signals.

Unconsciously, the three leaned closer together as they crouched in the shadows. His finger flicked to his VEIP in a hushing motion. Antigony nodded understanding. Carole's ears laid flat, her tail swishing in abrupt slashes. Bodie could see the muscles tense in her shoulders and haunches. She was close to bolting into the fray to meet the danger head-on. Damn, he loved that horse.

Bodie issued another silent radio burst, and this time, the image of the Pantera was near fully obscured. He came away with nothing his audio circuits hadn't already provided. Something weighing in the hundreds of pounds—something roughly Carole's weight—was working its way through the underbrush. Something the devil would have kept as a pet. *Zilich*, he corrected himself. *Zilich would have kept as a pet.*

Bodie was feeling the need to get north. And to do that, he had to survive the night. Sounds further on pricked his circuits. Carole bristled.

Something unholy was in the forest. A loud but indistinct moaning issued from the direction of the watering hole. And then another, closer in. And then there was wailing. Unholy wailing.

He had never been audience to such a racket. *Maybe the Wun-dee-go*, he thought, but this had a different sort of tone to it. This was snarling and wailing and moaning, as if the creature, *creatures*, he corrected himself, were tortured and in the mood to do some torturing of their own. It would have sent a shiver down his spine. Instead, Dmitr started riffing. He had no idea what was out there, but he tried mightily to put a face to the danger. Images and illustrations of various animals, domestic and esoteric, flashed through Bodie's tertiary OS level.

He noticed Helga, more and more, was keeping to herself of late. That was troubling. The last thing that Bodie needed was to experience some sort of robotic psychotic break. Losing his secondary OS level would seem roughly equivalent to that.

"Oh no," Antigony whispered, "I know that sound..."

Bodie turned to face her. She couldn't see him, but with his enhanced vision, he could see the terror in her face. It was the most honest emotion he'd seen from her yet. She shivered visibly from head to toe. Of course, she was also wearing just a wet button-up shirt and bandoleers.

"What is it?" he whispered back while removing his hat and then his poncho, which he pushed her direction. In the minuscule light of his visual emotive indicator panel, the bundle was discernable. She grabbed it with both hands, one of which landed on his own. He felt an electric charge, though he knew that if he were in fact a man, this woman would have a multitude of red flags as a potential mate.

"Thank you. That's very sweet," she whispered as she pulled the poncho over her head and replaced her hat. "That rustling out there, it's the sound of the undead."

With this new information, Bodie pinged Helga and Dmitr both. They came back with nothing useful. Dmitr was rifling through a myriad of images ranging from biblical texts to popular fiction. After a moment, 0.013 seconds of processor time, Helga offered up a postulate.

<Zombies. Ghouls>

Ummm ... say again.

Dmitr provided sketches from a handful of highly questionable sources. Mostly wild imaginings from authors and illustrators of the time. These were monsters born from the twisted psyches of broken men, it was safe to conclude. And yet...

"They crave—and bear with me here—brains," Antigony told him.

Bodie had to deny the urge to scoff or stare down at her disapprovingly. What rubbish. Right? Instead, he played along.

"Brains?"

"Well, not yours, obviously."

"What's that supposed to mean?"

"Not that you're dumb or nothing, but they crave *human* brains. That means me. One of the dangers of the Witch's Knickers is—so the medicine men or shamans say—if you get yourself killed while under its influence, you'll be resurrected as a ghoul. A zombie."

"But it's just a fungus."

"I don't care what it is. I just know what I know."

"But it's just a fungus," he repeated, feeling somewhat at a loss. It was a strange new emotion for Bodie.

<Fungi, molds, et cetera, have been known to have extreme psychotropic effects on human anatomy. Particularly human consciousness. See squirrels>

Antigony replied, "Yeah, you said that. Doesn't mean it ain't true."

The screeching and wailing continued, only now the chorus was clearly accompanied by others, a quintet possibly. A mewling whimper issued from the direction of what he'd suspected was the Pantera's location and then there was a ruckus in the undergrowth. The creature, now a mere dozen or so paces away, bolted.

"What could cause such a creature to flee?"

"Bodie? Time to go. That pony of yours ride two?"

"No different than one. Come on," he said and grabbed her arm. He was astride Carole in a blink, and Antigony was behind him almost as quick.

"Ride!" he whispered into Carole's ear, and she lurched forward even as the wailing sounds began to close in from all sides.

"Those creatures must have very sensitive noses," he yelled over the din of snapping tree branches and galloping hooves, "to be tracking us just on account of what resides within yer head." He chuckled.

Antigony didn't say anything but wrapped her arms around him harder as they cut between the boles. He was sure she wouldn't let such an abuse go unanswered. Later. She'd certainly have something to say later.

Shafts of moonlight began to penetrate the canopy above as they tore through the grove. They made a terrible racket and somehow could still hear the sounds of wailing and of pursuit behind and to either side of them. Bodie didn't have to use his fancy new echolocation technique to ascertain that they were in as much danger, if not more, than they had been from the devil cat. Carole was fast, but the underbrush formed a sort of maze, and she was forced to follow it or risk getting tangled in the fallen tree limbs and thick foliage.

Just ahead, something burst from the bushes to their right, and Carole cut hard in that direction. They watched a creature fly past them, just out of reach. Its arms flailed desperately as claw-like hands scrabbled for them. Bodie noted the shredded body, the rolls of fat, and the hairless features and recognized them all as belonging to one of Antigony's former wards.

"Dammit, Clement," she hissed, breathless.

Another of the ghouls leaped at them and missed. It hit the ground and maintained its momentum by running on all fours. Somehow it kept pace with Carole through the trees and then leaped again. Bodie leaned and twisted so that both Walkers lined up with the creature's head and fired. It exploded like a ripe melon, and the body bounced off Carole's hindquarters, nearly knocking her off her line through the trees.

Bodie was just returning his attention to the trail ahead when yet another ghoul sprang from the brush and ripped Antigony clean from Carole's back. Bodie dove straight to the ground in a dive roll and came up, twisting and firing. His sensory array told him where the creature and Antigony both were before he ever got eyes on the two.

Antigony hit the ground first, and the two had tumbled, locked in combat. As they rolled and finally landed with her back pinned against the ground, she'd kicked hard to launch the creature over her head. That's when the bullets caught the ghoul in the side of the skull, much to the same effect as before.

Bodie was just thinking that this could be manageable if they continued to attack one at a time, but then the human creatures stopped doing exactly that. Three of them burst from the bushes on all sides. Antigony reached for her gun but had lost it in the scuffle. Bodie got one clear shot off, which dropped that target, but two other bullets must have hit nonessential parts. The two creatures hit the ground and bounded off between the trees.

By his count, there was one more unaccounted for. Maybe the Pantera ate that one whole and there was no body left to resurrect.

"Tig, you okay?"

There was no response. He looked over and saw her holding her arm with a fearsome look on her face. Bodie thought he'd not like to be the object of that look any time if he could help it.

"Shoulder's outta place, I think."

He could tell that's exactly what it was. He kneeled down near her, brushed the hair from her face, and yanked her arm in exactly the right way.

She screamed in pain and rage and surprise and then got up and stomped away from him.

"That was an asshole thing to do."

"You were right. It was dislocated. I thought the best thing to do was to get it over with before you tensed up and made it worse."

She sucked in a deep breath as she rolled her shoulder tentatively to feel out the damage.

"Never ... ever ... touch me again without my permission," she scolded, glaring at him with exactly that face he'd wanted to avoid.

"Noted, Miss Von Riche. I offer my deepest regrets for any offense I may have caused. However, we should vacate the area—"

Wails and screeching assaulted them from within the tree line. The two remaining ghouls launched from the shadows. They'd been sneaking, and Bodie had been too caught up in the emotional turmoil to keep his brain in the game. He lashed out with a spinning back kick that caved in the head of the closest ghoul and let the moment carry him into the other, catching him in the midsection just before he connected with the surprised Antigony.

Bodie and the merchant-turned-monster somersaulted, hitting the ground in a heap. Bodie managed to roll to his feet while the ghoul scrabbled onto its hands and feet, eyes searching for Antigony. Bodie lunged, wrapping it up in a bear hug, and drove it into a tree. It thrashed and snapped at him with its teeth, clawing at his face. He ignored teeth and claws and crushed its skull with his bare hands. The thing collapsed onto the exposed roots of the tree. Bodie turned to see Antigony's face, jaw slack, eyes wide. She blinked a couple of times, closed her mouth, and then turned away to hunt for her misplaced hat and gun.

They didn't speak. Within a few minutes, they exited the tree line and were back on the road, though the going was not easy for Carole. In just a few hours, the snow had stacked up to a foot-and-a-half with no sign of stopping, and the wind ripping past stacked it up into tall drifts.

Justine swallowed hard, her head down, eyes focused on the beat-down footprints before her being swallowed up by the steady fall of half-dollar-sized snowflakes. The meager light cast by her kindling wood torch spilled across the blanket of snow in hues of pale gold. Shadows bobbed and weaved as she stomped along.

"Goddamn."

A minor pang of fear yanked at her core as if her mother could have heard her curse words. She wished that were true. Would gladly take the lashing and a thousand besides just to have her and her father back. But then, a foul tongue was the least of her sins, wasn't it? "Least by far."

The woodshed door emerged from the shadow as she drew closer as if on legs that were not her own. The cold stung what wasn't numb already on her face and ears, but inside, she was a furnace. Fear energized her even though she couldn't remember her last meal. *It was in the mine*, she thought but couldn't be entirely sure. Some of what had transpired there still eluded her. As if it were done by someone else, but she knew better. Her stomach growled, but she shoved away the discomfort and nestled back into that fire within her.

Now was all that existed. This thin wooden door between her and…whatever lay beyond.

What was it exactly? She really didn't know. That wolf creature, the stuff of nightmares, seemed to laugh off her presence but sure seemed to dislike whatever it was that was locked up inside this shack. What could it be that could put a predator like that off its appetite?

Justine had heard talk. Once. Maybe twice. About things unholy. The bad kind of injun magic.

If she was honest, she herself could be labeled as such. What she was when the magick was upon her. When the furnace of hate billowed and spilled out from below. Was she like something other than what the medicine men spoke of? Nothing she would have learned within the walls of Preacher Caldwell's parish, she was sure. This was injun business. For that, you had to travel a bit further abroad.

No further than the outskirts of Heavy Feather township. She'd never made the journey herself, but some had. The apple-cheeked, Chastity Berhardt being notable among them. Apparently, she wasn't much in the magick, otherwise she'd have been in that wagon with the rest. Could be her folks' money had a thing or two to do with that. It usually did in Justine's limited experience.

Chastity had told her and a couple of the girls about people who were dead but not dead. Justine's eyes went to the latch of the door. It jiggled slightly. She felt her insides turn to jelly. What if it was one of them? Could they be killed? She just needed firewood, for Christ's sake. Justine heard a faint jingling. Through the snow, a serpentine strand of coldbright coursed toward her. It burrowed under and then rose above the snow as it made its way to her. She was so thankful. There was more out there. Further off.

How much would she need? A lot probably. The door jiggled again. There was definitely something in there.

She dropped her hand down to the ground and let the coldbright pool in her palm. It really wasn't enough to do anything with, and besides, the magick inside her was so … not absent, but it might as well be. But she was going to freeze to death before the night was through. Even if the sun came up in the morning, she would still just slowly grow more and more lethargic until she went to sleep and never woke up. Her pa had explained how exposure worked. There was frostbite, and then there was just dying slowly because your body ran out of fuel to keep it warm. That's what would happen to her.

Even now, her teeth chattered, and her meager torch shivered in her grasp.

"Nothing for it but to just do the thing," she whispered under her breath.

She reached for the door. It bumped, and she screamed and then cursed herself for being so jumpy. *Just face it. Whatever it is. Just face it.*

She grabbed the latch and heard the rasp of metal on metal as the mechanism lifted free of its catch. She ripped it open, thrusting the torch forward. A smell like rotting flesh assaulted her, and then a creature leaped from the shadows, screaming and gnashing its teeth. She pulled her arms up to protect her face and body, but the creature lurched in midair and came crashing down on the dirt floor.

Justine heard the clank of chains as the creature, something human-like, hissed and cursed in phlegmy rasps. Others joined it, howling and whimpering and crying. She strained to see what they were, when she caught the reflection of glassy eyes further back in the darkness of the shed.

The stench caused her to almost lose control of her stomach. She looked again at the creature and realized it was wearing a shredded pair of dungaree overalls and a filthy red shirt, torn short at the forearms. The man-creature snarled at her, its yellowed, rotting teeth bared. And then it seemed to crumple within itself, all anger and angst sucked out of it.

She'd never seen anything like it. The two other sets of eyes in the back continued to rage and snarl unchecked. Justine turned her attention back to the creature before her and could see now that it was chained. That's what had saved her. It had just enough slack to reach the door with its foot but no more. That explained the thumping.

Just inside the door, a lantern hung, and she was able to reach it without endangering herself, but now that the initial shock was wearing off, the cold was settling in again. She needed to get to the bottom of this issue, get whatever wood was in there, and get back to the cabin immediately.

The lantern glow rose, and she could see that what she took for a woodshed was actually a small shop. No wood in sight, until the light grew brighter. Then she could see the back wall was stacked top to bottom with dry, cut wood. And snarling in the dirt before it were two more of the creatures, only they looked far more gone than this poor soul before her.

"K-k-ki-iilll," it gurgled at her. *Yeah*, she thought. *That sentiment is pretty clear.* She looked at the creature, bile rising in her throat as she realized his intestines were threatening to spill out from several gashes across its abdomen. Open wounds swollen with puss riddled its forearms, and now she could see its legs and neck as well. *Ugh, what happened to these people?* That's what she realized she was looking at. People. Just like Chastity had said.

The creature thrust out its arm, its hand cramped into a claw, but it wasn't trying to reach her. It was pointing maybe? Her eyes followed the imaginary line to what it reached for. On a high work table shelf was a scrap of paper. The paper, just like the table itself, was covered in dried blood. She arched her neck to see what was on it, not willing to budge an inch closer.

The writing was small, rough cursive. But orderly. At least the top third of the page was. She looked again at the creature before her and had to conclude that he was a man. Or had been. The shriveled creatures chained to a stake in the floor in the back room—she paused and sucked in a breath—looked like they could have been his wife and daughter. Only they'd succumbed greatly to whatever illness had taken them.

"Kk-k-k-ii-lll," it gurgled again.

Justine darted a glance at the man. She stretched for the note, and he made no move.

What's with all the kill talk if you don't really want to do it? She wondered.

She couldn't make much of the letter. The beginning was easier. It degraded precipitously from there. The gist was that his daughter had been sick. Meningitis maybe. They'd sought help from a multitude of sources and then, in the end, from the man in the north. His daughter had seemed to take a turn for the better, but that was short-lived.

Other symptoms cropped up. Fever. Lethargy. She grew thin and anxious, and her disposition changed completely. One day, the farmer had come back from town to find his wife had come down with similar symptoms. Within a week, he'd had to confine them to the woodshed as each had attacked him, lashing out with teeth and nails. Their symptoms had degraded, and then he noticed that he, too, had come down with a fever. When his daughter and wife had gone after the family dog, mauled and mutilated it, he knew that there was no saving them from the sickness that had taken over.

He'd thought to kill them—to put them out of their misery—but found he could not. As his symptoms progressed over days, his mind grew foggy and his hunger for raw meat, insatiable. They had some livestock ... a pig and a goat and a few chickens. They fed on them but found that they yearned for something else. He realized that he craved human flesh.

In a moment of clarity, he shackled himself and scribbled the note for whoever might find them.

"K-ki-ki-ll," the man whimpered, his twisted fingers pressed to his chest.

Justine suddenly understood. The man wasn't stating his intentions ... it was a request. To put him and his family to death. To end their torment. And possibly to save others as well.

That was all fine and good, but Justine would still freeze to death by morning. There was no way she could make it to the back of the shed and grab some of the dry wood without being torn to shreds by his family, even if he, himself, didn't try to do it.

She guessed that maybe there was a way to meet all their needs. And then she tossed the lantern inside and closed the door.

The shrieks were the worst. They continued for far longer than she could have imagined, even after the roof had begun to sag and then finally collapsed and flames clawed from within glass windows that'd blackened, cracked, and then fallen apart before the heat of the blaze.

Two walls were still standing when morning broke. The rest was a charred mass of smoking timber. The shrieking had died off hours ago, and the shack had burned itself out over the intervening time. Justine was cold again, but little by little, she felt her strength returning. She'd returned to the cabin and found the pantry still full of dry goods, at least. She'd gorged herself on oats and nuts and canned apricots and peaches and now found that she could summon the coldbright and it was compliant again.

Justine thought of the man and his family and the tribulations they'd gone through. They'd thought they'd found a cure only to discover that the man from the north had sold them a bill of goods. Though she was bone tired, she found her feelings of hate and lust for revenge had returned in full force. He was at the center of all of this. He was the source. And he had to die. Easy enough, she imagined. He may be smart.

He may be from another planet, even, but he was no match for her.

Coldbright snaked in writhing streams from the woods, shimmering in the morning sun. It came to her. Even more than before. Some untapped deposit must have made its way to the surface. Good. She wouldn't underestimate him. She would come ready. And he would meet the end he deserved.

Justine stepped up, and the mercurial metal poured beneath her foot, forming into a shield-like circular platform. And then she rose up into the gray of the Alta Estranyazie sky.

CHAPTER 7
THE ROAD TO PURO PURA

Bodie and Antigony rode for three hours. Carole forging her way through the deep snow, Antigony saying little, and when she did, it was through chattering teeth. It was clear to him that they needed to take a break, but it was hard to accommodate. He felt the pressure of the clock. For all he knew, Justine was already in Puro Pura confronting Zilich. And who knew how that was going to turn out?

He'd seen firsthand what the girl could do. She was only fourteen years old, and she'd single-handedly not just taken out, but *dismembered*, a gang of desperadoes. Bodie wasn't sure if Zilich stood a chance. But then the memory gifted to him by the coldbright illustrated just how devious, crafty, and completely devoid of compassion he could be. Plus, he'd had years to prepare his defenses, which Bodie, somewhere deep down in his circuits, also felt was a very Zilich thing to do.

Justine, on the other hand, had the element of surprise. No one could get from Low Camp to Puro Pura faster than she could. Especially not with the blizzard of the day and night before. Bodie could only hope that it had slowed her down, too.

What if he got there first? Did he have what it took to take down Zilich and force him to reveal everything he knew about his past? Odds seemed slim on that.

He, too, had the element of surprise. Zilich might not even know of his existence. Chances were that he did not. That was one positive in a long list of negatives. The first of which was being slowed down by the needs of his traveling companions—even though Carole could make up for it with her speed and stamina.

It was hard to say whether or not Antigony would prove a worthy companion in the prosecution of his current mission.

Directive? Did he just give himself another directive? That concerned him. The last one had gone so far afield. He'd have to ponder that.

His attention turned to the rocky, snow-covered trail ahead. It was just beginning to peel away from the windswept ridge they'd been following and nestle down into a twisting, serpentine gulch of smooth, colorful sandstone. This area was unlike anything he'd seen before. A veritable marvel of nature, with arches and all manner of bizarre geological shapes. Maybe, in one of these bends, they could make a quick camp and start a fire. They were out of the wind, at least for now.

Minutes later, they tucked themselves away into just such a place. Luck placed a fire pit and an abandoned claim right where they needed it. But in Bodie's experience, luck could be a fickle mistress.

A brief while later, an energetic fire still seemed to produce little heat. Antigony and Carole were pressed up so close that he feared they might catch fire themselves. To be honest, he didn't think they'd much mind if they did; they looked so miserably cold.

Even though the sun was high in the sky, it was barely visible through a dismal bank of low gray clouds. Before long, even that was engulfed by fog. Through the fog, snow fell in tiny flakes that were too dry to stick and instead just swirled around on an uneasy wind.

Bodie had to admit that conditions were pretty miserable. This concoction of dry snow and fog was called pogonip. It was harmless enough, but the fog could get quite thick, and with snow on the ground and no sun to use for reference, one could get lost quickly. Especially in these windy canyons.

This was Bodie's fear when he urged Antigony to quench the fire so they could get a move on.

"Sorry, robot. Not happening," she said through tight, blue lips, shuddering now where she'd been shivering before. The fire did not seem to be helping much at all.

He felt for her. He really did, but they had to keep moving.

"Miss Von Riche, you need to keep moving to stay warm. Plus, we could get lost in these canyons in this fog."

That wasn't a complete falsehood. It was highly unlikely that Bodie could get lost anywhere with his internal guidance and sensory systems, but there was always a chance.

<0.0234 percent> Helga provided.

Dmitr presented an image of a snowball and then one representing the gates of Hades.

Okay, I get it but I need them to keep going in order to survive. Holing up here without fuel for that fire is a death sentence.

Antigony didn't respond but started to poke around at the fire to spread out the coals and glowing chunks of wood that remained, kicking up a profusion of smoke that caused her to squint and wave it out of her face while muttering curse words under her breath.

Bodie checked his Walkers. He didn't know why, he'd already reloaded them on the ride, but it gave him comfort. Stowing the guns on his exposed torso caused him to remember the fact that he was mostly naked. He wanted his poncho back at least but knew that his new companion would die without it. She could really use a better outfit.

As they were about to mount up, something like gunfire echoed through the canyon, quickly followed by a second. They ducked instinctively and scanned their surroundings but realized that there had been no ricochet or visible strike.

"What do you think that was?" Antigony whispered.

"Not sure. But I think we should remove ourselves. I'll cover the fire. You two get up into that tunnel opening and stay out of sight."

Antigony nodded and grabbed Carole's reins before heading up the hill in a low crouch. Bodie spread out the remaining coals with his bare hands, and they cooled quickly from red to gray. He barely made it to the claim before another of the loud pops reached their ears. It was closer, and the way that it echoed, it seemed certain that whatever it was lay just around the bend.

As they waited quietly, sounds of a wagon could be heard but no horseshoes. Instead, there was a sort of chugging clatter of machinery. Bodie had uprooted a large sage and pulled it into the entrance of the mine. He peered through its branches, and the source of the noise came into view even as it popped again loudly.

Two automatons walked ahead of a horseless wagon. At the front of it, two more of the robots sat on a bench, and just behind them, a loud engine of sorts rumbled and chugged and belched smoke out of a wide stack in its center. Beyond that, there was nothing in the wagon at all.

"What is it?" Antigone whispered, though she doubted that the robots could hear anything with all that racket behind them.

"It's a horseless wagon."

"I heard of the idea, but I ain't never seen one."

"Neither had I. This one looks like it belongs to Zilich."

"I wonder what they're up to?"

"Dunno, but at least we can follow their tracks. They're most likely coming from Puro Pura. Maybe we're close."

"Don't you have a map in your head or something? I thought all automatons had that. They always seem to know where to go."

"Well, mine's kind of broke. I don't have any information about the north end of the Estranyazie. Just what I've heard."

"Huh... Well, that's not very helpful."

"Tell me about it. But, the closer we get to Puro Pura, the more of these guys I think we'll see. It should be pretty easy to find, but we'll need to keep an eye out from here. I don't know what they'll make of me if they figure out I'm not like the rest of them."

The automatons with the wagon passed from view but not before Bodie noticed an odd piece of equipment at one of their hips. It looked like a six-gun but was smaller and more sleek. He imagined it was some sort of weapon, but he had no idea what it would shoot.

They waited a couple of minutes more before heading out. The trail was easy to follow, and they were lucky that it was there. Several times they came across branches in the canyon that seemed just as reasonable to follow as the other, which would have slowed them considerably. It was getting really dark by the time the high, narrow walls of the canyon diminished into low hills and finally spread out. The dark and the fog made it impossible to see what was beyond, but occasionally they could hear the passing of other wagons like the one they'd seen earlier in the day. Bodie helped Antigony make a shelter out of sight and then headed out into the darkness to scout ahead.

Klamath swore. The quarter horse he'd stolen from that express rider had been noticed in town and reclaimed. He'd been forced to take Blackie's rambunctious Morgan. An ill-tempered steed if he'd ever seen one. And inexperienced. Its deceased owner liked it because it was tall, handsome, and matched his outfit and handle.

What a buffoon. He'd met an appropriate end. Now the man's cursed pony had gone and broken its leg while trying to avoid doing what Klamath had told it to do, which was to step over a fell tree and climb a scrabbling sidehill trail. Any normal horse could have done it. But not a stupid one, which Blackie's horse definitely qualified as.

He'd put it down, as was appropriate, but he wasn't happy about it. Now he was too far away from town to walk back and too far from Puro Pura to get there before nightfall of the next day, which meant two nights on the trail in this wretched weather. Klamath grabbed his bedroll, saddlebags, and his .45-70 and started off on foot.

He doubted he'd run into a soul on this road outside of the stray robot on an errand for Zilich. It was going to be a long walk without a horse. He spat a long brown stream of tobacco into the virgin snow and put one boot in front of the other.

It wasn't long before the wind came up and the snow really started to fall, but he was still able to make out an odd substance trailing across the road and a set of large tracks. They weren't wolf or coyote. They were from a cat. A big cat, though he couldn't place the exact breed from what he could see.

In this temperature, the dark substance should have been frozen, but it wasn't. It appeared fresh, though the tracks could be an hour old. Another one of the Alta Estranyazie's exotic creatures, no doubt. One of Zilich's misplaced playthings. Which meant he could be in real danger. If he continued on, there was a chance—especially if it was some kind of alien cat creature—that it would find his trail and, sooner or later, find him.

The smart thing to do would be to turn around and go back to Low Camp and forget this whole thing. The other choice was to follow the tracks. From what he saw here, the creature was injured. That was good and bad. It would be desperate and angry and there would be no running away.

Klamath shoved his bedroll and bags under a juniper on the leeward side of a rock formation and then stepped onto the tracks leading up a hillside strewn with similar rock features as if he were the creature himself. It could be hiding anywhere up there. Every shadow was a possible vantage point where the creature could be watching him even now.

In fact, he was certain it was. Any creature worthy of Zilich's menagerie would be.

Good. Let it watch. Let it come find him. Klamath was somewhat of a monster himself. Besides, he had an idea of what kind of creature bled that way. Blood that didn't freeze narrowed the possibilities considerably. And he'd heard stories before of what lay north of town. It was time the devil met his match.

Klamath checked his breach and closed it again.

"Here kitty, kitty, kitty…" he whispered, his voice low as vapor escaped his lips and was swept away by the bone-cold wind. He squinted against that wind, his eyes scanning the shadows but with the aid of alien biological tech. A few spots stood out as obvious choices. He wouldn't consider any of those. They didn't call it the Pantera del Diablo for nothing.

The tracks disappeared for a moment. Klamath considered how deep the prints were and realized the creature had leaped up to the next ledge. He stayed low and let the natural terrain conceal him. No sense making himself too easy a target as he made his way further up the hillside. Higher up, he picked up the trail again.

An hour passed. Then another. He could feel the beast's eyes on him as sure as he felt his soaked duster weighing him down. He'd have to oil it again after the storm passed. And after he'd concluded his business with Zilich, the girl witch and the renegade robot.

He cocked the hammer on his long-barreled Winchester, certain his Peacemaker would do little but irritate the alien predator. Klamath hadn't only made the one load to finish off that miserable robot. He had a second, and it rested in the rifle's chamber now, ready to do its gruesome work.

The wind let up briefly, and flurries of ice crystals in the air around him paused with uncertainty before grudgingly following gravity's path to earth. A low growl gurgled and popped in a strikingly non-terrestrial way from somewhere up and to his right. His breath caught in his chest as he strained to hear more when something sensed more than seen burst from his left.

The rifle boomed deafeningly as it was knocked from his hands by something serpentine just as fangs and claws collided with him, knocking him off the path. He fell and bounced awkwardly off a boulder several feet below. Even as lights erupted in his brain, he tracked the creature's trajectory. Stars exploded again as he hit the ground, and this time, he was truly disoriented.

He rolled to his feet, bowie knife in hand, when that same growl issued from the darkness to his left. He felt certain the creature had landed somewhere off ahead of him as he faced the side hill but spun to face this present threat and cursed himself for moving too fast. A hand shot out to steady himself just as eight emerald eyes glimmered from the depth of darkness ahead. *Maybe nine paces*, he thought. *But what good is a knife gonna do?*

Then something heavy landed on the ground a dozen steps away to his right. There were *two* of the creatures, he realized. Or could he trust his senses? The Pantera seemed to have the ability to project itself or an image or sound, at least. The creature to his right poised itself to pounce. In the blink of an eye, it lunged while a tentacle whipped out to catch his foot. That tentacle met a pincer-like claw that sheared it in half even while Klamath's other hand drove deep into the great cat's abdomen, breaking off cleanly as the beast tumbled past.

It yowled and writhed as it hit the ground, the broken-off piece of Klamath's hand transforming into some exotic, boring creature that he couldn't name and had never seen in real life. But the alien cells within him held its genetic memory and assumed its form and gruesome purpose: to consume a living creature from the inside out.

Klamath pitied the creature as its yowls gave way to mewling agony.

"Sorry, but it could only ever have ended this way. At least the rifle woulda made it quick. Course, you wouldn't have done any different. You're a killer. Just like me."

He turned to face the cave, and a blast of psychic energy rocked him, pounded the inside of his skull with agony and despair. He felt it in his core. His guts trembled with rage and suffering, and just when he thought he couldn't stand it anymore, it stopped. Klamath was down on one knee, his hand grinding into the grit and sand to steady himself.

He looked up to see those eyes and saw them in a whole new dimension of understanding. The creature wasn't just intelligent. It was self-aware. And it was dying. Its last hope of carrying on its seed lay twitching just a few yards away. The creature before him had given it birth, and now it had to watch as that life was extinguished.

For the first time he could recall, Klamath broke down. Warm tears slid down his face as he crumpled to his butt on the floor of the Pantera's den. Snot dripped down his face, and he wiped it away on his sleeve. He didn't know where his own feelings and those of the creature began and ended, but the feelings were real. The sorrow, the bitterness, the loss. He could relate to all those things, but it'd been an eternity since he'd let himself feel any of them. He locked gazes with the creature through bleary eyes and felt a connectedness through the sorrow like he'd never known before.

Just as he let out an exhausted breath, a serpentine tentacle whipped out at his head.

Ah, there you are.

His one remaining hand reformed into a chitinous blade and sliced it apart. He rose to his feet, gravel grinding beneath his boots, and then stepped forward, forging a path against an avalanche of emotion. Another tentacle whipped through the air. He swiped it with a casual backhand as it came close to taking his head off. And then, without remorse or hesitation, he drove that blade right between the two sets of emerald, alien eyes. And the light behind them faded out.

Klamath turned and stared out of the cave. The valley floor was all but invisible for the fog and chaos of ice crystals cavorting on the wind. He'd vanquished the Pantera del Diablo. And her adolescent cub. And didn't feel any better for it. But he did feel. That was something. Something he'd lost and never expected to find again. And this time, the tears that wet his cheeks were not the kind induced by psychological deception but real ones. Bidden by real loss. Loss that could never be rectified or erased. It just existed. Just like him.

Vohl observed while the two beetles slowly tore each other apart. One leg, one antenna, another leg... Soon they'd not be able to fight any longer but slowly starve to death. He'd created them as perfect clones. Perfectly balanced on offense and defense so that one had no advantage over the other. He'd worked at this for some time to get it right. He was very pleased with the result.

A voice crackled over the speakers in his workroom.

"Vohl. Report your findings to me on the bridge at once."

The coal-black creature rolled its overly large, gold-flecked eyes and turned away from his dismembered pets. He laced his fingers upon his potbelly and strolled across the floor as he thought about ways to make the fight between his creatures a little less underwhelming. There should be more noise. And blood. He should make them bigger, and they should have sad little families that watched on in horror.

His eyes grew wide with the thought and then the lids slid down into slits as a smirk turned up the corners of his mouth. Later. He would do it later this very day.

And then, with a poof of thin smoke, he disappeared. Off to do the captain's bidding.

Zilich had taken the news well. He was displeased to hear that the outlaws he employed to keep his mines full of magickally imbued children had been, quite literally, torn apart. But his mood had shifted noticeably when he was told of the arrival of a new pilot. A girl, which was even better.

The ship ran better with a girl pilot for reasons Vohl was unable to deduce. Humans were distasteful enough, male or female. The fact that the ship preferred one over the other spoke to a level of intimacy that he found repulsive.

The only reason he endured Zilich's presence, let alone his demanding nature, was that he was equally as soulless as Vohl himself. He could at least admire that quality, even if it came wrapped in a repugnant shell of pink meat.

"This girl sounds exceptionally gifted," Zilich said in his peculiar drawling way of speech.

He cracked his neck side to side and scratched a two-week growth of salt-and-pepper beard before striding to the command console, somehow managing to make it look effortless in spite of his mangled right leg that would no longer bend at the knee joint.

Navy coveralls hid the extent of the damage done to the rest of him when the ship crash-landed into this pitiful, backward bit of cosmic detritus. Vohl pondered for a moment, trying to determine if there was anything that he didn't despise, and came up with nothing. His experiments, he guessed. But even those were too limited by their appalling lack of sophisticated technological equipment to be much more than a passing amusement. If he had even slightly better tech, he could create monsters to rival what they'd poached and set them off to rampage all over this disgusting little planet.

"Too bad about Blackie's gang. We'll just have to send sentries to do it from now on. We're getting close, Vohl. We've had breakthroughs in Two-Law's Containment, Warp Matter Transfer. We'll be able to reignite the main reactors within the week. We could ignite them now, but I don't trust the sci-bots' hobbled-together AI framework to tie their own shoes without five rounds of testing."

"Wise beyond your years, oh lofty one," Vohl purred.

"Stow your false flatteries, imp," Zilich snarled.

"Stowed, oh gimpy one."

Zilich's head snapped up, the jaw muscles rippling under his despicable pink flesh. Vohl looked on coolly and pretended to file his nails before smiling back in a way that he knew bared all of his needle-sharp teeth. In his own Nawri culture, this was a grave insult, amounting to nothing less than a solemn oath to kill the recipient and wear their face as a mask while systematically expunging their lineage from existence. Zilich, he knew, was more than aware of this.

"You really are a loathsome little creature, you know that?" the man said, returning his attention to the various displays scrolling through myriad operational metrics before him.

"One tries…"

Zilich studied the data before him for a minute in silence before continuing, not bothering to look back. "Do you think she's strong enough to draw the rest of the ship to her?"

"Perhaps. If not, maybe she could be made to be?"

At this, the man turned around to search Vohl's shark-like features. "*Made* … to be?"

"Perhaps she could be harnessed?"

"Harnessed? How so?"

"Just a little thing I've cooked up."

"This *thing*… Will it kill her?"

"Hard to say. Would that be bad?"

"Yes, Vohl. That would be bad."

"Shame. No, I don't think it would kill her."

"Will she be … recognizable afterward?"

Vohl studied the ceiling of the bridge, squinted while mathing in his head, and then came to a satisfying conclusion and nodded.

"Definitely unrecognizable."

"Vohl. That's also bad. After we complete the ship, we need her as a pilot."

"But you can fly the ship, can't you?"

"You know full well that it exacts a price. I don't have the body," he said, motioning toward himself, "or the years to spare to pay that price. So, yes, we need her, and we need her intact and pliable."

"I don't think she'll come willingly. She seems to have it in her brain that your head would look well on a pike." Vohl's eyes gleamed at the thought.

"I know you get off on that kind of thing, but you forget, you need me to get us off this planet and safely through Xixli Space."

The Nawri nodded grudgingly. He was very much intrigued by the pike idea, though. Could he figure out a way to keep him alive while he did it?

"Go work on your harness thingy. I don't think I can stand to watch you fantasize about all the ways you'd like to kill me for one more second. Wait… Before you do that, go find her. I'd like to know where she's at and how long we have until she gets here. I have preparations to make if she's as powerful as you say."

Vohl snarled quietly to himself. Step and fetch was his least favorite thing to do. It was *so* beneath him. He was royalty, after all. His exile for murdering his brothers … just a temporary inconvenience.

Do this one task, and don't suffocate Zilich in his sleep, he thought to himself.

He'd lost count of how many times he'd given himself this familiar command. It'd gotten him this far. He was days away from being able to return home and annihilate his detractors—his parents first among them. Long live Grand Imperator Vohl!

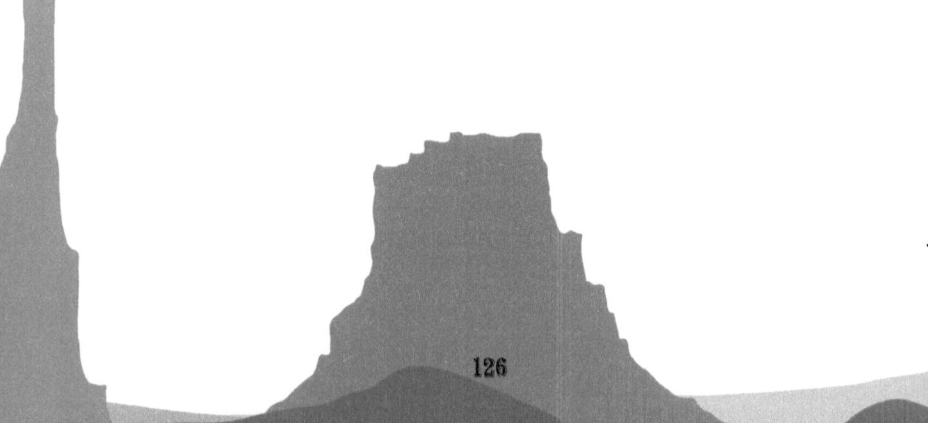

CHAPTER 8

DEAD BUT NOT BURIED

Vohl popped back into physical reality and was shocked to see a sarcophagus lying before him. This wasn't right. He'd homed in on the girl. Or so he thought. He thought he could just follow the carnage, but it had led him here. Peculiar.

He looked around. The room was dark, filled with black stone columns of alien origin. There were appurtenances as befitting a temple: gilded boxes, lampstands, that sort of thing. His eyes rested on a box on an altar, flicked back to the sarcophagus, and then back to the box. He was drawn to it.

His stomachs were doing flips, and he was, *what is this*, sweating?!?

Ughh. How unseemly.

His eyes flitted back to the box. He was definitely drawn to it. But he knew where he was now. The Rajak's cell. Special order. Otherwise, the sentries wouldn't have wasted the time or the space on bringing all this extraneous material. The cell was located in what was referred to as the menagerie: the massive containment area where all the creatures Zilich had curated were kept.

But the Rajak was special. A creature of supreme power and equal appetites.

He considered this, tapping his upper lip with his finger.

Did the box just shudder?

He'd heard movement, but this place was quiet as a crypt. He took a step toward it before checking himself and chuckling,

"Oh, I see. You want me to open it," he said to the sarcophagus. "I don't think I will."

A small line of light split the upper portion of the box, and then the lid lifted slowly, a warm glow spilling from within. Vohl's eyes grew wide, and he arched his neck to see inside.

"No."

He turned away, closing his eyes. He squinted and shot a glance in the direction of the box. It was closed, looking as though it had never been opened.

"Tricks, I see. Well, you'll have to find another stooge."

He poofed away from the cell, but in his mind, he recalled something from inside the box. Ceremonial bracelets. Coincidentally, about his size. He was sure he hadn't actually seen them, but somehow they were ingrained in his memory just the same.

Games, he thought. *The Rajak wants to play games. Hmm.*

Vohl wrinkled his broad, pointy nose at the stench of burned human flesh. A heap of smoldering ash and broken timber had melted the snow in a wide arc around what had been an outbuilding of sorts. Tree branches were bare and singed thirty feet up. Not far away, another building, a dwelling, stood untouched.

The habitation was nestled in a secluded spot on a forested mountainside with a little peek through the trees of the valley beyond. Peaceful but for the charred corpses with chains still wrapped around their bones. This last bit was hard to see through the ash, but Vohl had an eye for such things.

He'd found this place simply by desiring to find it. The same way he'd found the warehouse back in that vile Low Camp. Something about chaos and death drew him like a lodestone. The girl had certainly been here. There was no question about that, but there were also no coldbright remnants to query to get more specific details.

But this place did lay on a direct path between the carnage of the warehouse and Zilich's ship/fortress near Puro Pura. And it was obvious that this fire was only a few hours old. That was enough information to report back with.

Perhaps the girl had been forced down due to the blizzard? How strong could she be if something as simple as inclement weather detained her? But then, death seemed to follow her like, well, like this ... the cloying stench of burning bodies.

Vohl snorted, expelling wads of phlegm into the snow at his feet. He'd need to thoroughly cleanse his olfactory nodes when he got back.

Enough of this. Task complete. Now off to play with his toys and devise new and exciting ways to make Zilich's eventual demise even more entertaining.

Justine inhaled the plate of eggs, sausage, and toast and then licked the plate clean of the yoke. When she sat the plate down, she noticed some of it still on the tip of her nose. Rather than bother to find a napkin, she buried her nose in her tattered sleeve and rubbed vigorously. A muffled squeak made her conscious of what she must look—and smell—like. Her eyes flicked to the residents of the modest farmhouse, pinned to the kitchen wall and gagged by mercurial filaments of coldbright.

Their eyes betrayed so much. Fear, outrage, disgust, and ... something else. She scrutinized the two while tentacles of liquid metal brought her a cup of coffee and another toasted a slice of bread with butter.

The man, balding slightly, face creased by years in the fields, and the woman, trim and hard like any good frontier woman, could have been her own parents. They were similar, yet she didn't see signs of kids anywhere.

Oh...

She realized hers wasn't the only tragic story in the breadth and depth of the Alta Estranyazie.

To their left, she spotted a sepia-toned picture in a frame on a hutch. In the photograph, there were five people. In addition to the man and woman—presently restrained in their own kitchen—was an older woman, who probably passed in the intervening years, and two children. They could have been twins; a boy and a girl around eight years of age with dark hair like their mother and eyes framed by the same heavy brow as their father.

A knot twisted in Justine's stomach. It didn't sit well with her belly full of buttered toast, eggs, and pork fat. A tentacle brought the steaming cup to her lips, but she scalded them in her eagerness to wash down the sudden spat of guilt. The ceramic cup shattered and splashed steaming coffee across the floor.

"Dammit," she cursed and then instinctively shot a glance at the woman, expecting to see a look of reproach but finding instead a kind of sorrow.

"Don't look at me," she warned.

The woman nodded, as much as she could anyway, and closed her eyes tight.

"You lost your boy and girl?" Justine asked.

The man's eyes hardened, but the woman nodded again but barely just, as if it was too heavy a burden to give any more energy to that grief. Justine watched a solitary tear gather at the corner of her eye. It paused and then trickled slowly down her cheekbone before sliding down to her jawline where it held fast. Just one tear.

Justine wondered if she was capable of even that anymore.

"The mines?" she asked.

The man's iron gaze grew harder. The woman just slumped a little in the grip of the coldbright.

Before she realized she'd done it, Justine let them go. The farmer jumped to put himself between herself and his wife. His gaze never slipped, but the hardness seemed to leak out of it somewhat. Justine was good at reading people. She didn't want to see what she saw in his eyes. Behind the fear and anger was pity.

He didn't see a little girl like his own. Desperate. Lost. He saw a monster.

She couldn't blame him. He was right. Justine looked around the room. Plates were broken, a shotgun lay open-breach on the floor, shells scattered. He was still in his socks, for crying out loud, patches pulling apart where they'd been worn through, repaired, and needed fixing again.

She was a monster, alright. But she was also a hunter, and she would take the real monster down, the one responsible for all of their misery. She straightened in her seat. Flattened her part and braids with shaking hands as if preparing for choir at Sunday service.

"I'm going to fix what needs fixin'. The man from the north ... what caused all this turmoil, Zilich." She nodded toward the picture on the hutch. "No one else needs to see this kind of sufferin'," she assured them in a quavering whisper.

The woman broke down sobbing, her face in her hands. The man's eyes glimmered, his jaw jutting out, lips pressed flat, twitching under a torrent of restrained emotion.

After a long moment, he spoke, his voice tight and full of warning. "Take what you want and get. You leave us be. And you don't never come back."

It was Justine's turn to nod. The silver strands that billowed from her receded out the back door, and she allowed herself to be pulled along even as she continued to hold the man's gaze. This was another image that would forever be burned into her mind. The man, so much like her own father, protecting his wife ... from her.

She slipped out of the house and up into the pale light of a winter's day. Justine no longer needed the silver disk to support her; she just willed herself into the air the same way she willed the tendrils of cold-bright to move as she wished.

Fire burned in her belly, burned up her insides even though she felt so cold. And hollow. It was drawing near. The end of her journey and whatever fate held for her. Either she'd kill Zilich, or he'd kill her. Either way, she'd be done with it. She realized it was a burden she didn't wish to bear any longer. Couldn't bear. This *needed* ending.

She rose up further, and off in the distance, a haze of smoke stained the sky. Beneath it, a town with taller buildings than she'd ever seen. It sprawled across the northern edge of the valley, climbed up the red rock cliffs beyond, and eventually met a structure that dwarfed everything around it. The thing, not quite a building and too impossibly huge to be what looked like a ship, rested at an angle in the cliff. In fact, it extended well up into the sky above it, almost as if God himself had driven it into the rocks and then left it to play with later.

Fear gripped her throat at the awesome spectacle of it. But then rage burned it away.

"There you are. I'm coming for you. But not just me. The ghosts of my parents and everyone that have suffered at your hands. They're coming with me ... to sit in judgment."

A pang of loss bloomed within her as she pressed forward against the wind. But there were no tears. She was right. That part of her was broken.

Good, she thought. *Justice can't bide a weak will.*

Bodie had seen enough. Even at night, the terrain was crawling with Zilich's robots. They were certainly up to something. Dozens had come and gone just in the few hours he'd spent scouting the area ahead. His little party would have one heck of a time crossing the valley without being seen, so he figured they'd just have to be seen. Just waltz right into town as if they owned the place. Why not? It could work…

"You wanna do what?" Antigony demanded, hands on her hips.

"There's no avoiding the robots. I think we should just ignore them and mosey into town," Bodie drawled. Sometimes he felt like this affectation made his arguments more convincing.

"That sounds like suicide. Won't they be able to tell you're not one of them?"

"Perhaps. But, from what I can tell, they're somewhat single-minded of purpose."

He kind of envied that, having wandered for so long without a proper direction, and then once he had finally chosen one—inadvertent as it was—it had gone less than spectacular.

"I don't like it," she said, running a finger inside her appropriated clerical collar. She'd finally gotten warm after all those hours of misery, and now she was near to sweating, yet still wouldn't move away from the fire.

Carole had moved on and was standing near the tumble of granite that formed the back wall of their campsite, eyes closed but ears betraying a heightened level of alertness. The Pantera del Diablo had really done a number on all of them. And nothing needed to be said about the gory troupe of undead that had chased them through the woods directly after.

"Well, we could put it to a vote, but seeing that it's just the two of us, I 'spect it'd come up a draw."

"So what do you suggest?" Antigony asked, cocking her head and crossing her arms, clearly expecting to like this next course of action even less than the last.

"Well, I suggest that we just wait till dawn and head out then. Anyone tries to stop us, we'll regroup and change tack. If they don't, then straight on to Puro Pura, and Zilich beyond that."

Antigony mulled it over. "Sounds reasonable," she grumbled, sulking a bit and then brightening as she had a thought. "What do ya wanna do until then?" she asked with a knowing smirk, the light from the campfire softening yet highlighting her striking features. Apparently, her libido had thawed with the rest of her.

Bodie was certain it didn't show outwardly, but he was blushing again on the inside. He shook his head.

"N-Now, Miss Von Riche…" he stuttered but paused when she placed her index finger on the row of lights where his mouth would have been. Of course, this wouldn't have done anything to stop him from talking, but out of respect, he chose to comply with the non-verbal cue.

She stepped in close, and he could feel the heat from her body pressed against his. A curious tingling ran up from the bottom of his being and flooded into his chest.

This was not a typical sentry bot response to external stimuli. He was certain of it. Helga and Dmitr were oddly quiet.

"Miss Von Riche, this is never gonna work…" he said softly and without an ounce of conviction. She leaned in closer until they were nearly nose to nose. That tingling sensation inside him blossomed into a warm, churning tumult of sensual energy. And then she pushed away and turned back to the fire.

"I s'pose. But sometimes it's fun to pretend," she said, throwing a wink over her shoulder and swinging her hips in a way that drew Bodie's attention down to her well-shaped rear end. He averted his eyes hastily as she chuckled at his expense.

"G'night, robot. Sweet dreams," she said as she sashayed past the fire to find herself a spot where the rocks had soaked up some of the heat so she could catch a few hours of shut-eye.

Bodie, with his insides still roiling, turned to face the open valley floor. He kicked up his sensors to scan for dangers. This took a fraction of his processing power. The rest of it was spent trying to untie the knot of mixed emotions inside him that this dangerous and unscrupulous woman had so deftly crafted.

Helga, I already know the answer to this, but is there anywhere in my programming that allows for such a … carnal response to Miss Von Riche's feminine wiles? I know that I can learn, but … can I learn emotion?

<…>

I take that as a no. And as your vote of disapproval.

Dmitr splashed a quick image of a man and woman entwined in that most primitive of activities. It was clear what *his* vote was—misguided as it was.

Bodie continued to chew on the conundrum until early rays painted the sky purple, then lavender, and finally blushing tones of amber. Antigony was snoring, gaucho hat tipped low over her face, hands and arms tucked under the poncho Bodie had lent her. Carole lay beside her, sharing body heat, her ink-on-parchment coloration cast in tones of buttermilk as a thin line of molten gold spilled over the eastern peaks.

Across the valley, pockets of fog adopted those same hues while geese and ducks took to the air from their nighttime shelters. Bodie sighed at the idyllic beauty as his eyes came to rest on the brilliant structure jutting out of the rocks at the furthest reaches. He felt a tremor of anticipation and, if he were honest, dread. This was the final showdown.

No delaying it. It was time to move. He didn't know if the girl Justine was in Puro Pura yet, but they had to get there in order to find out.

An hour and a half later, they were just reaching the outskirts of a town that even from a distance was clearly like nothing they'd ever seen before, or maybe existed anywhere. There were buildings here five and six stories tall. Factories belching smoke into the sky from chimneys that soared well above that.

He didn't know what all of it was for, but it was easy to imagine it had something to do with the hulking vessel wedged into the red rock cliffs above.

Puro Pura's main avenue ran just under a mile, hit a dogleg, and then appeared to continue on about a half-mile beyond that. There, the town didn't stop but somehow mounted that impressive edifice of rock, climbing hundreds of feet until it melded with the base of the structure at its top.

Bodie was still taking it all in when he had a flash of memory: inky black space dotted with stars, the blue, green, and brown sphere of a planet streaked with clouds before him, and the glowing tail section of a large craft looming into view.

In this vision, the view before him diminished, and he realized he was seeing the scene through what looked like a window that took up an entire wall of a large dark room. Chairs with consoles before them dotted the interior space. He saw looks of excitement and trepidation from the crew, and then a voice that he recognized as his own cut the silence. "Helga, Dmitr, gather the boarding crew. Meet me in hangar bay four."

And then the vessel ahead of them drew closer and closer until its engines passed beyond the lower corner of the viewscreen and the true size of it became obvious. To Bodie's recollection, it pushed the limits of what could be called a medium transport. He knew it for what it was: an ark filled with all the most dangerous xenobiology in the known galaxy.

"Lock on starboard grapplers and match speed…"

And then the vision passed.

Bodie didn't know if this was some bit of info the coldbright had provided that he'd somehow missed or some latent memory dislodged by seeing the vessel in person.

Upon reflection, he realized it had to be an actual memory, something buried in his OS. The coldbright would recall the encounter from the vantage of Zilich's vessel, since that's what the coldbright was. What the kids with their magick called back to the surface was just the shredded and scattered remnants of the cataclysm that had caused that vessel to crash in the first place.

"You still with us, metal man?" Antigony asked, looking at him with her chin resting on his shoulder as the two rode along on Carole's back. Humans were an odd bunch, but this one? He didn't know if he possessed enough processing power to ever understand the convoluted tangle of motivations rustling between her head and heart.

Did he need to? Couldn't he just accept her company and her help at face value and not give it any more thought than that? It didn't seem likely. She had a way of forcing the issue. Kind of like a hurricane in a haberdashery.

"Yes. I'm still with us. Just thinking about what we're going to do when we eventually come face-to-face with Zilich. And Justine, for that matter. We're a sight short on intel."

"What's that mean, intel?"

"Um, reconnoitering. Tactical information. Specifics of the terrain ahead."

"Ah, *intel*."

"That's what I said."

"Yeah, but when you say it, you make it sound weird."

The two sat in silence after that as they rode on up the main avenue.

Sunlight spilled between the tall buildings to their right, casting the snow and mud on the street in alternating swaths of light and dark. Automatons strode along wooden sidewalks or drove carriages that were either horse-drawn or driven by billowing engines.

There were no humans to be seen, besides Antigony that was. The reality was that he was one of them, an automaton himself. No matter how he dressed or how he felt on the inside.

Bodie tried to straighten up in his saddle a bit but found a certain kind of melancholy pressing him down. Somehow, in an effort to find himself, he'd lost a whole other part in the process. But then he wondered at the root belief. What was the body, anyway?

If he were a robot *mind* contained within his original body, would he in any way be the man he knew himself to be? The answer was no. He'd be that robot.

The mind that had somehow been introduced to this body was the real Bodie. *He* was the real Bodie, no matter what *body* he possessed, metal or flesh or otherwise. And if he could somehow regain the memories from his former life, well then, that would really be something, wouldn't it?

A carriage backfired and the two of them had pistols in hand, ready to lay down lead before they realized their error. All the robots on the street stopped and stared at them but didn't engage. Bodie was certain that Zilich was receiving news of this imminent threat now that they'd shown their hand, so to speak. He felt stupid for not doing a better job of staying alert and keeping a cool head.

They looked on as all of Zilich's bots stepped aside or guided their wagons away from the main path to allow them through.

"Bodie. What just happened?" Antigony whispered as she leaned into him from behind.

Why'd she have to do that? He wrenched his focus from the feeling of that contact back to the situation that was unfolding around them.

"The robots seen our guns. I'm sure every single one of them is transmitting the news of our arrival, or at least of some sort of threat, back to Zilich in his ship. And they're clearing the way to let us through. Shows how much he thinks of the threat we represent: a woman, a horse, and a rogue robot."

"I resent that remark. I may be a woman, but I am most certainly a threat!" she said and then sat back and crossed her arms. He could feel her glare boring into the back of his head.

"I never said such. I was just saying that Zilich seems to think that we're not—"

"I'm sorry. You still talkin'?" Antigony interrupted.

Bodie dropped it, and they rode in silence to the end of the street. Muddy wagon ruts and dirty snow gave way to something more akin to artificial gray rock, and then a great arching gateway made of metal and glass led to a series of mechanical lifts beyond. He saw now that much of the structure that ran up the cliff was actually these elevators leading to staggered sets of platforms higher and higher up.

The whole thing reminded Bodie of mining operations he'd seen where ore material that had been pulled from the earth was then maneuvered up the shaft to a location where it could be further refined or shipped somewhere else for smelting.

Antigony couldn't maintain her facade of aloof indifference any longer at the sight of such wonders. She tapped on Bodie's shoulder. "What is this? All of this. What's it for? What's it *made* of? It looks like steel and glass but not like anything I've ever even heard before. If this guy made all this... I don't know. What are we walking into?"

This was the first time he'd heard anything come out of her that wasn't bravado, opinion stated as fact, or bald-faced seduction. Antigony was a lot of things, but timid was not one of them. It made him a little uncertain himself if he were being honest.

Carole's ears twitched as she clopped along the oddly textured surface. She didn't like it either.

"Zilich has certainly been busy. He's using off-world tech. And maybe recreating some of what he lost when his ship was destroyed. Well, most of his ship anyway."

"So, this is all alien stuff?"

"Technically speaking, I suppose so. But really it's just future science using indigenous materials. And then there's the coldbright. But he needs all of that he can get in order to put his ship back together. Though, I don't know how he's going to do that exactly with it sticking half in and half out of the rock like it is."

Carole drew close to the first elevator, and they dismounted. Antigony stomped her feet and rubbed her sore buttocks.

"Sitting on the back of that pony with no saddle is no way to travel, let me tell you."

She stretched her back as she turned slowly to take it all in. Sunlight streamed through soaring glass. It truly was a sight to behold. And then the ground beneath them shuddered before they felt the whole thing rising up. They'd been standing on one massive lift without even realizing it. Carole spooked, and Bodie had to hold her reins and pat her neck to calm her down. Antigony, on the other hand, lit up like a kid at a carnival.

"Oooh, it's like a ride!" she crooned, spinning again to take in the entirety of the experience.

In that moment, Bodie envied her easily diverted nature. He was finding it hard not to settle into a sort of defeatist mindset. There really was no way they could come out of this on top. Either Zilich or Justine would be the victor, and they would just be bystanders, lucky to escape with their lives. He was tempted in that moment to turn around but realized he didn't even know how to operate the lift. In fact, he wasn't sure how it had started on its own. That tightness in his throat and chest returned. For a robot, he certainly was feeling the weight of his own mortality.

As the elevator rose, the town of Puro Pura dropped away and they could see the valley beyond with mist still clinging to brushy hollows and meandering creeks. Beyond that were the hills where they'd slept the night before. In the background, Helga was piecing together all the fuzzy bits of the OS's internal mapping and guidance systems, corroborating visual data with everything observed on the trail—which, given the snow and fog, hadn't been all that much.

The elevator stopped with a lurch, and there was nowhere to go but left, where another series of lifts sat ready for use. Bodie could see tunnels diving into the cliff face that made up the back wall of the space. Off to the side were what looked like ore carts but the fancy Zilich version. He strode over to these and confirmed his suspicion. They were full to brimming with a material that looked like shards of silver. Coldbright.

Bodie shuddered at the thought of what Justine could do with such an immense supply of the stuff. That jogged his memory and not in a good way.

Where is she at anyway? If she'd already gotten here, he imagined the place would be burning.

He was getting too distracted. The whole plan was to head Justine off at the pass, so to speak. He just hadn't put much thought into what that would actually look like, since—he realized now—he hadn't really expected to be successful. That was an error in judgment. Speaking of errors in judgment...

He looked over at Antigony, her eyes still wide with wonder. It had been a mistake to bring her here. For all her bluster, she was still a fragile human being. And, he realized, one who he did not want to see come to harm.

Just then, a shadow passed over them, and he spun to see the very thing he'd been afraid of all along.

There she was, just beyond the glass, tendrils of silver undulating like sea grass but deadly as serpents. Justine, blocking the sun with her coldbright tendrils spread out all around, looked like some sort of ancient god but portrayed as a young girl in a dirty, tattered prairie dress.

The look on her face held all the fury of one of those gods.

"Devil's Jackelope, what is that?" Antigony breathed out. "Is that... Is that the girl?"

"I'm afraid so."

"She looks *mighty* upset," Antigony observed while drawing her pistols and stepping back into a fighting stance.

"I'm sure she is. The last time we saw each other, she warned me not to come here. And then she tore me limb from limb just to make a point."

"Whoa ... shit."

"Sure enough."

Carole whinnied and stamped nervously right before Justine sent a flood of tendrils shattering through a cascade of glass. Horns blared and lights flashed as a shimmering wall of what seemed like raw energy rose up around their platform. Serpentine strands of cold-bright slammed into it but to minimal effect. The tendrils reared back and slammed all the harder and still couldn't break through, instead just creating crackling arcs of electricity with each blow.

Bodie let out an uneasy sigh of relief, and then the floor shuddered and they started sliding along the floor to the next vertical shaft where the platform came to a sudden halt and then lurched upward again. All the while, Justine's tendrils beat upon the energy wall, making a racket so loud it was hard to hear or be heard over it.

"What are we going to do?!?" Antigony shouted. "We can't compete with that!"

"I don't know. But I'm suddenly glad Zilich's defenses are up to the task."

They rose farther and farther up the cliff, and Justine continued to fly alongside them, pummeling their defenses on all sides until she finally got sick of wasting her efforts. She pulled back, looked one last time at Bodie and his small party, and then flew up and out of sight. Just her tendrils could be seen trailing behind her until, after a moment, those too disappeared.

There was a long uneasy silence, and then Antigony grabbed Bodie's shoulders and turned him to face her. They were traveling ever higher on the elevator platform so that Puro Pura dropped from sight and the mountains and plains far to the south, beyond the canyons, were visible beyond.

"Bodie. Maybe it's best if we just leave this be. Keep our hides intact. Maybe we won't get all the answers you're looking for, but at least we'll see another day. And who knows, maybe you'll decide the life you have to live is better than a hollow memory of the one you're trying to resurrect?"

She looked into his eyes with such earnestness, for a moment he could almost believe that she really did care. That he was somehow something more than a shiny toy to be played with and then discarded.

"I mean, look at you. You're a robot. Do you think whoever you left behind somewhere up there in the stars is going to see you for who you used to be instead of the way you are now?"

That struck Bodie as hard as if she'd hauled off and pistol-whipped him with one of his own five-pound Colts.

"That was a cold-blooded thing to say, Antigony."

"Maybe. But it's true. How long you been away?"

"I don't know. The download of info I got from contact with the coldbright indicated that the event with Zilich's ship happened about twelve years ago. How long I was chasing him before that, I don't know. That's why I need to talk with him. Find out what he knows about me. Who I was. Maybe then I can make a decision as to how to proceed. I just feel... Well, I don't know." He bumped the brim of his cowboy hat up and held his jaw as he thought about it. "I just feel that I wronged someone in all of that nonsense, the way I was carrying on—like a man possessed.

"I was consumed by bringing this man to justice. And judging by how he's conducted business, stealing kids to put them to work in the mines, hiring outlaws with no qualms about killing to do it? He needs to be brought to account for his actions. And maybe I do, too."

She grabbed his face in her hands. "Listen to me. You're a good man. You think I'm silly the way I keep carrying on, toying with you just to make you sweat a little. Well, it's fun, I have to admit, but at the same time, I can see right through that metal skin of yours. All the way to your heart. You use it more and better than anyone I've ever met. We all make mistakes, Bodie Nine. We all make mistakes. Believe me. But we can't let ourselves be *defined* by them."

With that, she let him go and patted him on the chest where his heart would have been if he'd been equipped with one. Bodie stared at her, somehow coming up short on processing power. Helga and Dmitr, too, were silent.

She nodded and dabbed at the corner of one eye. "Well, okay then. Enough of the mushy stuff."

She looked up and smiled sadly. He followed her gaze and saw that they were nearing the top. Flashing lights illuminated a room choked with roiling black smoke.

Bodie heaved a sigh. At least Justine would be easy to track.

Klamath turned in his seat and steadied the long barrel of his .45-70 against one of the few surfaces of the steam engine that wouldn't melt the flesh off his forearm. He sighted in the bobbing metallic head of his pursuer as it ran to catch up. The horseless carriage he'd stolen bucked and then settled momentarily as it rolled over the terrain, slow and steady but faster than he could have jogged on his own.

The gleaming dome of the automaton's head popped back up into view, and he paused briefly before pulling the trigger. The shot boomed over the chugging of the engine. The head slipped out of view again and then popped back up just in time for the bullet—which had traveled a sizable distance—to cleave it nearly in two.

"And that's the last of you," Klamath said out loud to an audience of one, namely himself.

He'd run across the four robots on their way to Low Camp and decided the specialized pistol that one of them carried, along with their carriage, would be put to better use in his employ.

The first two robots had succumbed to their injuries just north of the Pantera den, where Klamath had paused to collect himself after his exciting and emotional encounter with the alien beasts. The third had taken cover behind the still-moving wagon but, once a well-placed shot through a wagon wheel had torn off its leg below the knee, was unable to maintain cover. Klamath easily picked him off.

The last one fired a shot from its pistol just as Klamath had squeezed the trigger on his Winchester. The robot's shot was true and amazingly had covered the distance quicker than the rifle. It caught Klamath off his feet and threw him deep into the den. He lay there for some time before his body could heal itself enough for him to regain use of his legs.

Once he could walk, he saw that the wagon was nearly a mile farther on and the fourth robot was some distance from the road and largely headless. He rarely missed. Except when it came to that damnable robot, Bodie Nine.

He was looking forward to their reunion.

It took an hour for him to catch up to the wagon, figure out how to get it turned around, and return to the scene of the ambush. A couple of hours later, he caught sight of his pursuer. Apparently, robot number three, who had suffered from a kneecapitation and a shot to the torso, had removed that leg entirely and replaced it with the perfectly functional one robot number four no longer had use for.

Two hours after that, the agitating automaton had drawn itself into rifle range. Klamath warned him so by removing an arm and causing the robot to tumble down a ravine. He was getting desperately low on bullets and would need to hand-pack another two dozen when he had a chance. Meanwhile, he'd just use his pretty new pistol. It was a tiny thing, but it packed a heck of a wallop.

Half a day later, the gleaming dome of robot number three bobbed into view again. Klamath was near the outskirts of a town the likes of which he had not seen in quite some time. Puro Pura had many of the hallmarks of a civilized planet. Barely, but still. It felt a bit like coming home.

Theirs hadn't been the only carriage he'd seen. Along the way, he'd passed no less than five other parties: four headed south and one he'd overtaken on his way to the north. This last had been a caravan and looked to be packing a large quantity of something other than coldbright. In fact, unless Klamath missed his guess, those wagons were filled with many of the esoteric creatures so common to the Alta Estranyazie.

Zilich, it seemed, was bringing all his pretty creatures back to the ark—the Ars Arcanum, as it was known across the galaxy.

Klamath placed his rifle behind him and turned back around in his seat. He slowed the carriage by pulling back on a lever that acted as the engine's throttle. It ratcheted back and stayed put. After a couple of minutes, he entered town.

What lay before him was peculiar, to say the least. The broad, muddy street was lined with robots identical to the ones he'd dispatched, only these were just standing still. None were working or headed off somewhere to do their master's bidding, whatever that happened to be. They all stood or sat off to the side and watched him come through.

It was eerie. At first, he thought it was because of what he'd done, but then at the far end of the street, he saw movement on up the cliff wall. There lay a system of elevators that looked like they were established to deliver material and personnel to various levels. What was on each of those levels he could only guess, but the town seemed to grow steadily more technologically advanced the further he ventured in. So much so that the far end almost looked to be an extension of the massive ship resting at the top of the cliff.

It was bigger than he'd expected. Having been stuck on this planet for a couple of years now, he'd grown accustomed to its ways and level of sophistication. The ship was a throwback to times he'd deliberately tried to forget.

Living amongst these people without revealing who and what he was required a constant effort. In fact, he hadn't used any of his special abilities for nearly his entire exile here, up until the girl Justine happened. And then once more with the Pantera del Diablo and its cub.

A shadow passed overhead and caught him out of his reverie. Above, and moving quickly, was what looked like a great chrome-dipped octopus or jellyfish. Tendrils thirty to forty feet long trailed behind a central point that he couldn't see from this vantage, but he knew what, no, *who* it was. It was the girl, and she was headed directly for Zilich's ship. What was left of it, anyway.

A smile turned up at the corners of his bushy mustache. He pushed the throttle lever forward, and the carriage splashed through puddles and patches of dirty snow before they transitioned to some sort of pavement.

"And now for the showdown…"

Klamath didn't know who would win out in the end, but he did know one thing: a scenario where Zilich, the robot, and the girl were all dead was the one he favored most. And he'd do whatever needed to be done to make that happen.

After which, he'd get off this god-forsaken planet and collect his well-earned bounty.

CHAPTER 9

TOOTH AND NAIL, ANTLER AND TENTACLE

Vohl watched as a dozen sentry bots struggled to wrangle the Wun-dee-go into its containment cell. It was scheduled for cryo later that afternoon. Dozens of other recaptured creatures had already undergone the treatment, but these things took time. Otherwise, when they thawed out, they would just render into a lifeless puddle of protein.

That was bad for business, and Vohl was counting on business being good. His rise to power depended on it. That and Zilich's death.

He'd fashioned his plans meticulously, so that element factored significantly in the final outcome. He didn't want to owe anyone a single thing when he finally sat his cushy little ass on the Imperator's seat. And besides, he despised Zilich and his self-important air. He'd know his place before this was all said and done.

A bellowing roar echoed through the containment area corridors, followed by heavy thuds as one of the more well-known residents expressed their frustration.

Ahh ... the Golem.

Vohl shuddered. There was one creature that they did not set free into the world to graze and be re-collected later. One creature that both he and Zilich feared above all else: the Golem.

For all intents and purposes, it was just a big, stupid lump of rock. But, unlike the other creatures whose exotic forms and myth-shrouded abilities were little more than exaggerated expressions of natural—and sometimes unnatural—evolution on their respective planets, the Golem was truly and inexplicably magickal.

For all of their collective knowledge on the topic— and it was vast—neither Zilich nor Vohl could understand *how* it existed. What they did know, however—and this was the truly terrifying part—was *why*.

The Golem existed to punish.

And not just anyone. Only those who had practiced an immensely, no, exorbitantly unjust life. Those who profited greatly from the suffering of others. Evil-doers.

For that, he and Zilich had much to be afraid of. The fact that the Golem could pass through any material substance—rock being, of course, its preferred medium, but spaceship material being equally viable— meant that there was quite literally nowhere to hide. Except space, which was impractical, to say the least. Vohl loathed discomfort. Especially being cold. And space was very, very cold.

So, the only way to truly keep the creature confined was to encase it in a vacuum. The Golem Containment Unit was a box suspended by gravitics within another box that contained such a vacuum. Besides being elusive, there was another reason why it could not be left to its own devices in the wilderness of the Alta

Estranyazie. It was imprinted on Zilich. And, most regrettably, on Vohl as well.

This seemed unfair since everyone Vohl had ever harmed had most assuredly had it coming. But such was life.

The fervent banging increased in tempo and ferocity, which was impressive considering vacuum containment's ability to insulate from noise and vibration. The creature could sense that Vohl was near. He shuddered again and then sneered at the unconscious sign of weakness, however justified. Still, no sense in loitering about and further aggravating the thing. There was much they didn't know about the creature, and who knew what it was capable of if it got mad enough?

Besides, it looks like the sentry bots have things under control, he thought as two of them went flying across the room and another was being alternately slammed into the floor and then the corrugated flooring above, over and over again. At least the Wun-dee-go was preoccupied.

It truly was a sight to behold, its ghastly gray skin stretched tight over skeletal features, its massive rack of antlers adorned with dried blood and ... entrails of its victims. It would fetch a handsome sum at Barqur's Bazarr in the Middleplex system.

Vohl's special ability to sense carnage and mayhem ensured that he always knew where these beauties were. The Golem? Not until after it had found its victim, and then, since it would just melt back into the rock or walls or whatever, it was impossible to track until the next victim, which could be weeks or months and possibly even be Vohl himself.

Another sentry bot went flying. Vohl decided he'd need to intervene. But what could he do? Then, before he realized what he was doing, he'd sauntered forward, paused, and then reached out tentatively into the air as if feeling for something invisible hanging just before him.

He blinked in confusion, and in the split second that his eyes were closed, he could swear he'd seen glowing bracelets like manacles wrapped around each wrist.

Fear clenched his chest. But then, one of his hands curled into a fist as if clutching something invisible.

The Wun-dee-go roared in surprise and anguish. It clawed at its chest and threw the sentry bot aside, forcing Vohl to duck, which momentarily broke his concentration.

The creature cast about wildly, hunting for the source of the attack, and then it spotted him. It stampeded forward, head down, eager to impale its presumed tormentor.

Vohl frantically fished in the air with both hands this time until he found what he was looking for and wrenched. The creature skidded to a halt, rearing back in agony, unable to even vocalize. Vohl chuckled nervously, smiled, and then twitched his hands again. The behemoth groaned as air expelled from its lungs and its back contorted viciously.

Vohl held it there. The sentry bots that had just dusted themselves off exchanged concerned looks. He saw their faces and raised an eyebrow before letting the Wun-dee-go free. It crumpled to the ground, panting short, shallow breaths.

Big, dumb animal...

Vohl dusted off his hands and walked past the creature and the robots. He observed cooly as the Wundee-go panted shallowly, its eyes tracking his progress.

Good. Let him sulk. He'll remember me next time, he thought, but part of him was preoccupied by what had just happened. What was it exactly? The power of the Rajak was what it was. He'd be ecstatic at this new-found power if he wasn't equally terrified.

A voice crackled over the intercom, breaking the following silence.

"Vohl, where are you?" Zilich asked in a forced, sort of offhand, way. "We have a situation."

Ah, the girl.

He'd sensed her nearby. *Time for the fun to really begin...*

Justine fumed. *That stupid robot.* She really didn't want to have to hurt him again.

Her tendrils stretched forward, gripping the walls as she exited the vertical shaft that led up the cliff and entered what she figured was the base of the spaceship. The corridor ahead twisted sideways so that the floors and walls and ceiling were off-kilter by thirty degrees or so. That seemed to match up. This was where the man-made structure ended and the ship began.

It was a good thing she could fly, but this was still going to be a little weird navigating within the massive vessel with it all at a slant. She wondered how Zilich and his robot crew managed it.

She flew toward the bulkhead; this was just a piece of the information provided to her by the coldbright in random bursts and at random times. The coldbright was a memory metal after all, but the interface wasn't perfect. She wasn't perfect, she corrected. There was still much she had to learn before she could gain complete access to it. Even her ability to manipulate the metal was incomplete, amazing as it may be.

She passed into the ship and everything cranked sideways. Her brain struggled to catch up to the fact that she now felt oriented to this new floor rather than the gravity she had grown up with.

She paused and turned around. Sure enough, the corridor she'd come from was twisted back the other way. New coldbright information trickled into her mind. This was a manipulation of gravity. She would maneuver through the entirety of the ship as if it were resting flat on the ground. The direction down inside the ship was different than down outside of it. She cocked her head as if hoping the knowledge would settle somewhere useful.

"Okayyy..." she said out loud.

There was so much that had been strange and wild over the last few days, but this was just plain disorienting. She'd never realized how much she took for granted the laws of nature. Of course, she didn't seem to have a problem with flying, but that was something that she was doing herself. Through magic. That somehow seemed to be justification enough. But this wasn't magic. It was science that was so amazing it *looked* like magic.

Fear began to percolate inside her. For the first time since giving herself over to the powers within her, she began to doubt herself. Really doubt herself. Could she compete with knowledge so great?

A voice pierced the silence and seemed to be coming from everywhere at once. "Hello. I'm Zilich," the voice said in easy, comfortable tones. Whoever this man was, he seemed to feel that she was as little a threat as she had just feared. "I am the owner of this vessel and proprietor of the township of Puro Pura. I imagine you've heard of me?"

Justine's mouth was dry. She settled to the floor, and the metal beneath her feet wasn't as cool as she imagined it would be but warm. She licked her lips and swallowed.

"I'm Justine," she yelled, not sure if he'd be able to hear her. "And your reign of terror and oppression has come to an end." She said this with as much conviction as she could muster but feared that it came off as hollow as it felt. Where had all the fire and venom gone? She was still angry, that was certain. But here, suddenly, she felt like the little girl she was.

Zilich chuckled. "My dear ... you have spirit. That's good. Space travel isn't for the faint of heart."

"What do you mean?" she asked, still yelling.

"You don't have to raise your voice. I can hear you as easily as God himself," he admonished gently. It was as if he were a teacher with a key concept but wanted his student to come to it on their own terms. She detested that familiarity. This was the man ultimately responsible for the deaths of her mother and father. And so many more. Maybe even the children of that couple she'd scared nearly to death. Their looks of fear and pity flashed into her mind again, reminding her of what she was. What she'd become. And ... what she must do. She held on to that kernel of righteous anger and let it strengthen her resolve.

A faint shuffle emanated from somewhere ahead, and she realized that the corridors ahead *and* behind her were slowly filling with more of the robots like Bodie Nine. That was okay. She didn't expect this to be easy. But she had no qualms about killing these new players. She continued the conversation while readying herself for the battle that was about to ensue.

"I asked, 'what you mean by space travel?' I ain't going anywhere with you."

"Mmm, that's where you're wrong, I'm afraid. You see, you're a pilot. And I've been waiting a very long time for you to show up. Twelve very long years, in fact. Since the last one died, resulting in the crashing of the Ars Arcanum, my beautiful ship."

The robots shuffled almost nervously, she thought, and then a small metallic cylinder rolled down the corridor in her direction, just as doors slammed down at either end of the corridor.

She whipped out a tentacle and batted the cylinder away just as it exploded in a burst of light with a deafening bang. Stunned and blinded, she sensed the robots closing in and lashed out, grabbing bodies and smashing them together in a torrent of disoriented rage.

She was still struggling to blink away the effects of the blast as more and more crowded in. She pulled in her tendrils, creating an impenetrable wall, and then burst them out, blasting the bots away and scattering them down the hall. This tactic could work. She did it again, only instead of the sentry bots collapsing on her again, another cylinder came tumbling in.

She spared a tendril to swat it away, but when it connected, rather than exploding with light and sound, it did so with electric energy, blowing Justine back against the wall and causing her to crumple to the ground.

She was blinking away stars when cold hands clamped down on her arms. Her mind was fuzzy. Pushing the bodies away would likely result in tearing her own body apart, so she did what was now quite familiar and separated those bodies from the arms that grabbed her. The corridor erupted into chaos as the bots fought back or tried to get away. There was barely enough room for her train of tendrils and the roughly dozen robots scrambling and diving to get their hands on her.

One grabbed an ankle and wrenched hard. She cried out and ripped it apart, but she had to let go of two other bots to do it. They came at her fast, and she struggled to swat them away. She was barely holding her ground. Still, fewer and fewer of the robots were functional. Maybe she could hold out?

She huffed with exertion. It was getting harder to keep them at bay. And then it was getting harder just to breathe. She realized too late that this was the tactic. The robots weren't the trap; they were the distraction.

Justine sucked in large gulps of air but felt like she was drowning. The robots that were left crowded in. She struggled vainly to push them away. And then she hit the floor. The warm metal against her face was the last thing she felt. Slack tendrils sprawling across dismembered metallic bodies was the last thing she saw.

Some indeterminate amount of time later, Justine woke with a horrendous headache. She tried to lift off the ground using her coldbright tentacles, but it didn't work. Blinking away the cobwebs, she pushed herself up and saw the problem. She didn't have any. All the coldbright was gone, and she was alone in a small dark room.

Justine slid her feet around and backed up to the wall. There was a small amount of light coming from rectangular strips in the ceiling as well as a tiny amount from a window high up on the solitary door. The whole thing was maybe ten by ten and echoed thinly as she scuffed around.

The grogginess slowly seeped out of her brain over twenty or thirty minutes. And then that same voice from before emanated from a corner of the room where tiny holes perforated the metal wall.

"I see you're awake. You'll have one hell of a headache, I imagine. Sorry about that. Couldn't be helped. You did a number on my sentry bots. Your ability to manipulate the coldbright is impressive indeed, but you still have much to learn before you can master the ship."

"You're insane if you think I'll ever work for you," she replied in a rasp, the words booming in her head, rattling like rubble from a mine explosion. She tried to swallow. Her throat was dry and her mouth tasted foul.

"I'm sure it's understandable that you feel that way, though I don't rightly know what I've done to deserve your ire. Come to think of it, I don't even know your full name."

Justine didn't respond immediately. It galled her even to be speaking to the man.

"It's Sever. Justine Sever."

"Well, Ms. Sever, I imagine you've suffered at the hands of the outlaws in my employ? Perhaps in the coldbright mines?"

She stared at the speaker, eyes narrowed. "Those men are all dead," she whispered. "Every last one of them. The ones who took me. The ones who transported us kids to Low Camp. Every single hand at the mines. Anyone I could find who took part in it. And especially the ones who killed my ma and pa," she said, her voice quivering with rage.

She wanted to keep things calm. Businesslike. She wanted to maintain a cool detachment. It was her rage that caused her to rush into the Zilich's ship like some pigheaded fool. And look what that got her.

But she couldn't keep the emotion out of her voice. She was just too tired and wrung out from all she'd been through over the last several days. Near on a week, she realized. And here she was. She'd found the man responsible for the deaths of her parents, and now she sat in a cell, impotent to do anything about it.

"Well, that is a tragic story. Truly. Not unlike my own really. Though I never wielded the power you have to exact that revenge...

"Still, I feel compelled to express that the means and methods by which the men operate are beyond my purview. I simply make the requests and provide the tools necessary. The men, a bunch of knuckledraggers with nary a handful of brain cells between them, do the rest. It's not ideal, but you work with what you've got. To be honest, I should be angry that you've so crippled my operation. I imagine it has set us back weeks if not months. Not to mention the cost. Near incalculable. But, it sounds like justice, at least, has been served. I could be convinced to overlook your transgressions in light of this."

"Excuse me?!?" She sprang to her feet. "*My* transgressions?" she roared at the speaker, almost unable to believe what she'd just heard.

"Yes. Even now, I'm in the final stages of retrieving my cargo—the esoteric creatures that I have curated from across the galaxy. And now, they will be delivered to a ship that isn't complete. Delayed for an indefinite amount of time. By you. We will have to figure out a way to round up the last of the coldbright in order to complete the necessary repairs. I guess there could be a way, but your training will have to be expedited to do it."

"Training? You're insane! I told you I would never, ever work for you, and I mean it. I'd rather rot in this room for the rest of my life than ever help you!" she yelled at the speaker and then pushed herself back into the corner, holding her legs tight to her body.

"Sweet Justine, I admire your conviction, but we have ways of making you do it. Personally, I'm against it, but ... it can be done. What I'd prefer is to come to some sort of agreement.

"What if I told you I could bring your parents back?" he asked.

She leveled a hard gaze at the speaker. "Bring 'em back? That's devil's work. I saw what happens to the people you bring back." She spat on the floor in disgust.

"Oh, you mean the liege, those whose bodies have been reanimated by a parasitic fungus? That can be an ugly business. No, this is nothing like that, I assure you. It's just science. Vohl's battery of gene fabricators should do the trick nicely if we're able to retrieve a sample of their DNA. If you don't mind me asking, how long have they been...?"

Justine's mind was reeling. What was he talking about? Could he really bring them back? Good as new? Or was he selling her a bill of goods like he had the man and his family from the cabin? She had no reason to trust this man, but if there was a chance...

"Dei Ennay? What's that? And what do you mean, sample?"

"Focus Justine. How long have your parents been dead?"

She thought for a moment. "About a week. Five days, I think. Maybe six. I'm not sure."

"Well, good news. If we can retrieve their bodies, I think we can have them back to you in ... just a few months."

"A few months?!? Why so long?" She was beginning to feel panicked. She realized she was getting caught up in his insane scheme, but she couldn't help it. What if he could do it? He certainly had technology that defied anything she understood. Robots. Anti-gravity. Who was to say that he didn't have the power of resurrection? And why shouldn't she use it? She could still kill him after she got what she wanted.

"These things, like all things worth doing, take time to do right. In the meantime, you will undergo training in how to operate this ship, which we will then use to extract the remaining coldbright to complete it and make it ready for interstellar travel."

"I don't know. I don't know if I can trust you. In fact, I'm certain I can't. And I'm not certain you can do what you say you can do."

"Well, you can have the day to think about it. I'll have someone deliver you a change of clothes and a meal. And a bed, even. It looks dreadfully uncomfortable in there. Did you know we had to put you in one of the Golem units?" He chuckled. "That's our most formidable containment for only our most powerful creatures. You are powerful, Justine. And someday, the very stars will be at your disposal."

There was a click and Justine realized that her connection to the outside world had been severed. She was alone again. And she had a lot to think about. What if it was true and she could have her parents back? Would having to work for this monster of a man justify that? Anything would be justified to bring her parents back.

She sat back against the corner of the cell and reached down inside herself to that burning mass of energy. The hate washed over her afresh. There was a part of her that knew the coldbright amplified that emotion. That with the power of the coldbright, she could lose herself to it. What would it be like if she learned more about how to use it? What was she really capable of? Could she hang on long enough to get her parents back and get her revenge on Zilich?

She would have to. She would play along until the opportunity presented itself. And it would. It had to.

CHAPTER 10

OLD ENEMIES

The lift reached the top of its track. Bodie and Antigony turned to take in a large glass- and steel-encased atrium. Whatever fires had caused all that smoke minutes before had been squelched. The smoke itself was strangely absent, but the remnants of its acrid stench hung in the air.

Walls were scorched black in places where equipment lay ruined. Bodie hadn't the foggiest idea what all the panels and piping were for, but their loss didn't seem to affect the lifts in any way. Helga rifled through information in the background, possibly sorting through some of what the coldbright had provided, or maybe taking inventory of memories that kept erupting into his consciousness as he interacted with things from his previous life.

His ocular circuits were drawn upward. Through the ceiling glass, the ship's flatly glinting metallic skin arced up and away above them. It was improbably massive from this vantage. To the right, it angled up into the sky with just the skeletal frame of some kind of scaffolding that rose up to meet its underbelly and then continued a short distance up its side.

The large room was empty, but at the far end was a bland wall that funneled into a corridor. Halfway down that corridor, the whole thing twisted thirty degrees, presumably to match the angle of the ship, which made sense. Justine was there, standing perpendicular to that off-kilter floor as naturally as anything. That *didn't* make sense.

He increased magnification and found that there were sentry bots farther on doing a poor job of staying concealed. They, too, were standing perpendicular to the floor without any difficulty.

Gravitics. The thought just bubbled into his consciousness as if it'd always been there. <Gravity manipulation technology>

Uh-huh ... I guess this is just the new norm? Future stuff everywhere? And, we're on speaking terms again? That's nice, he thought to his tertiary OS level.

It was good to have Helga back.

Bodie could see that Justine was talking, or rather, shouting at someone. Then, from the sides of the near end of the corridor, a handful of Zilich's sentry bots appeared. They crept into the twisted corridor behind her.

Bodie thought she noticed the movement but couldn't be certain. Things were about to get dicey.

"What's going on? Does Zilich think a couple robots are going to go toe-to-toe with that? The girl, I mean," Antigony asked. Bodie could tell she was surprised but also eager to see how things would play out.

"I don't know. I think she knows that they're there."

They stepped off the platform and started in that direction. Carole clopped along with them until Bodie placed a hand on her muzzle, signaling for her to stay put. Her ears twitched, and she shook her mane but did as she was instructed, wandering off to inspect the damaged equipment as if she imagined there was some fresh hay to munch on over there.

He really did love that horse.

As they drew near the corridor, doors slammed down between Bodie, Antigony, and the robots ahead. The two raced forward to catch a glimpse of what was going on through a small window in the door. What they saw was pure chaos. Silver tendrils thrashed wildly and bodies flew, crashing into each other and the walls of the confined space.

The robots were taking a beating. Bodie remembered being on the receiving end of Justine's fury and did not envy their position.

They watched, captivated, as Justine pounded the sentry bots relentlessly, but they just kept getting up and coming after her. She ripped a couple of them apart, but in the cramped space, she was unable to really keep them at bay. The battle raged on, but after a while, Justine's vigor began to lessen. The robots steadily closed in and finally, she was engulfed by their numbers. Still, it seemed wrong.

"It's like she just ran outta steam. Or ran outta breath maybe," Antigony offered.

"I think you nailed it. The robots don't need air, but she does. I think Zilich choked her out somehow."

"How could he do that?"

"Simple," a new voice provided from behind them.

They spun to find Klamath, big hat, bushy handlebar mustache, and all. He was holding a long rifle at his hip and it was aimed at Bodie's head.

"He can seal off the area and purge the oxygen. Or pump it full of something else. Some other gas that would cause a human to suffocate just the same as if they were in a bad mine. Done it myself more than once," Klamath told them.

It was Antigony who spoke up first. "Who are you? And what kinda cowboy knows about spaceships?"

"His name's Klamath," Bodie told her. "He's an outlaw, and there's more to him than meets the eye." Then to Klamath. "Last time I seen you, you were in a mess of pieces. In fact, so was your whole gang."

"So you say. But those men were not my gang. I'm a solo operator. And not really an outlaw, since I spend most my time bringing outlaws to justice. Outlaws like Zilich," he said, nodding in the direction of the corridor.

"What're you saying? You're here to help us?" Antigony asked, looking him up and down with a raised eyebrow. Her skepticism was obvious and Bodie appreciated her judge of character.

"Nah. I'd much prefer to see this here robot's head as a trophy on my bookshelf, but, by the way you two were carrying on, I have to assume the girl wasn't up to the task. I have no delusions of trying it myself, especially on Zilich's turf. So, as much as I truly would enjoy dispatching this troublesome tin can," he said, nodding toward Bodie, "*again,* I might add, I'm inclined to discuss terms."

"Terms? Terms of what?" she asked.

Bodie was certainly not comfortable joining sides with the ill-tempered rifleman, given their history.

"Well, not of a partnership. But maybe a truce of sorts. Short-term, of course. The sooner we can get back to blasting at each other, the better." He said all this without taking his gray eyes off Bodie.

"I don't know, Klamath. I don't much care for rogues and scoundrels. Present company excluded, of course, Miss Von Riche."

"I know," she said sweetly, with a playful tilt of her head.

"However—"

Just then, Carole, who had been meandering slowly across the room, bumped into Klamath's back. He jerked in surprise. Bodie drew and fired, hitting Klamath's rifle near his hand. The man cursed and put his fingers to his mouth, but as he turned, he spun and dropped to one knee, firing a small silver pistol with his offhand. The shot hit Bodie square, pitching him end over end and depositing him on his head several yards away.

At Klamath's first twitch, Antigony broke to the side. She came up with pistols blazing, catching Klamath off his guard. He took a round or two as he dove the other way and managed to slip behind the cover of an angular metal column.

When Bodie hit the ground, he carried the moment into a roll that brought him up to his feet, Walkers in hand. He didn't have an angle on Klamath but could see that Antigony was unhurt. As the echoes of gunfire faded, the whine of one of the elevator platforms filled the space.

Bodie hazarded a glance across the atrium through hazy layers of gun smoke. The platform rose into view. On it was a cohort of sentry bots and a small black creature whose large golden eyes were visible even across the seventy feet or so between the two groups.

Antigony called out to Bodie, "Bodie, I think we better vamoose…"

He was inclined to agree. The brim of Klamath's hat peeked from behind the column. Bodie fired off a shot to keep him pinned down before leaping to Carole's back. They bolted toward the closest wall of the atrium. Bodie pulled Antigony up as they passed and then fired at the glass wall ahead.

Sentry bots scattered with the gunshots and started to return fire. Bodie could hear that Klamath was doing the same with that powerful little pistol of his. He didn't imagine even Klamath would do well against these odds.

The wall came up fast and Carole leaped over the low section of it and out onto the red rock plateau. But ahead, the path pinched down between the ship's hull and the edge of the cliff. The only way before them was a ramp that was part of some kind of scaffolding system.

Bodie spurred her on just as shots rang out behind and electrical flashes ricocheted around them. The ramp only ran about thirty feet before it made a tight 180. Carole slid sideways on the metal grating, her rump slamming a cross member and knocking it loose. The whole scaffolding shifted with a loud snap as she scrambled up the next ramp. Bodie watched as a metal support member from below sprang out into the open air, fluttering down the cliff face before striking the rock wall and bouncing off out of sight.

Antigony clenched her arms hard around him and buried her head in his back. Carole crested the next platform and, having learned from her first pass, made a perfect barrel turn around the corner just as the screech of metal filled the air and the scaffolding yawed sickeningly away from the ship.

Bodie shifted his weight as Carole corrected for the slant of the rampway and charged upward. Movement caught Bodie's eye just as a sentry bot burst into view ahead.

"Dammit. They're climbing up the outside."

Bodie's Walker rang out, and the bot flew end over end off of the structure, just to be replaced by another. Carole was halfway up the next ramp and charging for the turn. Bodie fired behind him and saw that the sentry bots were climbing up both sides now. Two bots crested the platform railing ahead, and he fired, knowing he'd only get one of them and have to take the full brunt of the other one's shot to protect Antigony, but she slipped to his side and got the shot off first, ducking back just in time as a support member whipped by.

Both bots fell away as Carole rounded the corner and started up the next ramp. Another strut pinged and shot off the side of the scaffolding as it groaned and leaned further out over the cliff. As they climbed, they were getting farther and farther away from the ship. They'd either run out of scaffolding, or the whole thing would topple over the cliff. Bodie might survive that fall, but he couldn't say the same for Antigony and Carole.

As the next platform came into view, Bodie could see the curve of the ship's hull had a contour that flattened out and headed up toward the tail end of the ship. *Last chance*, he thought. He fired into the railing and it swung away to leave an opening and a gap of nearly a dozen feet. He steered with his knees into the gap.

Antigony screamed as Carole leaped, and for one precarious moment, they hung in the air between scaffolding and vessel. Bodie realized the scaffolding was falling away from the ship and he'd misjudged the gap. Electrical arcs splashed across the ship's hull as Carole landed, sure-footed as a mountain goat.

He reined her right, and they began to lurch up the narrow pathway before them.

"What are you thinking, you crazy tin-ass?!? The *outside* of the ship?" Antigony screamed as she pressed in close again while firing blindly behind her. He watched the scaffolding fall away with a half-dozen bots on it as her pistol clicked uselessly, the ammo all spent.

"Dammit. I'm gonna need to reload, but I can't do it back here like this."

Bodie reached behind him and snatched the pistol, ejected the clip, and loaded as he rode, continuing to guide Carole with pressure from his knees. The plateau dropped away below them as they raced along the side of the ship, ever upward toward the tail end where the engines were.

Bodie used his sensory array to get a bead on their pursuers as they barreled along the side of the ship. Several of the sentry bots had followed onto the lateral channel feature on the ship's exterior and were giving chase.

<Sentry bots en route>

Helga? There you are! You still mad at me?

<...>

Fair enough.

"Antigony, switch me places."

"Wha?"

Without time to explain, Bodie slapped the reins into her left hand and stepped off to the right with a hand still on the saddle horn. Antigony, out of self-preservation, bumped forward in the saddle as Bodie did a quick double step that bounced him back up behind her ... he landed facing backward ... Walkers blazing.

"Yeee-haaa!!!" he hooted as the shots rang out one after the other.

The robots in pursuit either caught lead or dove off of their own accord. And then it was the relative silence of wind rushing by and Carole's hooves pounding a steady cadence.

Bodie had a broad smile of glowing lights pasted across his face. He spun his six guns and slipped them into their magnetized holster slots on his torso.

"Well sheeyit, Antigony! Some fun, right?"

There was no response. Bodie twisted to find her slumped over the saddle horn, face buried in Carole's mane. Her arms flapped loosely as Carole sprinted ever upward.

"No, no, no, Tig."

Bodie spun and pulled her up. The raven hair strewn across her face had blood in it near her temple. She must have been grazed or caught some sort of ricochet.

Carole slowed to a canter then a trot. She was a smooth ride, but after that hard of a workout, she didn't have much smooth left in her. Bodie patted her side, and she slowed further to a walk. They were out of trouble for the moment. He looked around to get his bearings and saw a cluster of exposed mechanical equipment and sheets of siding stacked off to the side.

They were doing repairs. *Obviously*, he chided himself, remembering that the ship was still nose-down into the plateau. But maybe there was another way inside? He was sure there had to be. He scanned the area around him. Here, the channel they'd followed flared out for one of the massive engine assemblies. The upper portion of that flare was huge, big enough for a rodeo arena. At the point where the flare returned to the angle of the ship's side, he saw a painted rectangle around what appeared to be a door. Bodie guided Carole to it and pulled loose strands of hair away from Antigony's injury.

She had some cuts and scrapes and the whole area was raw and beginning to swell. The good news was there was nothing life-threatening about it, what he could see. The question was just how hard did she get hit? Knocked out, concussed, or worse? He knew she could have internal swelling or even a brain bleed.

Antigony groaned and Bodie realized just how deeply relieved he was.

"You okay, kiddo?"

"Who you … callin' … kiddo?" She mumbled out. "Damn, it's bright up here. Are we … in heaven? That can't be right…" she said, shaking her head slowly and massaging the uninjured side. She looked off to her right at the sloping metallic skin of the ship and the valley, far, far below. She made a gulping sound as if she were going to be sick.

"Take it easy."

Bodie guided her attention toward the vertical section to their left and the door outlined in white paint. "We're going to find a nice spot to sit down, gather our wits, and think. That sound good?"

She nodded and then grabbed her head with her hand. "Did you get me drunk, robot? Did we…?"

Bodie laughed, shaking his head.

"Nah, Tig. Yer virtue's still intact."

She chuckled weakly and then groaned at the exertion. "Okay, good. Cuz, you know I'm a lady and shit."

Bodie slid off of Carole's back and reached up for Antigony's hand. "M'lady?"

She beamed a pained smile, reached to meet it, and fell right past. Bodie scrambled to catch her, but she ended up in his arms, looking up at him dotingly.

<...>

Don't do it, Bodie warned his lower-level OS, knowing where Dmitr would be headed with his archive of imagery.

Bodie had been surprised that the door opened for him when he'd neared it. Then he realized he was technically one of the crew. He'd just been away for a long, long time.

No alarms went off when they entered. It was just him and Antigony since he'd pulled Carole's saddle and bridle once he saw that entry wouldn't be a problem. He didn't know how things would turn out and didn't want her stuck in the ship if something happened to him. It was better if she just made her way back down to the plateau or maybe the valley below. She was an exceptionally smart horse. She'd find her way.

Bodie took the lead as they followed a narrow path hedged on either side by convoluted piping and machinery, boxes and tubes with glowing things inside. Large critters scampered in the shadows. Occasionally, he'd see a couple of long metallic appendages peaking from around a corner. It made him think of a daddy long-legs spider, but much, much larger and made of metal.

"You seeing these things?" Antigony asked in a breathy whisper. "I don't much care for spiders. Especially bigguns."

She closed the gap between them until he could almost feel her breath on his neck.

"It's okay. I think they're just maintenance bots. Random bits of memory keep popping up in my head. Stuff I didn't know was there. Plus, Helga's been sorting through all the knowledge the coldbright's given me."

"Sorry. You lost me at Helga."

"Oh, yeah, sorry about that. Helga is just a name that I gave to my third-level operating system. Mostly has to do with memory and stuff?" He said that last bit ending it with a question. It was a soft skill that humans used sometimes when they were uncertain if what they were saying was about to get them in trouble.

"So, you're saying there's a woman in your head? All the time? Sounds like cheatin'."

"Um ... I don't know how that's cheating. It's just a name. I have a feller, too, by the name of Dmitr, if that makes it any better?" He did the question thing again, even though it didn't seem to work at all the first time.

"No, that just makes it weird. To each his own, I guess."

He stopped and turned to her, oddly concerned about what she thought of the peculiar arrangement of personalities inside his brain.

"Look. I have to interface with parts of my sub-conscious in order to access memories and data. It's the way the programming structure works within my operating system. I named those two lower OS layers after my former crew mates before I even knew I had crew mates. Helga is not some other woman to compete with. She was my—"

<Oh yeah?>

Not now, please? We can talk about this later.

<Good luck without me>

Wait, what? Why!?!

<...>

"Ughh, women," he groaned.

"Really?"

"What?"

"You said that out loud, you dumb robot." She brushed past him and then spun around. "And to think. You had a chance ... at this." She gestured at her feminine curves and tsked before stalking away down the narrow aisle, stomping loudly on the grating as she went.

Bodie stood there, dumbfounded for a moment. Even with his vast processing power, women were still an enigma.

Vohl surveyed the damage. He felt his lip curl until his face twisted into a perturbed sort of sneer. Between the girl pilot, the mustachioed cowpoke, the priestess in the bandoleers, and the rogue six-gun-wielding sentry bot, he was down a sizable number of the ship's security detail. Twelve in all. Nearly half of the retinue he'd retained.

There were still eighty or so of the less equipped drones out there, rounding up the last of the creatures.

At least, the ones that could be rounded up. Some ... they would have to go and find themselves. Like Jef the Traveler. He was as slippery a skinwalker as there was. But even they had their weaknesses. They could shapeshift to an extent and travel dimensions but only through the thin spots between worlds. Those were easy enough to find and all manner of traps would work.

Meanwhile, there was his bot problem. A handful were already in his lab being put back together, but the girl had known what to do to slow down that process. She was obviously pulling information from the coldbright. That meant that she was learning things without being taught, or rather, without being guided by him and Zilich. Which was not preferable. Still, she'd have a very long way to go before she could manipulate the ship in general and her containment unit in specific. They still had time. But not much.

As for security, he had an idea. It involved sentry bot scraps, a reanimator, and a handful of corpses still preserved by a winter storm that kept Low Camp colder than a meat locker. The stench of human carnage in his lab would be dreadful, but the end result? Could be quite spectacular.

There was a convoy headed through there now. The bodies could be in his lab by tomorrow, mid-morning at the latest, since the bots would travel through the night and the weather was vastly improved over days prior.

It was settled, then. He would go prep the reanimator. It, unlike much of the scientific equipment crowding his laboratories, required more arcane ingredients to operate. This was why Vohl's particular skill sets so suited Zilich's ventures. They tended to shy away from the traditional and plumb the depths of the esoteric. Vohl, as a creature of the arcane himself, was quite fluent in its natures. And what he didn't know he augmented by hunting other such creatures.

Zilich had little use for pixies, but Vohl, on the other hand, had squeezed out tomes of knowledge from the little buggers. The creature named Jef the Traveler, he was certain, had much to offer as well. His time would come. But for now, Vohl would keep his focus narrow. Begin training the girl. Build his army of reanimated cyborgs, one that would, unbeknownst to Zilich, be loyal only to Vohl. And then hunt down some of the creatures on Vohl's list—Jef the Traveler being at the top.

What he hoped beyond hope was that the skin-walker would give him information that would help him unlock another machine. Something he called a ghost box.

Someone started laughing a deep, devious laugh. Vohl spun before realizing it had been himself. He grimaced. That was a habit he'd have to curb. He'd carefully cultivated an image of the eccentric scientist with Zilich. One whose morbid habit of plotting his benefactor's death was cute and slightly disturbing, but not a true threat. He couldn't do anything to raise the man's suspicions at the deeper intentions behind it.

The truth was he desired to kill Zilich with every fiber of his being. But, the man had great knowledge of the galaxy at large, and once Vohl was Grand Imperator, he'd need that knowledge in order to upgrade his planet to merchant class, thus gaining access to the system of hyperholes and establishing his legacy for generations to come. But, with the ghost box, he could have both the pleasure of killing Zilich and access to everything he knows. Best of all, he could think of no better means of torture and humiliation. There were many people destined for the box. And with each addition, he would grow in power.

The laughter started again, Vohl jerked his head but then let the laugh soften into an amused titter and poofed away.

Moments later, he was in his lab. It was a massive space. In fact, it was a converted hangar. Row upon row of fabricators hummed and gurgled as he walked among them.

They sat on tables designed for humans, but he'd had a catwalk constructed along one side of each row so that he had easy access. Although, he just as frequently walked among the machinery on the tabletop. It was his, after all, he could do what he wanted.

He strolled past machines, currently printing sentry bot parts, and on to the experimentation area. Here there were animals in cages. Some sentient, which of course was against whole slews of short-sighted interstellar conventions.

"Skreebulix! Pecard ul vimit!" One creature cried, reaching out a small, furred appendage with three thick fingers. Vohl stopped, turned to the creature, and then pressed a button on the containment. The creature, upright and not dissimilar to a monkey of this planet, contorted into convulsing spasms before dropping to the floor.

Vohl smiled and resumed his journey, humming something from his childhood.

After a few minutes, the surroundings grew decidedly darker, the equipment more sinister and the silence crypt-like. He walked past a row of high-tech sarcophagi, all linked by tubing and chains to a tall box that actually did look quite like a crypt. It was made of a black stone material that reflected little light. There was a door in the center, hedged by fluted columns with what looked like lanterns. But, within the lanterns, there was a softly glowing, pale amber liquid.

Hearts. He needed hearts. Live ones, in order for his reanimator to work. That monkey creature would work to get things started at least. He realized he'd never even asked it what it was. Just something he'd grabbed from some anonymous planet at the time. Well, he could ask it now, for science's sake. And then sacrifice it.

Vohl smiled again. He quite enjoyed his job.

CHAPTER 11

REANIMATED

"**G**ood morning," a cheerful voice greeted Justine from the speaker in the corner of her cell. Zilich.

"Is it? I wouldn't know. I'm in a cell," she deadpanned.

"I dare say it is. Today begins your training. You have decided to go on with it, have you not?"

Justine looked down at her hands. She'd chewed her nails to the quick. But the clothes she'd been given were clean, though it was weird wearing boy clothes, meaning trousers and a shirt, rather than her typical cotton dress. The material was oddly stretchy, too, but not unpleasant. Additionally, along with a full meal, she'd been able to give herself a sponge bath, so felt somewhat like a human being again. But all this couldn't do anything to take away what the man was responsible for. Even if he hadn't pulled the trigger himself, he was the one who turned those men loose in the countryside to take children for the mines.

He was right, though. She was going to go through with it. She had to see if it was possible to bring her parents back. That familiar hollow ache reemerged.

"Yeah. For now."

"That won't do. There must be a contract. Ten years, minimum. You have no idea what it costs to do what you're asking."

"Ten years?!? You're insane. You can fly this thing yourself. Or is that what this is all about? You *can't* fly it yourself?"

"I could. But it's not ideal. A ship like this requires a captain *and* a pilot."

"Two years."

"Ha! That's cute, but no. It's ten or nothing. Another pilot will come along sooner or later. Besides, in addition to losing the opportunity to ever see your parents again, if you refuse my offer, you'll just grow older much, much faster than the people around you. You have noticed, haven't you?"

Justine's eyes darted back to her hands. And then to her feet. During her brief bath, she had noticed that they seemed different. She'd thought they looked rather elegant in spite of her ragged nails. Truly, she thought she was just growing up. But then the hem of her dress, what was left of it anyway, had also ridden a little higher above her ankles before she changed out of it. She'd noticed but was just too preoccupied with current events to put much thought into it.

Now she realized it was the coldbright. It was causing her to develop faster than she should. She felt it, subtly, in other ways, too. The way her mind worked. The emotions she was experiencing. Again, she thought all of this was brought on by the intensity of her circumstances, or even just hormones, but now it seemed painfully obvious. This was accelerated development. She was experiencing loss and tragedy and pressures she had no frame of reference for, and it was all being amplified by teenage angst.

Her stomach did flips. She was terrified and also thrilled at the same time. Then her attention slid to the most telling outward sign of all, her chest. That nagging ache... She crossed her arms and held herself tight.

"What did you do to me?!?"

"It's not me," he chuckled. "It's the coldbright. The magic. The element itself. To be honest, I'm not really sure how it works exactly. Conundrum is a peculiar metal."

"Conundrum?"

"Coldbright, my dear. Conundrum is its scientific name. Are you familiar with the table of elements?"

"Some. I've never heard of the one you're saying."

"That's because it doesn't exist on your planet. That's why we must find all of the original material rather than just mine for more of it. Also, it's a memory metal, so it remembers what the ship requires. Any little bit of coldbright can go anywhere in the ship and it will know what to do. Very useful. Does any of that make sense?"

"Not really. That sounds like magick or witchcraft."

"Well, then I've come to the right person, haven't I?"

Justine's gaze dropped to the floor.

"Has the coldbright told you things?" he asked. "Can you hear it speak to you?"

Justine thought as quick as she could. She didn't know if she should say yes or no. This man seemed to anticipate so many of her questions and answers. She didn't know if there was a benefit in holding back this knowledge.

He continued despite her silence. "Of course it has. You're strong with the magic. That will only cause you to age quicker. If you ask, it will tell you."

A pang of fear gripped her gut. "Can it be stopped? The aging?"

"You probably won't believe me, but yes, by piloting the ship. That will slow your aging near to zero. While you pilot the ship, you will stay anatomically the same. But don't take it from me. Ask the coldbright. That's your lesson for the day."

And then there was a click, and Zilich was gone.

Justine sat there for a while, rocking back and forth on her bed, not sure what to think. Ten years of service, but she could get her parents back. Could she wait that long for justice? Or would an opportunity present itself before then? What would she see in all that time, sailing the stars? It would be a dream if it wasn't such a nightmare. She'd dreamed of what her life would be like. Finding someone, settling down, and raising kids. But navigating the stars? She hadn't dreamt of it because it was impossible.

She sat back and closed her eyes, hanging one leg over the edge of the bed the bots had brought in. She breathed in through her nose, but there were none of the smells she was used to; sage, pine, wood smoke, dust, the manure from the livestock pens, the earthy goodness of the glen with the aspen trees where they rode sometimes in the summer...

The hollow inside her came rushing back. They were gone. But maybe ... maybe there was hope.

The small door-within-a-door where her food trays came through opened. A small circular tray slid through it. In the center of the tray was a mercurial marble. Currents of light and dark metallic liquid seemed to roll upon the surface. The door slid shut, and she stared at the object.

She closed her eyes again, and a whisper, like a breeze through tiny chimes, tinkled in her mind. She reached out a hand, and with her eyes still closed, she sensed its movement, up into the air, across the cell, and then gently landing in her palm. The weight of it nestled into the crease of her open hand. And then it spoke.

It wasn't a voice, but a thousand voices, muted, distant like when the Indians got together in the springtime down in the low valley. The multitude of voices would carry on the wind up onto the plateau some nights.

This was like that, but then solitary strains rose above the others. Like the Indian songs, these were stories. Only these stories were of ships and space and far-off worlds. And then they were stories of how things worked, how they went together, and much of it was so far beyond anything Justine had ever even imagined she had to pick and choose between the voices, only taking in what she could understand in the moment.

Hours stretched on, and Justine was rapt with fascination and a growing lust for this new knowledge. All of it at her fingertips, like all the world's libraries combined and then some. That times a thousand. A food tray slid through the door. And then, sometime later, another. But she couldn't stop, she was so close to an understanding, a meaning to it all, but then the voices diminished, as if the coldbright itself understood she had limits.

She scrambled and searched for more, stretched her inner self, straining to hear just one more thing, but it was silent, and suddenly, she felt even more alone than she had before. She realized there was a certain kind of community when she was with the coldbright. A ... belonging.

Justine's stomach grumbled, and she felt the acid in her stomach gnawing at her. Absent-mindedly, she flicked the coldbright away, and it slid underneath the tray. She willed it back to her, but the amount of coldbright wasn't enough to do anything more than rattle the tray on the stone-like floor.

With a huff, she stood and stretched out the kinks in her muscles and joints and picked up the tray. The old-fashioned way. Someday soon, she'd command the coldbright like she had before. The power of it was intoxicating. But beyond that, there was more. This entire ship would be hers to command. She felt the inner turmoil of exacting vengeance for her loss and the great tug of destiny that stood luringly just out of reach. Who could imagine sailing the vast expanse of space? Visiting the stars? A warm rush flooded through her at the thought. It was tempered by a feeling of guilt, though. What would her mother think? Of all of it?

A wave of emotion washed over her and she realized she was crying and couldn't quite pinpoint why. It wasn't just her parents, or being held captive in a spaceship, or being forced to work for that monster Zilich against her will, or the lives she'd taken—so many. What would her mother think? The thought echoed through her mind, and warm tears rolled down her cheeks anew. The waves upon waves of emotion rolled over her. Part of her knew it was everything she'd experienced, and another part knew it was the hormones. She was experiencing the transition from puberty to womanhood at an accelerated rate. She wrapped her arms around herself and pulled her knees in tight, rocking back and forth. She started humming a tune her mother used to sing but couldn't quite get it right. God, she just wanted to climb out of her own skin!

Then something caught her attention. A faint smell like ... rotten eggs? She looked up and there was a creature standing in the middle of her cell. Justine jumped and sat upright against the wall.

Standing there, looking at her with large, calculating eyes, was a creature of little more than three feet tall. It was black and had a broad pointy nose that dominated its face but for those eyes.

"Wha ...what do you want?" she asked. Secretly, she was shaping the coldbright into a tiny blade. It hovered near her hand just above the blanket on her bed, shielded momentarily from where the creature could see it.

It blinked. "I am Vohl," it said, elongating the pronunciation of its one-syllable name and raising an unamused eyebrow when she didn't respond, whether in recognition or fear or who knows what it was expecting. And then, before her eyes, it poofed away into a little black smudge of vapor before that too vanished.

Justine blinked as well. Did that just happen? What or who was that? Besides what it had called itself, of course. What was it, Vole? Wasn't that a rodent of some kind?

She wasn't sure what to think, but what she was certain of was that she was suddenly feeling the fatigue from her hours of training. She guessed it was. Her mind was numb. Her emotions were ragged. All she really wanted to do was sleep. And cry. Sleep seemed more constructive.

She faded off with thoughts of outlaws with guns, dark things creeping in the shadows, liege-zombies, and that constant theme of helplessness that plagued most dreams.

Antigony turned around at an intersection of aisles. Blue spots of light illuminated yellow and orange raceways that ran crosswise above her and off into the distance in every direction. On the knurled floor, green arrows proliferated and seemed to point in contradictory directions to one another.

Despite the visual chaos, she was sure she'd been to this exact spot before. Every direction held miles and miles of convoluted piping and racks of equipment with even more of the glowing lights. It was like being in the belly of some gigantic factory but many times beyond that. Above her was a grated catwalk just like where she stood now, and below that, she could see another level and levels below even that.

At one point, she'd taken a ramp, and then there was a ladder. The fact was, she was just so angry and hurt she'd just kept going without having any idea of where she was headed or how she'd get back. To be honest, she didn't care to. Bodie was just a stupid robot. She knew this, but there was something to him. Something more human than just about anyone she'd ever met. Certainly more so than most folks she'd encountered since coming out west. Come to think of it, that was largely why she'd left Chicago in the first place. The people there were shallow and self-absorbed, and she was becoming just like them. Too late, she guessed.

It was crazy, though. He was just a robot. She'd told herself it was just good fun getting him all twisted up, but really, was it just that? There was something beneath that "aww shucks" demeanor that was … she wasn't sure, heroic? She felt safe when she was with him. Even in the midst of all this, she looked around again, amazed by the otherworldliness of it, the magnitude of the construction for one. She'd been to a barn-raising or two. That easily took a dozen men. What surrounded her was something she couldn't begin to fathom. And then there was the technology. It might as well be magic. And there was that, too.

Antigony walked past another intersection and something in the shadows caught her eye. It was almost as if the shadow itself had moved. Shivers went up her spine and her hand slid to the semi-auto at her hip. She'd grown accustomed to the oversized, metallic daddy longlegs thingies creeping about, wrenching on this and that, but this was something else.

Did she actually see it? She didn't know, but now, things just felt different. Off.

Antigony spotted a ladder off to her left and darted for it. Her boots slipped, bouncing from rung to rung as she sped down the ladder. Her hands gripped the rails hard, but she couldn't slow down. And then, with a thud, she was on the next level. She scanned both ways and then bolted down an aisleway to another ladder and took that down with little more care, fear fueling her flight. Then she cut back beneath the way she'd come, looking up at the grating above to see if she could catch a glimpse of whatever it'd been in the shadows.

She heard softly padding footsteps but couldn't see anything. A thunk from behind her caused her to spin, but there was nothing there. The knot of dread swelled in her chest.

What was stalking her? In this alien environment, it could be anything. She started walking softly but still hurried. She couldn't help it as she moved even faster. Before she realized it she was running, full sprint past intersection after intersection, hazarding glances behind her. She thought she saw a shadow but couldn't make it out.

A corner came up quick, and she bounced off the wall as she rounded it. She heard the sounds now of pursuit and a growl, which caused her to pour on the speed again. Way faster than was safe. Another ladder was to her right and to her left were a pair of vertical tubes that were so large a catwalk disappeared around the curvature of the closet one. She bolted down the narrow path skirting its perimeter, intending on circling back around, but as she came to the far side, she stopped in her tracks.

A tall, black, wolf-like creature stood eye to eye with her. The creature's mouth hung open as it panted, slavering long strings from wicked fangs.

"Stay back," she stammered, pointing her pistol. She could barely keep her sights trained on it as she remembered to breathe and gulped air to catch her breath. Her pulse pounded. The pistol grip felt slick in her hands.

The creature's toothy visage seemed to be twisted into a kind of amused smile. It stepped closer. She gripped the pistol with both hands to keep it from shaking, but it did little to help. It stepped closer again, and the pistol barked, the noise deafening amidst all the hard surfaces of machinery. When the flash cleared, the creature was right in front of her. Her pistol fell from her hands.

She'd never felt fear like this. Palpable fear. All-consuming fear. Then, before her eyes, the creature morphed into something humanoid. It was thin, long of limb, and covered in bristly black hair. Its face was almost human but still bore traces of its former canine appearance—narrow-set eyes, a long nose, and teeth that filled its mouth. Still hanging open. Still panting. The hunger in its eyes was tempered by that ever-present amusement, as if it could think of nothing funnier than eating Antigony's insides while she watched.

Antigony drew in a shuddering breath. So, this was it? This was how it ended? She guessed that old gypsy had it wrong. She'd said she'd fall to her death on a cloudless, sunny day. Oh, well... Antigony closed her eyes, expecting any second to have her throat torn out and her insides opened to the air.

Seconds dragged on and nothing happened. She cracked one eye open and was stunned to find that there was nothing there. She opened her other eye and spun around in place, but there was no one there either. She was all alone. Again.

"Okay, Tig. Keep it together. Maybe that didn't really happen? Maybe you just made it up?"

But, she knew it had happened. She picked up her pistol from the catwalk grating. It was still warm. She ejected the clip and there was a bullet missing. She had actually fired. And missed. At point-blank range.

Only, she was sure she hadn't missed. Antigony shook her head in bewilderment. Oh well? There was nothing to do but find her way out of this mechanical maze and back to Bodie if she could. She really wanted to find him now. More than anything.

She heard steps of someone coming down a nearby ladder and then dropping to the floor. She stepped out from around the corner of the large tube and saw Bodie's familiar silhouette.

"There you are. Listen, I'm sorry about—"

Bodie spun around and Antigony realized too late that it was not Bodie after all, but one of the sentry bots. Her encounter with the wolf creature had so rattled her that she completely failed to notice that this bot wasn't wearing Bodie's typical cowboy hat and clothes.

It squinted its eyes and the lights of its mouth drew across in a thin line. It drew a sidearm in a flash, but something dark whipped out of the shadows and ripped its arm clean off, sending the sentry bot down the side aisle in the process. Antigony only barely caught the suggestion of a wolf-like body before it tore into the bot, sending limbs everywhere and a head that rolled to Antigony's feet. And, just as quick, the creature was gone into the darkness of the machinery.

"Glad to know whose side yer on, I guess," she said, not a little bit shaken.

Bodie had accessed a data terminal on a whim and was shocked at the mountain of information available to him. He'd located the crew cabins, the bridge, the mess hall, a laboratory and found that the lower levels of the ship were dedicated to containment units of various types. The whole length of the ship from the midline down was storage for the exotic and esoteric. Roughly half of the cells were filled.

He didn't know if that meant they were still gathering creatures they'd lost or if that many had died or not been able to be recovered, but given what he knew of some of these creatures, the Wun-dee-go and the Pantera del Diablo in particular, he was happy to know there were fewer to deal with if something were to go terribly wrong. Because even though he was something of an optimist, in his experience, something always did.

With the terminal, he hadn't been able to locate Antigony, strangely. And with the mass of machinery taking up this section of the ship playing havoc with his sensors, almost as quick as she was out of sight, she became impossible to track.

However, there had been a sentry bot that was dispatched to check out a possible intruder in the engineering area's lower section on level thirteen. Bodie had been on nineteen at the time but was making his way down even now. Halfway down, a solitary gunshot rang out. That was never good. Anything worth shooting once was usually worth shooting twice. A single shot usually meant something bad had happened. Or maybe someone was trying to signal someone else. He wanted it to be the latter but didn't hold out hope.

Bodie hustled, but it still took several minutes to get down near to where he'd heard the pistol's report. He hit the grating of level nine and found the severed head of a sentry bot. He picked it up and stared into its blank face, the twinges of an existential moment beckoning.

The eyes sprang open, and he almost dropped it. Then an oddly familiar voice burst from inside.

"Who are you and what have you done to my robot? Correction ... robots, since you've clearly co-opted one of their bodies. How are you doing it? Hostile program? Remote signal? No, a remote signal would have a terrible time trying to penetrate the hull of the ship, let alone all this machinery and radiation."

Bodie looked nervously from side to side, experiencing one of those rare moments of uncertainty.

"Responsive? Wait. You're *not* operating remotely, are you? You've actually impressed your persona into the sentry bot's hardware. That's really ... something..."

There was silence for a moment or two before the voice continued. "Few species have that technology. And none that would care to use it on one of my Neinhelen bots, except ... Arkhver, maybe?

"Well, isn't that a coincidence? Why, there was a certain Arkhveran Marshal dogging me when my ship was run to ground on this very planet, costing me the use of my leg and nearly my life.

"It couldn't be. Tell me it's you, Bodura Duc."

Bodie chucked the robot head and blasted it with his pistol, sending its sparking remains sailing down the aisle and over the ledge of a mechanical shaft. It clanged off into the distance, deeper and deeper into the belly of the ship.

He spun his pistol and holstered it before lifting a quivering hand palm down in front of his face. Why was he shaking? And a new realization slid into his consciousness. He was now completely certain he would kill that man. That was bad for karma. He didn't care. There was so much he couldn't remember, but there were a few things he knew. He just wished he knew *why*.

For instance, he knew that the voice coming from the robot's head was the man called Zilich. He knew that Bodura Duc was his own birth name and that Bodie was just what everyone called him. His crew mostly.

Then he sought the memories of his crew. Helga, his XO or executive officer, and Dimitr, his security officer, had filtered up through his memory circuits first, but then he remembered Pineel in Engineering, Periman on coms, and Palastroya in Ops. There were others, but those had been his leadership team. Plus, Gilhar Gurik in logistics. Then he remembered that Gilhar, the funny fat man, was dead. Along with nearly half of the others.

Someone had turned a very large, very poisonous— and nearly invisible—reptile loose in a cantina. Bodie remembered that they had tracked Zilich to the exact spot based on intel obtained from an associate of his. Whether it was a setup to begin with or Zilich had found out afterward was uncertain, but it was clear that it was an intentional act of sabotage.

Bodie himself had been there only minutes before. Zilich knew that he and his crew were tracking him. They'd crossed paths in Selerby-Xelos and then again at a wormhole station on the outskirts of the Tandook A/B system. Thinking on it now, it was definitely a setup.

Other memories flooded in. From where? He had no idea. But with them came feelings, and the more he remembered, the angrier he got. It would be really hard to keep the man alive long enough to find out what Bodie needed to find out. As it was, he was beginning to understand why he had chased the man to the edge of the known galaxy and been willing to hunt him down while the ship he was on went into a self-destruct sequence. In hindsight, that was pretty extreme.

But then he'd taken it even further. Abandoned his own body, the one he was born with, in order to make absolutely certain the man was dead. That—despite the extravagant cost in Arkhveran familial magick known as ... Mahna Noostra—was a one-way trip. Bodie reeled with the inrush of so much information and the deep emotions that came with it.

He understood now that his intention had been to infiltrate Zilich's sentry bot guard and assassinate the man before he realized what had happened. It was a suicide mission.

So much for that plan.

Whatever happened to Bodie during the crash had buried any memory he'd retained from that one-shot soul impression spell. That was the only plausible solution, since things kept on popping up unbidden.

Zilich, on the other hand, didn't seem to suffer any such issues. So now, Zilich knew Bodie was still alive and inhabiting the body of one of his sentry bots. What did he call them? Neinhelen bots. Bodie Nine? His consciousness was a stew of shredded memories. Was this where his fascination with karma came from? This was where the names of his lower OS levels came from. This was why he was struggling to find his prime directive. It had all been scattered to the winds with the explosion and resulting crash.

Who knew how long he'd be wandering the plains of the Alta Estranyazie, completely oblivious? If he hadn't run into the Severs and subsequently the cold-bright, he probably would have watched Zilich's ship take off into space and wondered at the magnificence of the spectacle. Never the wiser.

Bodie's thoughts were drawn back to the moment. Zilich would be sending another detachment to this location even now. That would not be good. He needed to find Antigony and hunt down a safe place to hide and make a new plan. What happened with Justine ... well, he wasn't really sure what to do about that right at the moment. He still hoped there was something he could do to help her, but you could only do so much for someone that was trying to kill you. As it was, they had a common enemy. Come to think of it, Klamath could be described similarly. The more thinking he did, the less he liked where things in his mind were headed. But then, of everyone on this spaceship, Antigony was the only one who *didn't* want him dead. Of course, with Antigony, one need only wait five minutes.

Bodie recalled a large area on the detention level called...

<The Terrariums>

Oh, thank you.

But something niggled in the back of his mind. He knew the two of them could hide there, but the thought of being surrounded by hundreds of the galaxy's most deadly creatures ... that seemed less than prudent.

The sound of marching feet echoed down the corridor. Oh well, he'd figure it out later.

CHAPTER 12

BLACKIE REDUX

Vohl was pleased. Despite the putrid smell of human meat. It would be impossible to rid his lab of the stench, but it *was now* the birthplace of a new creation. A beautifully twisted form. The desperado known as Blackie Lung, melded with spare parts from his Neinhelen sentry bots and a few other organic and inorganic odds and ends and then reanimated through a particularly dark form of witchery.

An eerie mist poured from the blacked-out crypt with the glowing lamps on either column. He'd had to sacrifice eleven of his favorite laboratory creatures just to fuel the machine, but the result... He sighed with paternal pride.

The creature, hulking and dark, stood with its head pressed against the wall, panting rapidly. Its wounds wept where flesh met machinery.

It must be in terrible pain, he thought. *Good.*

It'd be driven to pursue that which it was set to. He could use suffering and it's promised relief as an effective tool.

The creature roared in anguish and smashed its fists into the bulkhead, leaving large dents in the metal. It resumed its tortured panting.

"Blackie," Vohl commanded.

The abomination spun, its hands curled into claws, its eyes... Well, it didn't really have eyes to begin with, but its weeping eye sockets focused intently in Vohl's direction. It breathed a deep, ragged breath.

"Do you remember your name?"

"Ughhh," it responded, flexing its fingers and balling them into fists over and over again as if fantasizing about tearing Vohl into smaller and smaller pieces of Nawri meat.

"Do you remember the robot you struggled so hard to capture?"

"Uggghhh. Bohh-deee," he responded in a long, drawn-out rasp.

"After poking around in your brain, I think he's here on this ship." In fact, Vohl was certain of it. A wonderful stroke of luck, really. He'd had no idea that the girl and the robot were linked. But this rogue sentry bot, Bodie Nine, seemed to be quite taken with their new pilot. He was probably here to save her. How sweet. He wondered how this could play into Vohl's grand design. He wasn't sure, but after all the damage he'd done, Vohl was quite certain he didn't want him getting in the way. "Blackie, I'd like you to find him. And the woman he's with. And then I'd like you to bring them to me."

The creature that was Blackie flexed its fingers again. This seemed to be agreement. "Here, take this." Vohl threw a silver Peacemaker revolver at the reanimated cyborg. It bounced off its chest and fell to the ground. Blackie looked down at the gun.

"Pick it up. Shoot it," Vohl told it. Blackie continued to stare at the weapon. *Huh.* "Never mind. Go. Fetch."

The cyborg smiled a gruesome smile and tore off through the lab on all fours like a gorilla, jumped up on a table, scattering thousands of credits worth of equipment, sniffed the air, and then tore down the long table at a full primate sprint before disappearing through a door that, luckily, was keyed to its network signature.

Vohl massaged his earlobes to soothe himself. He'd need to provide at least some rudimentary ground rules the next time he created one of these things. "No breaking Vohl's things." That would be rule number one.

Now, how many more of these meatbots could he make? He'd have to raid the menagerie for sure. And then there was the ghost box... He was getting better at this dark form of witchcraft that bordered on necromancy. Well, who was he kidding, it was enough like necromancy that he needed to guard his steps well. One little slip and he was toying with damnation. Damned to what or to where? Well, these were delightful questions he'd rather not find out through trial and error. Perhaps the intelligent little furry primate thing could be coerced into performing the rites? For scientific purposes of course...

Antigony poked her head from behind the corner and looked up and down the corridor. This was different. Instead of the level upon level of corrugated flooring, ladders, and mechanical equipment, it was well-lit, smooth, and curved away, out of sight in either direction. A pulse of light traveled down the corridor, slowly fading through the entire rainbow of colors. Along with it, a clatter of wood trinkets and a pleasing chorus of chimes followed the soothing pulse.

Huh?

Antigony couldn't divine a purpose for this, but every ten or so seconds, the kaleidoscopic wash of light and sound would pulse and fade away through the spectrum in either direction. She wasn't good at things like distance, but it was easily a hundred yards in either direction. Maybe twice that. This ship was huge.

She felt like she was lost inside some gargantuan machine and realized that was exactly what this was. There was no hope of being found by Bodie. There was no one coming to save her. She was alone behind enemy lines.

Alone and without a plan, she corrected. Other than just trying to stay ahead of the sentry bots. She'd almost been caught twice. Once when that wolf creature had saved her from that bot she'd thought was Bodie, and then again, a few minutes ago, she'd pressed herself in between two large pieces of equipment that roared with a high-pitched whine. She thought for sure she was caught, but the group of five or six sentry bots just jogged right past her. She suspected that all this machinery messed with their sensors. Bodie's sensors worked great out on the plains and even in the canyons, but inside here, she'd lost him and he never found her again. And she knew he'd be looking. This was one of her gifts. People just liked her. Or hated her. There was no in-between. But Bodie, he was special.

That was her other gift. She knew stuff sometimes. Back at the hot springs when she'd been soaking and tripping on ground squirrel, she'd seen a vision: a knight in shining armor. Then the knight was a naked man astride a painted pony. And then the knight and Antigony, both naked, rode a magick carpet above the earth, and they held hands and stared into each other's eyes. There was more to the vision, something ominous, but then Bodie had walked right into her camp with that same horse from the vision. She didn't know what it all meant, but she knew they were destined to be together. And that there was more to him than just metal and circuits.

Something moved behind her, and Antigony jumped, but it was just one of the spider bots. It looked her over with telescoping red eyes on stalks of varying lengths and must have deemed her as not requiring any maintenance since it moved on across the corridor. The wall opened up where she hadn't even realized there was an opening, and before it closed again, Antigony shot across the corridor and through it. The knee-high bot casually sauntered up the wall, leaving Antigony all by herself.

This new space was dark and cavernous. Rows upon rows of large metal containers were interspersed with corrugated walkways and washed in low blue light. She didn't have a great vantage since she was on the ground level and there were at least four or five levels of walkway surrounding the larger containments. She realized that not all the containers were the same size. They were multiple of the smallest containers so that they could be stacked in a modular fashion. Some containers were twice as big as the little ones, others were

4, 8, or maybe 16 times. Something people didn't know about her was that she was quite good at math. Bad at distance, but good at math. She couldn't imagine what they kept in those bigger boxes.

A dull boom echoed from somewhere far away—farther on in this hold. The noise was followed by a mournful wail. Other screeches and screams echoed throughout. A chill ran down Antigony's spine.

"What the..." She trailed off as her mind reeled around what kind of nightmare creatures could be responsible for all the terrifying sounds. She shivered again and turned to look for the door she'd entered from, but there was nothing there. Most of the doors she'd seen had control pads next to them and were lit up with overhead lighting, but this must have been something just for maintenance bots.

She turned again. She'd just have to go through it. The walkways had to lead somewhere, didn't they? Directly ahead, a wash of amber light spilled from inside one of the containments. Morbid curiosity drew her to it. She stayed off to the side as she neared the window, the source of the light. Inside was mist, illuminated internally from a source she couldn't discern. She stepped forward without realizing it and before she knew it, she was standing with her face nearly pressed against the glass. Within the swirling mist, she could swear she saw movement but nothing she could make out.

She swallowed with a dry mouth. She didn't know when she'd eaten last or had anything to drink. She did have a small flask. She reached for it, when something slammed against the glass and caused her to jump. She looked up, and a woman was inside, desperately pounding against the glass, her hair slick. She was nearly naked and was bleeding and screaming.

Antigony's hands went to her mouth as she realized the woman looked just like her. She fumbled for her gun, but then a tree-like tentacle reached out of the mist and yanked the woman back into the murky depths. The screaming continued and grew louder and louder until it was all Antigony could hear. It was deafening. She had to cover her ears, and then she had to run away down the corridor to escape it. She kept running, turned at an intersection, and then turned again, running and not stopping until it faded. With the last strains, she could swear that the horrifying screams turned to laughter.

Antigony was on the ground, curled up with her back to a container wall. She was sweating and breathing hard.

"Madre de Dios, what ... was ... that?" she asked between panting breaths.

She clutched her pistol to her chest and wondered what good it would be against any of the creatures locked in here with her. In this ... warehouse, she guessed it was? This was the ship's hold. All these containers held creatures.

Bodie had told her a little about what Zilich had been up to, collecting terrifying creatures from other planets. Alien planets. Circling alien stars. She understood that the creatures that roamed the Alta Estranyazie probably came from these planets. The Pantera del Diablo was one such creature. The stories of the Wundee-go feasting on humans and stringing their remains through the forest as trophies came to mind. It was surely contained within these boxes as well.

Another heavy boom echoed through the low hum of machinery that was the ship's constant background. A haunting wail followed. That's what she would have imagined the Wun-dee-go sounded like. What else was in here? And what would happen if they got loose? Antigony got up and got moving. She looked back over her shoulder, remembering the chilling image of herself inside that containment with the creature in the mist. That was just a vision, right? There was no one in there with that ... that ... thing. Was there?

She told herself there was not. Logic said that there was not, but still. The image and the noise were branded in her memory now.

She kept moving. There were windows on most of these, she realized, but they were shut. Suddenly she was assaulted by heavy thuds and the wooshing of equipment. Some of the windows opened up and light spilled from inside. The lights varied in color. She wondered if they mimicked the suns of the creatures' homes. Not all suns were the same, were they? In a universe this large?

After her last encounter, she was reluctant to look inside the nearest window, but she found she couldn't help herself. Inside this double-tall and wide containment was a jungle forest. The light was pale yellow, and the plants were a riot of colors. She stared and could not see what was contained within. After a minute or two, she caught subtle movement but still could not see what was inside. She waited. A minute later, she again saw movement but couldn't discern its source. And then something blinked and the whole thing came into focus. It was invisible. Or something like that. The creature had large eyes which she could now make out easily. The rest of it... She could make out a silhouette that was ... different. A subtle color difference from the leaves and trees behind it. The creature was some kind of large lizard. It leaped from quite a ways back and landed on the glass, still transparent, its outline barely visible. It was easily as long as a man was tall, with long talons and a long tail that appeared to be tipped with a stinger like a scorpion.

The creature dropped to the floor, and all of a sudden, its true coloring faded into view—pale blue and vermillion scales with orange eyes and a shaggy brown coat of fur around its shoulders. It was terrifying and majestic. Almost a shame that it spent so much of its time invisible. One red-orange eye stared at her placidly from just above the windowsill. The creature flashed its tongue and then began climbing the window wall, fading back to transparency as it did so. Within moments, it was gone, or it was still there and impossible to detect.

Antigony's morbid curiosity propelled her onward. What else did Zilich have in this nightmare menagerie?

The next illuminated window was one level up. She climbed a set of spiral stairs. This containment was tall and narrow—four units high by just one unit wide. There was very little light coming from inside. If anything, it was a dark purple. The bright white square of her priest's collar glowed in the reflection. As did her teeth. Inside there were tall trees like pines or cedars, but after a moment, she realized one of the trees moved. Before she could focus on it, a small blur of light whisked into view, like a hummingbird. As it hovered before her, she made out a small human-like form. It was like a faerie.

What was so scary about faeries? she wondered, but then a large moth-like creature whooshed into view, snatched it out of the air, and fluttered off into the treetops. The dark violet light made its wings glow with an eerie light, but as soon as it landed, it folded up its wings and became nearly invisible. Oh, so maybe the faeries weren't the monsters. They were the food. That was ... disturbing.

The tree thing in the forest shifted again but did nothing terrifying. It just watched. Or she thought that's what it was doing. Who knew?

Just then, a shudder ran through the whole of the ship. Creatures from the various containments howled and shrieked and moaned and made any number of terrifying sounds. She wondered what had just happened. Was the ship about to fall off the cliff or finally crash down onto its belly? She realized that was probably close to where she was now. Maybe there were floors below, but not many. If it fell, it could break a bunch of these containers. Or if the power went out, would they just open up? Probably not, but still, she didn't want to be here if they did. She licked her lips and realized again just how dry her mouth was. Patting for her flask, she realized she must have dropped it earlier at the amber window. A shiver ran through her. She didn't want to go back, but she was mighty thirsty.

She *really* didn't want to go back. But she would. It wasn't all that far.

Antigony retraced her steps and found her flask where she'd been standing before. Nothing jumped out at her, but she could feel its eyes on her. Whatever it was lurking in the mists. She hurried back and was just passing the invisible lizard containment when she caught the scent of something off. It smelled woodsy but not like pine. It was damp smelling, and there was a strong undertone of mold. She glanced at the window and was horrified to see that it was no longer there. The opening was there, but not the protective glass.

"Oh shit."

Was the lizard out? If it was, how would she ever find it? What did a creature like that eat, anyway? Would it stalk her? Her instincts told her it definitely would. She slinked quietly by and made a beeline for the spiral stairs, taking a sip from the flask as she worked her way up. When she reached the top, she scanned the whole area, looking and listening. Who would have opened the containment? How many of those creatures were in there? Just the one or dozens?

Antigony picked up the pace and took another sip, only to have the bottle swatted away by nothing she could see. It clattered to the ground with a puncture hole clean through both sides.

"Oh shit" was right.

She bolted forward just as a spray of some sort of yellow substance splashed across the wall near where she'd been standing. She drew and fired in the direction of where the goo had come. A splatter of blood smeared in a streak going up and to the right on that wall. She'd hit the reptile, and it was on the move. She fired again and ran just as more goo erupted from just ahead of the streak of blood. It took off her hat, but she kept running. Better to lose her hat than her head.

CHAPTER 13

XENOZOOLOGY

Bodie sprinted for the railing and leaped out into the open air. He cleared the twenty-foot gap, his arc carrying him just over the railing of the next level down. He hit the corrugated floor and rolled with the momentum. He slammed into a cluster of conduits, but it allowed him to change directions and sprint down the aisle parallel to the vertical shaft.

The sounds of heavy objects hitting the floor behind him told him that the sentry bots had followed suit, although a hard impact and quickly fading scream suggested that one of them didn't quite make it across the shaft. There was a lot of interference due to electricity, magnetism, radiation, and a slew of other factors, but with nothing directly in the way, his limited sensor capability confirmed that there were still five sentry bots on his tail. He darted left down an aisle just as a concussive wave of energy blew past.

"Geez! These guys are madder than a hyena in a hoop skirt."

The bots had come prepared to fight. He guessed his little show at the elevators and subsequent chase up the scaffolding and side of the ship had tipped his hand that he was a scrapper.

Bodie spun and fired just as the lead bot cleared the corner behind him. As he was well aware, .44 ball ammo to the face would easily initiate a bot's sleep mode. The sentry tumbled as the one behind it leaped across the opening and fired its concussion weapon.

Bodie was already over the machinery separating this aisle from the next and sprinting back toward the main aisle. Just as he neared the end of it, one of the other bots stepped into view. He tackled it high and the two of them toppled over the railing and out into the empty air beyond. The difference was Bodie had been expecting it.

As they went over the rail, he caught the lowest bar and was swinging back so he could drop to the next floor down. Only, the enemy bot wasn't going down like that. It caught Bodie's foot. The two swung back and bounced off the metal structure and railing below. Bodie pulled his Walker with his free hand and was about to clear the troublesome hanger-on when he saw its eyes go round. He holstered and swung under the structure just as the sentry above fired. He couldn't have planned it better. The shot blew the bot off his foot, and he heard it hit metal time and time again as it tumbled to the lower levels.

"Scratch two, no … three," he said under his breath.

That still left three to go. A loud thud from his right had him pulling his Walker again. The robot sprinting toward him had no chance whatsoever. Bodie fired, and it spun from a shot to its shoulder just as a metal foot caught Bodie in the jaw from his left.

<Watch out>

Haha, very funny, he thought to Helga as he tumbled through the air like a rag doll.

<No. Watch out>

Bodie puzzled over the statement, thinking that she had deliberately warned him a fraction of a second late in order to make a statement. Then, as he spun, he saw a familiar yet unfamiliar face.

Blackie caught Bodie by the neck, and he jerked to a halt. But this was not the outlaw boss man that Bodie remembered. This new Blackie stood a full head taller, had hulking cybernetic muscles, and appeared to be part gorilla.

Blackie smiled. Behind curled lips were shiny metallic teeth punctuated by pointy canines. Just like the old Blackie, blood wept from vacant eye sockets.

Bodie struggled against Blackie's vice-like grip, his feet flailing inches above the ground. One of the other bots stepped in from behind, and Blackie grabbed its face with one hand and folded it down toward the ground until its back snapped backward. Bodie continued to struggle. He couldn't believe how strong this new cyborg version of the outlaw was. It carried him across the aisle and extended him out over the empty shaft. His smile grew bigger as he drew back a huge metallic fist.

A shudder ran through the entire ship, causing Blackie and the other bots to sway with the movement. Bodie snapped his Walker to the meat of Blackie's elbow and fired just as he kicked off of Blackie's chest. The cybernetic outlaw roared in pain as Bodie tumbled through the air, bouncing off a large conduit two floors down before he could grab the railing of the floor below that. One of his Walkers cartwheeled away, smashing and clanging as it was deformed into what would be a useless hunk of junk far below.

He reached for his other gun but thought better of it when the conduit above crumpled under the weight and force of cyborg Blackie as he followed. Bodie scampered further underneath the large conduit to get out of direct sight, dropped another floor, and tucked in above the railing to land on the corrugated metal. There were still two sentry bots in addition to the massive cyborg. Resurrected cyborg, he realized. Blackie had been dead for days. But then, so had Klamath. Was Blackie an alien, too? Seemed a little too coincidental. No, what had brought Blackie back to life wasn't biology. It looked like a cruel experiment.

He needed to run and hide until he could figure out a way to defeat Blackie or maybe get hold of one of those concussion weapons. He didn't know what it would do against Blackie, but it would help in his fight against the sentry bots at least. He'd have to figure that part out. For now, he needed to get lost, and quick.

<Change your ID> Helga offered.

What?

<You need to change your identification tag>

How do I do that?

<Switch it out for one of the bots you terminated>

Dmitr provided images of the first bot that had found him. Bodie had been hiding between pipework in the ceiling, had dropped down and separated its head from its body. But before he knew it, he had five others to deal with. Then Dmitr showed the one that he'd let get blasted by its buddy before tumbling to the bottom of the shaft. The other one wasn't dead, just knocked out. It was probably fine now.

If I can get to the one down below, how do I get its ID?

<If we get close enough, I can strip it. Even if the main power is destroyed, it has hardened residual power to keep memory functions operable and capable of being salvaged> Helga told him.

Really? How'd you know that?

<What do you think I've been doing all this time?>

I thought you were just mad.

<I am. But I don't want you dead>

Well, thank you, Helga. That's mighty decent of you. And what about you? He thought the query to Dmitr since he had also been quiet for some time.

Dmitr flashed images of an armory, maps of the ship, and specifications of futuristic firearms.

Okay, okay, I get it. You were busy, too.

Above, Blackie lunged from the conduit to the side of the shaft wall and then jumped to the floor above. There wasn't a good line of sight due to piping and large rectangular ducts routed overhead. Bodie moved with the silence of an Indian brave down the aisle and then to a ladder that took him a couple of floors down.

<I've disabled your identifier signal>

Oh, that's a good idea. What's that?

<It's how the sentry bots keep finding you>

Huh. That's how they're doing it?

<It's also how you're able to access doors and call elevators. You won't be able to do that until we strip that bot's ID>

Okay. I guess that makes sense. Any idea where Antigony is at?

<...>

Come on, you can't be like that.

<No. But, I may have found Justine>

He stopped in his tracks for a second and then kept moving, slowly and quietly navigating his way to the lower floors.

Show me.

Dmitr flashed through maps of corridors and then a massive, multi-level space. It was the ship's hold, and it was ... very large. She was being held there. It actually made sense. If something could hold a Wun-dee-go, it could probably hold Justine. Maybe.

He still needed to find Antigony but—

A ruckus up above reminded him he was trying to stealthily steal someone's identity and exit the area before being rendered down to his smallest components by the cyborg outlaw, Blackie Lung. He just realized that whoever had put ol' Blackie back together again had replaced everything but his eyes. What kind of sick individual would do that?

Bodie reached the lowest level, and the battered remains of the sentry bot weren't hard to find. There was a pit that extended another level down and the bots broken body was at the bottom of it. He'd have to be quick and hope that no one up above saw him.

Bodie slid down a pipe and scooted close to the broken bot.

You got it yet?

<You'll have to get closer>

Closer? If they spot us, we're going to be in big trouble.

<If you go through the doors to the exterior corridor, they'll know you're there anyway>

Fair enough.

Bodie crept closer, slowly. He was within a foot when a roar echoed down from above, "Bohhh-deeeee!!!"

Ughh.

Got it yet?

<Done>

Bodie leaped up, grabbed the rail, and was through the door to the exterior corridor within seconds. The corridor went left and right until it curved out of view. Then a rainbow pulse of light swept from one end to the other, accompanied by tinkling chimes.

"What was that?"

<Mood enhancement. It's for morale>

Huh? Who's morale? Isn't it all bots on this ship?

<Beats me. That's just what it says in the ship's operations and maintenance manuals>

Okay, so no Tig, huh? And Justine is somewhere in the hold?

Dmitr flashed schematics of the corridor, and directly in front of him was a highlighted access. Bodie heard the sounds of pursuit in the mechanical space on the other side of the bulkhead behind him. Then he heard the sounds of stomping feet from his left, further on down the corridor. Time to go.

He stepped up to the blank wall, and a crack appeared that spread into a low vertical opening. Ahh, it was for the spider bots. Bodie ducked through.

<You should know that some of these containments are open>

"I'm sorry, what was that?" he verbalized out of shock.

<Some of the holding cells. They've been opened remotely>

With monsters in them? Who would do that?

<I think Zilich. In order to eliminate intruders>

"Well, sheeyit."

Bodie stared out into the darkness dotted with blue lights along the corridors and bathed in varying colors of light here and there for as far as he could see. He pinged his sensors and a variety of signals came back. Some were large. Very large. Some were barely visible at all. That meant they were small, or maybe only partially there. He knew from experience that many of the creatures of the Alta Estranyazie didn't show up very well on his sensors. There was no way this was going to end well.

He flipped open the cylinder on his remaining Walker, ejected the spent casings for reloading later, and replaced them with fresh cartridges from his belt. He didn't know what mere bullets would do against most of the creatures Zilich had curated, but he didn't have much choice.

Bodie shook his head in resignation, pushed his Batterson down on his head, and then started jogging. There was an amber wash of light up ahead, and he detected the scent of a wet forest. Not exactly like anything he'd smelled before, though. It was foreign. Looking at the plants inside the containment, he understood why. They were literally not like anything from this planet. Something about that smell stirred up memories, though.

<The massacre at the station> Helga provided.

Bodie had just come to the same conclusion. He'd lost half his crew back before he'd traded his human body for a robotic one in his zealous quest to capture or kill the man named Zilich. The wet foresty smell was from the creature that'd been let loose in a cantina.

He remembered something from before. That was good. The memory itself? Not so much. A large, invisible reptile with a poison scorpion tail. And wings? He vaguely remembered something about wings. That was very bad. But it could still be the best thing he could bump into in the dark of Zilich's monster detention center. Of course, Zilich would probably refer to it as an exotic creatures' containment area, like it was some kind of zoo. He pinged his sensors, but before he could review the information, a strangled scream echoed down the corridors.

"Antigony!"

Bodie bolted into action, racing down the corridor, scanning the map for the most direct, least monster-y path.

<Right>

Bodie lurched right, took two steps on the container wall, and pressed on even harder.

<Straight. Then Left. Then up>

He tracked the directions in the overlay map provided by Dmitr as he sprinted. He was going to be dangerously close to somethin—

A massive, skeletal head with antlers poked around the corner in front of him.

"No, no, no, no. Not that," he blurted out.

The smell of rotting meat assaulted his sensors as he lunged off the wall to his left, bounded right, and then again, just barely clearing the railing of the upper-level walkway. The Wun-dee-go roared in frustration and beat the ground with its fists. Bodie raced along the walkway, but the Wun-dee-go easily matched pace beneath him, all while hunched over so its antlers wouldn't catch on the structure beneath Bodie's feet.

Another scream echoed from up ahead, and he and the Wun-dee-go both looked for the source of the noise. The huge beast burst forward with even more speed. Bodie tried to keep up, but the creature was insanely fast once it got up to speed.

<Ahead two containers and right>

Bodie rounded the corner right after the Wun-dee-go below him and they both came to a sudden halt. Before them, the catwalk ended, and suspended in the air was a creature Bodie had never seen before. Vaguely human, with long black hair, dark skin, and claws. It was garbed in faded black robes that looked like shredded gauze. Its hair was haloed around its head, wavering in emanating waves of energy, and draped in its arms was Antigony.

The Wun-dee-go stomped its feet and bellowed in challenge, but the creature hanging in the air was unphased. It screeched back. Then its eyes rolled back in its head, and as it roared, blazing white light shot out of its mouth. The beam of light hit the Wun-dee-go in the chest, where its stretched-tight skin began to sizzle.

It reeled in pain and roared back. The first creature, looking like some kind of voodoo vampire mummy, burst the blazing light from its mouth again, and it struck the Wun-dee-go, but this time, the creature didn't stop. Smoke and fire rose from the Wun-dee-go's body as it slowly stumbled to the ground, curling into a ball to evade the horrible light.

The sound was all-consuming. Bodie drew his Walker and shot, but the mummy creature raised a hand and the bullet stopped mid-air within inches of its mark. It stopped blasting the Wun-dee-go and its eyes rolled back to normal, only now Bodie could see that they were slit-like cat's eyes.

The creature smiled as it stared at Bodie. Then it rose higher in the air, it sucked in a large breath, and its eyes rolled back once more. As it began to shriek, Bodie stared down its throat where a pearl of light grew into a blinding miasma. He realized he was about to be incinerated, but then thudding steps from behind him caught his attention right before he was blindsided by something big, heavy, and moving with the speed of a freight train.

"Booohhh-dddeeeee!!!!!" Blackie yelled as he slammed into him from the side. They flew through the air as white light vaporized the catwalk where Bodie had been standing. He saw this happen as he and Blackie tumbled through the air and right before they hit the ground with a massive thud.

They hit with momentum. Blackie and Bodie tumbled a couple of times, and then Bodie felt himself thrown into the air with great force.

<134 feet to impact. That's a new record>

Wow. That is pretty good, Bodie thought, just before hitting the ground and blacking out.

CHAPTER 14

TELL ME YER SECRETS

Justine woke from a frightful dream and was glad to be awake. That was until she looked around and realized she was still in a cell. She shuffled across the few feet to the bathroom, which was an infinite improvement over the outhouse 25 yards from her family's cabin, since it wasn't cold and full of spiders.

Her family. Was the cabin hers now that they were gone? Was it even standing after those wretched men had been there looking for her? She suspected not. Not that she'd ever be going back. She fully expected to die here on this ship. It was a certainty, as far as she was concerned. She would either be killed by her captor or she would be killed by the sentry bots after she killed him. Zilich that was.

He came off as so congenial, but she knew he was as much a monster as any of the creatures he collected. That reminded her of the dream. The creatures had escaped. She was controlling the ship, and the creatures were out of their containments and taking over the ship. Then she remembered a curious fact. It was her that had let them out...

Her thoughts went to the coldbright and the connection she had with it now. She knew that most of the ship was made from the stuff, and yet she couldn't access that material. Not yet anyway. There was a secret to it. There was a way. She just hadn't figured it out. She used the restroom, washed her hands, and looked in the mirror.

"Look at you," she said to her reflection, marveling at the transformation. She must be the equivalent of fifteen or sixteen. She hadn't stopped aging when she'd come aboard the ship. That's what Zilich had suggested. That she'd stop aging once she was more in touch with the ship itself, or the coldbright that was the ship. Conundrum or whatever he'd called it. But looking in the mirror, she was clearly taller, and her face looked different. Thinner mostly. Prettier. She looked more like her mom, who was a humble beauty. And her dad now, in a way. The eyes. The set of her jaw. Her stomach clenched with the pain. It didn't hurt any less now that it'd been almost a week. The opposite was probably true. It hurt more. She was just accepting it.

Yes, she was definitely going to die on this ship. No way she could make it through Zilich's terms of enslavement. Ten years. She'd be lucky if she could go ten days without trying to kill him. Still, she'd try. Her mom and dad depended on it. Could he bring them back? She doubted it. Probably just lies, but then, if anyone could... Just looking at the marvels of technology all around her. If anyone could...

She stared into those strange but familiar eyes in the mirror as her resolve solidified into a plan of action.

"Com'ere," she said to the mercurial ball of cold-bright she'd left on her bedside. It whipped through the air into her hand. She opened her palm inches before her face.

"Tell me yer secrets."

And it did.

"Fascinating," Zilich said as he watched the myriad screens of the control room wall. Drama played out on all of them as monsters attacked monsters. Or robots. Or in one or two cases, a couple of meddlesome intruders. "Truly fascinating. I wish I'd thought of this," he said in awe.

Of course, it was an unspeakable waste of resources allowing the battle royale to play out, but on so many levels, it was truly an awe-inspiring sight. He was baffled that he had never thought of it: an arena where all the most terrifying creatures could battle to the death. And to put one or two heroes in the midst. What splendid entertainment! Again, he tried not to think of the cost.

Vohl groaned. He knew it pained him even more. The vile little creature had an angle that Zilich hadn't quite figured out, but he suspected that in some way he thought he was going to benefit from the sale of all the creatures in his menagerie. Not likely. Vohl would see the outside of an airlock before that ever happened. He was truly gifted, but Zilich had a giftedness of his own, and its greatest attribute was the ability to save his own skin. He knew that it was only a matter of time before the wretched little Nawri turned on him. Maybe it was finally time to punch that ticket. Once the ship was airworthy.

Something unusual caught his eye on one of the screens.

"Vohl. What is that ... thing on screen 6A?"

"Hmmm, why, I'm not quite sure. Haven't seen it before. Do you think the bots brought something back they weren't supposed to?"

"It looks like something you would have cobbled together in that lab of yours."

"Oh no. I think I'd remember if I did something like that," he responded sagely. "Hmm. Well, I better check on the new bots." Vohl poofed out of sight before Zilich could say anything to the contrary.

"Blasted little worm. He built that thing and he's lying about it." Zilich zeroed in on the creature. It looked like a man but cybernetically enhanced and ... well ... maybe not entirely a man. He tried to zoom in even more, but it leaped over a railing as a bolt of bright white light blazed past it, swung back underneath, and tore across the floor below on all fours. Like a monkey of this planet. Or more accurately, a gorilla.

"Oh, yes. How very Vohl you are." If he wasn't mistaken, that was Childers Lung—or what was left of him. Apparently, his new pilot, Justine, had rent him and the rest of his crew limb from limb less than a week ago. And now here he was.

That meant that Vohl had finally got that damnable machine to work. The reanimator. Zilich shivered and grimaced. Well, at least now he could say that he hadn't lied to Justine about her parents. They could "technically" be brought back from the dead. But he hadn't been kidding about the cost. He'd just failed to mention that it had nothing to do with credits. He wondered whose soul had been sacrificed to bring back the outlaw boss man "Blackie" Lung.

The ship shuddered again. He would have to figure out what was causing that. They were in no present danger since the ship's gravitics were fully operational and the whole thing had been properly anchored years ago. Still, Zilich didn't much care for things he didn't understand, and the timing, with monsters running free range and this new, powerful pilot onboard. Even if she was in a modified Golem Containment Unit...

"Oh, no."

He scanned the screens for unit V213. There it was. Still intact. It would take more than some idle tinkering to crack that one open. If a request to open the door was initiated, it had to be answered by Zilich himself. A process that required biometric authorization in person. And that was *never* going to happen. That was the worst decision he'd ever made, allowing Vohl to talk him into capturing an actual golem. Of course, it had imprinted on him and Vohl almost immediately. Vohl might as well have said, "Here, hold this grenade while I tinker with this pin."

He went back to watching the mayhem play out on the screens before him. He looked for the robot that had been co-opted. His old nemesis, Bodura Duc. There were robots or robot parts scattered to hell and back, making it all but impossible to find him. Then he remembered the IDs. Certainly, he could find him that way.

"Artis, show me the ID for the intruder robot from earlier."

The ship's computer complied.

"Artis, find this sentry bot."

The computer displayed a pile of battered limbs connected to a caved-in torso with a head lolling uselessly to the side of it. It was at the bottom of a mechanical shaft in the engineering section.

"Hmm. That's not like that little cockroach at all. Artis, is there anything unusual about this sentry bot?"

The computer displayed a code entry where the bot's ID had been swapped within the last few hours. "Bodie. Still so clever," he said while raking his salt-and-pepper beard with his fingers. He steepled them and brought them up to his lips. "Where is this new ID now?"

The computer highlighted a screen on the control room wall. A spider bot was attempting to salvage an incapacitated sentry unit in the midst of the mayhem in the ship's hold. It was dragging the unconscious robot along one of the detention corridors and away from the chaos of shrieking monsters, alien witches, and nightmare creatures. There was too much going on to get in there now. Perhaps the maintenance bot would be successful?

Zilich watched helplessly as something invisible punctured the side of the gangly robot and then something else resembling a harpy swooped in and hauled it off. The unconscious robot—most likely his old enemy and the one responsible for his being marooned on this backward little planet—just lay there. And then, something invisible started tugging it the other way.

Zilich's eye twitched. He switched to thermal imaging and easily made out the shape of an Eerd's Dragon. One of the stealthy, winged lizards he'd smuggled off of Catalpa. Cateelpa? He couldn't remember.

So many worlds. The same lizard he'd used to kill Bodie's crew was now unwittingly saving him. What sweet irony.

Zilich sighed. It would all play out. Bodie would die amidst the monsters, or Zilich would kill him once and for all. And what about this other intruder, the woman? He searched the screens but couldn't pick her out in the chaos.

"Artis, where is the woman?"

The screens all blanked and then worked in unison to create one large image. It was focused on the darkened opening to a large containment unit. He recognized it instantly.

"The Rajak." A mummy or a deity of death, depending on what folklore you gave credence to. For sure an embodiment of death for the Kholh'teps people, and for good reason. When it got started, it was a destructive force to be reckoned with. It being freed on this ship... Well, that could be the end of all of them.

The ship shuddered again, more violently this time, and Justine's eyes flashed open. That was her. She had done that; she was certain. The little glob of coldbright had told her a great many things. A lot of it completely incomprehensible, but some of it well worth the price of admission.

She closed her eyes and concentrated. "Hello, Artis."

"Hello, Justine. How may I assist you today?" came a feminine voice over the cell's speaker.

"I think I'd like to go flying."

CHAPTER 15
FLIGHT OF THE ARS ARCANUM

"**M**orning, sunshine," came the slow drawl of Klamath Pettibone.

The woman in the priest's collar and bandoleers' eyes fluttered.

After a moment, "What're *you* doing here?" and then her eyes grew round with concern as she glanced around, searching desperately for the creature that had brought her here. Wherever here was.

"Don't worry. The Rajak is gone."

"The what?"

"Rajak. It's a kind of deity of death. Sounds real scary." He shrugged. "Okay, it *is* a bit frightful. But it's gone. For the moment."

"Where'd it go?"

"Back into that sarcophagus," he said, nodding in the direction of a large, ornately inscribed stone coffin on claw feet a couple of yards deeper into the containment.

"Sarcopha-what?"

"It's a coffin. The creature is still weak from its confinement. It needs to feast, but I think it had a little too much fightin' to do before it had a chance to feed. Needed a rest first. You got real lucky. You're not a virgin, are you?"

Antigony leveled an unamused gaze at him.

"Yeah, didn't figure as much." He smiled. "That's a good thing."

"You're saying that thing eats ... virgins?"

"Mostly. Though I 'spect you'll do."

Antigony huffed resignedly. "Well, I'm flattered and all, but I don't presently, or ever, intend to be a meal for some creepy bag o' bones with a chastity fetish." She started to get up, but Klamath poked a sturdy forefinger into her forehead, effectively pushing her back down onto her butt.

"Hold your horses, little lady. You've got that shackle on your leg, and I'd bet if you try to remove it, it'll wake your admirer. I don't think you intend to do that."

She looked down and saw the black iron clasp around her leg that was attached to a chain that ran to a stout ring on the lid of the rajak's coffin.

"Oh shit."

"Got that right."

"Well, what're you going to do? You didn't just come in here to tell me I'm gonna die, did you?"

"No. I'm looking for your robot boyfriend."

Antigony stared daggers at Klamath. "He's not my boyfriend. And what do you care? You said yourself you'd soon enough see him dead."

"Yeah, well, that may be true. But, as much as I'm vexed by the fast one he pulled down there when the imp showed up with his posse, I still believe that the only way outta this ship alive is if we team up. I need to find him and form a plan before Zilich finds us or one of his monsters does the job for him." He cast his gaze meaningfully at the sarcophagus. "Truth is, if we don't act soon, these creatures are likely to tear this ship apart and us with it."

A violent shudder ran through the vessel, and the whole thing lurched.

They both shot concerned glances at the coffin. After a long moment, they returned their attention to the conversation.

"What's going on?" Antigony whispered, meaning the tremors within the ship.

"Dunno. Maybe they mean to move it. Maybe it's ready enough, though near as I can tell, the whole front end is still missing and they don't have enough material to put it back together."

Everything lurched again, and they both shot concerned glances at the Rajak's resting place. Then the whole ship groaned as it felt like it tried to lift into the air.

"Yep. That's exactly what's going on. Though, I can't imagine this thing is even close to spaceworthy."

"Spaceworthy?!? Like *space*, space? *Outer* space?"

"Exactly like that."

Antigony chewed a fingernail.

"Listen. We don't have time to waste. Where's the robot?"

"I ... I don't know. I lost him. Or he lost me. Not sure which. Both maybe." She shrugged.

The ship dropped and then lifted again as if its engines weren't entirely ready to carry the whole load. Klamath growled. Things were getting way out of control. He didn't much care to die because someone didn't know how to pilot their own ship. But he'd come this far.

The chain attached to Antigony's ankle shifted on the sarcophagus lid, making a loud *clink* and *thunk*. Antigony grimaced.

"I'll find him myself, I guess. What about the girl, Justine, know where she's at?"

Antigony shook her head. "Well, you're not much help, are you? If your stupid robot boyfriend shows up, tell him to find me so we can deal with Zilich before things get even worse. I'm going to make my way to the control room. I'll be waiting there."

"Hey, you can't just leave me here."

A low groan emanated from inside the large stone coffin.

"Ya see, that's where yer wrong," he said and turned and strolled out the door.

"Klamath!" she hissed. "Klamath! You no-good son of a sidewinder, you—"

But he couldn't make out anything else once he'd turned the corner. Didn't matter, anyway. He needed to be on his game as he made his way through the ship's containment area. He'd smuggled himself in here on the bottom side of one of the wagons bringing Zilich's critters back from grazing in the high plains. Getting in, it turned out, was the easy part. Now he had to find a way out. But not before he made sure that someone took care of Zilich.

He turned another corner and there, blocking the entire corridor, was a massive skeletal body with a rack of antlers that was half again his height. The creature looked pretty dead, though it was hard to tell with something that looked like a skeleton with skin on it. It was a Wun-dee-go, just like the one that'd chased him a few days before. Klamath was no bleeding heart, but to see the magnificence of the Pantera del Diablo and its cub brought low, and now this, it was a travesty. Made worse by the knowledge that Wun-dee-go were peaceful creatures on their home planet. It was when they were removed and the symbiotic relationship with the moss-like fungus that covered their bodies was destroyed that they became aggressive and ... well, downright surly.

"Shame," he said as he stared at it, then his face soured when the stench of rotting carcass hit him. He pulled his kerchief up to cover his nose and mouth before turning and heading up the corridor toward the front end of the ship where the bridge was located.

<001020xx1213?a00...001020xx1213?a00x110100... 001020xx121_a00x110100xxbxx01111> The alpha-numerics scrolled across Bodie Nine's ocular circuits before the background resolved from darkness to a dim, monochrome, night vision-filtered image of his surroundings.

<Detention Area floor>

<Multiple monsters>

<Significant physical trauma. More on that in ... 3.533s>

<Subjects of interest (Antigony, Justine, Zilich) ... Still unaccounted for>

Bodie's ocular circuits focused on the space where whatever was dragging him across the floor should have been but wasn't.

<An Eerd's Dragon. You may remember from earlier>

Yes, I remember. I'll make this quick.

<No! They're majestic creatures> Helga implored.

???

Bodie reached for his Walker and found it missing. The lights on his VEIP drew into a flat line.

<Rub its belly>

...

<Trust me on this>

He reached for the creature. *I can't believe I'm doing this.*

It hissed menacingly.

<Not right now. Are you crazy?!? It'll tear you apart. You have to wait until it takes you back to its nest>

You're kidding, right?

<...>

Bodie shook his head and watched helplessly as the containment cells slid by, one by one.

Antigony watched Klamath disappear through the entrance to the Rajak's containment unit.

That man is going to suffer for this.

If Bodie didn't put a bullet up his backside, she was going to.

The sarcophagus lid bumped again, and her head snapped to the source of the noise. She needed to think quickly. No more waiting for Bodie to save her. She'd gotten rather caught up in the damsel in distress charade. It was fun for a minute, but now it was time to get back to business. Besides, she was more than used to dealing with the surly, jealous types. She patted her holster and found it empty.

Of course.

She examined the chain around her ankle. It looked like iron. It extended about a dozen feet, where it connected to a large ring that was attached to the sarcophagus's lid. She could try to pull it away, but it was heavy-looking, and then she'd be exposing the Rajak, which would likely wake it and make it angry.

She'd only seen it briefly before she was ripped across the air from where she'd been running blindly away from the invisible lizard thing. Out of the frying pan and into the fire. She didn't know how she'd come to be unconscious, but she didn't have a headache or anything that would suggest she'd hit her head. At least not again.

She rubbed her temple where it was still tender from earlier that day when they'd only been running from robots and not a rogue's gallery of the galaxy's most nightmarish monsters. The ship shuddered again.

Damn. She didn't have much time before that thing woke up. She looked down. What did she have to work with? Boot knife. Bandoleer full of bullets. Good enough. Now she just needed fire. Behind her, on either side of the sarcophagus, were two lampstands flickering with a sinister-looking green flame.

"Probably do the trick," she whispered to herself and started to make her way toward the nearest one, but the grating of chains across the floor sounded like an earsplitting racket in the quiet of the containment. She froze in place. Gently picked up the chain as much as she could and tiptoed over to the lampstand. She laid it down on its side, but there was a wide bowl beneath the part that held the wick that wouldn't let it touch the ground where she needed to do her work.

She scanned the space and the only flat working surface she could see was, sadly, the sarcophagus itself. She breathed a sigh of resignation and carefully placed the stand near the Rajak's resting place. But, if she had to do it here, it gave her an idea. It sure would be nice if the Rajak couldn't chase her down after she escaped.

She looked again at the black stone box. It was raised on sculpted feet like a clawfoot bathtub, and there was just enough room underneath for her to squeeze through. She got down, crossed herself, and shimmied underneath. The ship bumped again.

Who's driving this thing anyway?!? she wondered in desperate concern.

A groan escaped from inside the stone casket and she held her breath while she listened for movement. After a moment, silence resumed. She slid out from under and realized now she was trapped on the wrong side of the sarcophagus with the lamp on the other side and not enough chain to reach the other lamp.

She'd have to go over. There was enough room for that. Antigony rolled her eyes and crossed herself again. Twice and through in a quick Hail Mary. At least, as much of it as she could remember. Slowly she climbed up and dropped her leg over the other side but that's as far as the chain would go.

Dammit.

Now she was straddling the sarcophagus with Rajak inside and her chain hopelessly wrapped around it. Now would be a terrible time—

The ship lifted and slammed back down.

No, no, no...

Another groan emanated from inside, louder this time, and there was a thump on the lid. Antigony felt it through her butt and thighs.

She pulled off one of the .44 bullets and used the knife to lever the lead from the casing. The black powder spilled all over the top. She hastily swept it into the middle near the big chain ring and did another one.

Another big thump from inside, followed by a seething hiss. Antigony's stomach did backflips, and she dropped the next bullet.

"Unggghhh," came from inside.

She picked up the bullet and emptied its contents hastily while grabbing another and another. She was going to need a couple more. The lid lifted entirely off the lower portion of the sarcophagus and thudded back down. She yelped in response.

"Unnnggghhhh!" And then louder pounding. The lid lurched each time, causing the chains to shift. Then the ship shuddered and thunked down again, causing the lampstand to tip away. The Rajak started to shriek inside and light bloomed from the edges as the lid lifted again and again. Taloned fingers poked out from under the lid, and as it settled back down, the thing shrieked even louder. Antigony yanked her leg back, but one of the talons sliced along the inside of her calf and ankle.

"Dammit," she yelped, grasping her leg and trying to maintain balance on top of the Rajak's coffin as it bucked violently from within.

The lampstand tipped back her way. She grabbed it and hastily pulled the chain taut against the lid right as the flame touched down. A massive flash whooshed and her leg was free, but the whole ship yawed, throwing her off the sarcophagus to land hard on the floor. She tried to catch the breath knocked out of her as she stumbled to right herself, but the ship was tipping away again, almost spinning like gravity itself had lost its grip. Just as she was getting oriented, gravity shifted again, but this time it slid underneath until she was right side up and the ship was flat. Or, at least, that's what it felt like. All she knew was that she was free, down was beneath her feet, and the Rajak was pissed.

A bloodcurdling shriek burst from the stone box and the lid slammed against the welded chain on its lid.

"Ooh, that was lucky," she exclaimed and then raced for the door before she remembered the cut on her leg and tumbled. The pain was intense. So much worse than it should have been. She sucked it up, cried out as she stood again, and hobbled for the door. She turned the corner and didn't look back. With any luck, she'd avoid anything worse. But then, that's how she'd run into the Rajak in the first place...

"You can access and manipulate any of the ship's systems from anywhere within the Ars Arcanum, but the ship's bridge is the nexus of those systems," said Artis, the vessel's AI, via the speaker in Justine's cell. She was giving Justine quite the education.

Justine closed her eyes and "felt" the systems of the ship through her relationship with the coldbright, the memory metal that made up most of the vessel and the material she had somehow bonded with early in her childhood. The coldbright itself was quasi-arcane, meaning that it had inherent magickal properties, but there was something about humans. Their special characteristic of being panarcane, meaning able to utilize the magick of any world or system, was unique within the galaxy. Who knew?

As such, Justine, having grown up in the presence of the coldbright, had a magickal bond with the element. Amongst the human children of the Alta Estranyazie, she was particularly gifted. The coldbright didn't know why. Artis didn't know why. It just was the way it was. The power of the Ars Arcanum's systems pulsed and vibrated within her: propulsion, gravitics, defenses, environmental, analytics, systems upon systems upon still more systems. It was mind-numbing even while it felt somehow ... familiar. There was an inherent quality to it all because she knew the coldbright and the coldbright *was* the ship.

A ripple ran through the vessel. She perked up. Someone was trying to control it. To contain her control on it. To squeeze her out. She chuckled. *How cute.*

Justine reached through the systems and allowed them to soak into her mind and body. Artis hadn't taught her this. She had just intuited that this was the proper way to connect with the ship. She followed the path of the commands, tracing them back to the bridge to a console, to a person.

"Good morning, precious," she purred over the ship's intercom.

She watched through the Ars Arcanum's internal surveillance camera feeds. She hadn't quite gotten the hang of polling the various systems, since she wasn't entirely sure what they all were or what they did, but she was beginning to get familiar. Her captor's grizzled, bearded face came into view in her mind's eye. The look of surprise and—satisfyingly—terror gave her an immense amount of joy.

"Artis?" Zilich called out tentatively while shooting glances in either direction, presumably eyeing possible escape routes.

"'Fraid not, pumpkin," she said sweetly.

He drew himself up. Squared his shoulders.

"Why Justine, you're certainly everything I'd hoped for. Your training has come along quite nicely."

"Has it?" She shifted focus to the propulsion system and juiced the engines just a tiny bump. The ship jumped, anchors in the red rock of the plateau exploded while ceramo-metal braces rent with horrific screeches. She routed this external audio back to the bridge. It was difficult and a little bit sloppy, but she managed it.

He covered his ears. "Whuh, what are you doing?" Zilich asked breathlessly, unable to contain his surprise and growing trepidation.

"Me? Oh, nothing ... much," she replied devilishly. "Just thought it was a lovely day for a joyride is all."

The ship's aft, already extending nearly half a mile above the plateau, began to fall, careening toward the flat rock with increasing speed. She shifted focus and called on Artis for help. The ship's propulsion and gravitics systems both cranked up to multiples over max to keep the back end of the ship from crashing down and imploding on itself. Something that, Justine realized too late, would cause catastrophic reactor failures and likely decimate the better half of three territories.

Zilich's eyes grew round as he braced for impact. The whole front of the ship cantilevered up as the back end plummeted. The engines, reactors, and a myriad of other systems all spooled up frantically, dimming the lights as the ship struggled to arrest its downward momentum.

Justine's stomach was clawing at her throat as she felt the ship lift off the ground and then rock back down with all power and gravitics shifted momentarily aft. The room swayed, gravity shifting underneath her, causing her to first fall into the bed and then away from it to land on the floor. She slid toward the bathroom and then slid away from it before gravity settled underneath her and the whole ship rested in vacant space above the plateau.

The view from the external cams was just a red cloud of dust. She queried Artis.

"The weight, momentum, and corresponding thrust of the Ars Arcanum has collapsed a large section of the cliff wall. It appears to have destroyed several blocks of the town of Puro Pura." Resultant booms from below seemed to emphasize her point. "I imagine that was not the intended result."

"No. Not exactly," Justine conceded.

"However, the vessel appears to be stable. It is not anchored and therefore is no longer geostationary."

"Layman's terms, please, Artis."

"The Ars Arcanum is flying. Relative altitude, 100 meters. Velocity, 2.5 meters per second."

"Convert to feet, please. And miles per hour. At least until I can get used to things."

"Averaging 347 feet in elevation and 5.6 miles per hour."

"Okay. Halt speed. Park at 500 feet. Does that sound about right?"

"That should be quite fine," Artis responded. She felt the ship shift under her feet, if only slightly. The gravitics systems, she realized, were being manipulated to offset inertia. She'd been taught that this was a large part of traveling with organics. Speaking of which, the animals in the detention area. She'd forgotten about them entirely. She polled the internal cams and was horrified to see the chaos that her initial attempts at control of the local systems around her containment had caused. As much as these creatures were monsters, many of them were still exactly that, creatures. They were no different from bears and tigers and crocodiles from her own world. Okay, maybe they were a lot different from that, but turning them loose on each other was equally barbaric. It was—a pang of guilt pierced her—wrong.

"Justine!" Zilich's voice came to her through the intercom speaker of her cell. "Stop it this instant. You're going to kill us all!" She was sure he was trying to sound authoritative, but she could hear the terror in his voice.

"Calm yourself, Zilich. Everything is quite under control."

"Is it? You just destroyed half of Puro Pura. There's much-needed fuel and stores down there. Not to mention tons of coldbright needed for the completion of the ship," he pleaded.

Coldbright. Hmm.

"But the ship is flying. And now we can begin to put the rest of it back together. Get it shipshape," she said with a smile. She had to admit she was enjoying herself.

A stab of remorse jarred her memory. Ma and Pa. She needed to keep things in perspective. She needed cold-bright to complete the ship. She needed the ship to find the remains of her parents. She needed the creatures alive in order to have leverage to force Zilich and his minion to rebuild and resurrect her folks.

"Justine, listen to me. You need to stop and take things slow. You don't know what you're doing yet—"

"You listen to me, Zilich," she warned him in a low, cold tone, "I run this ship. I *am* this ship. We have an arrangement and I intend to fulfill my part, in as much as these creatures will be gathered up and this ship will be capable of transporting them. You will fulfill your part, which means we will be retrieving my parents' remains and your little minion will begin to put them back together again. Then, and only then, will we consider taking this ship off planet, but you will in no way dictate to me how I go about my training as pilot and when I deem that we are ready to move to the next phase of this operation. Do I make myself clear?"

"Hoo-hoo," he crowed. "Sweet Justine. If you knew half of what you were talking about."

She slammed down the bridge's defensive measures, effectively sealing Zilich in the large command room. He jumped.

"I'll make this short. I. Am. The ship. And what I know is enough to make me dangerous. Think on that. I'll have someone deliver you to your quarters."

He shook his head. The look on his face was one of tolerant patience. "My dear, just because you can manipulate the systems of the ship doesn't mean you're in charge. You aren't the first pilot to get a little puffed up on their own power. The sentry bots are mine to command, and I have other means to assert my authority…"

She assumed control of the display screens on the bridge and fed the external cams to those displays. While they'd been talking, she had used her little glob of coldbright to defeat the lockouts of her containment cell, allowing her to step foot on the material of the ship itself. That had given her even greater control. Then that same little glob had navigated through the ship and out the exposed portion of the bow. There, it had extended in a nearly microscopic filament down into the rubble of the cliff face, creating an easier pathway for the trapped coldbright ore to follow once Justine was ready to shift focus.

Justine called the coldbright, and it flowed up the filament, resolving into a handful of humanoid shapes before filling in gaps in the shattered structure. She was going to need a lot more coldbright, but this was a start.

Zilich watched, mouth agape, as the humanoid creatures headed in the direction of the bridge. They looked every bit as mercurial as the coldbright itself and as menacing as his own sentry bots. He paled visibly.

Then the feed to the bridge glitched. Justine reestablished the connection, but when she did, Zilich was nowhere to be seen. She unshuttered the defensive system and her own sentries stormed the room but, after minutes of searching, found no trace. Her hands clenched into fists as she watched nervously.

"You slippery sonofabitch," she whispered as the sentries concluded a second and then a third sweep of the entire space. "Artis, do you know where he went?"

"I'm sorry. Who are you referring to?"

"Don't play games with me, Artis. Zilich, of course."

"I apologize for the confusion, but there is no one on the ship by that name."

"I see." She steepled her fingers and tapped them on the tip of her nose as she thought. "New tack. Let's go see this command center for ourselves."

She guided half the sentry cohort to her position in the detention area. It took several minutes, and when they arrived, only two of them were left, and one of those was missing an arm. *Oh yeah, forgot how dangerous it is to be wandering around in here.*

She absorbed the remainder of her sentries into herself. Six long mercurial tendrils emanated outward from her back, while a host of shorter ones filled in the gaps between them, forming something of a protective shield. At least from behind. They could shift around as necessary. Hopefully, she was up for the task of dealing with whatever it was she'd loosed in Zilich's hold. Her thoughts went to the zombie family at the cabin. And that strange wolf creature that had laughed at her and disappeared as quiet as a ghost.

"You are in considerable danger in your current location."

"That's an understatement," she said, looking around and listening to the shrieks and wails echoing through the cavernous space.

"I can provide a certain amount of warning using the ship's internal sensors, but many of these creatures were never intended to be allowed to roam free inside the vessel."

"Can't imagine why."

"Well, because they're very dangerous and difficult to track."

"Figure of speech."

"Noted," came the pleasant voice. "If I may, there are other, unauthorized individuals within the detention area who also may be at risk. How would you like to proceed with dealing with these interlopers?"

"Interlopers? Show me."

She closed her eyes and monochrome images of one of the outlaw bandits appeared. Then the renegade robot Bodie Nine. Lastly, the woman he had with him. They were each in different locations in the detention area. Bodie was the closest.

"I'll deal with them," she told Artis. "You find anyone else. Especially Zilich."

"Again, I am unfamiliar with anyone by that name."

"Okay. Find anyone else on the ship. Actually, tell me where that little imp creature is. Vole."

"The Nawri, Vohl, exiled heir-imperator and first science officer of the Ars Arcanum, is located in his laboratory."

"Is he now? What's he doing?"

"I'm afraid I don't know. Part of his working arrangement demands that ship security has no access to that space."

"Is that so? So, Artis, you don't strike me as the sort who wouldn't know the goings-on on this ship. Would you have any ideas as to what he might be up to?"

"Well, I could speculate with a reasonable amount of certainty that it involves the repair and or creation of some of his ... reanimated beings."

"Reanimated?" Justine perked up. "Like, resurrected reanimated?"

"I could surmise with 99 percent certainty."

"How?"

Artis replayed a video sequence directly into Justine's mind, though she didn't have the foggiest idea of how. It was like a waking dream, the same way that the other images arrived.

"What is that? Is this happening now?"

"No. This occurred about an hour and a half ago. There was an altercation between one of Vohl's reanimated creatures. The first such creature." She rolled the video back, and there was Bodie, getting tackled from behind by a large man-like creature and then thrown an impressive distance. When Vohl's creation, which bore a striking resemblance to an outlaw she'd met in Low Camp, went to retrieve the robot, another creature, this one looking like some kind of space mummy holding the woman she assumed was Bodie's new partner in crime, shot a beam of light out of its mouth and chased Vohl's creature—which she was quite sure was that outlaw boss man—out of the containment area.

Justine rocked back on her heels and rubbed her face. "Vohl made this?"

"Yes. He calls it Blackie."

"On account of his predisposition for the color and the bandana over his bloody eye sockets, no doubt." She held her jaw with one of the mercurial strands while she lifted into the air a foot or so. "Earlier, you said beings. Plural. 'Zat right?"

"That is only a supposition. But there were approximately a dozen human bodies delivered to Vohl's lab, and there are an excess of that number of sentry bots that were sent there for repair. Judging by the composition of the reanimated cyborg called Blackie, I would conclude that Vohl intends to make roughly a dozen of the creatures. Though I don't know if referring to them as creatures is entirely appropriate."

"Nah. You're not far off. I met 'em in real life and they were little more than savages then. But what did you call 'em, cy-borgs?"

"Yes. As in a cybernetic organism. An antiquated idiom, but a persistent one."

"Well, so we got monsters, aliens, mummies, inter-lopers, mad scientists, *and* zombie cyborgs to worry about?" Her tendril slid from her jaw up to scratch her head while another one came around for her to rest her chin on. She conformed the other tendrils into a loose representation of a large throne and drew her legs up into a cross-legged position beneath her. Justine pulled her braid over her shoulder and began to redo it as she lifted into the air.

"Artis, illuminate the corridors from Bodie's location to mine. Keep everything else dark. Warn me if anything ... creepy comes lurking about."

"Very well. I understand you're assuming the role of pilot for the Ars Arcanum. Is there something you'd like me to call you?"

"So glad you asked. If there's no one by the name of Zilich on this ship, then you can call me captain. Captain Sever will do, Artis."

"Very well, Capt. Sever. And, Capt., it appears that we've depleted the coldbright stores available in the carnage of Puro Pura, but we're a long way off from making the ship spaceworthy. What is your suggestion?"

"Well, Artis, I believe we should scour the territory for the remaining coldbright deposits we need. I will draw it to us, I think. After I speak with Bodie, that is."

"Very good, ma'am."

"Oh, and Artis, can you whip me up a new uniform? Something with some gold scrambles on the shoulders or some such thing? Just to eliminate any confusion when the time comes."

"Certainly, ma'am."

CHAPTER 16

REACQUAINTANCE

Helga had been right. Petting the belly of the Eerd's Dragon had done the trick. Of course, Bodie couldn't see that it was sleeping, but he could certainly hear its snoring. It'd taken the better part of twenty minutes to silently creep down the tree thing, onto the big mushroom-thing, and across the massive lily pad-things to exit the containment, but he'd finally done it.

He was working on his next steps when he came to an intersection. It was dark to his right and straight ahead, but to his left, there was a containment whose window bathed the catwalk in a deep amber. He remembered it from when he'd first entered the massive detention area. Having lost consciousness and been dragged through the hold, he didn't have a great sense of his location. At least from here, he knew where to start.

He walked cautiously over to the glowing containment and saw nothing but thick mist inside. Then there was movement, but it was so vague it was impossible to tell if it was real or just a trick of the light. Then it happened again. He noticed that the plas separator was still in place and realized he was grateful for that one tiny little thing in a day of deeply disappointing events.

Before he realized it, he was standing facing the window. Out of the mist came two shapes. They were dark and humanoid, and he couldn't make out their faces until they were mere feet away. He was just beginning to think that there was something familiar about them when they lunged for the glass and slammed up against it, pounding and screaming in terror to be let out.

He stepped back. Their faces were covered in blood. Their hair was wet with it. In fact, it seemed like the whole interior of the containment was wet with it, though he knew that was an impossibility. But what was even more impossible was that these two people, screaming for their lives, were Helga and Dmitr.

Bodie lunged forward, pressing his hands and face to the glass.

"No, no, no... No, this can't be happening. Helga! Helga!" He slammed on the glass and then something like a thick vine whipped out of the darkness and swiped Dmitr away into the mist.

"Dmitr! Nooo!"

Bodie slammed the containment plas until it cracked. He was palm to palm with Helga when she, too, was pulled away. He slammed harder and harder, the window spiderwebbed across its entire length but wouldn't break. He pounded relentlessly, with little improvement. The containments were built for this kind of abuse.

After minutes of this, Bodie slid to the floor, weeping bitterly, but no tears would come. He slammed the floor in frustration before pushing himself back against the wall. There was a dangerous thought lurking in the back of his mind. So dangerous, he couldn't fully give it acknowledgment. But it was right there in front of him. Clear as day.

His friends weren't inside the containment. He knew this because he'd seen them die.

There. You happy?

There was no response from his lower OS levels. In truth, there wasn't actually any distinction between one layer of his OS and the next. It was only ever him … and what he wished were true. That he still had Helga and Dmitr's companionship. Their love. Their loyalty. The things he'd sacrificed in his maniacal pursuit of the man that had, in the end, taken everything from him.

His mind flashed back to the boarding of the Ars Arcanum. The starboard grapplers had locked. The breaching team had met resistance. He'd been first through the temporary airlock. Helga and Dmitr behind him. They'd taken flak and concussion weapons, but they were veterans and within minutes had overrun the sentry bot defenders.

Section by section, they'd pursued their quarry. The planet below grew closer. The two ships, locked together, struggled against the unfamiliar mass and the grapplers failed. Catastrophic decompression savaged sections of both ships. Bodie's own ship strayed too close to the Ars Arcanum propulsion system and took unresolvable damage.

He'd instructed his remaining crew to scuttle the ship and use the jump shuttles to get home. A decision that left the boarding crew with no recourse but to take Zilich's ship, filled with the galaxy's deadliest creatures, damaged and tumbling through a quickly decaying orbit around an unknown planet.

Bodie's hands covered his face as the memory played out; how they'd hunted for Zilich and were unable to find him, how they'd stumbled on a stronghold of sentry bots and gotten pinned down. Dmitr had taken considerable damage. He was severely wounded and his armor was in bad shape. It froze up. Bodie provided covering fire while Helga assisted Dmitr out of his broken armor. Then a grenade banked off a wall and landed right in the midst of them. A one-in-a-million shot.

Helga had already sprawled on the grenade when Bodie turned. When the smoke cleared. The sentry bots had already charged past him, assuming he was dead. Helga was dead. Dmitr, in bad shape to begin with, was clinging to life. They shot him while he was unable to defend himself.

Bodie had gotten up, still barely able to see. Barely able to stay upright. He rushed the sentry bots. Executed them all but for one when the alarms blared, proclaiming an imminent crash. Bodie was bleeding all over. Helga and Dmitr were dead. Zilich was MIA. The lone sentry bot lunged for him, and that's when he'd pulled his final card. The Mahna Noostra familial magick that allowed him to project his consciousness, his very self, into another being. He didn't know if it would work with a robot.

Apparently, it did. But he had no memories after that. Not until he was dug up in that Chinese camp at the south end of the Alta Estranyazie.

Bodie sighed heavily. He hadn't just let them down. He'd failed them. They were dead because of him.

But there was still more to the story. He wasn't even supposed to be looking for Zilich, but his pride wouldn't let him leave it alone. The prince marshal couldn't leave it alone. His father had begged him to come home. To marry.

He realized he wasn't chasing Zilich as much as he was running away from responsibility. And his friends were dead because of it. They'd followed him to the end of the galaxy and he'd squandered their loyalty.

Zilich is still alive.

So what? Was he going to make the same mistake? Throw away everything for this man?

His thoughts went to Antigony. As misguided as her interest in him was, he couldn't let her die because of him, too. And Justine? Well, that was something else entirely. She'd ripped him limb from limb after he tried to save her and her family. He figured they were even. He didn't even care how that factored in his karmic ledger. That whole thing was just a sham, anyway. A way to soothe his guilty conscience.

Suddenly, the lights of the corridor came on. But just the corridor. Just in one direction. He looked around, and it appeared that it was lit up just for him...

He didn't have time for games; he needed to find Antigony and, he assumed, that mummy thing as well. He polled Dmitr, but there was no response. *I guess I'll have to do things myself.* It was easy enough. A 3D map of the detention area overlaid his visual circuits, but there was nothing labeled "mummy thing," so results weren't exactly jumping off the page. There was an entry for Wun-dee-go, a handful of others he didn't recognize, a

Golem, whatever that was. It was in a highly fortified containment. Heavy thudding sounds came from that location even now. That seemed about right.

He found the location for the Eerd's Dragons. Dragons. Plural. He hadn't even thought to check thermal scans. He did so now. The area was clear, much to his relief. Then he found the containment called Brittlebark. That was the location where he'd seen the horrific vision of Helga and Dmitr. He'd assumed it was some kind of psychic projection. An imposed hallucination of sorts. He was still of that mind, but the name did not fit the experience. Terror Trees. Warped Woods. Something like that at least did it a little more justice to the horrifying experience.

He was getting distracted. Antigony was the focus. Where had he seen her last? It was more toward the middle of the detention area. He and the Wun-dee-go had been racing to find the source of her screams. He looked that direction. It happened to be the same corridor that was lit up. And it was in the direction of the pounding coming from what he assumed was the Golem Containment Unit. One of the units anyway. Those, at least, were locked up tight. Bodie scanned, researched, and plotted, all the while walking and keeping a keen eye on the path ahead.

After a minute, the lit corridor turned away to his right. He did need to get over one more row but wasn't sure he wanted to follow the lit-up path to do it. He walked past, only to have that corridor go dark and the one he was in getting lit up instead. At least until the next cross corridor. This, he didn't like. Someone was responding to his movements.

He bounded off the walls to either side and up to the walkway above. The lighting shifted to match his new path. But this was the path that he'd been following when he'd heard Antigony's screams before. He hoped she was okay. He didn't think he could take it if she wasn't. He had to admit: he missed the excitement of having her around. As uncomfortable as it was at times. But there was no way things could work out between them. He was a robot now. And she most certainly had *very* human needs.

Well, one thing at a time. He needed to find her first. Then he'd need to figure out how to defeat whatever it was that'd taken her. He tuned his audio so he could catch her voice again.

Bodie was listening intently when he turned a corner and realized he was at the intersection he was looking for. His olfactory senses should have warned him. The smell of death was thick on the air. The Wun-dee-go's body was crumpled on the floor below him. Whatever it was that took Antigony had killed the Wun-dee-go. Bodie's stomach sank. He was so out-gunned. Even if he had his guns. Now? Things seemed thoroughly hopeless.

"'Bout time I ran into you."

Bodie spun to see Justine with her silvery tendrils arranged into a throne with a halo of smaller tendrils behind her. She hung suspended in the air above the second-floor walkway. Bodie stepped back, hands at the ready, but he had nothing. Nothing except the bowie knife, at least. He pulled it in a flash and crouched, ready for a fight.

"Now, now, Mr. Robot. Is that any way to treat the captain of the ship?"

"Captain?" Justine nodded with a cat-who'd-eaten-the-canary smile. "What's that mean, you beat Zilich?" he asked in surprise.

She shook her head. "Nah, he just up and left. But I am running things around here. I got my minions hunting him down while I rebuild the ship and find the rest of the coldbright so we can get this thing ready to travel."

"Travel? Where do you mean to go to?"

"I think I'll return these creatures where they came from. Give me an excuse to get around a little. But first I need to deal with a little problem."

Bodie's fingers fiddled on the knife handle as he readied himself for the attack he'd been expecting all along.

"Nah, it's nothing like that. I need you to deal with something for me," she told him.

Bodie's eyebrow rose skeptically. He slid the Wost into its sheath and stood up. "What kind of something?"

"Well, Zilich doesn't work alone. Besides his sentry bots, he has a scientist who deals with all these animals and dabbles in some very ... obscure research. I think you may have met one of his creations?"

Ahh, that's what she was getting at. "You mean Blackie?"

"Yes. And that's not all. The scientist, Vohl, is resurrecting more of his gang. So, if you didn't like Blackie, don't be surprised when he rolls up with half his entire posse."

Bodie sighed and adjusted his hat. "Where are they now?"

"Back at Vohl's lab. But I don't expect them to be there long."

"Huh. And what about Zilich? You said he was missing?"

"Yeah, one second he was there, next he was gone."

"Sounds familiar. Where'd this happen?"

"On the bridge. Why?"

"Dunno. Just thinking there must be some sort of secret passage or something."

"I'd know if there was. I can feel every inch of this ship through the coldbright."

Justine and Bodie locked eyes. "I better get up there and see what I can find," she continued.

"Justine. Are we good?"

"You mean, am I going to tear your limbs off and leave you in a puddle of your own fluids? Nah. I didn't want you screwing things up when it came time to kill Zilich, but I'd say we're well past that. You deal with Vohl and I'd say we're good."

"Yeah, well, I don't know about this Vohl guy, but Zilich is a lot slipperier than you might expect. I thought I had him cold. He wiped out my crew and blew up his own ship to get away. And yet, here he is, ship and all."

"Don't worry. I won't repeat the errors of your past. He killed my parents and now he owes me big. But listen, I don't know how you're going to deal with that Vohl character and his gang of zombie cyborgs." She looked at him. "Yeah, I know right? Anyway, you can't *kill* Vohl. I need him for something."

Bodie put his hands up. "Hold on a minute. First thing I gotta do is find Miss Von Riche. She was taken by—"

"The Rajak," Justine interrupted, "some kind of deity of death. Looks like a space mummy if you ask me."

"Space mummy?" He thought about it. "Yeah, I guess that kinda fits," he said shrugging. "Still, that ... Rajak thing is mighty fearsome. Killed a Wun-dee-go and everything."

She was about to respond, but a booming voice broke through the silence from somewhere off in the distance. "Boohhh-deeee!!!"

"Sounds like your cue."

"What do you mean? We should deal with him together."

"Sorry, robot. I gotta find Zilich before he pulls some shenanigans. You said it yourself. He's slippery. He even said as much. That he has ways of knocking me down a peg or two. I'm not going to give him the chance. Good luck," she said with a wink before her throne turned and she sped away into the darkness.

"Well. That's no good," he said just before the lights went out.

Zilich was still alive, which, even though he'd told himself it didn't matter, it did matter in as much as he was dangerous and ornerier than a two-headed timber rattler. Blackie and his gang were on their way. He was weaponless except for a high-quality bowie knife, and he still didn't know where Antigony was. Oh, and a deity of death called a Rajak was still on the loose and not likely to give her up. That about rounded up his inventory of issues. Also, there were monsters everywhere and a young girl from the plains was now piloting an interstellar spacecraft with the intention of leaving the planet sometime in the near future ... because, why wouldn't she?

He heard the sound of feet padding down the walkway behind him and turned just in time to watch as Antigony ran headlong into him. Something was wrong. He stumbled backward to absorb some of the shock and make the collision softer on her but ended up tripping on his own feet. The two of them fell to the floor with her on top.

Her eyes went round with surprise and then narrowed in a sensual way before she remembered she was mad at him. She pushed away from him, but she was weak. In fact, she looked downright ill. Her eyes were sunken, her skin pale, and there was a thin layer of perspiration on her face.

"Miss Von Riche."

"Don't say it like that. I'm mad at you and I like it too much when you say my name like that."

Bodie wasn't sure what to do with that information, but it was clear she was hurt and in distress. "Antigony, are you okay? You don't look well. Was it that Rajak that did this to you?"

She looked at him. "How do you know about that?"

"I saw that it had you, but there was a fight with a Wun-dee-go, and then I got attacked by a zombie cyborg and lost track of you. Then I was dragged off by an invisible flying reptile called an Eerd's Dragon. But I got away from it by petting its belly before I was psychologically attached by a spooky tree and then I ran into..." He faded off. The look on her face made it clear she didn't believe a word he was saying. "You don't believe any of this, do you?"

"No," she said, shaking her head solemnly. "You didn't come for me, and I had to escape the Rajak all by myself." She pointed at the manacle and melted chain still attached to her ankle. The gash in her leg was covered in dried blood but was puffy and angry. "And now, you wanna make up some cockamamie excuse rather than admit the truth. You don't really love me."

Bodie wasn't really sure what to say. He'd never considered it because he'd only met her the day before last. He did the only thing he could do: create a diversion.

"Oh my goodness, Antigony, your leg. Are you okay?" He was legitimately concerned, and based on her weakened state and ghastly pallor, it seemed likely that it was infected.

"Oh, that…" She waved the injury away, but Bodie could tell she was a little out of breath, too. Now that the initial excitement of their collision was wearing off, she was running down fast.

"Booohhhh-deeeee!!!!" boomed Blackie from somewhere closer than before.

"Damn, he's gonna be on us in no time," Bodie said.

"Who is?"

"Blackie. The resurrected cyborg outlaw that's looking for me. He and his posse are coming and I haven't got anything but a bowie knife."

"That's not good," she said sleepily. She looked like death. He had to get her to safety and then figure out what to do about Blackie and his gang.

"Come on. We gotta git," he said, peering around the corner, but when he looked back, she was fast asleep against the containment wall.

He checked her pulse. It was weak. Her breathing was fast and shallow. Now the sweat peppered her skin in big droplets.

He breathed out a sigh. "Dammit, Tig. You gotta hang in there."

He searched the 3D maps and found a sick bay between the detention area and the bridge, conveniently located near Vohl's laboratory. He scooped her up and started jogging as quietly as he could. All while scanning the surroundings with his sensors.

One thing didn't look right at all, Antigony's own signal was faded. He didn't know what could be causing that. But it couldn't be good. One thing that was good, however, was that the signals of Blackie's gang were pretty clear. At least he thought it was Blackie's gang. There was a line of red dots coming up on him from behind. He cut left to get to the farthest edges of it, rather than get caught in the middle and easily surrounded.

He paused at the corner and listened as the sound of boots scuffing down the corridor below grew louder and louder. Bodie laid Antigony down on the grating and waited for Blackie's zombie minion to pass by. Then he slipped over the railing. The outlaw looked up just in time to see Bodie's size tens connect with his face.

Bodie hit the ground off-balance because of the way his target crumpled beneath him. He rolled with it, but it was still loud. The man wasn't out, but Bodie drove his knife temple to temple through his head. He wasn't sure how to kill these things and figured that had to be the safest bet. The body flopped and flailed. He struggled against it, trying to minimize the racket, but it was no use. Instead, he withdrew the blade with a foot pressed to the outlaw's head and then removed the head with one surgical slash. The body dropped and lay silent. *Noted.*

"Callahan! Is that you?"

Ugh, not this again. Bodie bounded up the walls to the floor above to collect Antigony, but she was gone.

He searched frantically before remembering to scan with his sensors.

A faint dot was tracing its way back the way they'd come.

"Dammit, what're you doing?" he whispered, dumbfounded. He headed back in that direction but had to pause when another one of the outlaws passed below, presumably looking for his counterpart. Bodie let him pass by and then continued on around the corner where he thought Antigony had gone. He saw her just ahead.

"Tig," he whispered as loudly as he dared, but she didn't respond. She just kept drifting forward. That's when he realized that she wasn't actually walking and her feet weren't touching the ground.

CHAPTER 17

POSSESSION

Bodie circled around in front of Antigony as she floated just above the walkway. Her hands were out and her eyes were closed.

"What in the world ... Tig. You awake? Tig," he said again, a little louder than he wanted to. He waved his hand in front of her face. She didn't respond, so he just grabbed one of her hands and guided her the other direction. She followed, still hovering above the ground a couple of inches, sleepwalking without actually walking.

"This is easier than carrying you, I guess." He didn't want to think on the implications of what was happening to her, that maybe the cut on her leg had something to do with the Rajak and that she had absorbed some bizarre alien powers. Or, something far worse: that she was becoming like the monster itself. There was no telling, but he knew one thing: they had to get out of there and get her some help.

Zilich hurried along the narrows of the secret passage. It was made from an element other than coldbright and it ran from the bridge to his private chambers. Trailing his fingers along the wall as he went, he smiled. Best investment he ever made was this. It'd saved his butt numerous times. Most notably from that damnable Bodura Duc. And now from that meddlesome pilot, the prairie simpleton Justine.

"Thinks she's the captain now, does she?" He chuckled and then his face twisted into a grimace as he fought the tortured muscles and tendons in his leg. A constant reminder of his near-death experience caused by that same Arkhveran marshal that now inhabited the body of one of his sentry bots. Well, he'd have to deal with him, too. And then his expression soured further. And his science officer.

What was Vohl thinking, creating that abomination? The resources needed for reanimation were sizable. And then wasting perfectly good sentry bots, and who knew what else, on piecing that no-good outlaw back together...

He curled his hand into a fist and pounded the scanner that opened the door to his chambers. It would recognize his palm print as well as anything. The door whooshed open and there in the middle of his office was Vohl, digging through books on his desk. *Why, that little worm...*

Vohl spun to face him, eyes bright, a smile on his face. Zilich knew what that meant, by the way, the insult that a smile was in his culture. That smug little imp thought he was so smart.

"Can I help you, Vohl? Or have you already helped yourself?" he asked, looking at his desk to determine what it was that Vohl had been after.

"Um, no. I just thought I'd left something here, but it doesn't look like it. My mistake," he purred. His eyes were bright with mischief.

Zilich scanned the space, looking for anything amiss, and there was a handful of things but nothing that stood out as a likely target of the foul little creature's desires. He limped across the plush textile floor to his desk and sat down in his chair, thankful to be off that leg. He pretended to massage the muscles where his thigh met his knee, all the while grabbing his pistol. He held it pointed at his science officer below the tabletop.

"Seriously, Vohl. What are you doing in my office? What are you looking for that's so important you'd risk your life for it?" he asked as he lifted the weapon into view.

Vohl's eyes went even more round, which Zilich wouldn't have thought possible except for his familiarity with the creature's duplicitous ways. He knew Vohl wasn't surprised. He just hadn't figured out what the angle was yet and was playing along until he could.

"Well, Zilich, I'll come clean," he said, turning, folding his hands behind his back, and pacing casually as he spoke. "I intend to kill you and put your ghostly form into a little box where I can torment you till my heart's content and exploit you for your knowledge and your network of criminal colleagues throughout the galaxy." When he finished, he stopped pacing and smiled again for effect.

Well, *that* was a surprise. He actually believed every word. He just couldn't believe he'd said it.

Zilich pulled the trigger and realized his mistake. The weapon had been fiddled with. A bright flash engulfed him, and that was the last thing he saw.

"Hmm. I always wondered how he did that," Vohl said, looking at the spot where Zilich had just appeared in his office. It was a good thing he'd already sabotaged the pistol he had hidden beneath his desk. What a stroke of luck.

He turned back to see his former employer, head flat on his desk, drooling like an idiot. Ugh, humans were so disgusting... He poofed away to the infirmary and grabbed a floating gurney and guided it out the door and down the hall, back to Zilich's chambers.

Next, he would take him to the laboratory and set up the ritual that would incarcerate his soul in the ghost box. Hopefully, things were progressing well with Blackie and his crew. He needed to get things wrapped up with the intruders and the girl pilot as quickly as possible. Now that Zilich was out of the way, he needed to renegotiate terms with the girl before she got too out of control and decided to do something stupid that could get them all killed. Plus, he needed to get all the remaining monsters rounded up. They played a pivotal role in his plans for his home planet.

His eyes darted back to the gurney. He really couldn't wait to get Zilich tied up and prepared for the ritual. The look in his eyes after he learned what was in store for him would be ... priceless.

Bodie scanned the darkness ahead while pinging his sensors. Blackie's gang still pressed forward in a line ahead of him. He was following at a safe distance, but there were still plenty of other things to be worried about. Foremost among them, the detention area had grown silent. He hoped that meant that all the creatures that had been let out, having had the opportunity to size each other up, had now established some sort of pecking order. Maybe the mayhem would die down. But he was certain that did not mean that the area was, by any stretch of the imagination, safe.

He was thinking this even as a set of eyes in the distance ahead of him glimmered. He stopped in his tracks. Antigony glided to a halt beside him. Still unconscious. Then a growl emanated from further ahead and one or two aisles over. He heard one of Blackie's gang screaming and hollering as something got hold of him. The other outlaws yelled and one or two pulled to assist. Good. Maybe he could use this diversion.

When he turned his attention back to his own path, the glimmering eyes were gone. He didn't like that one bit. He pulled Antigony left down the next available walkway and made his way for a door he hoped he'd be able to access without making too much of a racket. As they crossed the next intersection, he saw that the creature with the glimmering eyes was paralleling their path one aisle up. Bodie's stomach dropped. There went any hope of getting out of here quietly.

As they crossed another intersection, he turned quickly around to go the other way but stopped when he saw another set of eyes down the corridor from which they'd come. *Great. There's more of them.* He pinged his sensors, and judging by the last location of the eyes he'd seen, there were maybe five … creatures? Another set of eyes glimmered near the second pair, and that confirmed it. Bodie flipped through a handful of visual filters trying to find something that could help him gauge what it was that was following him, but none were particularly helpful.

A red filter revealed something interesting. A vapory body coalescing around each set of eyes. He looked down each corridor and there, at the next intersection, was one of these new creatures. They were surrounded. Off in the distance, the growling and screaming continued, only now there were at least three different people involved with whatever it was that was going on. Bodie didn't hear Blackie's voice. He would have been more concerned about that if he didn't have this new dilemma to sort out.

He had no choice but to pick a direction and try to go through whatever it was that was stalking him. "Tig, you ready for this?" he asked, even though he knew she wasn't likely to respond. He was right. He turned and raced for the creature closest to the exit. The creature waited for him. As he drew close, a third eye opened, a muzzle full of gleaming teeth yawned open, and two scythe-like arms stretched wide to either side.

Bodie let go of Antigony's hand as he lurched forward and leaped into a flying sidekick. His boot connected with the creature's face before it had a chance to react. Its face crumpled beneath his foot as he landed on the walkway, but one of the vicious blade-arms caught him in the shoulder. Despite his arm being made of some sort of high-tech alloy, it sliced him as easily as if it were muscle. He cupped the wound as metallic green goo dribbled out.

Antigony came floating toward him at speed. He tried to grab her with his bad arm, but it didn't work and she slammed into him. He stumbled while she pirouetted gracefully on down the hall. "Tig! Wait!" he yell-whispered as she spun away. He bolted after her, still holding his bleeding arm. He hazarded a glance back. The now three-eyed ghostly scythe creatures had converged and were closing in. He poured on the speed, straightened Antigony out, and yanked her around the next corner.

The creatures screeched in discordant harmony as they blew past.

"Boohhh-deeee!" a familiar voice boomed from somewhere ahead and to his left—between him and the door. *Of course.*

"Sheeyit," he cursed as he barged ahead. The phantom choir behind him reoriented themselves and was barreling up from behind. He didn't bother looking back. His sensors told him there were seven now, closing in, and from his right were other signatures, probably Blackie's zombie cyborg minions, and to his left was Blackie himself. This would have been a great time to remember some of that family magick. Maybe how to disappear?

"Woulda been nice," he huffed as he swung Antigony up into the air and slid on his hip as they hit the intersection. Everything converged, cyborgs, scythe ghosts, Blackie... Everything that was except Antigony and Bodie, who skated right through, high and low, like poop through a goose. Screeches, screams, and the clash of contact all erupted as the bodies went flying.

Bodie's boot found purchase as he slid and he popped up, just in time to catch Antigony's hand as she floated down to the ground. He whipped her down the next aisle and there ahead was the door he was looking for.

"Lucky day!" he exclaimed and then immediately wished he hadn't. The massive door split down the middle, and beyond it was a handful of robots escorting a large flatbed transport carrying something that looked like a huge wooly octopus. Or decapus, he surmised when he realized it had ten arms rather than the traditional eight.

The transport slid forward into the doorway and he leaped on top of it, running right over the creature. Antigony followed as easily as if she were actually awake. The creature roared in outrage, but all of its appendages were clamped down to the trolley. The robots scattered as the stragglers from the previous pursuit began to emerge from the darkness. First Blackie, covered in streaks of blood and roaring in rage, then two of the scythe creatures, followed by two of the remaining cyborg outlaw minions.

Blackie leaped up onto the transport and then quickly away as the scythe ghosts slashed through the air where he'd been just fractions of a second before. The blades sliced through a manacle and one of the decapus's tentacles flailed freely, grabbing the three-eyed creature and smashing it into one of the decapus's robot keepers.

As Bodie and Antigony careened up the outer corridor, Blackie smashed into the wall, missing them by only a foot or so. One of the robots tried to stop Blackie, but he grabbed its arm, spun around, and hurled it down the hall. It collided with Bodie, sending him flying through the air, while Antigony just drifted on behind.

Complete chaos ensued around the wooly decapus creature as it began to free itself and other monsters started pouring through the open doors. Plasma rounds from the robots sliced in every direction before they were overwhelmed. Bodie wished he'd grabbed one of those guns. He watched as Blackie charged down the corridor toward him and Antigony floated by. At least she was kind of safe. But if he was going to save her at all, he needed to face the music. It was time to face Blackie. Again.

Bodie stood up just in time for the massive cyborg to smash into him at full speed. The two tumbled through the air. Blackie's teeth sank into Bodie's damaged shoulder, but he'd had his bowie knife ready. It was hilt-deep in the cyborg's abdomen. Blackie roared with rage as he realized the deception. Bodie slammed the pommel with his hand, trying to drive the blade all the way into Blackie's spine but was interrupted by the floor as they hit hard and tumbled.

Blackie rolled to his feet, but one of his legs crumpled beneath him and he dropped to a knee and one hand as he ripped the blade out of his body. He looked up to see Bodie's foot careening into his face. Bodie made perfect contact, but the cyborg was so solid he just bounced off, flying over his head to land in a heap on the other side.

Bodie put his good hand down to push himself up, and the knife pinned it to the ground. Then Blackie's huge fist came down on Bodie's neck, pinning him further.

"Boohh-deee," he exclaimed, relishing in his victory.

"Is that all you know how to say? What have they done to you Blackie?" Bodie asked, his face pressed to the floor.

"Boohh-deee die now," he articulated.

"Oh, well, that's a little better, I guess."

Down the hall behind him, he finally heard Antigony smack into the wall at a T intersection. He winced. That was going to leave a mark.

Blackie drew back his other fist and was about to flatten Bodie's skull when a screech echoed through the hallway and a scorpion-like stinger dented in part of Blackie's head. Bodie could hear the flapping of wings but couldn't see anything until a dragon-like creature slammed into Blackie, talons first, knocking him down the hall, back in the direction of the detention area door where mayhem was still in full bloom.

Blackie roared as the Eerd's Dragon attacked again, slashing his face and chest before flapping away out of reach. Bodie couldn't believe what he was seeing. The very creature that had dragged him off to its lair was defending him now against his attacker. Magnificent creature indeed. *Thank you, Helga.*

Bodie spun on his heels and raced for the end of the hall where Antigony had collided with the wall. She was spinning in lazy, slow-motion circles, her arm and head cast over to the side like a drunken ballerina.

"Poor darling." He pulled her to a stop and gently brushed a strand of black hair away from her ashen face. Her skin was pale but with a dark, almost metallic cast beneath. Her lips, instead of the deep crimson he was used to seeing, were black. He lifted an eyelid to see if her pupil would react to the light and was shocked to find her irises were a vibrant green and her pupils were slit, just like the Rajak's own.

He sighed deeply. "Beautiful Tig, what're we gonna do now?"

"You called me beautiful," she murmured and her lips swept into a soft smirk, but she didn't wake further. Bodie just looked at her, eyes wide, speechless.

Behind him, the shouts and shrieks continued but were growing rather than lessening in intensity. He turned and saw why. The decapus was free, its tentacles thrashing and dragging its body along the too-tight corridor. Robots and other creatures were fleeing in front of it and they were all heading their way.

In the foreground, Blackie and the Eerd's Dragon were still going at it. Blackie looked bad. He was bleeding and limping, but the Dragon swooped in close and Blackie caught it with a backhand, sending it cartwheeling into a wall. As it hit, it disappeared from sight. Blackie lunged and slammed the spot with his fists, but nothing appeared to be there. The Dragon had escaped, which Bodie was happy about, in a very mixed sort of way.

He pulled Antigony along with him around the corner before Blackie saw them. He'd have to deal with him another time. And the creatures escaping the containment? He just hoped they could capture Zilich and Vohl before the ship took too much damage or they were all overcome by the ferocious and completely terrifying assortment of creatures.

They worked their way toward the bridge but were forced to take an alternate route when they turned a corner and saw a cluster of sentry bots headed their way. Bodie had thought they were all wiped out, but there were apparently still more. Or maybe these ones had finally been repaired. Who knew?

A long hallway brought them to a door. He opened it and was buffeted by a gust of wind. Beyond was a large section of the ship that laid open to the elements. The superstructure of the vessel extended outward in chunks with skeletal cross members filling in the gaps like webbing. Silver tendrils of coldbright extended from the broad valley floor hundreds or maybe thousands of feet below. The filaments were filling in gaps in the external sheeting, extending structural elements, and generally mending what was missing. The opening was still ten or eleven stories tall and equally wide. There were tons and tons of material still needed to fully repair the ship.

Bodie was about to turn around and go back the way they'd come when he heard someone coming down the corridor. He thought better of it and closed the door. Besides, what better way to make their way up a couple of floors without having to risk being found by sentry bots or monsters or Blackie himself? Heck, maybe they could make their way all the way to the bridge. It was nearly straight up from where they were now.

He looked around for something to jam the door with but found nothing that could work on a sliding door. Instead, he smashed the access pad with his fist. Hopefully, that'd do the trick. He had to admit; he was missing Helga and Dmitr's constant companionship right about now. Even if it'd been all in his head. And with Antigony quiet, which ironically was something he'd quite literally prayed for on several occasions, he was feeling more alone than ever. But he owed it to her to find a way to fix whatever was going on with her.

The only way he saw that happening was through the help of Zilich or his scientist, Vohl.

He wanted nothing to do with either of them. He just could not see any other way. Justine wanted Zilich's head on a pike, but the man, crafty as always, had disappeared. Bodie knew he needed Justine's help to get Zilich or Vohl to play along. Plus, there was something else that Justine wasn't telling him. He'd kept his mouth shut at the time, but he was good at reading people. And, as astonished as he was to see this radical change in appearance and personality, he had still caught the slightest hesitation in her voice. Her sudden altruism, returning the creatures to their homes, seemed, maybe, not false, but definitely incomplete.

What could Justine want if it wasn't just Zilich executed for his crimes? She'd said she needed Vohl alive. That was the clue.

Bodie pulled Antigony to him. He removed one of her bandoleers, bound her wrists together with it, and slipped her arms over his head. This way, she could just float along behind him as he climbed. Seemed like it ought to work.

He'd just made it to the nearest wall to begin his climb when he heard pounding at the door.

"Oh no, better get moving."

He started climbing but was slowed by his damaged arm. The wound he'd received from that first scythe ghost earlier had healed some but was far from 100 percent. Still, he pressed on, regardless of the pounding. By the time he'd reached the third level, the door buckled inward and flew off, out over the edge.

Bodie looked down to see Blackie's silhouette in the ravaged door frame. "Doesn't this guy ever give up?"

he mumbled to himself, confident that he couldn't hear him with the rushing wind all around. Still, he shifted a little to the left to get out of Blackie's line of sight. His foot slipped and he and Antigony swung wide like a barn door before swinging back where he could catch hold again. He shot a desperate glance down. Blackie hadn't heard or seen a thing. He breathed a sigh of relief.

He watched quietly as the bruised and bloodied cyborg limped out to the edge of the construction. If ever there was a chance to end this, the time was now.

Dammit. He pulled Antigony's arms from over his shoulders and leaned her up against the wall. She was going to float away if he left her here. Sun was pouring through a hole in the siding here. He took the other bandoleer and looked for something to tie her off to, but there was nothing this far in. He didn't want to get any closer to the leading edge, but that was where the only exposed structure was.

Again, dammit. Bodie scooted the two of them along, trying to avoid the open sections so as not to cast a shadow below, and finally got to a spot that wasn't too exposed to the elements and still had rough structural members to tie off to. He looked over his shoulder. Blackie was still down there, but now he was joined by someone else. It was the black, imp-like creature from earlier that morning. That must be the science officer Justine was talking about. Vohl. He was the one who resurrected Blackie and made him into a monster. He was also the one that Justine needed alive for some reason.

Bodie suddenly had a terrible feeling that maybe Justine wanted him to bring back her parents. Had she seen Blackie? Did she have any idea what kind of butcher this twisted little creature was? That reminded him of his own needs. To reverse whatever it was that was happening to Antigony. He looked over at her and saw that the sunlight had cast across her arm and it was beginning to blister and blacken. She turned her head fitfully, mumbling something unintelligible, and then Bodie watched in slow-motion as her eyes flashed open, the catlike irises blazing green, and then they rolled back.

"Oh, sh—"

A shriek so loud it hurt his auditory circuits burst forth as a beam of light shot out of her mouth. He dove to the side. Large sections of the reconstructed ship wall across from them burst into molten metal as the light swept across it. Down on the lower level, Blackie and Vohl spun to see what all the racket was. Then they spotted Bodie just yards away.

"Booohhh-deee!" Blackie growled lustfully and bounded toward the wall beneath him. Vohl smiled a nervous smile and reached out a hand toward where Antigony was still tied to the structure. Bodie lunged forward to help her and she hissed at him with bared teeth. Not-yet-pointy teeth, but it was terrifying just the same. He backpedaled, not sure what to do, when Blackie appeared over the edge of the floor, grabbed his ankle, and whipped him over the edge.

He tumbled end for end and hit the deck a few feet from where Vohl was standing. Bodie looked up at the vile little creature that stared down at him, amused, but then Bodie saw Blackie hurtling down to land on top of him. He rolled away at the last second.

Antigony shrieked again and sliced through her bonds with the blinding light before leaping into the air. She shot a beam of light at Blackie, who roared and leaped away to find cover. Vohl stood his ground, reaching out again toward Antigony. She thrashed in pain as if she'd been stabbed. Bodie saw the Nawri twist his hand and watched Antigony writhe in response. He swept a foot out, knocking Vohl from his feet. Vohl hit his back hard and seemed stunned.

Antigony recovered and shot a beam of light at the imp, which began to sizzle his already black skin. Bodie ripped the little creature out of the blinding beam. He couldn't let her kill him. They needed him to fix her. Or at least help them figure out how. Bodie grabbed him by the neck and pulled the evil little scientist up to eye level.

"You're going to tell me how to fix her."

A beam of light whooshed by and stopped a foot or two away. Did she know what she was doing? He wasn't sure. He moved Vohl closer to the deadly beam. The Nawri clawed and scrambled, trying to get away.

"Okay. Okay!" he cried and Bodie pulled him away. But then, as he did, the creature smiled and poofed into nothingness. Bodie looked at his hands in disbelief, and then from behind him, there was a loud roar. Bodie turned to see Blackie launch a large crate at Antigony. She turned in time to take the full force of it. Her body flew away from the impact, tumbling end over end out into the open air.

"Nooo!!!" Bodie cried and, without a thought, ran and launched himself out into the void after her.

CHAPTER 18

THE DARK WITHIN
THE DARKNESS

Justine entered the bridge. There was no one there but her two mercurial minions.

"What did you find?"

They shook their heads. Justine massaged her temples. "Want something done, do it yourself," she paused, tilting her head. "Or get an AI supercomputer to do it. Artis?"

"Yes, Captain Sever?" Artis's warm, professional voice filled the large room.

"Show me a map of this ship ... but highlight the areas that are *not* made of coldbright. Start with this room."

A 3D schematic blossomed into view on the wall of screens. Plain as day, a channel bisected the bridge and exited toward the back wall. It was right beneath her feet.

"Zilich, you sneaky son of a goat. Artis, expand."

The schematic expanded until it was obvious that a secret passageway led directly to the captain's own chambers. Her chambers now. But no doubt, the escape route Zilich had taken. Now, how to open it?

The coldbright throne unraveled from around her and she slid gently to her feet. The tendrils splayed out and then drove down, ripping huge, ragged holes in the floor and peeling back the metal to expose the narrow staircase beneath.

"That'll do."

She floated down the steps with her silver tendrils trailing behind. Within minutes, she was faced with a door. She placed her palm on the access panel, and even though she'd had Artis key all the encryptions to her own biometrics—she'd learned quite a bit from the coldbright in her short amount of time onboard—the access panel failed to open.

She huffed out a breath and then drove the coldbright tendrils through the door, blowing it off its track entirely. Stepping through the ravaged frame, she glanced over the space. The well-appointed room and adjacent office were empty. There was debris everywhere on the floor, which was regrettable, but there were no clues as to where Zilich might be that she could see. At least nothing as interesting as the pistol lying on the desk. It was partly obliterated, which looked a lot like sabotage to Justine.

"Who would have done such a thing?" That creepy little creature that was making all the zombie cyborgs seemed like a likely suspect.

"Artis, where can I find Vohl?"

"Moments ago he was in the construction area at the fore end of the ship, but he's disappeared. As he has appeared nowhere else, I would assume he's either exited the Ars Arcanum or gone back to his lab."

"That's what I figured."

The wind whipped past Bodie's face. He scanned the broad panorama below him for Antigony. It felt like an eternity as he searched for her with the knowledge that the ground was rushing up to meet them at 3.8 meters per second. But, after a moment, his finely tuned tracking and acquisition faculties pulled through and her diminutive form rose from the background.

He tipped himself her way and instantly began tumbling end over end. Instinctively, he put his arms and legs out in a spread eagle and his fall stabilized. The ground was beginning to coalesce into fine detail. He didn't waste time gauging the distance but reacquired Antigony's position and, carefully this time, tipped toward her.

It was working. He was moving toward her faster and faster and had to rear back and extend his arms and legs fully to slow down, which caused her to whisk away.

Damn, this was tough. He tried again and this time had to just go for it. They connected, and he pulled her in close. Her eyes fluttered open and then closed again. She buried her head in his chest. This was how they were going to die.

Something bright caught his attention. A shimmering vertical filament like a lone strand from a shiny metal spider's web lay a couple hundred yards away. Maybe...

He tipped them both in that direction and, after a moment, snatched the coldbright strand. It flew through his hand, but he gripped it hard as they swung around. His hand began to glow red-hot. He kept on the pressure, slowing them as much. The ground rushed up fast, and he was just able to pinpoint the mining shack on the hillside before they crashed through the roof, with Bodie taking the brunt of the impact with his body.

<001020xx1213?a00…001020xx1213?a00x110100… 001020xx121_a00x110100xxbxx01111>

The familiar hexadecimal sequence scrolled across Bodie's ocular circuits, but there was no status provided by his lower-level OS. There was only silence. And darkness.

Above him, shattered timbers revealed a ceiling and beyond that another ceiling, or roof perhaps, for beyond that were the first stars of the evening surrounded by a lavender sky fading into a deeper black.

He was lying on bare rock and clay. It was cool and smelled of earth. A scent that was surprisingly strong after the time spent on Zilich's ship. He searched the small space and found Antigony hovering in repose a few feet away, mumbling fitfully. A thermal scan revealed that she was cold, yet somehow covered in fever sweat. He was just thankful that she was alive, though, considering that she'd been infected by some kind of space mummy vampire thing, he might have to broaden his definition of the term.

A low growl emanated from the darkness beyond her, and Bodie was suddenly aware of a set of yellow eyes. Hands flashed to torso and hip, but neither his gun nor his bowie knife were there. The growl deepened as a large black wolf stepped forward, baring its teeth. Bodie slowly rolled from his seated position into a low crouch, expecting the creature to lunge at any second. But then, once the wolf had placed itself between Bodie and Antigony its body shifted into that of something decidedly more human-like.

It still had black fur covering its body, and its facial features were still vaguely canine, but it was definitely more like a man.

"Hello," the creature said in a rasp that started to smooth a little as it continued, "I am Jef."

Bodie was speechless.

"J-Jef?" he stuttered.

"Y-Yeah," the creature mocked back in a near-exact replication of Bodie's own voice.

"What are you?" Bodie asked, truly dumbfounded.

"I am Jef." The creature shrugged. "A traveler. An observer. And, rarely, an actor. But not in the sense that you human types refer to actors, but in the sense that sometimes certain situations require action. But mostly I try to stay out of things."

"Us human types? So, you're aware that I'm not entirely a robot?"

Jef shot Bodie a look. "Well, duh. Any other mind-blowing insights Prince Marshal Bodura Duc?" Bodie again was speechless. "Listen, I haven't got all day to chat," Jef continued. "I really just came to see for myself the state of Ms. Von Riche."

"Really? Why?"

Jef scrutinized Bodie as if weighing whether or not telling him would be revealing some big, galaxy-shattering secret. "Well, I knew her grandmother. Sweetest gypsy lady. She'd con the fur off your back if you weren't paying attention, but, you know, good people."

"You'll have to forgive me, but did you just say you knew her grandmother? Aren't you one of Zilich's monsters?" Bodie asked.

"Eh," he tilted his head side to side, "in as much as it was convenient. I said before that I'm a traveler. I visit exciting places. Someone rounds up all the galaxy's most horrific creatures into one place, there's bound to be some excitement." He smiled a toothy smile and then settled down into a squatting position, where he pushed around a rock with a clawed finger.

Bodie was still struggling to catch up. "So, you knew Antigony's grandmother?"

Jef looked up and nodded. "Yup. We had a bet."

"A bet?"

"Are you going to just keep repeating what I say or…"

"Yes, well, no. I just… I'm having a hard time following all of this. You're from someplace else. You were captured by Zilich, but kind of on purpose, yet you can travel about freely. And, you knew Antigony's grandmother with whom you have a bet? What kind of bet?"

"Well, Madame Zondra Von Riche—a beautiful lady, by the way, much like her daughter—was also quite gifted with precognition. She told me once that her granddaughter would fall out of the sky and become a god. Naturally, I scoffed at this. But…" he said, nodding in the direction of the woman floating in the corner of the room.

"Wait, what're you saying? What do you mean, God?"

"No, not God with a big G, but god, like deity. Like, you know, something a little more local." Bodie shook his head in bewilderment as Jef continued. "Well, even then, this is more of a win on a technicality since it's only the Kholh'teps people that call the Rajak a deity.

And half of the lore suggests he was really just a king with some wildly fanatical followers. The stories say it took 10,000 souls to bring him back from the dead! I doubt even one of those people was remotely willing to be a part of the whole thing. Bunch of sickos really if you ask me," Jef said, grimacing.

"Wait, so the Rajak is really just some dude that killed a bunch of folks as part of a magick spell?"

"Yeah, something like that."

"So does that mean that what's happening to Antigony can be reversed?"

Jef grimaced again. "Oooh, I dunno. That's some pretty big magick."

"Then what are you doing here? Just observing?"

It was Jef's turn to be quiet for a moment. "Ya know, ya got me there Bodie. I did want to check in on Zondra's progeny. Turns out, I owe her money. Course, she's been dead for nearly twenty years now, but... Oooh! I know..."

He produced a pale coin and flipped it through the air at Bodie. "Give this to Ms. Von Riche, will you?"

Bodie tried to catch it but realized his hand was still melted together and non-functional. The coin bounced off it and hit the ground. It spun on the ground, and rather than coming to rest after gravity and friction dragged it down, it just continued to spin.

He looked up to question Jef, but the wolfman, who referred to himself simply as a traveler, was preoccupied, sniffing the air.

"You smell that?" His eyes narrowed.

Bodie sniffed the air in the way that he could, which was to draw a sample of ambient air across wafers of substrate located within his olfactory sensory array. He did smell *something,* but he couldn't quite place it.

"Anyway, as I was saying," Jef continued with a puzzled grimace and rubbing his ear distractedly, "I really try to stay out of things, but this particular plane of existence is ... peculiar. Discordant."

"Once again, Mr. Jef, I'm at a loss. Discordant? Planes of existence?"

Jef looked at him. "You don't know any of this?"

Bodie shook his head. "Look, my," he looked at Antigony floating in the air just a few feet away, "friend is maybe a god. I only just found out I was something other than a robot. We just fell out of a spaceship. And I'm talking to a monster. No offense."

Jef shrugged. "Lotta people say that. It hurts, ya know?"

"Really?"

"No. I'm a super cool, interdimensional traveler. I see things that no one else gets to see. I mean, the cosmos ... it's a symphony, man. That's what I was saying about this plane. It's out of sync, or maybe not that. It's just out of harmony, but maybe not even in a bad way. I just can't tell."

"What do you mean, the universe is a symphony?"

"Yeah, well, God is the only one that can experience the whole thing. It must be ... I don't know. I don't think anyone but God could understand it, but me? I get to see parts, get to experience this one little piece here, that other piece there, and over time, I can piece it together, some small part anyway. It's brilliant."

"But you're saying there's something wrong with our bit?"

"Yes. And no. It's just different. It doesn't fit, but I know it has to fit, so I'm just not hearing the whole thing. These planes, they're the same but different in ways. Like, you exist over and over and over, but in each dimension, there're subtle differences. They diverge and come back together again ... a harmony. But this one is," he shook his head in apparent wonderment, "off."

"I exist in other planes?"

"Well, of course, you do. You have a very big role to play." Jef's eyebrows shot up and he covered his mouth. "You don't know. Do you?"

"Know what?" Bodie asked, his eyes narrowing.

"Well. I ... I ... don't really like to get involved in things, I just ... observe. It's not really my place ... but maybe ... maybe that's what's different. What's wrong?"

"Now you're just speaking gibberish."

"No. Maybe that's it. Vohl. He doesn't factor much in the other planes, so I haven't given him much thought, but here... I told you the planes diverge and intersect, the histories and activities, ultimately they shadow each other. They're all part of the same song but this one is so... I mean there's you and the fact that you don't have any idea what your true role is going to be, but then Vohl, there's an ... energy, a deep, resonant malevolence... Maybe—"

He stopped mid-sentence and shot a glance over his shoulder. A low growl emanated from his throat. "Back in a minute," he said, his voice cold and full of violence. And then he stepped back into the darkness, his form shifting into something from a gothic novel even as he faded into black.

Bodie stood alone, surrounded by silence. The sky, visible through the hole in the floor and roof above, was deep violet. The stars ... brilliant. He heaved a sigh and rubbed his head, realizing he'd lost his hat. Again. No gun. No knife. No hat. No *horse*.

His gaze flitted across the rock-hewn room. Antigony, still floating in the corner, tossed weakly. Her condition was getting worse, he could tell. He wondered if it had to do with how much time had passed since her infection or if there was something to do with proximity to the Rajak. When he'd found her, she was floating back toward its containment. On the ship, when exposed to sunlight, she'd awoken and brandished some of the power of the Rajak itself. Now? She looked small and weak.

He just wanted to take her and run away somewhere safe. Forget the whole thing, but in his gut, he knew he needed to get back up to the ship and see this thing through. Not at the *expense* of everything he held dear, but this time, in order to save it.

What had she said earlier? We all make mistakes, but we can't let ourselves be defined by them? Yeah...

He was just beginning to realize that as crazy as Antigony was, he found a certain kind of peace in her presence. He took strength in that.

He needed to do this for Antigony. And maybe, in spite of everything that made sense, for a chance at something more. He looked at her pale skin and black lips and then at his own malformed robotic hand. His self-healing circuits weren't making much headway on repairing the damage. It would be better if it was just a clean break.

Bodie realized Jef had not returned. How long was a minute to a creature that could walk the space between planes and sample the symphony that was the multiverse? Surely, nothing could have happened to him. Could it?

Then a flash lit up the interior of the shack above. The light was from outside. A second later, a low boom shook dust from the rafters and rocks.

"What was that?" Bodie asked in surprise before he realized it could only be one thing: the Ars Arcanum. Either Justine had gone ballistic or the monsters were running amok. Or both.

Jef appeared from the darkness. "We have a problem."

"I know. That was the ship, wasn't it?"

"No. I mean, yes. That was the ship, but the problem… It's much, much worse."

CHAPTER 19
GHOSTS OF THE AGES

Vohl's eyes could barely see over the edge of the table supporting a box that was roughly the size of an android's head. It was black wood or stone, much like the Rajak's sarcophagus, he thought. It was covered similarly in archaic scrollwork. The ghost box. It was a thing of dark beauty. And soon it would be Zilich's prison.

The hair stood up on Vohl's arms and he had to repress the urge to purr, a despicable behavior and way below his class. With the power of the box, he would return to his home, enslave his detractors, and take his rightful place in the galaxy.

Muffled fits of rage came from somewhere off to his right and he smiled and closed his eyes. Listening to the screams as if they were a soothing lullaby.

"I'm sorry, Zilich, but you'll have to speak up. I can't quite hear you," he said over his shoulder while staring at the box in fascination once more.

It was like it called to him. It's beauty. It's power. He had his sacrifice, now all he had to do was finish deciphering the last bits of glyph. His smile melted into a frown. That was the damning part. He had no idea what they meant. What he'd deciphered so far referred to something he'd never heard of. None of the pixies had any clue either. He was certain of that. He had extracted a heavy toll in his pursuit of the magickal knowledge required. Greater than any of them were able to bear. But science required sacrifice.

Zilich shouted into his gag, thrashing against his bonds. Vohl knew that would only draw them tighter. The pain would be intense. The faintest hint of a smile crossed his lips. He brushed the glyphs on the box's surface with his hand, and a faint luminescence lingered. His eyebrows raised. The box seemed to enjoy the suffering of his guest nearly as much as he did. Interesting...

Vohl reached out, his hand gripping something invisible, and gave it a slight squeeze. Zilich bucked and thrashed, his screaming redoubled. The glyphs glowed more brightly and then faded. Vohl's smile broadened. This was immensely pleasurable, but still, he knew that the box needed to be opened in order for it to consume a soul. There was something missing, and he didn't know how to get it.

He drummed his fingers on the tabletop as he thought but was ripped from his musings as the ship lurched beneath him, causing him to stumble to his left to regain his footing. The creatures. They were wreaking havoc on the vast ship already. He was running out of time to commit Zilich to the box. Soon they would be everywhere and the ship itself could be harmed.

And then there was the girl. He would deal with her when he had the chance. He needed her alive, after all, and that wasn't really his strong suit.

A faint jingling danced on the air. His ears perked up. "Ooh, how fortuitous."

One of his traps had been triggered. One of the traps he'd laid for the shapeshifter. *He* could unlock the box. If anyone could, it would be the traveler known as Jef. Vohl walked over to Zilich. The man's face was bloodied and swollen; one eye was closed completely. Vohl had not treated him kindly. He patted his face, and the man recoiled.

"Be right back, old friend," Vohl rasped before he vanished into a faint smudge of sulphury smoke.

"Whadya mean?" Bodie drawled out slowly, eyes squinted as he struggled to understand what the skin-walker was trying to communicate.

"I mean that the ship blowing up is bad, but Vohl? He is part of this cosmic discordance. And so are you."

"But how?" Bodie asked, massaging his forehead and trying not to wonder whether or not he'd ever find his beloved Batterson.

"I don't know precisely. It's up to you to find out through action and decision-making. I'm just an observer. I have too much knowledge to participate directly. I would simply create the simplest solution. But what's going on here is ... beautiful, I just can't see it yet," Jef said, staring dreamily off into the darkness of the hewn rock shaft beyond.

"You make less and less sense the more I talk to you."

Jef simply nodded in agreement, his stare never wavering until something caused him to bristle.

Bodie felt it, too. They were not alone. The faint smell of sulfur tickled his senses.

"My, how you keep popping up," said Vohl in his breathy, child's voice from high up in the corner of the room.

Jef uttered a low, dangerous growl and shifted into his wolf-like form when Vohl's hand shot out and gripped the air. The skinwalker stiffened and let out a strangled whimper. The small black imp floated down slowly. Jef was frozen in pain. Bodie stepped in between them.

"Why are you doing this? What has he done to you?"

"You mean what *can* he do *for* me? Much. So, very much."

Bodie pivoted into a fighting stance.

"Don't worry, robot. You'll get your chance," the imp promised.

Then a groan issued from the far side of the room and Vohl's attention shot in Antigony's direction. "Ooh, what's this? A pretty, pretty plaything! This the Rajak's doing, yes?" His eyes lit with intrigue.

Bodie was silent. He didn't want to give the creature anything to work with. Jef's whimper turned into a weak growl. "What's that? You have something to say, traveler? Good. We have much to talk about."

Jef growled deeper and Vohl's hand clenched harder, cutting the growl into a sputtering cough.

Bodie couldn't stand it any longer. He lunged to the side and leaped off the rock wall in a spinning round-house kick that should have split the Vohl's skull, except it was no longer there. Instead, Bodie cartwheeled uselessly through the air and hit the ground gracelessly.

He didn't wait to let his circuits settle but managed to roll to his feet. But then Jef was there. His posture stiff, teeth gritted in pain, he swiped a clawed hand, knocking Bodie across the room and into the rocks. It took a moment for Bodie to clear his head and realize that Jef must have been coerced in some way by Vohl to attack him.

"Good fun, wouldn't you say, robot?" Vohl crooned.

Bodie darted a glance in the creature's direction as Jef charged forward, clumsily slashing at him. His teeth ground as he struggled against Vohl's control, but there seemed to be nothing he could do. Bodie leaped back and stumbled into the adjoining tunnel. It was narrow, with little room to maneuver. A quick scan told him it only extended a few yards before opening to a shaft. He hoped it wasn't deep.

"Goodbye. It's been ... entertaining at least," Vohl said with a shrug. Bodie had nowhere to go as Jef approached. The last thing he wanted to do was hurt the skinwalker, who was the only other person he'd met recently that wasn't trying to kill him ... until now at least. Bodie struggled to find another way, but then Jef drew back and slashed. Bodie caught his wrist and Jef roared in fury or frustration, Bodie couldn't tell which, but then Vohl's influence took over and the skinwalker wrenched his arm free and thrust forward with a vicious kick.

Bodie flew back and ground to a halt at the edge of the pit. His heels hung over the edge, arms windmilling to regain balance, when Jef lunged forward again, this time with an arm outstretched to help. But then he convulsed in pain and yelped as he clutched his chest, his face a mask of agony. Their fingertips brushed, but then Bodie tumbled back into the darkness, toppling end over end before colliding with water and rubble below.

The impact was hard. His system struggled but didn't quite have to power cycle. He wished it had. Jef's agonized cries echoed off the rock walls from above. Vohl questioned him about some sort of device—something he called a ghost box. Jef was adamant that he would not provide what he wanted, but only for a while. In the end, the skinwalker caved. After the anguish of what he'd been subjected to, Bodie couldn't blame him. Not one bit.

Then there was silence. Bodie's sensors showed only two bodies in the chamber up above. One was barely there, which he assumed to be Antigony. He took that to mean that the skinwalker had perished. Too bad. Then the remaining signatures disappeared. His shoulders slumped.

"Tig..." he whispered plaintively before rolling over onto his back and looking up into the darkness above. The barest flicker of light preceded another dull boom that emanated through the rock.

He didn't know exactly where Vohl and Antigony had gone, but he could guess. Somewhere aboard a monster-infested ship that was slowly being torn apart from the inside out and that would most likely end up worse off than he'd left it nearly a dozen years prior. Right now, he needed to rescue Tig. And Vohl...? He needed to die.

Bodie lay there in the dark for a while, listening to the water trickling down the walls into the murky pool that he was lying half in and half out of on a low pile of cast-off rubble. He wasn't basking in the pathetic as it would probably appear. Well, maybe he was a little, but mostly he was thinking. Thinking about how things had come to this. Thinking about what he could even do about it.

The honest answer was not much. Since this whole thing began, he'd succeeded at very little. Now he needed to figure out how to get back up to the ship.

"No idea how I'm going to do that. Sprout wings and fly maybe?" he mused bitterly.

Bodie lay there quietly, dipping into a semi-meditative state. Seeking a place inside himself where answers to the hard questions that faced him might be somewhat less elusive. The space felt lonely without Helga and Dmitr, even if they were just the constructs of a shattered mind and a guilty conscience.

Water trickled. From far above, he heard metal sheeting creaking in the wind and the wood structure groaned. Crickets made cricket noises. He searched his memory banks for just what that sound was called and missed Helga's thoughts layered in with his own even more. His idiotically single-minded focus had gotten them all killed and here he was, still trying to complete that mission. The only difference now was that it was no longer about pride.

Ouch. He realized that's what it had always been about. Zilich had made him look the fool. The Prince Marshal of Arkhver ... unable to catch a lowly smuggler.

Trill. That's what crickets did.

Well, not giving up. That's what Bodie did. Even when it wasn't the best course of action. And despite everything, he was still alive, and he was still on Zilich's trail. He only lost now if he gave up. The loss of his friends and crew was only meaningless if he gave up. And now … he had more to lose, maybe even more than before. Antigony was, well, maybe not a *helpless* victim, but a victim just the same. And while he may not be able to do anything to save her from the Rajak's thrall, he could at least keep her from being some kind of lab experiment for that sadist Vohl.

And Justine? Well, maybe she could find her way back to something good and wholesome, like the girl he'd met who had entrusted him with her biology experiment.

His mind went back to her tearing him limb from limb with her coldbright tendrils and scattering the remains throughout the carnage of the warehouse in a completely coherent rage. Maybe that was a big ask, but you just never knew.

Bodie listened again for the trill of the crickets and instead heard the digital slithering sound of the coldbright. This must have been a significant deposit for so much of it to have been left over. He checked his sensors again and realized that his ability to hear it through the rocks and soil was not something provided to him through the suite of sensors that came with this particular type of robot body.

"Wait … that doesn't make any sense at all," he mumbled, trying to sort through the fog of disparate facts.

He remembered how he'd been aware that Justine only had a little magick. Of course, he'd been quite wrong about that, but he'd had an awareness of it. She must have suppressed it somehow, because he could definitely feel it now when she was near.

Bodie paused as the realization settled in. What was it, then? His own inherent magickal ability that gave him access to that information?

"That's the only thing that makes any sense. The Mana Noostra."

The family magick. He searched his processors. Why couldn't he remember more about it? He palmed the side of his head a couple of times as if that'd knock something loose.

Oddly, other memories bubbled into his mind.

He remembered it being monsoon season, and they were barricaded deep down inside the palace keep while the flood waters rose and rose. He'd ditched his studies to sneak down to the armory. Dmitr was there. Years his elder, he recalled now. A hollowness grew inside his chest. Of course Dmitr was there. He was always there. He didn't agree to Bodie's course of action in chasing down the smuggler Zilich, but he was loyal to the end. And always up for a good fight. Had he known how it would turn out?

Bodie turned his attention to other memories. He may have shirked some of his magickal studies, but it didn't change what he was born with. The birthright of the Arkhveran governing family. He listened to the grating of coldbright as it slid through rock, bubbling to the surface before lifting up into the air in gossamer strands, straining toward the Ars Arcanum.

"At least the ship will be easy to find."

As if on cue, another dim flash was followed by a dull boom several seconds later. Roughly seven miles away by his count. Could he ride one of those strands right up to the ship? He looked down at the deformed glob of metal that was his right hand. That would not do.

Bodie levered himself up and rolled into a seated position. He looked around the rock walls of the shaft. A lift mechanism against the wall was erected to shuttle ore from this level all the way up to the top. A quick scan told him how to proceed.

He loaded the bucket with rocks, clumsily ratcheted it up a dozen feet overhead with his good hand, then shoved his damaged hand through the support works. He paused, took a calming breath, and kicked the failsafe bar until it snapped. The loaded ore bucket crashed down, shearing his hand free at the wrist.

He pulled the stump up to his face to take a closer look. Hydraulic fluid gushed out while random sparks illuminated the glistening rock walls before his systems took over and shunted supply to the missing appendage.

He expected it to hurt, but it didn't. That was just his human self at war with this robot body.

Well, maybe now he could do that trick again with the coldbright. Before, on the plateau, it had happened so naturally. He didn't even realize that it was he who had healed his broken foot and punctured torso. And after Klamath had shot him and fractured his skull, he'd done that as well. Or something inside him had done it.

Bodie called to the strand with his mind, reciting ancient words remembered from children's lullabies.

"Llew-Enall-Hal-Um
Tsi-To-Enak...
Ver-Un-Oh..."

He whispered it softly, closing his eyes and straining to recall the last line.

"Se Kip-So Vernaim... Yeah, that's it.

"Llew-Enall-Hal-Um,
Tsi-To-Enab
Jep-So Kip,
Kip-So Vernai-Im"

He remembered it more and more. The magick, his birthright, ignored but not completely forgotten. At least not anymore. An image sprang to mind of his mother standing in the doorway, nodding along with the melody while his nanny sang in soft but crystalline vibrato as the magick wove itself between the notes.

"Llew-Enall...

"It's a haiku!" he exclaimed, shaking his head in disbelief. "Not a 5-7-5 meter, but 5-4-3-5. Same thing. Basically..." He tapped his temple with the metallic forefinger of his remaining hand. The realization dislodged something else in his memory. This song, the one he was remembering now, was a minor spell of calling.

He closed his eyes and just let it all soak in as he repeated it in his mind. The cool of the mine shaft, the sky above through the broken floor and ceiling. The empty desolation of the Alta Estranyazie. The call of the metal. He let all those things seep into his being as he called back. And, in the absence of its master, namely Justine, it came.

"How did I do this before without casting?" he wondered aloud, but no good answer presented itself. Maybe it was the haiku he composed after leaving Justine's family's cabin. Maybe it was the vast lonesomeness of the Alta Estranyazie mixed with his desperation to find the Severs before something bad happened. Maybe there was a lot more to magick than he realized as a bored young man growing up in the palace keep of Arkhver. There was a link between suffering and magic. He remembered as much. Maybe in his posh existence as a child of the king, he didn't have much use for a magick system that ran on discomfort.

Nine of sixteen genetic subvariants of the king and his consorts. Bodie Nine. His hand returned to his brow to massage his temple. His subconscious self had been leaving breadcrumbs back to sanity all this time.

A subtle background noise rose in his auditory circuits. The digital slithering noise grew into a rush. Then it continued to build, the din of it, the flood of it. The sound filled the chamber. It came on like a king tide. Like a storm surge. And then it was on him, gobs of quicksilver, lapping and crashing in waves.

In the moment, his human self struggled to breathe. He couldn't think. He was slammed to the ground again, but then, without being quite sure how, he was suspended above it ... by the coldbright, much like Justine had been when the tendrils emanated from her.

This was similar but to a lesser degree. Not the radiant, goddess-of-death form that she assumed when she was in full bloodshed-and-violence mode. But, something like it, just a bit more modest.

He looked around, eyes wide. At the time, the magick of his childhood seemed a trifle. But this?

"This'll do," he said as the lights of his indicator panel spread into an amused smirk.

Bodie concentrated and pulled the undulating set of tendrils in toward himself as his sense of propriety took over. He consolidated the mass of it all onto his frame. There was maybe a way he could pack it on and not look like he was hulking with coldbright-enhanced muscle. That'd be prudent.

He wasn't certain, but it seemed better to play his cards close to his chest for this final encounter. Whether it was going to be with Zilich, Vohl, Blackie, Klamath, or even Justine, he wasn't sure. Maybe all of them at once. And then, there was still the Rajak to contend with.

There's no good way this is gonna end, he thought, shaking his head. He stared at the stump where his hand had been. It was dark with oil and gritty mud. He willed the coldbright into shape. At first, five hair-thin strands eeked out of the wound, forming a wire skeleton of a hand. But then more and more of the strands followed, building on the anatomical framework until, within a minute of its beginning, a fully formed hand sat where once there was nothing. He wiggled the fingers, inspected them thoughtfully, and then clenched them into a fist.

Light rent the clouds from one end of the sky to the other.

2.178 seconds later, a concussion wave swatted Bodie to the ground like a troublesome horsefly. He pressed up off the sandy trail and dusted himself off just as the thunder from the explosion boomed, echoing off hillsides and canyon walls. Streamers of dirt poured down the walls of the dry river gully he'd been walking along.

"How much more can that ship take?" he wondered aloud.

Seemingly in response, the Ars Arcanum canted sideways and began to spin slowly. It wasn't immediately obvious, but his robot senses told him that it was losing elevation.

"Shouldn't have asked."

Bodie had traveled a day and a night to catch up with the fractured and billowing derelict. It'd gone south, which was refreshing for a change. It was also quite clear that if Justine was piloting the ship, it was only just. Things were quite clearly, *not* in shipshape.

He couldn't imagine the chaos that must be going on inside with the once-captive monsters taking over. Ghosts, ghouls, vampires, mummies. Ghost-ghoul-vampire-mummies ... from outer space. And who knew what else? He was kind of glad he hadn't been aboard. But here he was ... sneaking back on. What was he thinking?!?

Another burst of orange blistered the sky and overloaded his circuits. Fire burst in a line from belly to backside and then the front half of the ship bent at the resulting fracture. Somehow the ship remained aloft, but the speed of its descent increased markedly. Double at least.

"What are you doing, Bodie? Seriously... At this rate, why not just wait for it to come to you?" he asked as the wind whistled past him. His thoughts went to Antigony and then to Justine. There was a chance the girl could make it back to the side of right. An outside chance, but a chance all the same.

He began to jog. During his travels, he'd been thinking, amongst other things, of a knot. It was actually just a short loop of rope, but when wrapped around another rope and passed through itself twice, it became something called a Prusik hitch. He could use it to lock in hand and footholds on a strand of coldbright. The strands were still somehow being drawn up to the great ship—instant elevator.

Bodie guessed that Justine must still be working to pull as much material back to it as possible, even while it was being destroyed from the inside out. She must be repairing everything she could with the material. She had her hands full.

Up ahead, a flicker of light in the air like a strand of spider's silk told him a coldbright deposit was near. He heard it, too. The filament twisted upward into the sky. A jolt of excitement coursed through him. It was possible that he could use the coldbright the same way that Justine did and just fly up to the ship himself, but there were two problems with that. One was that he didn't want to give away his new capability. The other was he didn't actually know how to do it. Justine had figured it out, so it was possible, but manipulating the shape of the coldbright was one thing. Using it to defy gravity was quite another.

But one thing he did know. Regardless of how ready he was for it, it was time for a showdown.

A vast shadow overtook him. It cast the gully and the hillside beyond in relative darkness in little time. He looked up to see the Ars Arcanum. It was black with a smoky corona of sunlight all around it. The darkened underbelly was dotted with fires, some billowed white smoke as they were being tended to by automated systems. Still others were roiling black, completely unchecked.

Bodie shook his head again and pulled out the loops of rope he'd prepared for the ascent.

He looked up again to size up the job he was about to endeavor upon, and a light dusting of ash scattered across his face. It reminded him of the snowfall after the Sever cabin had burned and of Downy the woodpecker. The tiny creature had trusted him, and he'd let it get eaten while he was off chasing his missing leg. Justine had trusted him, and so had Joe and Mer. And going farther back, his old friends and crew mates. Now, it was Tig who was trusting him. He couldn't let her down. Wouldn't let her down.

"Alright. Let's get to work. Tig, I'm comin'."

He wrapped the first rope loosely around the cold-bright strand and let it slide while he wrapped the second, larger loop, meant for one of his boots, just below that. He slid his boot into the loop and it yanked tight quicker than he was expecting, ripping him off the ground so that he was rising higher and higher above the ground, hanging by his foot and flailing to get his balance.

It took him a second to reach up and grab hold of the first Prusik hitch, but he finally did, and after a minute, he was standing on one knot and holding onto the other, looking much more like he'd envisioned it and less like the buffoon he felt like.

"Some rescue mission..." he mumbled.

His gaze dropped to the ground, and he watched as the sage and bottlebrush of the gully diminished below, growing into a fractured valley floor, and then again as that valley floor diminished into yet more ragged gashes through a plateau that stretched off in the distance. A song sprang into his mind.

"Ashfall the heavens
Bloodspell beckons
Deep to deep
Wing'd justice draws nigh

"Deep to deep... Hmm. I wonder what that means."

CHAPTER 20

ARCANUM FINITUM

Justine gulped one big lungful of air and thrust off the ceiling, diving back below the surface of the roiling water. The room below, nearly full to the ceiling, looked like a subterranean cavern filled with blinking lights and deep shadows as aisles of machinery disappeared into darkness.

She half swam and half pulled herself along through the underwater maze of what used to be the forward engineering room. Drive power was in the back of the ship and took up nearly a quarter of it.

Gravitics though, they were located here. They were what was keeping the hulking craft from colliding with the planet below. And it would be an understatement to say that they were in a state of extreme stress.

A deep shudder ran through the ship. The pressure wave pulsed through the rising water even as Justine scrambled forward. Then the far end of the room started to tip even farther away. She wasn't sure if the gravitic axis had shifted out of alignment again or...

She surged forward until she found the jar. Not a mason jar but a massive machine larger than her family's cabin. Held within the "jar" was something the ship's AI referred to as inverted space. She didn't understand the science of it, but she understood the ship at a level that one might liken to almost emotional, unconscious even.

Because of her relationship with the coldbright, she could deduce things about what was broken and what was needed to fix it that someone with several lifetimes of scientific knowledge would be scratching their head at.

Lucky that. The Ars Arcanum would have been a smoldering crater covering much of the region if she hadn't been here. Of course, she was the one with the hare-brained idea to fly the damned thing.

Her lungs burned. Bubbles escaped from her lips and blurred her vision as the room tipped further away. She had images in her mind of the massive vessel rolling over onto its side. She knew she could poll the coldbright for data on the status of the ship, but she just didn't have the time. Either she could fix it or she could not.

She reached forward with her tendrils, grasped the jar, and fused to it. This was the scary part. She'd discovered before that melding with the machinery had an allure that was hard to pull herself away from. There was no way to describe it, but there was a certain ... belonging. It was so easy to get lost in the complexity, the purpose and wonder of the machinery.

She closed her eyes and "felt" her way around the machine. It took no time at all to find the problem. A fracture. In a container that held inverted space within it. She didn't need a degree to know that was bad. Very bad.

Her lungs were screaming now. She broke off and raced for the surface even as the panic of drowning flooded her, pushed her to breathe even while she was still underwater.

Still kicking, she was completely out of breath. She couldn't think of what to do but started counting the seconds.

1-2... She kept kicking. 4-5-6... Her lungs ached. She felt like she was suffocating because she was. She stroked frantically for the surface ... 10-11...

Justine broke the surface and slammed face-first into the ceiling, gasping, sucking in huge lungfuls of what air was left.

There wasn't much of it. *The bubble might be gone when she came back*, she thought, completely terrified by the idea. She didn't know if she could convince herself to go back down. Right now, she couldn't even imagine it. She sucked in more air, panting raggedly.

She was going to die. There was no way around it. This was the end. Crash, drown, did it matter?

Panic surged in her chest again, making it even more difficult to breathe, and then the panic of not being able to catch her breath amplified that fear.

"Justine," Artis's soothing voice came to her from somewhere. Justine spun around, but no one was with her.

"I'm transmitting through the ship's hull. Only you can hear me."

"Oh," she panted out. "That's good!" she yelled over the noise of splashing and bubbling water, nearly ecstatic to hear another voice, even if it wasn't exactly another human.

"You're doing great, Justine. What did you find?"

"Uh … the jar… It's … broken," she managed while treading water with both her exhausted legs and the quickly fading coldbright tendrils. Manipulating the material on land and in the air was a snap. In the water, it felt more like the metal that it was. She really had to focus on staying afloat.

"That's bad," Artis provided. Apparently, there was no way to sugarcoat it.

"So I gathered. I need … to get … back down there … don't I?" Justine asked, though she knew the answer already.

"You're the only one who can do this. Of course, it's entirely up to you."

That was a surprise. The ship was giving her permission to *not* save it. As well as everyone and everything on it. It must understand the heavy burden placed on a pilot's shoulders. To either be master of the ship forever or die of old age decades before you rightly should.

Water splashed into Justine's face, causing her to choke, even as she realized the air gap was nearly gone. She was out of time. The decision had been made for her. Fix it or die.

She sucked in two more quick breaths, but before she could dive, something brushed her foot.

She recoiled, but too late. That something grabbed her and pulled her down.

Justine kicked and thrashed and pummeled with her fists relentlessly, only to realize there was nothing there. But something *had* grabbed her. She hadn't dragged *herself* down.

She took one more quick look around and kicked again for the surface, to that quickly shrinking pocket of air. But no matter how hard she pressed her face to the metal, she could only get a few shallow breaths. She pushed off, and as she turned toward the end of the room where the grav jar quietly bubbled, awaiting her return, she came face-to-face with someone else. A girl, much like herself, or at least much like she'd been only two short weeks ago. But this girl was deathly pale and her eyes were sunken and dark. Her lips, too, were dark.

Justine was so stunned, she just froze. The girl's expression, which had been sad at first, slid into a sinister grin as she lunged forward, claws out. Justine screamed, expelling precious air in a cloud of bubbles, but then once again, when the bubbles cleared, there was no one there.

She kicked up into what remained of the pocket and then the ship lurched and rolled even further. The meager pocket of air slid away through a grate in a stream of silvery bubbles. Justine tried to follow but was trapped. She grabbed the grate and thrashed against it, pulling her tendrils into play, ripping away chunks of metal catwalk, but even as an opening began to materialize before her, the light ahead shrank further and further into nothingness.

Justine lurched up, coughing and gasping for air. She rolled on her side and continued to hack and belch up water.

"Ughh … what in … Yazie's bloomers," she wheezed out.

She was wet and cold and all around her was the loud thrum of machinery gone haywire and rushing water.

She had no idea where she was, but to be honest, she couldn't be bothered. She was safe. At least for the moment. The last thing she remembered… She stopped, her attention drawn to the water. She'd drowned.

She'd been trying to catch her breath when the ship tilted again, causing what air was left in the pocket to trickle away.

She scanned her surroundings with renewed intensity. As near as she could tell, she was still in forward engineering, just in another section. The smell of chemicals was strong. How long had she been out? Minutes, she guessed. But then, how did she get here?

And then a chill gripped her. How *did* she get here? As if by instinct, her eyes were drawn to the far corner of the upended room bathed in shadow. Within that darkness was the form of a young girl, huddled in the corner. Her eyes shone a ghastly silver that was only interrupted when she blinked.

Justine remembered being dragged underwater. Remembered that girl up terrifyingly close, lunging at her with teeth and vicious claws. And yet, after she'd drowned, she found herself here.

"Did you save me?"

The eyes blinked, but nothing more.

"Thank you," Justine mouthed, somehow unable to give the words breath. It was just too surreal.

The ship shuddered and a massive rending and screeching of metal tore through the silence. Through her connection to the coldbright, she could feel the tortured metal in her bones as if it were her own body.

Justine looked back to where the girl crouched in the corner, only to find her gone once more, which was somehow even more disconcerting than when she had been there.

And then a new, more fervent clamoring sounded through the waters. An erratic hum that could only be the gravitic jar at the far end of the bay, maybe fifty feet down. She slid off of the bulkhead wall that had acted as her own personal marooner's beach and slipped into the water. With one big gulp, she dove with renewed vigor, pulling and kicking with the tendrils until the jar loomed into view. A large glowing blister on the sidewall opposite where the fracture had been was suddenly her main focus. There the metal glowed hot, sizzling the water around it as it grew. She had maybe had seconds. Justine reached down inside herself to a similar mass of molten metal and engulfed the jar with her tendrils, melding into it, binding it with all her strength.

Damned if it weren't near impossible. She could do something, but it wasn't much and it wouldn't be enough. She held on tight and prayed for a miracle as her lungs began to scream once more.

Klamath held on to the railing with one hand while his other hand stuffed his Peacemaker into his waistband before loosening his belt. Below his boots yawned a nearly quarter-mile plummet. With the ship tipped on its side, his hiding place in the mechanical mezzanine of one of the belly hangar bays that stretched from one side of the ship to the other was now a gaping chasm. It was narrow, filled with random obstructions, and a very long way to fall. One slip and he'd pinball his way all the way down.

At first, it hadn't been all that bad, back when the ship just had a modest tilt to it. But now, it was a legitimate hazard. And, to make things worse, he had company.

A hundred feet below, dark figures climbed their way toward him at an alarming pace. Blackie's gang of reanimated cybernetic outlaws. Reanimated *polygenetic* outlaws was more correct, on account of the fact that, in addition to robot parts, they'd been partially reconstructed from various marsupial species. RePOs he'd call them.

He slung the end of his belt over a nearby cable, lunged for the loose end with his free hand, and started sliding at a brisk pace toward the other wall of the chasm, which had previously been the floor. His stomach jumped up into his throat, but after a few seconds, he landed on two feet, slid for a ways, and ground to a halt. Still in one piece.

He ventured a glance over the edge of the short maintenance building he was now standing on the side of. Below him, the posse of RePOs was confounded but only for a minute or two. Eventually, they all scrambled and leaped to the opposite, shadowing their prey and continuing to close the distance.

"Dammit. I thought that'd get one or two at least," he said and stroked his mustache. He buckled his belt and holster and slid the Peacemaker back into its home. For such a low-tech piece of equipment, he sure enjoyed the feeling of safety and comfort it provided. Speaking of which...

He drew, leaned over the edge, and fired twice. Two distinct screams issued from below, followed by bodies tumbling and bouncing off of equipment, piping, columns, and various other solid and unforgiving objects. He breathed a sigh of delight and hazarded a quick glance over the edge. Four more to go. Blackie wasn't with them. Too bad. He wondered where he could be. Must be attending to some more important matter.

Klamath leaned back over and pulled the trigger again, only to be met with a dissatisfying click.

"Figures." He looked at the empty pistol before salvaging the spent casings and holstering it. He was all out of bullets, and he'd lost that wicked little pistol he'd stolen from the sentry bots a few days prior. Hiding out on the monster-infested ship had been dicey, to say the least. When presented with the option to save the gun but lose an arm, he'd chosen the gun, but then another infernal creature jumped up and took that, too. He'd been forced to retreat unarmed, in every sense of the word.

Quick footsteps from behind caused him to spin and crouch low. He made out Blackie's trademark bandana mask and bleeding eye sockets just before he slammed into Klamath's chest and the two flailed over the edge into the open air.

They tumbled end over end, locked in a mid-air wrestling match, exchanging fists and elbows, Klamath trying to get himself free, Blackie intent on crushing him with brute gorilla force, not seeming to care that, at any moment, they were going to hit something or hit the bottom.

Klamath's alien biotech took over. He felt his skin go squishy and moist where the outlaw held him tightly, while other portions of his anatomy grew flabby and diaphanous. In just a few seconds, he slipped free as his upper extremities billowed out into see-through, pearlescent wings.

Blackie roared in rage as Klamath slipped out of his hands and glided to safety, where he suction-cupped and flattened himself to a wall a couple hundred feet above the floor. He'd only heard Blackie's screams for a moment before they were cut short by a loud crash and thud.

Served him right. He was a piece of work when he was alive and even more so after his death and subsequent reanimation. Two more RePOs went screaming by, followed by even more heavy crashing and thudding.

"Lucky day. Looks like Vohl needs to work on a self-preservation upgrade for his monkey men."

That left two more, at least. He needed to find a better way to ditch these losers. One bulbous, translucent eye stalk spotted a water pipe. Some form of alien sensory organ told him it was cool, clean, and flowing rapidly.

"That'll work," he gurgled.

He fluttered to it, incised a thin breach, squeezed inside, and then excreted a film of day-glow eggs that hardened into a watertight seal. He let the current whisk him away to safety until less than a minute later, he slammed into a grating. The force of the water behind him threatened to extrude his body into half-inch tubes of translucent alien meat. He was stuck and about to die an undignified death somewhere in Zilich's plumbing.

That's when Klamath's biotech grew teeth where it needed them, and within seconds, he was floating free again but in a large engineering room completely flooded with water.

CHAPTER 21

ELEVATOR UP

The Ars Arcanum loomed into view. It'd taken a lot longer to close the distance than he'd expected. The ship was much bigger from this angle. He could see that it was at least a mile long.

The front end was still a cavernous opening where the ship had not yet been fully reconstructed from the crash. Hundreds of silver strands converged in a tangled mass just ahead and were closing fast. There was a good chance he could get smashed or tangled up in that mess. He needed to pick his point of entry and do it quick.

Before he had a chance, the silver strand he was riding quivered, paused, and then began to sag. In fact, all the other strands were reacting similarly. Bodie had a bad feeling about this. And then he started to fall.

"Sheey—"

Bodie shot the coldbright tendrils out and formed them into a makeshift pair of wings. Inelegant, rudimentary wings, but they were wings, nonetheless. He angled toward the lowest part of the ship, already judging speed and descent and knowing he wasn't going to make it.

He flapped once and nearly upended himself. What was he doing wrong? A tail, he needed a stabilizer! His thoughts drove the movement of the coldbright and some of the strands trailed back. He flapped again, made some tweaks to the shape, thinking of something like a hawk and then a vulture, and then finally settling onto the broader wingspan of a condor, the true masters of gliding. His descent angle rose. He was headed for the very lowest edge. A very broad and smooth edge with nowhere to land.

Bodie flapped again. The angle rose and there was something ... a communications array or maybe it was a weapons bay. Didn't matter what it was, it was where he was going to land. He made some more tweaks, started to get the hang of this flying, and then realized just how fast he was going.

"No, no, no, no..."

Bodie streaked into the opening, hit the back wall, and nearly slid back out into the void. He managed to catch an edge at the last second and hung there with his boots dangling in the wind. His heart felt like it was in his throat. As he pulled himself up, he realized he was struggling more and more between his two selves, the robot and the human. Robots shouldn't feel fear, but he did. Humans weren't made of metal with a processor for a mind, but he was. What a convoluted mess he was. But now was not the time to feel sorry or try to compartmentalize all these divergent thoughts and feelings. He was what he was now. For better or worse. All he could try to do was the right thing.

Right now, the right thing was saving Tig. And probably Jef. The skinwalker had done right by him. To save them, he'd have to deal with that maniacal little imp, Vohl. How he was going to do that he did not know. Just make it up as he went along, he guessed.

Something tugged at the back of his mind. A melody riding over the rushing wind.

A song of the Mana Noostra. He closed his eyes and listened to the strain. He breathed in and closed his eyes and just felt the melody in his mind and in his heart, contained within him and looking for a way to escape, to express itself out in the materium. The song was another call. But this time, it was a song of seeking.

With his eyes closed, he saw a faint green line tracing itself away from where he huddled in the weapons bay on the outside of the ship. It followed corridors that were broken and twisted sideways, some flooded, some choked with black smoke and chemical fire. The green line traced its way to a room filled with a tangle of broken equipment, past a chair with restraints lying open on the arms and legs.

The line shot forward down still more corridors, down a lift tube to another level, and through a set of broken double doors, massive doors. And then it was navigating between containment cells until it came to one that was made of black stone like dull obsidian. His heart sank. He knew what this was going to be. The Rajak's tomb.

The green line wavered and grew thin, but then at the end of the strand, a red heartbeat, but only just. That heart was Antigony's. In faint black-and-white outline, he saw Vohl and Zilich, and in the wreckage of lampstands and tapestry and other things befitting a temple, he saw the sarcophagus of the Rajak, bound in iron chains but floating above the chaos. The skin-walker was nowhere to be seen. But then, over in the corner, was a shape that was very familiar to him. Blackie. In his present form, at least: part gorilla, part robot, and all bad.

"What're you up to, Vohl?"

He had glowing bracers on his wrists in spite of being cast in the same black-and-white outline as everything else. What did that mean?

He sighed with confusion. The image slipped away the more he dwelt on it. He closed his eyes again and tried to reengage with it, but all he saw was the Nawri holding something, a box of some sort. And then there was a flash and the whole thing disappeared, replaced with the sound of the rushing wind and the ship struggling to stay aloft while it continued to tear itself apart.

Bodie pushed up to his feet and realized he was holding on to the business end of one of the ship's plasma cannons. He carefully followed it to the back of the bay, picking his pathway through a convulsing mass of pipes and tubing, since the ship was keeled over on its side and he was essentially walking on the wall. He found an opening with an access hatch inside.

"Okay. Let's go finish this."

Vohl breathed in the moment. This was pleasing on so many levels. Just one victory in a string of many, many more to come. He breathed out a long breath, smiled, and turned to his next victim.

"Okay, where was I?"

He was greeted by silence. It was to be expected from the girl and the stiff, but Zilich? He was usually babbling endless banalities.

He pretended to look around for possible people to answer the question, lingered, and then settled on his ex-employer. "Zilich. What's that? How did I cook up this ridiculously complicated and well laid scheme? Oh, it just came to me one day. Nothing to it really," he replied, admiring his talons, breathing on them, and then nonchalantly polishing them on his fur.

"What's that? What's with the bag o' bones in the rock box? So glad you asked. You see, the Rajak, it turns out, isn't just some historical relic but really is some kind of deity ... from where he's from, anyway. And he has some powers, but we've really clamped down pretty well on that. But he does have some handy little gadgets." Vohl rattled the magickal bracers on his wrists that only he could see. He preferred not to refer to them as manacles, which was really what they looked like. His ego wouldn't allow him to acknowledge the idea of being indebted to anyone. For anything. Let alone some long-dead, genocidal maniac.

Zilich's face betrayed his puzzlement.

Vohl rolled his eyes and reached into the air before him, his hand gripping something invisible. Zilich's eyes went wide. He knew what came next.

Vohl smirked dangerously and gave a twist. Zilich roared in agony, spittle flying from his lips, tears welling in his eyes before streaming down his cheeks as he rasped out breath after breath, trembling.

Vohl turned to the girl and mummy locked in the box, but they were unappreciative witnesses.

His smirk flattened. "Don't worry. You'll get your turn."

A clatter of movement from behind caused him to turn. "Oh. Monkey Man. You're still alive?"

The resurrected cyborg looked as though he'd been in a tussle with a starliner. The barest tilt of his head was acknowledgment.

"So?"

"The man, Klamath, has escaped," he grunted. Blood trickled from his nose and traced the contours between teeth and where they met the gumline.

"Of course he has, you Neanderthal. No worry. We have what we need. Almost. Why don't you just sit tight for a minute?" Vohl asked, nodding toward a spot between two columns near the wall.

Blackie, unable to do anything but what was demanded of him, limped away, leaving a mixed trail of blood and hydraulic fluid. Once there, he seethed with chaotic energy.

He'd tear me limb from limb if he had the chance, Vohl mused, then shifted his attention to the ghost box. It was glowing. His smile returned.

"If it doesn't work now..." He turned to Zilich. "You ready for this? Of course, you're not. You have no idea what's in store for you. You see this Zilich? This is your new home. But not for you as you are now. After. You're. Dead," he said with finality. "How do you like them apples, huh? You're about to become a gadget. A knickknack. Barely even a thing. I pity you. Or I would, at least. But ... you know." He shrugged.

"Well. Enough preamble. Let's get to the part where I suck your soul out of your body and jam it into this little box here."

Zilich, who was quietly trying to regain his breath, raised his head. Vohl just now realized he'd been uncharacteristically quiet for a while now. It was quite clear that his jaw was broken. Or maybe just dislocated. Honestly, he didn't really care which. The man's putrid human flesh was about to be aborted and his essence trapped in a magickal container that'd allow Vohl to coerce him to divulge anything he wanted to know. Locations of secret smuggler hyperholes. The man's exhaustive list of pliable bureaucrats—mildly out of date most likely but still... And then there were his alliances with various criminal enterprises, a network that was broad and deep and most notably extended to an exceedingly hostile region of space that resided just beyond this solar system. Zilich had lorded that knowledge over him these past twelve years, knowing that it was likely the only thing that kept a dagger from between the ribs in his back. He was smart that way. But those days were over.

The ship shook underneath his feet. What little lighting was left began to pulse slowly, dropping quickly to full darkness and then blooming over the course of two or three seconds before dropping away again.

The ship had never done that before. But then again, he'd never been forced to walk on the walls instead of the floor before, either. If that girl didn't get things under control soon, there would be no repairing this thing. And no escape from this horrid planet. He needed to get moving, no more drawing out his moment of triumph. Oh well. It was a shame, but the victory was the important part. There'd be plenty of time to gloat later.

Vohl walked up to where Zilich kneeled on the ground, his hands bound behind his back and connected to bonds that wrapped around his ankles as well. He sat the ebony-colored box on the floor before him. It rippled with a hazy green light that traced the inset symbols covering its surface, leaving no mistake as to whether it was just a pretty relic or something immensely more sinister.

"Zilich, meet Ghost Box. Ghost box. Zilich."

Vohl clanged his wrists together and the manacles, visible only to him, rang like ceremonial singing bowls. The box began to glow, slightly at first and then brighter and brighter. Vohl flicked a switch on a remote and Zilich's hands came free from the gravitic bonds. He planted them on the ground as he fell forward. The box bloomed and then faded.

"Grab the box."

Zilich looked up at him, nearly eye to eye, though he was kneeling on all fours.

"Grab the box, Zilich. Don't make me make you do it. Claim this tiny bit of self-respect. Choose your destiny. Do it for yourself."

Zilich stared at him uncomprehendingly. Vohl's hand shot out and grabbed his face. Zilich groaned but would not move. "Very well."

Vohl maneuvered the remote, using it as a guide for the gravitic manacles on Zilich's wrists. His hands slid forward, inching closer and closer to the box. He fought against it but was unable to resist their power, and finally, his hands rested on either side of it. The green light bloomed again and Zilich cried out, only this time it was accompanied by a breathy whistling sound that steadily grew into a sound like rushing wind through a narrow gap.

Vohl watched in morbid fascination as Zilich's face and then shoulders and arms and then torso and legs began to blur out of place as they were sucked in slow-motion into the box. Yet, his body remained fixed. It was as if two superimposed parts were being peeled away from each other. Embers lifted away from the split and as more and more of the perceived outer layer peeled away, the embers grew greater in size and number until, after a few more seconds, nothing was left of Zilich's body but a charred, smoldering statue of chalky carbon.

Vohl began to giggle and then stopped, suddenly feeling as though it was somehow irreverent in the face of the magnitude of what had just taken place. He chortled again. And choked on it. It was a sobering feeling. He was awed by the display. And delighted, but, yes, he could gloat later.

He looked down at the box, which was no longer glowing but occasionally rippled again with the ghoulish green light.

"Are you here with me still, Zilich?"

The box rippled.

"That's not quite good enough. I need to hear your voice. Are you here with me?"

There was a pause, but then after a moment, a voice like wind through reeds emanated from the box. "Yeah. I'm definitely here. Somewhere. And someday, what you've done will come back to haunt you."

"Ha! Says the voice in the ghost box. Good one!" he said, clapping his hands.

The ship bucked beneath him, and he was ripped back to the reality of the moment. The ship, and all the monsters that represented the payout he needed to reclaim the throne, were going down. He'd have to do it without the monsters. That was a lost cause. But, with the ghost box and the Rajak's powers at his disposal, he could do it. Easily.

Now, he just needed a way off this planet.

"Artis?"

"Yes, Vohl?"

"Where is Justine? I need her to build a smaller ship before this one destroys itself."

"She's currently trying to repair the gravitic engine. However, it seems unlikely that she will be successful."

"What if she isn't? We'll crash?"

"We'll explode. And vaporize a significant portion of northern Nevada or California, depending."

"Depending on what?"

"How far we make it. And how well-contained the engine is when it goes."

"What do you mean, how far we make it?"

"Well, Captain Sever instructed me to maneuver the Ars Arcanum toward the Pacific Ocean, in the hope that an explosion either over the water or in it would reduce loss of life and contain as much of the coldbright material as possible. It's a gamble, but we're approaching the Sierra Nevada mountains now. There is a very slim chance her plan can work."

"We need that craft immediately."

"Luckily, Captain Sever already thought of that. She had me cannibalize much of the starboard engineering module, but the modifications are nearly complete."

"What modifications?"

"Well, the craft you speak of, of course. In order to maintain continuity of the organic members of the crew, a craft would be required. It just makes sense. It would be impossible to build the craft, hold the ship together, and keep the gravitic engine from exploding all at the same time, except that Captain Sever is exceptionally gifted. Amazing that she came from such a primitive culture, wouldn't you say?"

"Yes. Yes, truly. And ... where would this craft be located, Artis?"

"It's currently docked at Aft Belly Bay 04. Do you require an escort to assist you with your ... things?"

"Yes. Excellent idea. How many sentries are left?"

"Just eighteen." A dull boom resonated through the hull of the ship. "Make that sixteen, no, fifteen. But they're all busy assisting with the fires."

"Pull them back. I want them all here, with me. Now."

"Very well. You should know that this will likely compromise our ability to safely guide the ship out to sea."

"Yes, yes, I know," he said, waving away the idea impatiently. "Just do it. Better yet, send five of them here and have the rest clear a path from here to Bay 04 and hold it."

"Of course, Chief Science Officer Vohl."

Vohl glanced at the sarcophagus. A small pang of fear gripped his insides. Was it safe to take the Rajak with him? The bracers were an extraordinary power in and of themselves. And then there was the woman. Could she be controlled? He'd just committed his long-time employer—the man known galaxy-wide as a notorious pirate and smuggler—to a magickal box. And now he had that man's knowledge forever at his fingertips. He'd unlocked the power of the ghost box. Surely, he could figure out a way to use the woman. Even if he just set her free in the middle of the imperial castle and let her wreak havoc with her deadly laser vision. She'd cut through the imperial guard in no time. He thought about how he'd been able to control the Skinwalker and coerce him to attack the renegade robot. Perhaps he could do the same with this woman?

Another boom rattled the pillars, causing one to crack and then split in half. The fact that the ship was still aloft was a testament to the power that the girl pilot wielded. He'd take her if he could.

You will take the girl.

"Who said that?" Vohl spun around, but no one was there but the enthralled woman and the monkey man.

Vohl paused. In that void of silence, he knew that the voice had been inside his head. Fear gripped his insides.

"Who's there?" he squeaked.

His mind burst forth with a chorus of sinister laughter. It was deafening and everywhere. He clutched his head, but it did nothing to diminish the sound.

He gulped dryly and pushed down the desire to retch. So, this was it, then. All that power. Of course there was a catch.

He straightened, dropping his hands and just taking all of it in. So be it. As long as he got what he wanted, he could share his mind with the Rajak. At least for now...

CHAPTER 22

GETAWAY

Klamath used the undulating fins along the sides of his sleek body to move forward through the submerged chamber. There was a dull hum underlying the rush of water. That, plus the current, plus the relative pressure, told his alien senses that the room was both filling and emptying. That meant there was a breach.

Theoretically, he could use that breach to exit and find a way out of the ship itself. It was more than clear that if he was going to survive, it would not be aboard the Ars Arcanum. He would have to find another way.

The room pulsed with light, but slowly, as he worked his way lower toward the far side of the chamber. At the end of it, he saw something that made him realize how dire the situation had become. If he wasn't mistaken, that large object was a gravitic engine—a jar containing unimaginable amounts of energy. The next thing he realized was that it was being held together by strands of coldbright. A pang of fear shot through him.

Oh yeah, the situation is much worse than I thought.

Then, his sepiidic eyes caught something else. The girl, Justine, floating limply at the nexus of the strands of coldbright. He propelled himself forward, grasping her with his thick, forward-facing tentacles. He detected the electrical signature of a weak pulse. Weak and getting weaker. Without a thought, he morphed between species, using his cuttlefish-like ability to generate gas and that of some unnamed creature to pass it along to the girl. A tube with five tentacles at the end grasped her face and began the flow of oxygenated air.

She bolted upright, coughing, sputtering, and flailing aimlessly until she caught sight of Klamath's horrific form, which caused her to thrash even more violently.

Shit. Stupid, stupid. I should have thought of how this would appear to her.

He morphed further until his alien biotech found the combination of features that would keep them both alive and allow him to speak to her—through her mind.

Justine, the thought boomed between them.

Her thrashing came to a sudden stop. She looked at her supposed attacker anew; her face still engulfed by the tentacles but for her eyes, which squinted as she struggled to comprehend what was happening to her.

"Justine. It's Klamath Pettibone. I'm sure I look very different from the last time we met … in that warehouse … back in Low Camp." He pushed an image to her of the graphic aftermath.

Her eyes went wide and her fear, through the psychic bond, was palpable. Her bewilderment was now tinged with flashes of fear and disgust. And shame.

He used that bond to push a subtle wave of calm in her direction. He watched as her posture relaxed a little.

This is a useful trick. I shoulda figured this out a long time ago.

"Hmph. I'd much prefer you'd play God with someone else's mind entirely. Even when you're saving my life," she said.

You are a sharp one. He looked at her again, realizing for the first time that she'd aged years since the first time he'd seen her just a few short weeks ago.

"Yeah. I'm older now. Smarter, too. 'Course, it won't mean much if I can't fix this space jar."

Her attention drifted to the now glowing blister, barely contained by the coldbright. "Ah, pig shit."

Yeah, oh shit is right. We should be thinking 'bout how to get off this rig, he thought to her.

"I made a craft. I had Artis help me. We were trying to get the main vessel out over the ocean. So's we can limit the explosion and better contain the materials for collection later. I would drop the carcass of the ship and carry just the jar if I could. I don't know. Hadn't figured it out entirely. I have all the sentry bots working to hold the fires at bay. Don't know how that's working out either."

"Actually," Artis interjected, projecting her voice as resonance through the ship structure, "the sentry bots have been commandeered by Vohl. He's making his way toward the escape craft as we speak."

"What?" Justine tried to ask but was unable to with the alien breathing apparatus suctioned to her face, and besides, she was underwater. She projected her thoughts through the coldbright, which she realized must have been how Artis had known what she and Klamath had been talking about. They'd have to talk about boundaries later. "Why?!?" This, she noted, was the weirdest conversation she'd ever had. Speaking through resonance with an artificial intelligence, and then telepathically to some kind of alien squid thing. This was a far cry from slopping pigs and scouting claims.

"As Chief Science Officer, he is the ranking member of the crew. I'm compelled to obey his command where it does not specifically pertain to navigation and flight."

Justine conveyed this to Klamath.

What about Zilich? Klamath asked Justine through the mental link.

"Artis has been hacked to believe that he doesn't exist. By Zilich himself, I'm afraid. It was his attempt to hide from me once he knew I'd taken over."

Sounds like a Zilich thing to do, he thought at her. *Probably had that planned long before you ever came along.*

A groan rippled through the water, and they turned to see the blister on the side of the jar bulge and strain at the coldbright. It grew in brightness until it was fully engulfed in roiling sheets of thick white bubbles.

"Oh, this is so not good. Artis, status? How much time do we have? Where are we?" Justine asked through the link.

"We've just crossed the Sierra Nevada. But with the sentry bots having abandoned their posts, I doubt we'll make it to sea. In fact, our current trajectory has us heading directly toward the human settlement of San Francisco.

"San Francisco? Is there any way to avoid it?"

"Prospects are not strong. I've lost any ability to navigate or alter speed. Vohl's decision has doomed us and the inhabitants of the city. The bay, too, is teeming with ships."

"That vile little swine."

In some way that she didn't understand, she could tell bounty hunter turned monster squid thing was in agreement.

Be that as it may, we still need to save our own skins, he thought to her. *And that craft is the best way to do it. Vohl will take it for himself. And then we die along with all those people.*

A wave of energy pulsed through the waters, and Justine thought she was going to be sick. She felt a similar disturbance through the psychic link. Another wave pulsed, and it confirmed her fear that it was coming from the grav jar.

That's real bad. Listen, girl, you can't survive underwater, but I can. I can hold the jar. You hunt down that little troll and keep him from stealing our ship. I don't like it, but there's no sense in me going after him just to have the whole ship go up. You just tell your AI to let me know when the deed is done and we'll figure it out from there.

Justine's eyes squinted again as she struggled to read his real intentions through the link but found it to be a featureless wall, obscured by fog and shrouded as if built of half-remembered dreams.

Klamath began to morph again. This time evolving along the lines of a huge squid or octopus but with powerful-looking tentacles and covered in obsidian-like scales. It was a thing of nightmares, and under any other circumstances, she would have been screaming and thrashing to get away. He rotated his body to gaze at her with a large, questioning eye. Justine gave a quick nod and began to loosen the strands of coldbright.

The jar swelled visibly, issuing another wave of energy, denser and more nauseating this time. Klamath responded by wrapping himself around the exterior skin of the grav jar and squeezing tightly. She marveled at the dexterity of the tentacles. They moved almost as if of their own volition. Her own coldbright tendrils looked clumsy in comparison.

Seeing the jar safely, at least in relative terms, enveloped, she started kicking for the surface, using the coldbright tendrils to speed her escape.

The grav jar stopped expanding. Klamath was able to move on to step two, sealing it in an egg sack with a unique chemical structure that was something akin to the diamond-hard concrete substance he'd used earlier to escape Blackie and his resurrected primate clown posse.

The girl was off to do her part, which was to stop the Nawri from stealing the getaway craft. As soon as she was out of sight, Klamath began excreting the millions upon millions of crystalline eggs. It took finesse to move around the jar while maintaining the magnificent amount of pressure needed evenly across its surface. Well, semi-evenly. As even as could be expected given the circumstances.

After a couple of minutes, he'd done as good a job of containing the grav jar as he thought anyone could have. It'd buy them some hours, anyway. Now, it was time for him to do what he'd planned on doing from the beginning: beat Vohl and the rest of them to the ship. Justine was just a distraction to slow the others down. If Vohl managed to make it to the ship at all, Klamath would be waiting for him.

If it turned out that only Justine showed up, well, good for her. She'll have proved herself a worthy sidekick, maybe. He'd never had one before, but given her particular skill set of manipulating coldbright and piloting a starship, she would certainly be worth keeping around. He might even give her a percentage of the bounty on Zilich. And who knew if there was one on Vohl. As wretched as he was, it was more than likely.

Klamath jetted down further into the gravitic system's forward engineering plant. He knew there had to be a breach somewhere. What he really needed was a map. Where did the ship's AI say that craft was? Bay Four? Belly Bay. *Aft* Belly Bay. That was quite a ways away if he had to guess, especially with the ship in the state that it was in. He needed to hurry.

Bodie raced along the corridor wall. The lights bloomed slowly and dropped to full dark for a second or two before building again. Supposedly, this was supposed to be some sort of warning signal, but the ship laying on its side was a pretty good indicator, he thought. Anyone walking along the walls to get from their quarters to the mess hall who didn't know things were in really bad shape didn't belong on a starship. Or anywhere, really.

He bounded over an intersecting corridor, and down there somewhere in the darkness, he thought he saw a set of glowing eyes.

Always with the monsters, he sulked. *Hopefully, whatever it was didn't see me. Or care. Wouldn't that be nice?*

Somehow, in spite of the size of the ship and its numerous levels, he'd ended up in the main cargo shaft. He knew from experience and from his memory files that he was getting close to the large hangar-style doors that led to the containment area known as the Terrarium.

He had a choice to make here. The song of locating was still active in the back of his mind. When he thought about it, he could see an image of the trail between himself and Antigony, and by extension, Vohl. It was vague but present enough for him to track.

That trail led to a place halfway along the containment area. So, he could waste time and try to climb up the corridor to get to the corridor that ran parallel to the terrarium where Antigony was now. Or assume they were headed to somewhere farther back in the ship and cut through the Terrarium to get there.

He had no desire to cut through the Terrarium. None. He didn't know what state that area was in now that it was turned on its side. Did some or all of the individual containments fall over and crash to the bottom of that massive, empty space? He didn't know. Did the creatures all flee to other parts of the ship, or did some remain? Also good questions.

The hangar doors loomed into view. Decision time. He stepped up to the edge, the doors before him across the chasm that used to just be a corridor. It stretched upward into darkness. And downward into ... not quite darkness. It was dark, but it also appeared to be moving.

Before he could switch to a different visual filter, a furry arm shot out of the darkness, wrapped around his leg, and pulled him over the edge. He deployed cold-bright tentacles to grasp the corner and the hangar door. It halted his descent, but then the creature attached to the furry arm started shuffling its body upward. The roiling mass of tentacles resolved into a shape that was still fresh in his mind: the wooly decapus. The creature that had easily put a beatdown on a handful of sentry bots just like himself.

He slipped a couple of feet closer to the creature as it closed the gap, using him and the walls of the corridor to pull itself upward. It filled every inch of this smaller space. That was probably Bodie's only saving grace, the fact that the creature didn't have much room to work with.

Bodie extended his coldbright tendrils further, searching for a better grip, but there was nothing that was going to help. The creature had to weigh two tons. He couldn't reach down to his ankle to dislodge its arm. But he could cut it. If only he had a long enough blade...

It was a small gamble. Bodie let go with one of the strands of coldbright, fashioned the end into something like a Japanese daito, and whipped it down at the creature's tentacle-like appendage. The blade cleaved it in half with surgical precision.

"Hoo-hoo, take that, ya wooly bastard!"

Purplish goo splattered the wall and Bodie alike. The creature bellowed a breathy, gurgling roar. With his leg free, he ripped upward, guiding himself through the hangar door and out into—slight misjudgment—another chasm filled with darkness. Bodie tumbled through the air in a tangle of spindly metallic arms. The lights came up slowly as he fell. He could just make out one of the containment structures, collapsed on itself, along with a bunch of other debris. Way far below. A couple of building stories below. Then the lights went out again. He hit it hard at an angle and bounced a few more times.

< 0 0 1 0 2 0 x x 1 2 1 3 ? a 0 0 … 0 0 1 0 2 0 x x - 1 2 1 3 ? a 0 0 x 1 1 0 1 0 0 … 0 0 1 0 2 0 x x 1 2 1 _ a00x110100xxbxx01111>

This again.

He polled his sensory systems for anomalies, missing data, etc. It was nice when Helga used to do this for him, even if she'd been a figment of a broken mind and a guilty conscience.

Consensus? Not that bad, actually. He'd just fallen a dozen stories or more. He could consult his internal maps, but it didn't really matter. He was lying in a puddle of some foreign substance or other mixed with some of his own internal fluids, but he really wasn't all that bad off.

"Must be the coldbright holding me together." Well, maybe he could face off against whatever was coming up next. That reminded him he was running out of time. He calmed his mind and let the song of locating echo in his mind. Antigony was nearing the end of the containment corridor. The exact opposite corner from where he lay currently. Vohl was there. A couple of sentry bots. Blackie. The Rajak's coffin. And there was something else… Something not quite with Vohl's little party, but Bodie could feel a tug. Something like an intention.

He brought a soft focus to the feeling. Letting go of emotion. Letting go of his worries. The focus of the spell slid along the corridor. Back the way they'd come, past a couple more sentries, and then it coalesced around another person. Moving fast. Justine.

She was coming for Vohl. It was in that moment that he realized that Zilich wasn't in the picture. And neither was Jef, the skinwalker. But he'd felt them, he was certain of it. He searched that feeling and it seemed ... bad. If a nasty end had come to Zilich, oh well, but Jef? He was an observer of history amongst dimensions and yet somehow he'd gotten entangled in this one. Was it because he'd helped Bodie? Perhaps participated a little too much?

He'd alluded to this version of reality being warped in some way. That Vohl and Bodie were always at odds with one another. And that the fate of the galaxy lay in the balance. How could that possibly be?

A very bad feeling settled in his gut. After all, he was a soul inhabiting a robot body, his somewhat romantic interest (misguided as it was) had been possessed by an ancient deity, and he was consorting with inter-dimensional entities. Those seemed like the sorts of things that people with epic destinies had going on. He was also going down in a flaming ship full of monsters while the bad guy was about to get away with the girl. As stories went, this one was not ending well.

The lights began to brighten again. He heard an odd shuffling sound above him before seeing the wooly kraken, formerly suctioned to the wall forty or so feet above him, leap out into the air. He was about to be crushed. Not ending well at all.

CHAPTER 23

COMEUPPANCE

The fire in Justine's belly was blazing hot as she raced down the corridor. Artis had told her right where that despicable little creature was, and she had a chance at reaching him before he got to the escape craft. But only just.

The lights were a terrible nuisance. She was going fast, and, in the span of one blackout, the corridor went from completely empty to not-quite-so-empty with two of the sentry bots standing there, plasma pistols at the ready.

She twisted left, away from a bolt of plasma. The smell of burned hair wafted by as one of the coldbright strands shattered, causing her to tumble to the floor/wall. A trail of plasma bolts coursed toward her and she rolled to the side, shooting out a strand to grasp the closest of the two bots. She spun it, wrapping it in a couple of coils until it faced its partner, and then the end of the coldbright strand slipped over its trigger finger. A flurry of plasma shot out and the other sentry bot exploded into multiple molten chunks.

The coiled-up bot struggled to free itself, but its own plasma pistol now drifted toward its head.

"You shouldn't," Justine said in a strained, breathy whisper. The bot fought to keep the barrel away, but it inched closer. "...play..." And closer until there was a flash and the bot's body went limp. "...with guns," she finished, sweating from the exertion.

She pushed up to her feet and started running again. A little bit more cautiously, but she still had to beat Vohl to the ship. She'd just have to be prepared. She poured on the speed, using coldbright strands to propel her along and extending a couple ahead as feelers.

The lights came up, and a sentry bot pulled its gun, but Justine had it wrapped up and ripped in two before it could fire. She cast the pieces aside, but as she passed, a flash erupted and she shrieked in pain. Fire burned in her side. She flicked a tentacle toward the bot and pierced its head through an eye socket, pinning it to the floor. It fired again, and she managed to save herself by sacrificing another tentacle. The arm exploded, peppering her face and neck with shrapnel.

"Die already!"

She plunged another strand into its other eye and then ripped the two apart, leaving the bot's head a mangled mess. The pistol dropped to the floor and she, herself, collapsed. Her side was a gory, cauterized mess.

"That was stupid," she hissed, grimacing as she hastily inspected the wound. If it hadn't been melted, she'd be bleeding all over the place, but still, she found herself weak and shaky. She just wanted to sit for a minute.

"No time for that. I know it's shock, which I can't control, but I can't stop just yet."

She drew the shattered strand of coldbright back to her and let it absorb into the wound. She screamed out. But when it was done, it only hurt a lot. She hazarded a glance down and the skin was whole, albeit silver in appearance. She could get by with that. Justine didn't know what long-term effects it would have on her, but right now, she just needed to survive the day. She and whoever was left.

She had her hesitations about joining sides with that outlaw, Klamath, and she really wasn't sure where things stood with the robot and the lady. But she'd do what she could.

Justine stood up on wobbly legs, but then the hairs stood up on the back of her neck. She spun around to find the corridor fully lit and empty. But when the lights dropped, there was a set of three glowing eyes in a pyramid arrangement. They were only thirty or forty feet away. A sound like steel grating on steel emanated from down the hall. The eyes blinked out.

She bolted in the other direction as fast as she could. Faster than before. Fear drove her. She didn't know from what, but it was something from another world, and it clearly didn't come with good intentions.

An intersecting hallway flashed by overhead, and she heard the metallic sound again like a sword being drawn from a scabbard. She hazarded a glance behind her as the lights dropped again, and this time, there were two sets of eyes. And they were gaining.

"Dammit."

She was sucking wind. There was no way she could go this fast for long. She returned her attention ahead of her. The lights bloomed and another sentry bot was there, but before she could react, it was sliced into pieces from behind. For the briefest moment, she saw a feminine-looking creature, wisp thin, white hair, ashen face, two green eyes, with a third glowing green eye just above them. The apparition wore a gauzy ceremonial-looking robe, and it held two long scythe-like blades, one up and one down in its hands. And then it was gone.

Justine flew right through the space. Pain sliced through her shoulder. Metal clanged off of one of her tentacles and she hit the ground again. She rolled with the momentum and came up clumsily to her feet. She kept moving but facing backward, still trying to catch up to Vohl while also maintaining distance between herself and the spectral, sword-bearing wraiths. The three materialized shoulder to shoulder. They were all similar but different.

They wore the same ceremonial robes. They were all inhumanly thin, and they all had those scimitar blades held in the up and down positions. They moved forward as one, crouching low, and then they struck. Justine countered; metal rang out as swords struck coldbright strands.

Pain lanced out again, this time on her arm, as one of the creatures sliced and twirled inside her guard. She tried to get out of the way, but the wraith creature was fast. It caught her forearm and drove toward her stomach, but she'd pulled in a strand and spread it out across her torso as armor.

The blade bounced off the plate, but she morphed the coldbright back into a tentacle that grasped the creature's blade as she sent another strand right through its eye. She was sure she'd hit home, but the wraith vanished at the last second. The other two shrieked and intensified their attacks.

That unsettled feeling returned, and Justine ducked just as a blade whooshed through the air above her. She pulled the strands back, encapsulating her body in a metallic shield. The wraiths collapsed on her, striking relentlessly over and over again.

The din of metal-on-metal contact rang through her ears. The wraiths shrieked in rage, and she dropped to the floor, curling into a ball and just doing everything she could to keep the coldbright between her and the flailing, shrieking ghosts.

This was all fine and good, but then she realized she was unable to breathe. Or see. A quick thought turned the surface covering her mouth, eyes, and ears into a screen. The noise bloomed into a roar as the creatures continued to pound on her and shriek in fury. The frenzy grew and grew, and then, in an instant, it stopped.

She looked up. It was dark and three sets of eyes looked down at her. But, as the lights came up, the wraiths were gone. Warily, she pushed to her feet and looked up and down the hall to find it vacant. She waited for the lights to drop and checked again just to be sure that they weren't going to jump out at her once more, but they appeared to be gone for good. She worked moisture back into her mouth, swallowed, and started jogging back up the corridor.

"Artis, where are they now?"

"Vohl and his entourage?"

"Yes."

"They're making their way down the corridor at the end of the containment area, but because the ship is on its side, that hallway is a vertical shaft. They're not moving quickly."

The ship shook violently, and a boom and the sound of tearing metal assaulted her. Suddenly, the corridor she was in twisted and burst. She shot out strands to hold on, but the wall pulled away from her, and she watched as a massive chunk of the ship broke off like a calving glacier. Parts of it were lit by glowing fire and columns of smoke. The sound of wind grew into a roar.

The fragment peeled farther away, and darkness grew above her. When she recognized tiny pinpricks of light in the darkness, she realized it was the night sky. The massive chunk of ship fell away entirely, and then the ship itself began to roll over even more.

She held on with her tentacles, keeping them short so she could maintain her body armor, which she only now realized would have been a great trick to learn early on. As the ship rolled over, she saw a line of snow-capped peaks off to her right.

"Those must be the Sierras." She breathed in a shuddering breath.

A grid of dim lights to the north was likely the capital city of Sacramento.

"Artis, are we still on a trajectory for Frisco?" she yelled over the wind.

"If we make it that far. There's a five percent chance we will impact in the hills above Alameda," she heard Artis's voice through the ship's structure, similar to when she was underwater with the gravitic jar.

On the bright side, Klamath must be managing if they weren't dead already.

"How much time do we have?"

"About forty-five minutes if we don't completely disintegrate or blow up first. Ten percent chance of that. Make that fifteen."

"What a cheery thought. Thank you for your kind words of encouragement," she yelled.

"You're welcome," Artis said, seeming genuinely pleased to have been of service. "By the way, Vohl's party seems to be making much better time now that the corridor is somewhat horizontal."

"Dammit. Didn't even think about that." She started running in a low crouch to keep her balance. "Thank you, Artis."

"Don't … mention … it," she heard with each step.

The wind ripped past her as she exited out into a more exposed portion of the ship's hull, causing her to realize that they were traveling at quite an impressive speed still. Sacramento to SF in forty-five minutes was about a hundred miles an hour. Easily as fast as the fastest steam engine, even if it was positively crawling by interstellar spaceship standards.

Of course, no one on Earth really knew anything about such things. Outside of this small group of people, anyway. However, Earth was about to learn a whole lot more about spaceships pretty quick. One was about to crash into a major metropolitan area. Not like anything on the East Coast or in Europe, but still.

Justine tried to imagine within the 3D model of the ship where Vohl was in relation to the escape craft when she realized that the chunk of ship that fell away might have had the craft in it. Fear pulsed through her. She searched the yawning void through the fire and smoke and saw what she hoped to see. The ship was intact from M-Line back.

The Aft Belly Bay was literally in sight. The part of the ship that ripped away was a blessing in disguise. Now she didn't need to catch up to Vohl. She could head him off at the pass.

She just needed to navigate fields of ravaged metal and fire to do it. She closed her eyes and imagined a pathway between where she was and where she needed to go. The coldbright of the ship slowly grew up into a bridge. Slowly being the operative word. The Ars Arcanum shook violently again as an explosion lit up the sky from somewhere beyond what she could see. The ship lurched and that horrific sound of rending metal erupted from somewhere ahead.

"Shit."

She started running. She couldn't wait for the coldbright to form into a simple, smooth walking bridge. She had to go before the ship fell apart beneath her.

The Rajak tore at Vohl's mind. Not outright. Not in plain sight, but from the edges, the recesses, and all the nasty places he veered from in the prosecution of his daily chores and rituals.

You really are a pathetic little thing, aren't you? Hardly worthy of my presence. Perhaps I should take my powers back and bestow them upon someone of more ... significance, the creature said.

Vohl steadfastly ignored him. He'd had a life's worth of practice. Remove the oily, serpentine residue of the Rajak's words in his mind and it could have been any day of his childhood and early adult years in the presence of his parents and older brothers. Vohl had always known what to do in such instances: keep quiet and wait. Well, his waiting was almost over. He'd taken care of his brothers. In their sleep, but certain that they'd woken enough to see his face before they slipped away under a tide of poisonous Tanglewrath. They were awake but unable to move, and then slowly, their organs began to shut down one by one.

He'd waited until the season's longest eclipse when every one of his race slept to renew their strength and vitality for the year to come. It'd cost him dearly, crippling him for years, but it had been so worth it. His parents were broken of course, which made the victory even more enjoyable. He couldn't wait to get back. After his decades-long exile.

So this trifle, this annoyance of the backwater deity trying to invade his mind? Well, he'd lived through worse.

Suddenly, his vision swam into darkness. He reached out and steadied himself against the wall. Laughter filled his head, his throat constricted, and his mind felt like his skull would not be able to contain the pressure.

Vohl grasped his head in agony, nearly collapsed under it, but found that inner well of strength from his childhood humiliations. He drew himself upright, breathed through the pain, and continued onward toward the craft. The laughter never diminished, but the pressure did slightly.

He turned drunkenly. "Hurry up," he snapped at Blackie and the remaining bots. "We're running out of time." The ship shuddered in seeming agreement.

They were lucky the ship had rolled over. It was strange and often difficult walking on the ceiling, but it beat trying to navigate a corridor that had turned into a 400-meter shaft. The ground bucked beneath him and then settled. He yanked on the chain that bound the woman and she glided forward. The sarcophagus of the Rajak, also chained to her, floated along behind. Convenient that. Blackie trudged along behind, but then sniffed the air. A sinister smile crept onto his twisted face. The hollowed-out eye sockets with coagulated streams of blood dripping from them gave even Vohl the creeps.

"What is it? Tell me it's not that blasted robot," Vohl sighed, pinching the broad bridge of his shovel-shaped nose.

Blackie nodded. His joy at this development expressed in every fiber of his being.

"Go if you must. But kill it this time. If you fail, don't come back. Strap yourself to the front of the ship and wait for death to meet you."

Blackie nodded again. Noticeably less joyful this time. He turned and disappeared back down the hallway.

Bodie watched helplessly as the two ton, furry, octopus-like creature—the wooly kraken as he found himself referring to it—plummeted toward him. At the last second, he shot out coldbright strands, like spears set against cavalry. The creature landed with a *whump*, impaling itself against Bodie's coldbright spears. It lay there, still. Bodie had killed it, but in much the same way that it was pinned by the spears, he was pinned beneath it.

Two tons is a lot. Not something that Bodie couldn't deal with, but when no matter where you push you meet squishy resistance, there's just no good way to move it. He tried everything, but he just couldn't get enough space to work with. Then, after what seemed like ages, he was able to shift the weight a tiny bit. He pushed, and the creature rolled ever so slightly. He used the coldbright to form a plate of sorts and still more of the coldbright to form something like a hydraulic piston to push against it. The floor buckled beneath it, but still, the monumental creature shifted and rolled until it finally flopped over.

Then Bodie saw why. Blackie leaped atop the creature, kneeling on a knee and one fist. The fingers of the other hand twitched in eager anticipation of tearing him limb from limb.

"Blackie. So glad you could make it."

The gruesome visage broke into a horrific smile. Bodie smacked it off his face with a coldbright tentacle before pulling all the strands back to himself. He imagined an enhanced musculature, plate armor, and two of the daito blades on the ends of stalks. The coldbright manifested itself in that way.

"Let's end this."

Blackie roared and lunged forward. Bodie swung the blades at him in a one-two attack, but Blackie caught them with one of his feet and the opposite hand before slamming into Bodie with his other foot. Bodie went flying before skidding to a halt against a shattered containment structure. A crumpled door read, "GCU-1." He didn't have time to consider what that meant before Blackie was hurling through the air in his direction. He rolled to his right as the cyborg gorilla outlaw smashed into the wall, making an impressive crater.

Bodie leaped backward, using his appendages to suspend himself in the air between larger containment structures like a waiting spider. He waited for Blackie to charge again but shifted at the last second, lashing out with one of the daitos. It struck home. Blackie roared as he flew by, but he managed to grab a tentacle as he did so.

He landed and used the appendage to whip Bodie into a wall.

Bodie's brain glitched but didn't quite shut down. He was still sorting his senses when Blackie's gorilla feet loomed into view. Bodie twisted and sprang backward, slicing the spot where Blackie was to ribbons. Blackie roared in pain again as the swords struck home.

A boom echoed from far away, causing Bodie to remember just how little time he had to play around.

"Damn. Blackie, as much as I'd like to stick around, I got things to attend to."

The cyborg looked up from his bleeding wounds and roared a challenge.

"Ah, don't be upset. I'll come back to finish things." With that, he shot out strands, clasping Blackie's arms and legs, and swung him around before catapulting him toward the back wall where the wooly creature lay in a pool of purple blood. The lights dropped to darkness as he heard Blackie hit the ground. Bodie turned and bolted while he had the chance. Saving Tig and getting off the ship were his number one priorities now. Killing Vohl was right up there, too. He hoped he could do both. Blackie would have to wait. Bodie leaped to the top of a containment structure and jumped again.

The lights bloomed to full, and he saw that many of the structures had not fallen. It looked like all the towers of Manhattan were pressing down from above. He shot out a coldbright strand and used it as a swinging vine like Tarzan. As he whipped up into the air, he shot another and another.

"Well, this is one way to do it." He swung up one more time and realized this time he needed to grab ahold of some railing and make his way to the doors at the end of the containment area if he wanted to get out. Otherwise, he'd be climbing a very tall, very flat wall, and as much as he could do with the coldbright, he didn't think he was quite equipped to do that.

He pulled himself up to the railing and began working his way along it like monkey bars. A familiar cell came into view. It was the one that had the creature in the mist that had presented itself as Helga and Dmitr. People from his past who had died. He tried not to look, but as he passed, the lights blinked out and he could swear he'd seen a form in the mist that looked just like—

Something slammed into him from behind, knocking him from the railing. He shot out a coldbright strand to catch his fall. A hurtling piece of metal intercepted it, and he tumbled away just as the lights went out again.

"Bohhh-deeee!!!" He heard the guttural roar of the cyborg gorilla.

Damn, but that dude's a pain in my iron ass...

He tumbled, twisted the coldbright into gliding wings, and aimed for the wall. He only had one chance here. Swoop up as high as he could and try to lasso something near the utility door leading to the corridor. He barely remembered where it was. The lights bloomed. He found his spot and shot out a strand. Blackie landed on his back and they swung into the wall, colliding with a loud metallic thud. Blackie slid down to Bodie's feet but held fast. Bodie was struggling to hold on, too. He shot out another strand as a backup.

"Last ... chance ... Blackie."

The cyborg gorilla roared. Large swaths of his body were covered in dark, slick blood and fluid. He reached up, grabbed hold of Bodie's thigh in one huge hand, and hauled himself further up.

Bodie'd had enough. There was a tiny amount of pity in his heart for the slain outlaw, now resurrected in a half-robot, half-primate body, still with hollowed-out eyes because his creator was a sadistic psychopath. But that tiny hesitation was dwindling fast, especially knowing that Antigony was being carried away by that same psychotic imp. To what aim, he could only guess. And ultimately, he had to catch up to find out. And he was running precious low on time.

Bodie's first strand slipped, and the two dropped a couple of feet before being caught by the other.

"In a way, I'm sorry Blackie."

Blackie responded by sinking his teeth into Bodie's calf. Half a second and two scythe-like swipes from his tentacle swords and Blackie stiffened. His lower half fell away and his upper half lay open to the air before the monstrous form of Blackie slipped away. Thankfully, the lights dropped out so Bodie didn't have to live with that image of the outlaw falling away. It was oddly sad. He couldn't say if it was the fact that he was part animal or if it was because, even in death, he was being used to advance the agenda of those more powerful than himself. He didn't have time to think about it.

He shot out two more strands and hauled himself up to the opening. He was very happy to put the detention area behind him.

Now, what was that again that he saw in the misty chamber…? That's right, it was his own image. He didn't know what that meant. Oh well, he had places to be. And a villain that needed a comeuppance.

CHAPTER 24

JUSTICE, JUDGMENT, AND JUSTINE

What luck! Half of the belly of the ship had been torn away, right up to the open cargo hanger of the Aft Belly Bay. Bays One and Two were gone. Only cargo bays Three and Four remained. But the only one that mattered was Four. That's where the escape craft rested—thankfully fastened to the ceiling upside down rather than resting in a pile of wreckage on the floor that used to be the ceiling. The wind roared past. It was a good thing the Ars Arcanum was going so slowly. It would be impossible to even stand in the exposed space if the wind were any worse.

Vohl realized it was time to use his newfound magick for real.

Child's play, the Rajak boasted from some recess in the back of his mind. Vohl doubted it was that easy, even for him.

"You three, stand guard," he shouted at the remaining sentry bots. Blackie had not returned. He wondered if it had been foolish to send him away to deal with the renegade robot. No matter, he was so close to what he needed to finally escape this wretched rock. His gaze drifted to the portion overhead that revealed an inky blanket of stars. Soon.

The ship shuddered and attempted to roll even more to starboard. Fear gripped his insides. He was running out of time. Of course, he could always just transport himself into the cockpit, but then he'd forfeit his prize and power. There was still so much to learn before he mastered the Rajak's power and rid himself of its nuisance spirit.

It snorted. *Soon your mind will be but a shell for my spirit. Soon you will grow tired of the fight and your body will be mine to command.*

Vohl gulped involuntarily and sneered. "Good luck with that." His hands stretched out, and he enveloped the craft in a magickal shroud. He was just grasping at straws here. Laughter erupted from the back of his mind. He focused again, wrapping layer upon layer of magickal power around the craft. He had no idea if this was going to work. The second he released the retainers, he'd know. And that would be a moment too late.

The laughter continued.

"You could help."

The laughter redoubled. A lot of good it was having an ancient deity inside your mind. Still, it was clear that this tack was not the preferred method, according to the Rajak. He wanted to do it just to prove him wrong, but he knew better. Vohl was a pragmatist.

Another tack, then. *Why not control the craft and use its existing systems?*

Silence. Well, alright then. Why not enlist the aid of someone who is actually helpful—the ship's AI?

He teleported himself inside the command module of the ship.

"Artis," he snarled, his voice projecting throughout the main area of the escape craft.

"Yes, Chief Science Officer Vohl?"

A broad smile crept onto his face. "Initiate warm-up and starting sequence for take-off."

The cabin bloomed to life. Two rows of consoles with a center aisle between them stepped down to a clear, circular area bounded by a handrail. Sheets of transparent material angled from above and around the circular platform so that someone standing at that railing had a 180-degree view above, below, and to either side.

Vohl strutted down the steps to this vantage point and grasped the railing, which, maddeningly, was nearly face level. He'd have the girl fix this when she arrived. Which he imagined would be any minute. Peeling the bots away from their duties saving the ship would have gotten her attention.

He looked through the viewscreen at the fires and wreckage playing across the Ars Arcanum's skin as it arced away above him. To his left, a dark swamp slid by before a couple of hilltops brushed alarmingly close to the current bottom side of the great ship. *Cutting it close, Grand Imperator,* he thought to himself while a tingle of fear and excitement swirled in his guts.

Through the viewscreen above him stood his sentry bots with his trophies: the sarcophagus, the ghost box, and the intriguing human woman under the Rajak's thrall. Time to get his getaway craft right side up and load his precious cargo.

"Artis."

"Yes, Vohl."

"Can you pilot this craft to land on the pad where it belongs?"

"Unfortunately, no. The craft was created in such a way that it requires a pilot, not an AI. This was an intentional countermeasure against theft."

He let out an irritated hiss. "Of course it was."

Suddenly, Vohl was aware of a presence in the cabin. He spun and there was a despicable human man with disgusting face fur. "Let's make a deal, Varmit," the man said.

"I don't make deals. And you have no idea who you're messing with," replied Vohl as he casually reached out and formed a fist, intending to crush the insides of this intruder, but then he was gone.

"Where did you go?" Vohl asked in shock, his eyes squinting as he searched the room, and then something grabbed him roughly from behind while something like a claw grasped his throat.

Fool! the Rajak accused from the recesses of his consciousness.

"Who are you? What do you want?" Vohl asked, his voice drenching with spite.

"I said a deal," the man replied, but his voice sounded different. It had a reedy quality to it. Vohl cast a glance behind to find some kind of large crustacean.

"Ooh, a shifter. How nice for you. As I said, I—" he started to say before the pincer began to construct and crush his windpipe. He struggled to swallow. "What ... do you ... want?"

"I'd settle for you dead, but all things in due time. For now, I want what you want, which is to get off this miserable planet. I overheard your little conversation with the AI. Sounds like we need the girl to do it."

"It seems," he choked out, "but like I said … I don't make deals!"

Vohl teleported off the bridge and back down to the landing pad. The robots jumped at his appearance and then settled. Vohl looked up at the ship's viewscreen and there was the man-alien, staring back smugly. He waved.

"He knows I'll be back. I will make him suffer for his insolence, but I don't have time to waste extricating him from my craft."

The Rajak snorted and Vohl rolled his eyes in frustration. Nothing was going according to plan. And then movement from farther down the cargo bay floor caught his attention. Silvery tendrils and a silvery form bounding through the wreckage. "What now?!?"

It had to be the girl but in some kind of armor. And then, off to the side, another figure arrived from where Vohl and his entourage had entered the shorn cargo bay floor. It was the renegade robot. So much for Blackie. Little loss. Vohl scanned right and left for an escape, but there was nowhere to go.

"Sentry bots. Sic 'em."

From above, a speaker crackled to life. "Ready to talk yet?"

Vohl watched as an access hatch opened on the roof of the escape craft. He darted a glance back at the two sprinting at him from the far side of the bay and then back up and nodded. The man smiled again, and Vohl couldn't wait to scrape that smile off his face with the man's own severed claw.

The Rajak drew Vohl's attention to the woman and the sarcophagus floating in the air where the sentry bots had been standing moments before. *Helpful all of a sudden, are we?*

Using the Rajak's magic, Vohl reached out telepathically to the woman, and surprisingly, he found a sentience there. But she was sleeping? He broke off his attention and desperately looked back to where the robots were engaging the girl and renegade. *Not well,* he thought.

He reached out again to the woman and found her staring directly at him, her rage smoldering just beneath the surface of the psychic link.

"Carry us up to the ship."

She smiled. Her eyes rolled back and her mouth opened wide. A piercing pinpoint of light inside her throat grew into a blistering white light. Vohl ducked and dove to the side as a beam of light, like plasma, sliced through the air where he'd been and started drawing a line of molten metal across the deck.

Bodie stepped out onto the hangar deck and was greeted by bright sunlight in a cloudless sky. The far end of the deck was a wall of black and gray smoke. The wind ripped at him, pushing him in the direction of a sleek, silvery dagger of a spacecraft, hanging upside down from what was left of the ceiling above an area that was clearly intended to be a parking bay.

Near the craft was Tig. *Great!* And Vohl. *Boo!* And a handful of sentry bots charging at him. *Bummer. Oh well, time to dismantle more bots.* Bodie charged forward, weaponless but confident. But then a movement caught his attention from his right.

Crashing to the surface of the hangar deck was another bot, he thought, at least. It was slim, but then it had streamers of familiar-looking tentacles that punched into the deck and pulled it along at a ferocious pace. Justine had learned a new trick. Armor. She was kinda scary like that. Just a few short weeks ago, she was a sweet, innocent young girl with her whole life ahead of her. Now? He didn't quite know how to categorize her, but within the hour, the dust would settle and he'd know if she was friend or foe. At least if the ship didn't explode or crash before that happened, and … if he were being honest, those were slim odds.

Three of the sentry bots veered in her direction. He was going to have to hurry up if he wanted any of this action. Bodie burst forward just as the sentries ahead raised their pistols and started blasting as they ran at a full sprint. He unfurled coldbright wings and launched into the air.

The bots didn't expect the maneuver and tried to correct, but Bodie, with the wind to his back, was on them, coldbright blades singing. He dismembered one, snatching its pistol from the air with a tendril and using it on the other while another tendril formed into a blade and ran the first bot through.

It was still alive, but then Bodie's foot planted on its chest and he morphed the blade into something akin to a four-pronged grappling hook and ripped it back out with most of the sentry bot's insides.

He snagged the other bot's gun while he scanned the deck. Justine was charging toward the escape craft, sentry bot parts scattered across the deck behind her.

Then a blinding beam of light slashed across the hangar floor and Justine had to maneuver away.

It was Tig. She'd gone dark again. He darted forward as beams of light slashed back and forth, leaving trails of molten metal in their wake. Vohl blipped this way and that, not willing to leave but unable to stay still. Bodie wondered why he didn't just blink his way into the ship, but then, it was hanging rather precariously from the ceiling. That was probably helpful when the Ars Arcanum was upside down.

The other issue Vohl had to juggle was not allowing Tig to destroy the escape craft. A beam shot at him and he lunged to the side. It appeared that the coldbright was a great shield against many things, but space zombie magick wasn't one of them. Is that what Tig was turning into? And could it be stopped?

Something was nagging at him. Why didn't Vohl use his telekinesis against Tig? He seemed to be fascinated by her, but that wouldn't stop him from killing her if she stood in his way, would it?

He saw Justine circling around to the right, trying to stay inconspicuous, which was comical given the fact that she was a shiny chrome being with billowing tentacles. Finally, Vohl just gave up and vanished. Tig looked around desperately, her eyes pure white, her raven black hair whipping in the wind. She was crouching low, hands claw-like with long black nails. She looked terrifying, bordering on animalistic, as she sought her prey. The Rajak's sarcophagus floated behind her on the heavy iron chain.

Was she too far gone to save? The only one that really knew was the Rajak. Maybe Vohl. The only way to find out would be to question him. That meant Bodie had to keep him alive.

He and Justine were converging on the scene, but Justine was a little ahead. Tig, sensing danger, unleashed her burning light. Justine dove to the side but kept closing the distance. She was going to take her out. Bodie couldn't have that either.

As he approached, Tig turned on him and the blinding beam swung perilously close, but one of Justine's tentacles wrapped around Tig's wrist and then the other wrist, causing her and the beam to jerk away to the side.

Tig spun to meet the threat just as Justine flew over her head. Tig's beam followed and a molten streak arced across the escape craft and then the ceiling above. The ceiling, structurally compromised as it was, groaned in response and threatened to buckle.

Tig, not completely driven insane by the dark presence within her, realized the danger as well and ceased with the beam, but that wasn't the extent of her power. She clutched the tentacles holding her wrist and ripped viciously. Justine yelped in surprise as she was whipped back over Tig's head and out onto the exposed deck.

Bodie seized his chance.

"Tig, stop it now." She snapped to him and looked as though she was readying another attack. He dropped his hands to his sides. "Tig. Sweetheart, you know it's me." Admittedly, he was laying it on a little thick, but he had to get her attention somehow. She hesitated and then shook her head as if to clear the warring thoughts and voices inside it.

Out of the corner of his eye, he saw a glint of movement. "Justine, wait. We're all on the same side here."

Tig saw Justine too and bristled, but Bodie stepped between them with his hands up. "Ya'll need to—" he was saying when a shriek of metal from above was followed by the whole ceiling collapsing with the escape craft attached to it. Bodie dove to protect Tig, encircling them with a cage of coldbright tendrils as hunks of jagged metal rained down on them.

When the debris stopped, she was okay, staring at him with her unnerving emerald eyes. At least she didn't look openly hostile or like she was about to slice him in half with her scary plasma beam, but beyond their tiny refuge, he could see movement between the cracks.

It was Justine. At first, he thought she was coming to save them, but then she floated up into the air to the ship, still suspended but barely above the floor.

And then he saw Vohl, there for a moment before he vanished. Bodie tried to replay the whole scene in his head to make sense of it but was struggling to do so. She hadn't just willingly opted to help Vohl escape, had she?

"The Rajak's power. The imp is using it to coerce her," came Antigony's voice. It was low and halting, but it was her. Bodie's heart leaped with excitement. He was so relieved to hear her voice and to see her calm, but then he could see the inner war playing out on her face. Her brow was wrinkled slightly, and pain was reflected in her eyes.

"Tig, what's wrong?"

"It's too hard, Bodie. Keeping myself myself. I can't..." She breathed a ragged breath. Before he knew what he was doing, he was holding her in his arms.

"You just hang on, Tig. We'll figure out a way. You just hang tight, you hear me?"

He looked her in the eye and it was as if two sets of eyes were staring back. A cruel smile twisted her lips but only briefly. He watched her tremble with the effort of pushing the Rajak's presence down. His heart broke at her struggle and her pain. But then a whirring sound turned into a dull roar as the ship above them began to slide forward.

He heard her hiss and saw her hands curl into claws.

"No! Don't do it, darling. Don't give in. It's not worth it," he cried. "It's not worth it. We'll figure this out, and Vohl? We'll just have to find him and deal with him then. Right now, we gotta figure out how to save this ship or get off it, and I'm leaning toward the latter."

The escape craft slid out of sight momentarily before reappearing as it lifted up into the sky and peeled away.

Bodie cursed under his breath but knew deep inside of him that losing Tig to his unbridled obsession for justice, or more aptly, revenge, the same way he had Helga and Dmitr was the wrong thing. He'd find a way to deal with Vohl. And Justine? Well, he needed her or he would have killed her already. She was a pilot now, infused with the coldbright. That was the most likely thing. Hopefully, that was enough to keep her alive until Bodie could find him and make things right. Or ... maybe the lesson here was to fight only the battles you could afford to lose?

He was tired of lessons. All that could fade away for the moment. For now, he would work with what he had. Tig was alive.

Kind of.

CHAPTER 25

THE STILETTO

Justine watched as a large chunk of the ceiling collapsed on Bodie and the woman. The section where the craft was attached too dropped low but then stopped just a dozen or so feet from crashing to the deck. That was lucky.

Then something clutched her insides and gave a gigantic twist. She cried out involuntarily and would have crumpled to the ground, but whatever it was held her tight.

"Justine, so good to see your putrid human carcass again," came Vohl's syrupy sweet husk over the rushing wind. He was right behind her. If she could just—

Her insides wrenched again and she couldn't even scream.

"Now, now. Let's play nice. I need you to pilot a ship, and I'd hate to have to shred apart your insides to do it. Let's go. Now that that troublesome robot is gone, it's time to make our exit."

He nudged her forward and she could do nothing but comply.

She entered the hatch to the craft, and he was already standing in the open corridor. His smile was smug, but there was something feral in his eyes that she couldn't quite sort out. He motioned toward the command module.

"Take us out of here. Now."

There was no reason not to comply other than Bodie and the woman being trapped on the ship. If they were alive, which didn't seem likely. A twinge of sadness gripped her. She hadn't meant for that to happen. Bodie was a good person, especially for a robot. And there was so little of that in this world.

Then she remembered the sacrifice that Klamath had made to stay with the ship. Maybe she could deal with this sawed-off scoundrel and come back? That would be the honorable thing to do. Of course, there was little honor in dying stupidly. Flying back to a ship that was a ticking time bomb? Well, one problem at a time.

"Artis?" she asked as she descended the steps of the command module. She felt a gentle squeeze around her organs as if Vohl needed to remind her of the ungodly suffering he could administer if she didn't obey.

"Yes, Captain Sever?"

"Carry us away."

"As you wish," the voice said, shifting slightly to something younger and more vibrant. "And you may refer to me now as Astrid while my persona is separated from the Ars Arcanum. Just to alleviate any confusion in the course of ship-to-ship communication. Which I understand to be unlikely as the Ars Arcanum is on a one-way trip to annihilation."

"Yeah, fair enough, I guess ... Astrid," Justine replied, realizing now what an incalculable loss that would be. She needed to make this quick.

The deck of the Ars Arcanum slid away below the viewscreen before her as the craft accelerated and arced away. She felt the subtle tug of the allowed gravitational force as the craft veered away and began to accelerate even harder toward thunderheads in the distance.

She understood that there was a necessary angle of departure when exiting a gravity well such as a planet. This was part of the knowledge she was acquiring from the coldbright. It was a constant flow of information. She couldn't possibly learn it all, but once accessed, it was always available for reference. As long as there was a suitable amount of coldbright from which to draw the knowledge. There were a lot of idiosyncrasies to the way the element functioned, she realized.

The world slid away below her and those billowing towers of cloud, moments ago so far away, drew closer. It looked as though they were just going to impale themselves into the side of them like an injun arrow to a big, fancy wedding cake.

"Well done ... Captain. Now, just one last little task—dealing with an unwanted guest."

She spun to see who he was referring to, but there was no one else in the open compartment. But then one of her tendrils whipped out against her will. It struck a console against the wall and a grunt issued from what appeared to be empty space.

Then the wall itself seemed to shift to the side. Her mouth dropped as she watched a man coalesce from the visual parallax. It was Klamath. He wiped away blood from his cheek. Before she could say anything, another one of her tentacles flew at his face, and faster than the eye could follow, his hand flashed up to block it, only it wasn't a hand but some kind of large chitinous claw.

"Now, Justine. No need to get all upset about me bending our prior arrangement," Klamath said.

"Oh, I'm more than miffed that you lied to me, but…"

"It's not her that's the problem. It's me," Vohl finished as several more of Justine's tendrils flew at the space where Klamath was. He severed the strand he was holding, and right before her eyes, he shifted into something undefinable, half lurching, half slithering away from the attack.

Then she was stepping forward, her tentacles pounding the wall, floor, and ceiling—everywhere Klamath went, destruction followed. Alarms blared and acrid smoke smelling of electronics and metal filled the air as the ship lurched beneath them. Klamath darted this way and that. Justine was still unable to recognize what kind of creature he'd become, or maybe he was some kind of hybrid between them.

Then a stream of stingers flashed by. One of them caught her in the shoulder and arm, piercing through her coldbright armor. She cried out, but her body wasn't hers to control. She fought against it as fire erupted from the injury. It burned so intensely that she had to glance down to make sure it wasn't actually on fire.

A growl escaped her throat as she pursued the man with even greater intensity, even though it wasn't her that was driving her body. He darted left and two of her tendrils morphed together to smash down on the spot, narrowly missing him.

"No offense, Justine, but given the circumstances, I'm going to have to presume our truce is over." A blade whistled past her head, embedding itself in the wall of the ship. Only it didn't look exactly like a knife. It appeared to be crafted from some kind of insectoid armor with little black spines bristling along the back of a wickedly jagged edge. She ducked to the side to avoid two more.

Justine struggled to track where the man went as he morphed between creatures with deadly darts or wicked armor or even camouflage. She heard movement behind her and spun to protect herself, when all of a sudden, she was smacked with something she could only guess was some kind of psychic impact. She saw stars and struggled to keep her balance, as if she'd been thrown from a horse, but nothing had touched her.

"Oh, not fair, that's cheating," whined Vohl from somewhere in the space.

Klamath appeared before her, and as he moved to fire some unknown form of deadly projectile at the imp, Klamath suddenly convulsed with pain and froze in place. Gripped, she could tell, by Vohl's agonizing mental power.

But then, when Vohl began to ball his tiny hand into a fist, Klamath smiled. She watched in shock as his body morphed into pink and purple, glistening surfaces that made it look like he was made up entirely of crystal. Justine saw his face twist into a bizarre crystalline smile, but then all of her tentacles shot at him, their ends sharpened to points, and they pierced his body, punching gaping holes in his hardened skin.

He convulsed in pain.

"I'm sorry," she whispered, before her tentacles ripped back out, exploding pink and purple shards across the command module.

Vohl breathed a sigh of relief and cracked a toothy, self-satisfied smile.

"Nicely done, my dear," he said as he floated down from his hiding place above the melee. He settled to the deck and looked up at her. "Now. You and I are about to come to an understanding." He stepped forward, and the smile turned decidedly more sinister. A faint tinge of sulfur tickled her nose and throat. His eyes, huge and golden, gained a malevolent cast. There was no doubt in her mind that if she double-crossed him, he would extract as much pain as was humanly possible to endure before dying and then resurrect her body just to do it all over again.

She swallowed as this realization settled in. There was no dealing with this creature. She'd been a fool to think that she could outsmart him or somehow compete against a creature that could crush her insides with a thought. Not even Klamath had been able to escape.

And then a shadow slowly grew up from the floor behind him. She thought it would stop at something roughly the size of a human being, but it continued to grow larger and larger until it was easily one and a half times that height and twice as wide. It was dark gray like granite and human-like, but as if it was in fact a version hewn from living rock.

Vohl spun and his eyes widened in terror as the creature grasped him with one gigantic fist. He struggled and squirmed, desperately trying to break free, and then there was a sickening crunch. Vohl's body crumpled and then poofed away in a thin wisp of coal dust and sulfur.

Justine watched in horror as the creature examined its palm, seemingly surprised by the sudden disappearance. It let out a long breath and muttered a prayer under its breath.

What just happened? Was Vohl dead, or did he just get away? If he did escape, she hoped he died from his injuries. It was obvious they were extensive. Maybe him slinking off to some hole in the ground and suffering a long, drawn-out death was a better form of justice than it just being over with in an instant. She was pondering all these things when she realized the creature's attention had turned fully to her.

A wave of paralyzing fear washed over Justine as she met the hulking stone creature's piercing gaze. She was next, and there was nothing she could do to escape. It stared at her with an appraising eye, and she couldn't help but feel as though every right decision and every wrong decision she'd ever made were being weighed against each other.

Casting its head one way and then another, it stretched out one huge hand, index finger extended, and poked her in the chest. It felt to her like being hit with a musket ball.

"I'm … watching … you," it boomed in a tone so low she could barely understand it, but the message was crystal clear. There had been a judgement made, and she'd escaped by only the barest of margins. On a technicality, maybe, like he had other more important people to kill at the moment.

She nodded solemnly. Then the creature did the improbable. A smile broke across his face, and she could almost believe it was genuinely happy at this positive turn of events. Then, it slowly sank into the floor, making uncomfortable eye contact all the way until its eyes dissolved into the material of the floor and the rest of it disappeared entirely.

"Astrid, what just happened?"

"Well, Captain Sever, you just met the Golem."

"Ah."

"My suggestion, though I believe the lesson is self-evident, is that you listen to him. But then, organic interaction and motivations often baffle me. I find them fascinating."

"Well, thank you for that."

Suddenly, the ship was engulfed in darkness as it entered the turbulent column of clouds. The bridge was smoking and sparks occasionally jetted from damaged wall displays. Oh yeah, there was that. It reminded her that the Ars Arcanum was probably on its way to crash into the San Francisco Bay or just go atomic somewhere out over the Pacific. The latter being preferential. Both would be bad for Bodie and his woman friend if they survived the collapse. Ordinarily, she would have assumed they were dead, but then Bodie was a sentry bot and she, well, she was possessed by some kind of demigod from another planet. If anyone could have survived that, it was the two of them.

The haunting last words of the Golem rang in her ears. "I'm watching you." The right thing to do would be to go back and make sure they were okay.

"Then again, who else in the world do I have?" she mused out loud.

"You've got me," said Astrid.

"Thank you."

Then she noticed a small, crystalline shard vibrating on the ground. As she watched, it jittered sideways and then skittered across the floor to a larger clump of crystal. Klamath. "Of course, you're still alive. Bounty hunter. Interstellar cockroach." Klamath didn't respond. Probably couldn't just yet. "Astrid, keep an eye on that lump over there. Tell me if it starts looking like a person."

"Of course."

Justine strode down the steps to the command module and stood before the arching viewscreen filled with the illuminated gray of the inside of the clouds. She shook her head. If only her mom and dad could have seen this. Her, captain of an airship, gliding through the heavens.

She had wanted so badly to have them back but knew it was wrong to disrupt the natural order. Play God. Bring them back. Of course, Vohl had done that with the outlaw and his gang. That was just like him.

Then she remembered something else. What was the artifact he was so consumed by? The ghost box? She turned and there it was, resting on one of the consoles. It gave her the creeps. As she looked at it, it almost seemed to shimmer with a ghostly light. That was something for later. She didn't even want to think about that yet.

Instead, she let her armor slip out into streamers of coldbright so she could grasp the railing with her own hands. It was warm to the touch. She smiled. Then with a thought, the Stiletto banked right to turn back and see about her friends.

CHAPTER 26

BLACK SANDS

Bodie reached over and grasped Antigony's hand as they sat on the black sand beach of some uncharted island. She very nearly crushed it in response. This was an odd courtship by any standards, but then these were weird times.

The Ars Arcanum, contrary to all outward appearances, had lasted a shockingly long time. Hours and hours after Tig had melted away, the collapsed beams encircling them, they'd coasted over the dark blue waters of the Pacific Ocean. And now they were here.

Bodie looked at Tig and found he couldn't look away. Her face was still pale with the ongoing effects of the Rajak's thrall, but she was captivating, nonetheless. Her emerald eyes reflected the last rays of sunlight until they were lit up with tandem pulses of bright white light from a far distant explosion.

It'd be minutes before the sound reached them. And it would. There was no saving the gravitic jar of the Ars Arcanum, and the resultant explosion would be on the megaton level.

He breathed a deep sigh but didn't take his ocular circuits off of the woman by his side, not even to cast a concerned glance in the direction of the sarcophagus floating behind her on its iron tether. She needed healing, but there was no source of adequate information on the subject. Not on Earth anyway. That was a situation that needed addressing, and soon.

Meanwhile, there was the massive ark of exotic alien monsters that still needed to be dealt with anchored just a few miles off the coast of this unknown isle. The Ars Arcanum had crashed down finally, and through a combined effort of all involved—Bodie, Tig, Justine, and even Klamath—had held off the creatures long enough to seal up the core areas so it was sea-worthy and remove the compromised gravitic component.

A glimmer of silver on the horizon grew into the sleek, chrome form of the Stiletto on its way back from disposing of the offending article. It circled once, hovered, and set down just up the beach a ways. Bodie squeezed Tig's hand, and the two stood and headed that direction.

Justine's familiar voice crackled over Bodie's intercom and he played it out loud for Tig's benefit.

"You two lovebirds done cuddling? We've got a bounty to cash in."

"And a load of extradition contracts to negotiate for all these critters," Klamath chimed in. "Though, for the life a me, I don't see why we just don't sell 'em. We got Zilich's spirit in the ghost box and he'll tell us where we can do it."

"We talked 'bout this, Klamath. These creatures have been separated from their homes for well over a decade. They survived this long, they ought to at least be turned back out to finish their lives on familiar soil."

"Throwing away a fortune..."

"It's the right thing to do." Justine cut him off. "And I'm the captain."

He grumbled his contempt for this new arrangement but ceased his argument.

"But before all that, we need to find out what can be done for Tig. This curse is a burden no one should have to bear."

Her eyes said it all, pain, longing, despair, and behind it all, a keen intelligence watching, waiting for an opportunity to take over. To escape? To kill every last one of them? Probably all of the above.

He admitted it was a little unnerving seeing all that when he looked at her. It was a heavy burden indeed, but he turned and kissed her on the lips, letting the last moments on a romantic tropical beach linger for a few seconds longer. He'd learned a thing or two with the coldbright, and one of them was how to manipulate his own material structure. He and Antigony had explored as much of that as was appropriate for a budding romance between a magickal element-infused robot and a space mummy vampire-possessed saloon dancer turned high-plains badass. Butterflies churned in his stomach. He couldn't wait to explore more, but as always, work beckoned.

"...And we need to find my horse."

END

1. Bodie's bizarre obsession with karma is a constant theme but seems to be more a product of a guilty conscience than anything else. How do you think he's doing in balancing good and evil?

2. The death of Downy, Bodie's woodpecker friend, weighs heavy on him even though he saved it from dying from exposure. Why do you think he takes it so personally?

3. After Justine loses her family, she meets two different families, the cabin zombies and the man and woman in the farmhouse who probably lost their children to the mines. Which of these encounters do you think impacted her more, and why?

4. Antigony is a source of constant perplexity for Bodie. Is this the most telling example of his true human nature or are there others?

5. What's up with Jef?

6. The outlaw bossman Blackie Lung goes through a couple of transitions throughout the story. Which is your favorite for a villain?

7. Vohl surpasses Zilich as the villain in the story. Do you think he sees himself as the villain in his own story?

8. The golem finally catches up with Vohl in the end, but it's unclear what exactly happens to him. What do you think happened to Vohl?

9. Justine is faced with the opportunity to bring back her parents from the dead but must forfeit a decade of her life to do it. Yet, the question of whether there is some sort of catch to the trade is very likely. It's this dilemma that ultimately drove her to take over the ship and take things into her own hands. What difficult situation in your own life drove you to do something you previously thought impossible?

AUTHOR BIO

Eric's base camp is at the foot of the oft-smoldering Sierra Nevada in NorCal where he enjoys surfing, snowboarding & mountain biking with his wife and three adult sons. You can check out excerpts for upcoming projects at his author page: enlard-author.weebly.com.

On his nightstand: *The Hitchhiker's Guide to the Galaxy* by Douglas Adams, *The Martian* by Andy Weir, any one of the Murderbot Diaries books by Martha Wells, or the Arcane Casebook series by Dan Willis. There's some Stephen King stuff, too.

**Discover more at
4HorsemenPublications.com**

10% off using HORSEMEN10